PIRATE NEMESIS

TELEPATHIC SPACE PIRATES

BOOK 1

CARYSA LOCKE

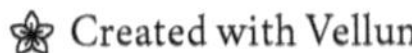 Created with Vellum

ercy didn't like the way spaceport security was watching her. It was a busy place, with half a dozen freighters offloading goods, and just as many uploading new cargo. Merchants shouted at dock workers to handle their crates more carefully, transport hawkers flashed bright screens showing their rates, and three Commonwealth Navy ships had docked this morning, men and women in uniform disembarking in a raucous flood of noise.

She ducked between two enlisted men arguing over where they wanted to throw their credits away – booze, gambling, or the local pleasure house. Maybe she could lose security in the crowd, but she wasn't counting on it. Verath 6 featured an enormous spaceport. The planet's colonies were split between farming and mining, and both provided exports throughout the Commonwealth. It was chaos, but for all the crush of people, Mercy knew she stood out.

She'd already been here too long, and the pressure to run, to flee, was a growing anxiety streaking heat up her spine and coating her skin in a thin sheen of sweat. She was running for her life, and the crowd was the only advantage she had. If security slowed her down...she couldn't dwell on that possibility.

For the past hour, she'd carefully looked over each ship, trying to stay unobtrusive. It wasn't easy. There just weren't many kids here, much less a thirteen-year-old girl, alone and unchaperoned. She needed to find the right ship, and fast, before the guard shadowing her decided he needed to do more.

Choosing which ship to catch a ride on was complicated. It couldn't have too much security. It couldn't be too official, too wealthy, too criminal, or too desperate. It needed a captain reluctant to turn her over to the authorities, if she was caught, and it couldn't be someone likely to sell her off to slavers. Half the "merchants" here operated as smugglers, and that sort of element was risky.

Stowing away meant extra weight, and most ships, whether cargo or passenger, were charged docking fees based on weight. Captains didn't take well to being charged extra, even if it was only by a few kilos. If a stowaway was found and couldn't pay, some captains would float them out the nearest airlock.

Her mother had drilled all of these things into her by the time she was ten, just like how to operate an aircar, navigate a star chart, or work the autopilot on a ship. Knowing how to run was half of Mercy's childhood education. The other half was how not to get caught in the first place.

Don't get noticed. Act like you belong, even if you

don't, and that means paying attention to everything, from the people around you to your own body. Her mother's words floated through her mind, and Mercy made a conscious effort to keep her shoulders and arms relaxed, to stroll along like she was bored and didn't care about any of the ships or people around her. Like her heart wasn't trying to beat its way out of her chest. She looked around like she was just another jaded kid dragged along on adult business at the port, desperately searching for anything in this place to entertain her. What she really hoped to find was a way to shake the guard's attention for good.

She found it in front of one of the transport hawkers. A couple stood there with a baby cradled in the woman's arms. Mercy noted their skin and hair color, the fit and cut of their clothes. Not an exact match for her own in either case, but close enough to suit her needs. Deliberately, she stopped and heaved a huge sigh, throwing in an eye roll for good measure. Then she marched her way toward them with every visible sign of bored teen apathy she had ever seen other kids use, and came to a stop just within the boundaries of personal space. Mercy made sure it was on the edge of the woman's line of sight, and when she glanced over, gave a quick, artless smile.

The woman frowned, and cast a quick look toward the man, but he was busy haggling with the transport hawker. When she looked back, her face was filled with uncertainty, just a hint of suspicion in her eyes.

Nothing to worry about here, thought Mercy, concentrating hard. *Just a harmless kid.* It helped that she looked young for her age, her green eyes wide and guileless. Her clothes were basic and serviceable, blue and tan synth-cloth treated to repel dirt and grime, the sort of thing every working class family bought for their children. It also wicked away her nervous sweat, which helped cool and calm her. Her skin, naturally tinted bronze from a mixed ancestry, could pass as darkened by working long hours in the sun. In short, Mercy could easily be some farming kid, dragged to the city by her family for the day.

"Waiting for my Mom," she said out loud, low enough that the woman would hear, but the words wouldn't carry. The woman's expression eased. She sent a quick, searching look around the space-port, but smiled when she looked back at Mercy. A warm smile. The kind of smile a mother used.

"She left you alone?" she asked, juggling the baby a bit as it fussed in her arms. Concern shone in her eyes, and Mercy thought quickly. She gave a careless shrug.

"Just for a minute. My brother's on leave from the Navy, and she didn't want me over there with all of the soldiers. They'll be along, and then we'll all go home together." For just a second, Mercy's throat closed, and she had to fight off the wave of fresh grief and panic at the thought that she might never see her real mother again. To cover, she nodded at the baby. "Doesn't all of this noise bother him?" In her experience, people were always happy to talk about themselves.

Sure enough, the woman's face lit up. "Oh, not even a little." She laughed. "In fact, I think he likes it. So much to see, everywhere he looks."

Mercy craned her head to get a better look. The baby was looking at her, blue eyes wide. His fist was stuffed into his mouth, drool coating his tiny hand. Inspired, Mercy screwed up her features, crossing her eyes and distorting her face in a ridiculous fashion. The baby squealed with delight and laughed, open mouthed, waving his tiny fists in the air.

Behind her, the security guard moved on, his gaze looking for something more interesting than this small family securing transport. Some of the tension in Mercy's stomach relaxed. She allowed herself a small, genuine smile.

"He's cute," she said, and the woman beamed with love and motherly pride. A moment later, though, and she was frowning at Mercy. *Uh-oh.*

"You should stay close to us," she said. "Until your family comes to get you. The spaceport can be a dangerous place."

"Sure." Mercy shrugged like it didn't matter, but her mind was scrambling. She couldn't stay with these people. This woman had decided Mercy needed looking after, and that meant she'd eventually get worried when her "family" never showed. And that would get her dumped into the same security office she'd just spent so much trouble avoiding. She cast her gaze around for a way out, and luck was with her.

Having secured transport, the man turned away from the hawker and said something to his wife. While she was momentarily distracted, Mercy bounced up on the balls of her feet and waved madly in the general direction of some tightly grouped uniforms, moving their way toward the exits.

"There they are!" she said, injecting her voice with breathless excitement. "Thanks, bye!" She dashed into the crowd, darting between people and weaving quickly, until she was sure she'd disappeared from view. The noise of the port swallowed whatever words the woman called at her back, but Mercy was already gone, already focused on the next task. Finding a ship.

She had to move quickly if she wanted to avoid drawing the attention of security again. Fortunately, she'd already narrowed down her choices to two frigates loading cargo. Both of them looked to be carrying perishable goods, even some livestock. That meant the cargo hold would have to be sealed and temperature controlled. It also meant Mercy might be able to put together a meal or two, either from what was being loaded as cargo, or whatever rations were being loaded to feed the livestock. She'd eaten worse.

Both ships looked like good options. Unfortunately, she had no way of getting a look at their destinations ahead of time, so she wouldn't be able to choose where she was going. That left the crew as the deciding factor. Both were small operations, as the smuggling type often were. Just a captain and one or two supporting crew members. One captain was a woman, and Mercy was leaning heavily in that direction. Women tended to be more sympathetic to kids, and if she was caught, that could mean the difference between life and death.

She started in that direction, dodging around

crates still being offloaded from other freighters, ducking the gruff hands and curses of dock-workers who didn't like a kid getting in their way. Then she saw something that made her stumble and hesitate. Just beyond the woman captain and her ship, a newly-docked vessel was offloading. It looked like any other small cargo outfit, the frigate old and scarred with decades of space travel and a few close brushes with pirates or smugglers. The hull bore marks from plasma burns, faded and old, but unmistakable.

That wasn't what had halted Mercy in her tracks, though. It was the crew walking out of the docking bay. Three adults, and what looked like two teenagers. Boys a few years older than she was. They looked like a thousand other people here, dressed in the ubiquitous flight suits and spacer gear common across merchants, smugglers, and transports. But they didn't *feel* like any of those people. They felt familiar, their presence warm and soothing in the same way her mother had been. But instead of being a comfort, that feeling washed adrenaline through her body. She actually felt the blood drain from her head.

I'm too late, and now they're going to find me and it will all be over. There would be no escaping if that happened. Mercy took a huge, shaky breath of air, trying to force down the terror so she could think.

It rooted her to the spot until a crate shoved into her hard enough to knock her aside, scraping her hip and arm in the process. She stumbled, the pain a distant distraction next to the sound of her pulse hammering in her head. The insult thrown at her by the dockworker as he shoved past was meaningless noise.

She caught herself before she fell, and straightened, ignoring the man even as he spat at the ground by her feet. All of her attention was still focused on the distant group, two docking spaces away, and nowhere near far enough. She couldn't approach the female captain now.

A second later, she realized her mistake. She was *too* focused on them. Just as she altered her gaze to look at something else, still keeping the five in her peripheral vision, one of the boys turned his head toward her. Not just toward her. *He was looking right at her.*

Mercy stopped breathing. She'd swum in ice-cold water once; one of the many escapes she and her mother had used during their years running. She still remembered the way the freezing temperature had burned against her skin, literally freezing the breath in her lungs so she spent the first few seconds wondering if she was going to suffocate, instead of drown. This felt exactly like that. The boy had blue eyes as cold as that icy water. She barely noticed his dark hair and sharp features, so trapped was she by that gaze.

He'd seen her, and in a second he was going to point her out to his companions, and then it would all be over. Ten years of running, all for nothing. Her mother gone, Mercy dragged back home to certain death.

Please, she thought. *Please just look away. Let me go.* She'd never tried her persuasion on someone else with Talent like hers. She didn't know if it would work. But she thought it as hard as she could. *You don't notice me. I'm no one. I'm nothing.*

That's not true. The new voice in her head shocked her. It was young, male, and definitely not her own thought. He was past her shields, inside her mind. Panic beat frantically inside of her, urging her to run even as her conscious mind knew she could never run far enough. *You're her. The one we're looking for.*

No! I'm not. I'm no one. Please, I'm no one.

But you are. She could feel the confusion in his tone. *Pallas is your mother. Isn't she?*

No! Yes. Mercy couldn't control the punch of emotion that spiraled through her at hearing her mother's name. *She's gone.* Her throat clogged and tears burned behind her eyes, but she fought them. She couldn't cry now, here. *Please, just let me go.*

Across the dock, with countless people milling between them, the boy stared at her. His companions ignored him, gathering around the other boy for some reason. Mercy had never wished so hard for anything in her life. Well, except the wish for her mother to come back. But she had no chance of that happening right now.

Go.

She thought at first she was imagining the word in her mind. A hawker stepped between them with his brightly flashing screen, and Mercy's gaze wavered from the ship she'd been doggedly focusing on. When the hawker moved on, her eyes met the boy's icy blue stare.

Why?

She could see the confusion in him, in the angle of his head and the set of his shoulders.

I don't know. Because you want me to, I think. A long pause. *You should leave before I change my mind. If my brother catches you...*

He didn't need to tell her twice. She should have been moving already. She turned, stumbled the first two steps because her legs were so shaky. But she found her rhythm quickly enough, and made straight for her second choice.

As his mind faded from hers, she thought she heard the distant echo of another conversation.

Nik, what are you doing? Who were you talking to?
No one.

The other frigate, the one with an older, no nonsense looking man as the captain, was getting ready to load the last lift of freight. Operating the lift was one of the crew, a girl, not much older than Mercy. Maybe not *any* older. Mercy hunkered down behind a convenient stack of crates and watched for a moment. Her instincts screamed at her to hurry, to get the hell out of here before it was too late. But she needed to be smart about this. Getting caught sneaking on board could be just as deadly as being found by spaceport security.

This girl had short blonde hair and wore an actual flight suit, like something a real pilot would wear, but kid-sized. Made for her. She was operating the lift like she did it all the time, letting the anti-grav thrusters take care of all the heavy lifting as she maneuvered it toward the ramp.

"Atrea," called the captain, "make sure those crates of chicken feed are loaded where we can get to them." He waved a datapad in her direction.

"Remember how much fun you had last time, climbing over half the cargo for it."

"Yes, Dad." Atrea rolled her eyes exactly like Mercy had done earlier.

"Don't roll your eyes at me. Chickens were *your* idea, so *you* get to take care of them." He muttered something else under his breath that Mercy didn't catch.

"Chickens are pure profit," Atrea said, but the words were spoken so low Mercy didn't think the captain heard.

"Damn nuisance, is what they are. And *your* responsibility. I won't say it again."

Both Atrea and Mercy winced at the same time.

"Yes, Sir."

Mercy eyed the captain. Only someone with genetically or mechanically enhanced hearing could have heard that over all this noise. She wondered which he was, thought about looking to find out, and immediately decided against it. *Your Talent is both an advantage and a trap.* Her mother's voice ran through her head again, as if she stood right next to her. *Use it only when you have to. Always assume someone could notice.* And someone already had. She couldn't risk using it again.

So she didn't use her telepathy to look inside the captain's head and see if she could find out more about him. It was enough to know that he had a daughter who worked with him, one Mercy's approximate age. A father would probably hesitate to airlock or enslave a girl if he caught her stowing away on his ship. Especially if his daughter was standing right there.

Decision made, Mercy used her Talent in the most passive way possible, projecting what she thought of as her *don't look at me* protocol. It was a risk, but one she had to take. It was a suggestion, really, a kind of pressure on the minds around her to look in any direction that wasn't right at her. It didn't always work, so she still had to be sneaky and careful getting aboard the ship. But she was small and fast, and it was enough this time that no one saw her slip up the ramp and crawl back over the crates already loaded. She hid right in the middle of the stacked cages full of chickens. They made enough movement and noise that it would be easy to remain unseen back here. She shifted a couple of them to make a box of empty space just large enough to crawl into and curl up in, the smooth floor of the hold pressed against her cheek. She re-secured the straps holding the chicken cages in place and finally felt safe, away from prying eyes.

They smelled a bit, an earthy, animal kind of smell that made her wrinkle her nose. Tiny feathers drifted everywhere, but it gave Mercy something to do, trying to catch them on the backs of her fingers as they floated through the air. She heard the lift moving into place, heard the girl tell her father the hold was secure. Her stomach rumbled, but she'd have to wait until they'd made the first jump before she dared look for something to eat.

When was the last time she'd eaten? Before her mother disappeared. Two days ago. She'd been too busy running ever since. She shied away from thinking about that. Couldn't dwell on what it meant, yet. Pallas had known this might happen one day, that she might not make it home. She'd done everything she could to prepare Mercy. *You have to run,* she'd said. *Run, get on a ship to anywhere else, and don't look for me. If I don't come back to you, assume I'm dead. They'll come for you, too. You have to run, and disappear.*

Her eyes burned, hot with tears she couldn't afford to cry yet. Not until she was away. She wondered what the boy and his crew were doing right now. Had he seen her slip aboard this ship? Would they go on looking for her mother? Would they find her?

Mercy rolled onto her side and squeezed her eyes shut. She pressed her sleeve against them as hard as she could, her jaw locked. Moisture gathered and spilled over, soaking into the mesh of her sleeve and drying instantly. A sound escaped her, and she curled into an even tighter ball. *Can't cry, can't make noise.* Not yet. She forced her thoughts away from the boy and her mother, and thought about how hungry she was instead, how her insides had this big empty hole in the middle of them, and her stomach seemed like it was trying to turn itself inside out. The burning heat of the tears receded, and she took a long, steadying breath.

Eventually, the vibration of the engines firing up rumbled the deck beneath her. Relief coursed through her, some of the tension leaving her body. Soon now, she would truly be safe. No record of a girl matching her description leaving the planet. No record that she'd ever existed.

When the ship broke atmosphere and made the

first jump in whatever journey it was taking, Mercy knew she'd made it. The boy had kept his word, and he and his crew would never find her. But she also felt like the last connection she had to her mother severed. The people hunting her wouldn't be able to find her, but neither would anyone else. Mercy gave in and cried. She let the tears come until she could hardly breathe, until her head ached and her stomach churned in a mess of grief that eclipsed any hunger she felt. Until she could do nothing but lie, exhausted and numb, watching the feathers drift slowly down around her.

The chickens suddenly stirred, squawking loudly in protest as the straps to their cages were freed and the crates shoved aside. Mercy tensed, but there was nowhere to go, no more room to run as light spilled over her and a blonde head suddenly appeared above her.

Blue eyes bright with curiosity peered down at her.

"Hi," said the girl, Atrea. "Who are you, and why are you on our ship?"

*M*ercy lost all sense of time. It was easy to do, trapped in a cell on a space station. The air was unrelentingly cold, as only an enormous hollow structure built of metal floating in space could be. Not hypothermia cold, though, just enough to never feel warm. Life support was set to keep the temperature regulated for sustaining life, but not for comfort. Mercy also suspected the holding cells were considered a low priority against the rest of the station. She sat huddled on her bunk, a thermal blanket wrapped around her, arms crossed, and her hands sandwiched beneath them to get some warmth into the tips of her fingers. The thin synth-cotton clothing she'd been given didn't provide much in the way of insulation.

She had no idea how long she'd been imprisoned. It could have been a Galactic Standard week, or months. Sometimes they sedated her, and the black void of drugged sleep could take up any amount of time. She couldn't even guess from the number of meals they'd given her, not when they could feed her body whatever nutrient solution they wanted while she slept, and not when the actual meals were the tasteless nutritional bars usually reserved for deep space voyages. No one sane liked eating them, but they did provide the body with all of the essential nutrients and vitamins for survival. She'd worry that she *was* being taken somewhere deep into uncharted territory, but the station didn't move outside of its orbital rotation. A ship's engine felt different, vibrated on a deeper frequency, with jumps through space that dilated time and left the head spinning like a night spent doing serious drinking.

Mercy could only assume the nutritional bars were the most expedient way of keeping her alive. That was the only good news, if one could call it that. They kept feeding them to her, so they wanted her alive. Which only meant they wanted to use her in some way. If she had to guess, it wouldn't be for her skills as a pilot or a smuggler.

No one came to talk to her. No advocate, no port authority, or agent of the Commonwealth. She wasn't in here for smuggling. No matter how hard she tried to come up with a reason, *any* other reason, she kept coming back to the worst case scenario. Her Talent. She was here, trapped in this floating tomb, because of her Talent.

She'd failed. After all this time, years spent running, hiding what she was, building a life constantly on the move to avoid exactly this situation, and she'd failed. Worse, she'd gotten someone else trapped in the same web. Somewhere, in another cell probably, was her only friend in the universe. And she was here because of Mercy.

If she was alive at all. If Mercy was here because of her Talent, they, whoever they were, could have no interest in Atrea Hades. In fact, as an officer in the Commonwealth Navy, Atrea was a liability to them. Officers didn't go missing without notice.

Bile rose in Mercy's throat just thinking about it. Wondering if they'd already spaced Atrea, her friend was nothing more than a frozen husk, floating through the endless vacuum of space. She desperately wanted to reach out with her Talent and find Atrea's mind, verify that she was still alive. But if she did that, she might be giving her captors exactly what they wanted. She couldn't risk it.

I'm sorry, she thought, careful not to reach out with her gift. *I'm so sorry, Atrea. What will I tell the old Wolf?* That thought came as a complete surprise, as it was predicated on several impossible things, starting with getting out of this place alive, and ending with finding Atrea's father, wherever he was currently making port. Mercy was pretty sure none of that was going to happen.

Her first days here had been spent getting her bearings and trying to think her way out. She didn't remember much of *how* she'd been taken. Drugged, she suspected. The drinks they'd been served in that hellhole on Yuan-Ki, where Atrea thought they'd find a contact who could give them information on where Talented people went when they were taken. Which meant the entire thing was a setup, a trap. A hysterical laugh threatened to bubble up, and Mercy fought it down grimly. The irony wasn't lost on her, she just wasn't in a position to appreciate it.

They'd found her. Drugged her. Taken her. The same people who took her mother all those years ago. Panic set in after that, and Mercy couldn't focus beyond the cold wash of terror churning her gut and making her hands tremble. An eternity blinked by before she was calm enough to think clearly again. To set it aside and look at where she was, with an eye for what she was going to do about it.

Unfortunately, there wasn't much opportunity to escape. Her cell door never opened while she was awake. A sedative was pumped in through vents in the ceiling. Whenever Mercy woke, her mouth dry and tasting faintly metallic and gritty, something would be different. Her clothes. A fresh tube of water. A new stock of nutritional bars. One time, her hair was cut. The heavy, dark length of it, threaded through with hints of copper without the necessity of a nano-treatment, was gone. The air prickled her skin, blew a cool shudder over her head and down her neck. She reached up with a tentative hand and found a short, prickly stubble covered her crown. She started inspecting herself after that, looking over every inch of dusky bronze skin she could see. Sure enough, she found evidence of needle marks and medical patches. They were taking samples.

Her gut churned again. Her fists clenched. What were they looking for? Proof of her Talent? Was there some genetic test that would show clearly whether or not she was psychically gifted?

None that Mercy knew of. None Atrea could find evidence of in her clandestine searches through Naval records. But as Mercy pointed out more than once, that kind of thing was sure to require clearance well above a captain's rank.

Her thoughts kept circling back to Atrea, but short of using her Talent, there was no way to know if her friend was here on the station. Between the desire to know and her continuing isolation, the temptation to drop her shields and reach out with her gift became greater with each passing moment. She clenched her hands into fists tight enough for the newly shortened nails to bite into her palms. Giving in wasn't an option. As horrible as this place was, how much worse off would she be if they could confirm who and what she was?

She'd become so used to isolation that it didn't quite register when the lock to her cell disengaged with a click. Not until the door hissed open did Mercy look up, blinking at the sudden wash of warmer air that flooded the room. Light from the hallway made her eyes water, and she realized for the first time how dim her own space was kept. Apparently no one wanted to waste station power resources on people being held prisoner.

"Not at all," said the man who strode through the door to her cell. Fit, handsome, and wearing the type of synth-silk suit that cost more than two or three of Mercy's smuggling runs put together. "We simply didn't want you feeling too comfortable."

He smiled as he said the words, a cold movement of lips that managed to be condescending and threatening at the same time, with no hint of warmth to soften it. He wasn't going to pretend to be her friend.

Then the meaning of his words registered, too slow, and Mercy realized he was answering a question she'd never asked, never verbalized aloud. He was responding to her thoughts. Adrenaline washed through her, so intense the nutrition bar she'd choked down an hour ago threatened to come right back up. Fear pounded in her throat, her heart a staccato rhythm through her blood, even as a comforting familiarity seemed to blanket her mind, and relaxed muscles in her back and neck she hadn't even realized were tense.

It was so completely odd a juxtaposition that she couldn't form a coherent thought until the man had finished entering the room, bringing with him a single chair that he placed across from her with careful precision. When he sat in it, regarding her with dark eyes as cold as his smile, Mercy realized she had far more immediate concerns than whatever warm fuzziness seemed to be encircling her mind. This man was everything sharp, cold, and cunning, and she had a feeling she would need all of her faculties for whatever lay ahead.

"I thought it was time we met," he said at last, his voice cultured and refined, free of any accent to identify what system he might be from. Here he was, her mysterious captor. She should ask so many questions, but was afraid she already knew the answers to most of them. Why was she here? *Her Talent.* What did he want? *To use her.* When could she leave? *Never.*

"Never is a long time, Ms. Kincaid."

Kincaid. It was the first alias she and her mother had used, all those years ago when they started running. He was telling her how much he knew. *Everything*. Suddenly, she wasn't sure if the voice in her head was her own, or his. That thought was the most frightening of all. If he was in her mind, directing her thoughts, he could make her do anything.

He smiled again, and her gut twisted sharply.

"Not anything, Ms. Kincaid. Or do you prefer Mercy? I wouldn't want to make you uncomfortable." He didn't need to inject a taunting tone. The words all by themselves took care of that. Her eyes narrowed. A thread of anger filtered past the fear, and she latched onto it like one drowning in a turbulent sea. She would climb that thread until it became a rope, life-saving and grounding in a place that threatened to pull her beneath the waves.

"Fuck you." She didn't know she was going to speak until the words left her mouth. She realized she meant them, every bit of bitter, impotent rage at her situation encapsulated in one short sentence. Her voice was rusty with disuse, but the words came out clear enough.

His smile didn't waver.

"Mercy, then. It seems ridiculous to have formality stand between us, given the intimacy of our connection."

"Sure," she said, giving a careless shrug. "I suppose being the asshole holding me prisoner is a kind of connection." The kind that meant she envisioned all sorts of ways to end him, and get the hell out of here.

"No," he said. "Not that kind of connection. I must admit to a certain disappointment that you don't sense it."

Sense what? Mercy leaned back, studying him. Was this guy some kind of psychotic freak, obsessed with her? Maybe she was the first Talented person other than himself he'd ever come across, and he decided to kidnap her to get to know her better. Somehow, that was a slightly less threatening alternative than what she actually suspected was true: that he represented an organized group who systematically hunted down Talented people, imprisoning them, controlling them, and somehow using their gifts for profit.

He looked sane enough, she supposed. Expensive shoes that looked like real leather, a suit clearly tailored to fit a body he either paid to keep toned and in shape, or worked at himself. Intelligence gleamed in the dark gray eyes, which observed her with a clinical detachment that belied his words. His black hair was neatly trimmed, and the skin of his chiseled face smooth but for one rippled length of scar along his left cheek. It was old, a pale line that didn't quite match the olive pallor of the rest of his skin. What kind of person wouldn't pay to have such a small thing sculpted clean? Especially given the expensive suit he wore. Surely he could afford the body alteration to get it fixed.

"I keep it as a reminder," he said, and yeah, this whole being inside her head, reading her every thought thing was getting old, fast. She could try to force him out. Why hadn't she thought of that sooner? She had shields. Sure, they mostly kept her from picking up every stray thought from the nulls who projected everything unconsciously, but surely they could also keep her mind free from freaks like this guy.

"Willem," he said. "My name is Willem Frain. Feel free to call me Will."

Mercy ignored him. Her focus had turned inward, and now that she was really thinking about it, she could actually feel his mind, so different from the nulls, the head-blind people she was used to. It was strange, but instead of feeling like an invasive, unwelcome presence, he felt...warm and familiar. Like coming home and sinking into a favorite comfortable chair.

That pissed her off the most. If this was the first step in some kind of brainwashing scheme, she wasn't falling for it. She was here against her will, pure and simple. And good old *Willem* was the last person she would ever give permission to be inside her head. She focused on building up her shields to shut him out. Unfortunately, a steady diet of isolation and nutritional bars hadn't exactly left her in top form. She started feeling exhausted almost immediately. It was one thing to block someone from entering your mind in the first place, but he was a solid presence already past her shields, and he felt...weighty and immovable.

"I wouldn't suggest that," he said, and Mercy glared at him. Of course he wouldn't; being kicked out of her head wasn't on his agenda, she felt sure.

"At the risk of repeating myself," she said, her voice thick with sarcasm, "fuck you."

If possible, his eyes chilled even further. "A

little civility wouldn't kill you, and may even work to your advantage."

"Yeah? If I'm nice to you, I'll get an extra tube of water? A second blanket?" She rubbed a hand over the stubble of her head. "New hair?"

He sighed. "This aggression isn't going to get you anywhere. I know the things you want most, Mercy. To be free, and to know the fate of your friend Atrea."

She went still. Desperately tried to lock down her thoughts.

Willem shook his head. He looked disappointed. "You are so much less impressive than I ever imagined. We know everything. We've had weeks to look through every thought, every hope, every dream, every memory. There is nothing about you that you can keep hidden, you foolish woman." He spread his hands. "Do you truly believe I would be sitting across from you now if I didn't already have the leverage I need?"

Leverage meant they wanted something from her. However much he might insult her, call her disappointing, foolish, even stupid, they still *wanted something from her*. He didn't, couldn't know everything. He was lying.

Willem angled his head. *I see you require proof.* He spoke the words in her mind, and at the same time flicked the fingers of one hand toward the door. *Show her. Now.*

Mercy tried to shut down her thoughts, raise her shields, shove him out of her head. She couldn't focus, couldn't manage any of it, and for the first time she wondered if they'd fed her more drugs than just sedatives. Maybe she couldn't keep him out because something was preventing her. The thought vanished as a memory surged up from her subconscious, swallowing everything else.

She was three years old. It was the man her mother sold their sloop to. The memory was vague, misted by time. More of an impression, one of towering size and the smell of fried food and engine grease. His thoughts were dark, malignant things that made her press hard against her mother's leg. So young, she had no words to describe the things he imagined, but they filled her with wordless terror. Pallas knew. She took his coin and his darkness, and left him a dazed shell of who he'd been, missing all memory of the woman and her tiny daughter, and what he'd meant to do to them. Others would come, looking for the ship, Pallas said. He would not be able to answer their questions.

Mercy came back to the present with a gasp, old terror receding under the more immediate concerns of the present. It was an old memory, one she'd all but forgotten until he – or they – brought it back to the surface. The image of her mother was so sharp it cut. The feeling of love and safety, of knowing she would always be protected. Mercy had almost forgotten what that felt like. To experience it again so deeply, only to have it ripped away the next instant, left tears prickling behind her eyes.

She'd be damned before she cried in front of this bastard. She clenched her hands into fists. "What the hell do you want from me?"

Willem leaned forward so suddenly, she'd have backed away if she had anywhere to go. But she was already pressed against the wall of her cell.

"We want you to embrace your Talent, Mercy. Become who you were born to be." He said it so intensely, it was obvious he meant every word.

It was so not what she was expecting to hear that it startled a laugh from her. *Seriously, who talks like that?*

"Who I was born to be? Is that a serious request? Because I think being a pilot smuggling agricultural goods to starving colonies is a pretty good job, really. People are always happy to see me, and they pay well. I don't think I want to be anyone else."

His eyes burned with more disappointment and anger. "Don't be obtuse. A job isn't who you are. You aren't just a telepath, whatever your mother told you. Your Talent is far beyond that, and from what I can see, totally wasted on you." His disappointment had settled into disgust. "It is unfortunate we didn't find you as a child, when your mind was more malleable."

Sure, thought Mercy, aware he'd hear it. *When you could mold me into whatever obedient little slave you wanted. No, thanks.*

He leaned back. "It doesn't matter now. We must deal with what we have, and what we have, unfortunately, is you."

"Hey, feel free to let me go anytime."

He ignored her, but Mercy saw the flash of annoyance cross his face. She took satisfaction in knowing she could at least cause him some discomfort.

"What you have," he said, "is a priceless gift. It is extremely rare. As you have guessed, we want you to use it on our behalf."

"Who is this *we* you keep referring to? I'd like to know who my enemies are. Oh, and since you know everything about me, let's talk about my mother." Mercy decided there was something liberating in throwing caution aside and saying whatever she wanted. "You *are* the ones who took her away fifteen years ago, right? Is she still alive? Do you have her stashed away somewhere in a cell too?"

She couldn't tell if that was a flicker of recognition in his eyes, or just more anger. His shields were like an Ivaldi ship's hull, smooth and impenetrable. It was just one more thing to keep her anger simmering, that he could be inside her head seemingly at will, but she couldn't see into his.

"You *will* use this gift," he was saying, completely ignoring her question.

She shrugged. "Sure," she said, smiling sweetly. "Just as soon as you tell me where my mother is."

He met her smile with one of his own, and something in it twisted her stomach with foreboding. *Now,* she heard him think, and with another flick of his fingers, the wall behind him shimmered, the smooth gray of carbon plasteel giving way to the projected image of a cell just like the one Mercy was in. It, too, had a single bunk. On it lay a familiar blonde figure, curled underneath a thermal blanket, eyes closed in sleep. Mercy stared at Atrea. She watched closely until she could see the rise and fall of steady breathing.

A cascade of emotions tumbled through her. Relief that her friend was still alive, disappointment that she had been taken, fear at what they might do to her. Until this moment, Mercy hadn't realized that some part of her still hoped Atrea had escaped. It was unlikely; they'd walked into that hostel on Yuan-Ki together, and been served the same drinks. Atrea would never have let someone take Mercy without a fight. It only made sense to take them both.

Despair filled her. She would do anything to keep her friend alive, and they knew it. *He* knew it. She tore her gaze away from Atrea and looked back at Willem. He was smirking. It made her hate him even more. She wrestled with the feeling until she had control of it, until she could trust herself to speak without screaming at him.

"What is it you want me to do?"

CHAPTER TWO

"Your friend is a perfect test subject. You will use your ability to unlock her latent potential. She will become Talented." He spoke the words in a calm, reasonable tone, as if he were asking for nothing more complicated than a routine jump to another star system.

She stared at him, struck mute. Surely she must have misheard? What he was saying just couldn't be done. But Willem Frain gazed back at her with flat, cold eyes, and Mercy knew he was serious.

"That's impossible," she said finally. "She's a null. Head blind. No Talent. You can't *unlock* it, like a treasure chest."

"You are correct that Atrea Hades is indeed a null, and as such she is useless to us." He spread his hands in a gesture meant to appear helpless. "I'm afraid we do not keep useless things."

Mercy hadn't thought she could hate him any more than she already did. She was wrong. She spent a pleasant few moments visualizing herself stuffing him out the nearest airlock. Watching the pretend version of Will float out into the cold dark was one of the more satisfying things she'd indulged in lately. Even better, in those few seconds, than her fantasies of escape.

He gave her a look. She supposed it was meant to be intimidating. Unfortunately for him, he'd already violated her on such a deep level there was nothing left for her to fear. He'd invaded every corner of her mind, observed every private dream, every personal hope and desire. It was worse than being assaulted physically. Thinking about it made her head swim and her stomach heave, so instead, she imagined his death. It was self-indulgent, irritated him, and it made her smile.

Will leaned forward, and a sudden force slammed Mercy's head into the wall. Bright spots danced in front of her eyes. Stinging pain radiated down the back of her neck as her muscles strained against the invisible grip that held her. He hadn't touched her physically. This was something else. Something Mercy herself had hardly dared play with for fear of giving herself away. Telekinesis.

"You may think you have nothing to fear from me, Mercy. But use that imagination of yours to think about what I might do to your friend. I don't particularly care if you succeed in my request. This is simply a test, to make sure you are what we believe. To prove, if you will, that you can do it. Atrea has no use to us beyond this, a fact you would do well to think on."

"You're insane. What am I supposed to do? And how?" She ground the words out between clenched teeth, since the grip he held her in effectively kept her jaw immobile.

Frain smiled coldly. "That is for you to figure

out. I can tell you that we believe you have this ability. Think of it as another Talent. Like telepathy. Sadly, we have no one on hand to teach you to use it. This will be trial and error, I'm afraid."

He held her like that, pressed uncomfortably hard against the smooth plasteel wall, until he'd picked up his chair and left her cell. Once the lock on her door clicked, the telekinetic grip released her. Mercy sagged forward, her eyes still on the opposite wall. He'd left the view of Atrea in place. He didn't give her any further ultimatums, didn't say another word, telepathic or otherwise. He didn't need to. The message was clear. Buy into this irrational request, or Atrea would die.

Mercy supposed they were giving her time to think about that. To come to the realization that she really had no choice. She closed her eyes. The painful truth was, there was nothing she could do to save her friend. Agreeing to try what they asked was a foregone conclusion; of course she would, if it bought them more time. If it bought Atrea a few more hours, or days, or weeks to live. But what they wanted just wasn't possible. It would fail, and then they would both die.

Whoever or whatever else they might be, these people were insane.

Mercy curled up beneath her thermal blanket and watched Atrea sleep. Only one small kernel of hope remained, a miniscule chance of rescue that was unlikely to appear. She couldn't help but hold on to it, nurturing it like a tiny flame about to be extinguished by a gust of wind. Wolfgang Hades would look for them once he realized they were missing. Atrea checked in with her father regularly, and the old Wolf was an ex-military man. Miss a check in, and he'd come looking. It had happened before.

Mercy smiled, remembering Windfall. Originally planned as some corporate head's private space station, the place fell to private investors when the business ran into trouble. They turned it into a gambler's paradise, outfitting the station with casinos, resorts, and private body enhancement clinics with the best tech and doctors that money could buy. They even ordered a batch of genetically perfect clones to work the tables, and provide more personal shows and services. That got the anti-cloning and clone rights activists up in arms, which pretty much guaranteed tons of free publicity. Windfall was one of the most popular just-this-side-of-legal getaway spots in the Commonwealth. As a privately owned space station, it didn't have to follow the laws and rules new colonies were subject to. She and Atrea spent a few days there once, celebrating Atrea's brilliant scores on the officer's entrance exam to the Navy.

Unfortunately, when they'd woken in their room after three days of resort hopping, the old Wolf was sitting there, waiting. With Atrea's new uniform in his hands. The uniform she hadn't yet told him about. Mercy winced, remembering. Wolfgang Hades had a complicated history with the Navy. He didn't ever talk about it, but Atrea warned Mercy he wouldn't approve of her choice, despite the fact that he seemed to have an endless supply of friends and acquaintances from his own military days, happy to help them out whenever their small smuggling operations needed it.

The old Wolf held that uniform, his face looking chiseled from granite, heavy and gray with a scruff of unshaven beard. The fact that he hadn't taken the time to shave when he'd come looking for them spoke volumes. He never took his eyes from Atrea where she sat with mussed blonde hair, bloodshot eyes, and her shoulders squared defiantly.

"Mercy, I'd like a private word with my daughter." He didn't raise his voice, but that was almost worse, somehow. She'd hesitated, not wanting to abandon her friend, especially when Atrea was doing this, at least in part, to help Mercy's search for her mother. Captain Hades looked at her then, and the disappointment in his eyes had her sucking in a breath like he'd kicked her.

"Please," he said softly, and Mercy couldn't refuse.

She'd left them alone, and never did find out the details of their conversation. What Atrea did tell her, however, was how she'd forgotten to send her usual check-in via ansible a day into their celebration. Two days later, and the old Wolf had found them.

"How?" Mercy wanted to know. It wasn't like they traveled by regular transport. Mercy had her own ship, equipped with a scrambler. Whatever ID it logged at docking wouldn't be traceable. Atrea just smiled faintly.

"It's Dad. Did you really think he'd give us a ship he couldn't find?" She'd gone on to imply heavily that even without the ship, Wolfgang could track them down. Atrea wouldn't specify how, just that he had "resources" and "contacts who can find anyone, anywhere."

Mercy found it disturbing at the time, but right now, she would give anything for that to be true. *Please find us.*

No one is coming for you, Mercy. Willem Frain's voice in her head was a stark reminder that her thoughts were never her own in this cold prison. She wanted to scream.

Stay the hell out of my head. You know I'm going to do what you want, so just leave me alone.

Maybe Frain wasn't the kind to gloat, because to her surprise, he did leave. Even the weight of his presence in her mind disappeared, and for a brief time, she felt truly alone again. She welcomed the return to isolation, a feeling that had verged on driving her mad such a short time ago. Now, the dizzying rush of relief overwhelmed her. A silent tear slid down her cheek, and she made no move to stop it.

Mercy had learned a long time ago that sometimes emotions cut so hard and so deep, physical release was the only way to survive them. Survival was her only priority now. Long enough for the old Wolf to come for them, or for an opportunity at escape. Her jaw tightened. She would not give up.

She stared across the room at the image of her friend. Atrea, who had risked so much to help her. Defying her father, giving six years of her life to the Commonwealth Navy. Risking that very career by digging into records she had no business searching, hoping to find some hint that would lead them to Mercy's mother.

It was a trail that had led them here. To this.

"Stupid," Mercy whispered out loud, watching Atrea sleep. "I never should have let you keep that promise."

She knew what Atrea would say, if she had the chance. *Like you could stop me.*

"I would try." Knowing what she did now, Mercy would do whatever it took. As badly as she wanted answers, it wasn't worth Atrea's life. She smiled faintly. "Plus, the old Wolf will kill me when he finds us."

She rolled over onto her back, unable to face looking at Atrea's image any longer. She didn't know what tomorrow would bring, but she doubted very much that either of them were going to like it.

*

MERCY DIDN'T MEAN to fall asleep. When she did, she didn't expect to dream. Maybe it was the memory Frain and his friends had pulled to the surface, because for the first time in years, she dreamt of her mother.

"Tell me who we can trust, Mercy," Pallas said. Mercy sat in a chair, her legs dangling over the edge, too short to reach the ground. Her mother stood behind her, running a comb through hair recently cut to shoulder length. The comb worked nanobots through the wet strands, changing the color from dark auburn to inky black. Mercy wanted a few blue strands as well, but Pallas didn't allow anything that might call attention to them.

"No one," said Mercy dutifully. She knew the answers expected of her.

"Why?" Every night, Pallas asked the same questions.

"Because the nulls are afraid of us."

"And?"

"And Grandmother wants to hurt us." Mercy felt sad at the words. She still didn't understand why her grandmother hated them.

"And who else?"

"Other people like us want to hurt us, too."

Finished, Pallas set the comb aside, and turned the chair so that Mercy was facing her. She knelt in front of her, taking both of Mercy's hands between her own. She squeezed them tight enough to hurt, eyes bright with worry.

"I told you never to come looking for me. Why did you disobey me?"

"I..." Tears pricked Mercy's eyes. Adult resentment and anger chased away her child self, and she was suddenly standing across from Pallas in a room much like her cell. "I had to find you."

"No!" Pallas shook her head, pacing away from Mercy as far as the small space would allow, and then back again. Her petite, slight form radiated agitation and that constant energy that no amount of nanobots could disguise. "No. I told you if I ever disappeared, it would be too dangerous to look. Why didn't you listen?"

"I can't. I can't leave you with people like this." Angrily, Mercy swiped a hand across her eyes, wiping away the moisture. "I won't!"

Even now, even if she escaped, she would never stop looking for her mother. She just wouldn't endanger anyone else with the search, ever again. She would have to leave, forget Atrea and Wolfgang Hades, pretend she'd never known them.

Pallas stopped pacing and came to stand directly in front of her. Mercy stood half a head taller, but that didn't stop her mother from taking her shoulders in an iron grip and giving her a shake.

"Stupid, stubborn child. I am lost. Leave me."

"No. I am not a child anymore, mother."

Green eyes a mirror of her own searched Mercy's. Pallas sighed, a sound as full of frustration as it was a capitulation. Her grip gentled, and she moved one hand to cup Mercy's face.

"Things are different now. Everything has changed. Be careful who you trust, stubborn girl. I was wrong." She hesitated, looking pensive. "Sometimes, we have no choice but to trust someone. Even family."

It occurred to Mercy that her mother still looked young, as young as the day she'd vanished. But this was a dream, and who could explain dreams?

"I *will* find you, Momma."

"Oh, Mercy." Pallas smiled sadly. "I hope not."

She woke with a jolt. Disoriented. Sad. Angry. Was the dream another trick, one of these bastards messing with her head, twisting her memories? No way to know. She glanced reflexively toward the wall that had shown her Atrea, but the picture of the other cell was gone, the plasteel back to unrelenting gray. Apparently they'd decided she no longer needed motivation. A thread of panic made her heart beat faster. Or they'd realized what they wanted wasn't possible, and spaced Atrea.

Mercy sat up, debated reaching out with her telepathy. Decided there was no longer any point at all in trying to hide. They knew everything already; what more harm could she do? Stealing herself, she dropped her shields.

And immediately raised them again when the lock clicked on the door to her cell. It opened, letting in another rush of warm air and enough light that it dazzled her eyes. She blinked rapidly a few times, and it was no surprise to see Willem Frain standing in the doorway.

He smiled. She hated that cold, insufferable smile. Then he stepped aside, and two people she didn't know moved into the cell. A man and a woman. Mercy eyed them warily. They looked as cold as Frain: expressionless, and locked down so tight she picked up nothing from them. They didn't touch her, but she felt a vise-like grip wrap around her body, holding her arms pinned to her sides and chaining her legs so she couldn't kick out with them. She was lifted, set on her feet between them, and walked out of her cell while she struggled futilely against the telekinetic grip.

"Struggling will only risk injury," Frain said mildly.

"Like I'm going to listen to anything you say," she snapped back, continuing to strain against her bonds. She thought about testing her own telekinesis, a gift she hadn't used since she was a little girl, floating dolls through the air to make them move like she wanted.

"I wouldn't suggest it," said Frain. "I would also point out that I have not lied to you once."

Did he seriously think she was going to trust him?

"Fine," she bit out, as they began to march her inexorably down the hall. At least the temperature was more friendly out here. She could feel some of her extremities starting to lose their constant chill. "Then tell me where we're going."

A spark of eagerness brightened his eyes, made them almost seem warm. "It is time for us to begin."

$\mathcal{A}$s uncomfortable as Mercy's cell was, it turned out things could always get worse. She was marched into a room that looked frighteningly like a medical lab. Cold, sterile, all gleaming steel surfaces and lights that shone too brightly. Her telekinetic bonds were not released until they'd maneuvered her into a chair and engaged a binding field to keep her there. The silent woman leaned forward and secured a generator to her chest, then stepped back and triggered it remotely. A gravitational field invisible to the naked eye snapped into place around her, the pressure keeping her anchored, unable to lift an arm, a leg, or sit forward.

Across from Mercy, Atrea sat in a duplicate chair, awake and straining uselessly against a duplicate field, her hair mussed even worse than before. She could see by the tightness of Atrea's jaw, the paleness of her face and vivid gleam of her eyes that her friend was furious. But when she saw Mercy, she went still, and anger morphed into shock and concern, her eyes widening and her jaw loosening.

I must look even worse than I thought. Which, given the shaved head and lack of recent meals, was pretty bad.

It's okay, I'm okay. Mercy sent her friend the reassurance automatically, reflexively, before stopping to consider that it might not be a good idea, given present company. Atrea couldn't answer her as a telepath could, but her thoughts were loud and clear, not only to Mercy, but probably to every Talented person in the room. Which Mercy counted at six.

Okay? This is okay? What the hell have they done? Her hair! What are those discolored patches on her skin? Bastards. Fuck this. No one ever thinks of everything. They will make a mistake. We are getting out of here.

While Atrea was thinking all of this, Willem Frain was lowering a full body scanner around her chair. It cut her off from Mercy's view, but that didn't matter. The tone of her thoughts reassured Mercy better than anything else possibly could: her friend was as well as she could be, under the circumstances. She was still Atrea Hades, smuggler-born, military trained, and all-around badass. People underestimated her a lot because she was tiny and unassuming, with a pretty face and blue eyes she could make guileless whenever she wanted. That was their mistake.

It might be more difficult to fool these particular people, since they could read her thoughts. On the other hand, Frain seemed to believe anyone not Talented was useless. If Mercy warned her, they would hear it. But it was best to assume they already knew everything about both of them. In that case, nothing Mercy said, short of "this is the escape plan" would make a difference.

Atrea, they can hear everything you think. They've poked around in my head so much, they know things about me that I didn't even remember. Assume the same is true for you.

Mercy couldn't see her friend's reaction, but she could hear it. It consisted of a lot of profanity. Growing up in and out of shady spaceports had given her a huge repertoire.

I hope a black hole opens up and eats them all, was her final thought on the matter. Followed quickly by, *just not while we're here with them.*

The burst of amusement surprised Mercy. A laugh bubbled up, aborted by the rigid hold of the binding field that held her so securely. Atrea's attitude brightened hers. A small, horribly selfish part of her was suddenly very glad her friend was here with her. Which only made her feel worse.

What the hell is this? Why are they scanning me?

Atrea's thought, driven by uncertainty and fear, drove all of the good feelings away. It reminded Mercy of exactly why they were here.

"This isn't going to work," she told Frain, the words difficult to form within the field. She wanted to say them out loud, though. Both as an act of defiance, and so Atrea would hear. Hopefully Willem Frain would reply in kind.

He stepped within Mercy's field of vision and lowered himself to kneel beside her chair. His eyes were just as cold as ever, the scar across his cheek stark under the too-bright lights of the room.

"It will," he said, smiling. "Trust me. Let's start, shall we?" He nodded to someone outside Mercy's field of vision. She could feel them, though. All of them.

Their minds were like Frain's – warm, familiar, and distinct. Six Talented people. Her mother's mind had felt like this. She suddenly remembered the other time she'd felt it – when she was thirteen, trying to stow away on a ship at Verath 6. She forced her thoughts away before they could fully form and Frain picked up on them. Instead, she wondered why; why did Talented minds feel so different from nulls? They were like puzzle pieces she hadn't known were missing, snapping into place and making her whole. She hated it. She didn't want anything to do with these people, and definitely didn't want to feel like she belonged with them in some way.

"But you do. You will come to see that, Mercy." Frain stood up. "Pay attention to the difference. Our minds feel different to you, I can see it in your thoughts. Look at Atrea's mind. Look as deeply as you can for any hint of that same feeling. It should be there, somewhere. Buried. Her mother was Talented, even if she is not. The ability is there, latent, dormant, genetically recessive."

Mercy stiffened, shocked. The sting of betrayal bit at her, paranoia raising its ugly head. Why? Why wouldn't Atrea tell her something like that, when Mercy had shared her own secrets? What else had she kept from her?

But she couldn't trust anything these people said. Maybe they were lying.

Then Atrea's thoughts registered, and she realized her friend was as shocked as she was. And just as skeptical. She didn't believe what Willem Frain was saying, couldn't believe her father never would have told her. Mercy wasn't so sure. She'd always felt the old Wolf had his secrets.

She took as deep a breath as her restraints allowed. "Look, even if what you say is true, I still don't know what you want from me. How do you expect me to do anything to a recessive gene?" It sounded crazy, especially when she said it out loud.

"I don't know." Willem gave her a long look. "But you have the gift to do so, and you will figure it out."

Atrea's panicked thoughts hit her like spikes, shouted so frantically Mercy winced and raised her shields unconsciously in defense. *What the hell is this guy talking about? He's crazy, right? He has to be insane, that's the only possible explanation. Mercy, tell me he's fucking insane. Tell me—*

Out of the corner of her eye, Mercy saw Willem raise a pained hand to his head, wincing. Nobody shouted their thoughts louder than a null in emotional crisis. They usually didn't even realize it, but it was one of the reasons Mercy always kept her shields up around other people. After a moment, Willem responded to Atrea himself.

"I assure you, Captain Hades, we are all quite sane. I'm sure, despite your unfortunate lack of actual Talent, that you have quite a developed sense of intuition. A sense when something just feels off, or when a deal is about go horribly wrong. A tremor down your spine when a particular man catches your eye at a spaceport, perhaps?"

It took Atrea a moment to answer.

"I—that's not—"

"Oh, don't bother denying it. I've been through your mind, seen every such incident for myself already." Frain waved a dismissive hand. "The most recent occurrence was on Yuan-Ki, of course. The clone who served your drinks; you knew there was something off about him, but you kept it to yourself. You felt guilty, wondering if the fact that he was a clone was bothering you on some level. It was not. He was not a good actor, and I'm afraid he was nervous that you would somehow sense the drug he used to spike your drinks. Fortunately, your own guilt kept you from reacting to what your intuition was telling you."

It took Atrea a moment to process what he was saying and respond.

"I really hate you," she said at last. "Stay out of my head." Her tone wasn't menacing. It was flat and matter-of-fact. It was the tone Atrea used right before things went really bad and she started shooting people. She used to carry two metal throwers, antiquated weapons that fired metal projectiles that would rip through flesh and bone in a messy explosion of blood and gore. Since joining the Navy, she'd had to switch over to standard disruptors. They stunned their targets, jolting them with enough electricity to knock them down and out long enough to throw restraints on them. Of course, Atrea carried a backup piece she'd modified herself. It burned through flesh and organs and left nothing but charred tissue behind. Stunning people was all well and good, but she'd been raised never to leave a real enemy at your back. If she survived this, she'd hunt Willem Frain to the ends of the universe.

Mercy thought of all the times Atrea had stopped in the middle of something to change direction, or said it was time to go right before a brawl broke out, or somehow knew port security was nearby when they were supposed to be clear on the other side of the dock. What Willem Frain was saying made sense. For the first time, Mercy started to wonder if he wasn't actually crazy. Fear skittered like ice through her veins, shuddered down her spine. If he wasn't crazy, if everything he said was true, what the hell did that make her? What did it all mean?

"Now." Willem turned toward Mercy. "If you would please drop your shields and do as I have instructed." He paused. "If you refuse, Atrea will not be returning to her cell."

The implied threat was clear enough, and unnecessary. Mercy remembered his threats without the reminder. She glared at him, but ultimately did as he asked.

She dropped her shields, and went into her friend's mind. She stopped just inside the natural shields every null had. They weren't like Talented shields, but built on instinct and the mind's unconscious need to protect itself. Usually thin and full of weak places that allowed thoughts to be projected out easily, or a telepath a route in. Atrea's were a little stronger than this, probably because she was aware of Mercy's gifts, and that awareness had led to her strengthening her shields without being conscious that they even existed. Not that Mercy invaded her mind often. But sometimes they used her Talent as a way to communicate silently when they needed to. Atrea knew Mercy could read her thoughts, and deliberately directed them at her sometimes, and Mercy actively used her telepathy to tell Atrea things. But she'd never gone past this point, the place where she could read surface thoughts, the things Atrea was actively thinking. Even that could be confusing if she didn't concentrate.

People really had no idea how chaotic and unorganized their thoughts could be, jumping like quicksilver from subject to subject, layered and overlapping. The mind moved at much greater speeds than the words someone stopped to consciously think to themselves. It could be overwhelming. But over the years, Mercy had developed her own technique for sorting them all out. She allowed the quicksilver thoughts to make just an impression, a flash of insight into what they were about, that quickly faded. She focused on the loudest, most present thoughts. It was a little like trying to focus on your friend's voice in a crowd if the other people were all talking loudly and at once.

This is impossible. They can't do this. Mercy can't do this. I can't be Talented. Atrea's panic made the thoughts come fast and hard, one after the other.

Atrea, it's me. Look, if I don't try this, Willem says he'll kill you. I know this isn't going to work, but I can't just do nothing.

There was jumble of too many thoughts at

once before Atrea settled on one. *I don't want to die, but I don't want this.*

I know. Mercy hesitated, conscious of those who were listening. *I don't think it will work. I don't see how it will work. But can you imagine me trying to explain to your father how I just did nothing and let them kill you?*

Another chaotic reaction made Mercy wince. Sometimes, talking to Atrea like this gave her a killer headache. She could just imagine what that was going to be like in this place.

No. I don't like it. What if you mess something up? What if you...break my brain?

There it was, the real reason Atrea was panicking. If she was honest, Mercy was worried about that, too. She'd never done anything like this before.

I'm going to be really careful. I have an idea of what he wants me to try. I probably won't even find what he's asking me to look for, so I doubt I'll be doing anything at all. Just looking. Okay?

This time, the jumble of mixed up thoughts went on even longer. Finally, a single thought emerged. *Okay. Just be really careful. This is the only brain I have, you know.*

Normally, the joke would have elicited a smile from Mercy. But right now it just amplified her anxiety. *I know.*

She stayed where she was for a moment. She allowed her awareness to extend beyond Atrea, and felt the six Talented minds in the room once more. It was comforting, even if she didn't want it to be. The brilliant warmth of their Talent melted away her fear and anxiety, each one a soft golden glow she could almost see.

Taking a deep breath, she plunged deeper into Atrea's mind, looking for the same warmth, the same hint of light. The deeper she went, the more thoughts sped past her. Mercy tried to ignore them. She didn't want to invade Atrea's privacy like this, didn't want to know her friend's most private hopes and fears.

It was impossible not to hear them. Suddenly, she knew how much Atrea loved the order of the military, the black and white precision of it. She knew how much she missed her father and Mercy, the conflict she wrestled with trying to decide whether to sign on for another tour of service. She knew about the man in Atrea's life she'd never mentioned, the one she'd spent the last four years in a relationship with until distance and secrets finally pulled it all apart. The loss and hurt were still fresh.

Memories started surfacing then, pulling Mercy even deeper into her mind. She understood, suddenly, why Atrea was so determined to help Mercy find her mother: because she'd never known her own, and the lack was this big empty hole her father would never talk about. She saw her friend's pride when she was selected for a special unit in the Navy, how her scores in gunnery were the top of her class, the top of her unit. She saw the first time Atrea figured out that her new best friend was Talented. She saw her fears, her shame and embarrassment that Mercy would know every secret thought, that she might not like her anymore. She saw when Atrea realized her new military friends would never understand her smuggler upbringing, and the evasions and lies she told about her past.

She saw the conversation with her father, on Windfall. How he left the military to be with Atrea's mother because it was too dangerous to stay in. He had to protect her, just as Atrea should be protecting Mercy by staying away from anything to do with the government. *Family comes first. Don't fool yourself into thinking you belong with them. Not every mission you're given is black and white. Not everything they ask is for the good of the people. Don't let yourself be used.*

Everywhere Mercy looked, there were personal things she didn't want to know about her friend. But nowhere did she see that hint of light and warmth she was looking for. She felt herself getting tired, starting to drift. It was becoming more difficult to separate Atrea's thoughts from her own. If she stayed much longer, she risked losing herself or harming Atrea. She pulled back, and was surprised at how long it took, how many layers she had to move through to reach that place on the surface of Atrea's mind again.

By the time she did, she became aware of a distant, pounding pain, a level of exhaustion that dragged at her thoughts and turned her sluggish. She struggled to leave Atrea's mind altogether, was alarmed to realize she almost didn't make it past her shields. Her awareness sank back into her own body, and the distant pain exploded into agony, radiating behind her eyes, through her jaw, her neck, her skull. Her stomach churned with it. The lights in the room seared across her vision. She had to close her eyes to block them out.

Disappointing, she heard Willem Frain say coldly. She felt him assessing her, couldn't drum up the energy to care. *Take her back to her cell. We will resume when she has recovered. This is what comes of not exercising one's gift. This is what happens to Talented too afraid to use it.* She could hear the sneering contempt in his words, had a distant desire to spit on him.

If only she could be sure her head wouldn't explode from the movement.

"What's wrong? What's happening?" She heard Atrea's voice as though from far away, echoing and faint. They must have removed the scanner. Mercy tried to make her mouth form words, because she knew she wouldn't be able to use her Talent right now.

"I'll be fine." At least, that's what she tried to say. She wasn't sure what actually emerged, because the voices around her were rapidly growing fainter and harder to make out. She knew what this was. Burn out. Too much with her gift, too fast. Her body was shutting down to recover. She'd fall asleep and stay that way until her mind regrouped. It had never been this bad before, but she'd never gone so deeply into someone's mind before, either. Never seen and assimilated so many thoughts and memories at once.

Dimly, she was aware of being lifted, carried for a time. It made her head spin and intensified the pain. She clenched her jaw and swallowed, trying desperately not to vomit. Not to spare whoever was carrying her, but because she really didn't think throwing up would help her head feel any better. Finally, she felt the cold waft of air that meant her cell, felt the solid, uncomfortable surface of her bunk and its single blanket. Nothing had ever felt so wonderful.

She curled up, still keeping her eyes closed. Waiting for oblivion to take her, or the pain to recede. She might have cried, she couldn't be sure. Then she felt the press of a capsulet against her neck, and didn't care what they were injecting her with if it brought her peace. It was the last thing she was conscious of, before oblivion rushed up to claim her.

WHEN MERCY WOKE, her eyes felt gritty and bruised, her head ached, and her stomach lurched in protest when she gingerly sat up. It felt exactly like that time she and Atrea got into her father's private stash of Bennethan rum and drank the whole bottle between them. When he'd caught them, too late, the old Wolf took one look and said the morning would be punishment enough.

He wasn't wrong.

She was surprised to find a tube of something other than water waiting for her, propped beside her bunk along with a nutritional bar. The liquid was translucent, green, and smelled faintly sweet. Since it was the only thing to drink, and choking down the dry, tasteless bar without some kind of liquid was practically impossible, she took a sip. It didn't taste bad, and the residual headache and bruised feeling around her eyes faded instantly. Encouraged, she drank more.

Whatever the stuff was, it definitely helped her feel more human again. Even her stomach settled. She leaned back against the wall behind her and chewed mechanically, alternating between the bar and sipping the drink until both were gone. She remembered what had happened well enough. Worried, she reached out to Atrea. Her mental touch was tentative, unsure of her reception.

Atrea? You okay?

Mercy! I was so worried. I—

Abruptly the connection cut off, and Mercy could feel nothing of her friend, hear none of her thoughts. Alarmed, she sat up.

Atrea? Atrea!

None of that, now. Willem Frain's mental voice was as distinct as the imprint of his mind. *You must save your strength for our next session. It appears you have very little of it to spare. We have a lot of work ahead of us, but rest assured, Mercy. We will not stop until you succeed, or Captain Hades is no longer a viable subject.*

That was exactly what Mercy feared most.

CHAPTER FOUR

*I*n an ideal situation, Reaper would use his Talent to search out every mind on the space station and kill them. In an ideal situation, he would separate out the target, kill everyone else aboard, and then his team could physically board the station and retrieve her. Killing came easily to him. It was the first solution to any problem. However, years of training made him stop and analyze. That same training assured him that killing was not always the *best* solution to a problem. It was not the most optimum solution to this one. No matter how he looked at the situation, that didn't change.

One, their target reportedly had a friend with her, someone Wolfgang Hades didn't want dead. Reaper really didn't care what Hades wanted, but his orders did. He didn't always care what his orders stated, either, and if orders were the only issue, he might ignore them. They weren't. The minds aboard that station were shielded, which meant they were Talented. Even if he attacked them using his gifts, he might not be able to kill them quickly enough to avoid a counter attack, which could include the injury or death of the target. That was an unacceptable risk.

It left him with one option: a physical assault. While the space station appeared to have no weapons, and the corvette he commanded could easily destroy it, that, too, was not a solution. They had no choice but to board it.

There was no ideal method for boarding a hostile space station. In many ways, a planet, a moon, even a colony on an asteroid would be an easier target. Unfortunately, their quarry wasn't in any of those places. She was here, at an abandoned storage facility for a now defunct mining company, a long-forgotten station floating in orbit around a moon that, according to scans, had rich deposits of a variety of metals.

"Log it." Reaper didn't look away from the view of the space station. He had no doubt one of his dogs would note the system, the moon and the materials for possible future retrieval. The Lomada system was too far inside Commonwealth territory to be an easy target, but if the potential rewards were great enough, it could be worth the risk. Pirates took their bounty where they could. Someone, probably Cannon, the current pirate king, would weigh the risks versus the rewards.

That was a different mission, for another day. Today, they had a space station to board, a retrieval to complete. And only one point of entry. Cutting another would take too much time, and would not be quiet. No way to enter without being noticed. That would also put the target at risk, but Reaper thought it could be controlled.

The enemy would be confident they could deal with an incursion, set up an ambush. The target's life would not be in jeopardy until a tipping point occurred. Until they realized they would not win.

"Something isn't right." Jaxon spoke from where he sat strapped into a jump seat.

The others were unbuckling safety straps, getting to their feet, checking weapons.

They were a good unit, handpicked by Reaper to serve as his dogs, the squad of highly trained men assigned to him. Dog units were for the highest ranking pirates, ostensibly a kind of protective detail or honor guard, and a show of overt power. Reaper didn't use his that way. This team had been with him for five years. Jaxon, Mateo, Knox, Titus, and Zion. Each one brought a specialized skill or knowledge to the team. Jaxon, tracking; Mateo, scouting; Knox, demolitions; Titus, medical; and Zion, weapons. Each of them could also pilot the ship, act as gunner, or board another ship to take it by force. Their Talent added another layer of ability.

Jaxon sat still, his head cocked as if he were listening to something far away.

"What is it?" Reaper asked. Part of his attention remained on the station. If anyone was paying attention, their ship's presence would be noted soon. A corvette was a smaller class of warship, but certainly not so small as to escape notice entirely. They were transmitting a merchant code, but one look at the ship's armament and shielding would make that suspect.

"Not sure." The Hunter paused, frowning. Reaper waited. Trying to rush Jaxon wouldn't get an answer any faster. "Something doesn't feel right. The target."

"But she's here?" Reaper's voice was sharp; they couldn't afford to waste time and resources being wrong. Not that Jaxon had ever been wrong before. But Reaper didn't make the mistake of believing a Hunter's tracking to be infallible. Nothing and no one ever was.

"Yes. No." Jaxon unclasped his safety restraint with a hard motion, betraying his frustration, and stood. He was a tall man, medium brown skin, a roughly masculine face made more menacing by the growth of stubble along his jaw, and exhaustion etching lines around his eyes and mouth. Jax's gift wasn't without a price, and he'd been using it nonstop for weeks. "She *is* here. She just feels different. I mean *really* different."

Reaper frowned. What did that mean?

"Are you sure your gift is giving you an accurate read?" He was careful how he worded the question. Jaxon's loyalty was certain, but he could be short tempered, especially as close to burnout as he was now. Unsurprisingly, the other man's dark eyes narrowed into a scowl.

"Once I have a psychic imprint, I don't lose it."

"And yet." Reaper let the two words hang in the air.

Jax ran a hand through shaggy, uneven hair that was multiple hues of brown. It often looked like a six-year-old had hacked at it with a knife. In fact, Reaper knew Jax cut it himself, whenever it got long enough to irritate him.

"I don't know how to explain it, boss. The imprint I picked up weeks ago isn't the same." He looked at Reaper unhappily. "It's her. Just…different."

Reaper considered for a long moment.

"If the subject has undergone severe torture, or had her mind damaged significantly?"

Jax shrugged.

"I once tracked a lost teenager on Rasvus. Kid fell down a ravine, cracked open his head, fell into a coma and never woke up. Doc said even if he did, he'd never have mobility or motor function again. His imprint never changed."

Interesting. A puzzle, but one that would have to be solved later.

"We need reconnaissance," said Reaper. "Ghost." Mateo stepped forward. His Talent was so unique he'd been given a nickname that represented it. Like Reaper.

"I'm on it, boss."

A moment later, a ghostly shimmer appeared next to Mateo, an exact duplicate of himself, down to the armored clothing he wore, the faint sheen of the black fabric visible beneath the lights of the ship as he moved. His short black hair was mussed from the nap he'd caught during transit, his dark eyes hooded and deceptively sleepy. Ghost had a habit of looking lazy, of being the guy in the back of the room looking half asleep, like he wasn't paying attention. Reaper knew that for a lie. Ghost was always paying attention. To everything.

Reaper gave him a nod, and the specter disappeared. It would reappear inside the space station in a few moments, but the visual would be more opaque, a faint outline barely visible to the naked eye. Ghost could project himself anywhere within his line of sight, and even more remarkably, he retained awareness in his actual body. Effectively, he was in two places at once.

It would be a few minutes before he had anything for them.

"Maneuver to the airlock. Prepare to board." Reaper paused, considering. He counted more than a dozen individual minds aboard the station. They were Talented, and he and his team had no idea what gifts they might possess. "Zion." He called forward the dog he considered the most dangerous. While Reaper had chosen each of them meticulously, and had no doubt of their loyalty to him, part of him would forever be wary of Zion and his particular Talent.

"You want me to back him up?" asked the other man with a good-natured grin as he shouldered his way into the forward compartment, past Mateo. It was not an unusual tactic for them to take, but Reaper shook his head.

"No," he said, and held out his hand.

Zion froze, the smile slipping away. He was usually the one Reaper sent in whenever they needed a face, someone to talk or negotiate. His chiseled features and blue eyes were considered a striking combination, paired with skin colored a dark, burnished gold, and the lean, toned build all of the dogs shared. Lean, so they could move quickly and flexibly, toned because they trained their physical strength as much as their mental. To this, Zion added an easy ability to laugh and joke, to be approachable in a way Reaper would never be. It put people at ease, and they liked him instinctively. Particularly women. But those were not the skills Reaper needed from him today.

To his credit, Zion didn't hesitate. He took Reaper's hand, and used his Talent to draw upon Reaper's, to mimic it. His demeanor changed. The laughter fled from his features, the very air around him becoming charged. The dogs closest to him moved back instinctively, giving him space the same way they did Reaper. Even Zion's eyes lightened, the intense blue fading to the ice of imminent death, becoming the same color as Reaper's. The eyes of a Killer.

"Ready," Zion said, his voice as expressionless as his face.

When we go in, said Reaper, speaking telepathically to all of them, *Zion and I will take point. Then Knox, followed by Mateo and Jax. Titus stays here.* They needed their pilot in place for a fast extraction in case anything should go wrong. *Once we've dealt with any immediate hostiles, Jax will lead us to the target.*

What if you need a medic? Titus did not sound pleased at being left behind.

Reaper gave everyone a long look. *Don't need one*, he ordered.

His tone did not leave room for dissent. In reality, any of them could manage field dressings or med-salve. If anyone was hurt beyond that, well, the situation would change. Killing everyone on the station with his Talent might just become the most expedient solution at that point.

Zion nodded to show he understood. Reaper had picked him for his team of dogs for just this purpose. Then he spent years training him for occasions like this, times when Zion would use Reaper's Talent to give them not one, but two Killers. An unstoppable force by any definition.

A Killer's Talent saw death. It pinpointed vulnerability, weakness, giving insight into the quickest, most efficient way to kill anyone. It was the first thing Reaper saw when he looked at someone, the first thing he thought of when he walked into a room, the thing that dominated his thoughts at any given moment. In the mental pathways of the mind, a Killer saw exactly where and how to strike. Sometimes a mental attack was the most efficient. Sometimes it was physical, or a combination of the two. Like a Hunter's ability to track, the Talent was extremely specialized. Killers usually only bred with other Killers, resulting in a line of gifted assassins going back to the creation of the very first Talented. But Reaper was different. Only his father had been a Killer.

It didn't make him any less deadly.

He'd trained as a child alongside his brethren. Like his brother, Dem, Reaper learned how to kill as efficiently as possible. He did not rely on his Talent, but used it to enhance the skills he'd spent his life training in. The fact that his mother was a powerful telepath and telekinetic, and had also passed her Talents on to him, only made him more dangerous.

He waited now in the calm before the battle. Still, silent, every breath measured and even. The corvette moved into position alongside the station, and he could hear the docking mechanism extend, the seal connecting to the station's airlock. If somehow those aboard the space station had failed to notice their presence before, they were surely aware of it now.

"They've split into two groups," Mateo said suddenly. "Half a dozen at the airlock, armed with disruptors and plasma shields. Another six in a central room, looks like some kind of lab. Both the target and secondary target are there."

Reaper let out a breath.

"Knox," he said, "pulse grenade." The dog who specialized in explosives and demolitions tossed one up to Reaper, who handed it to Zion. Pulse grenades served a dual purpose – the bright light they emitted when they went off would effectively blind anyone in the vicinity, while also detonating a short range EMP burst that should drain their plasma shields.

"We use only one," Reaper said. "I don't want to take out power to any of the station's functions." It would be extremely inconvenient to suddenly lose artificial gravity or life support.

Reaper looked at Mateo.

"Target status?"

"That's…hard to answer, boss."

Reaper frowned. "Explain."

"Both target and secondary target are alive, but…neither one is in good condition. Something is very wrong with our primary. They've got her in a full body scanner, and she started screaming about five minutes ago and wouldn't stop. Hostiles just sedated her."

That was not good news. A few weeks ago, Wolfgang Hades had asked them to find and re-trieve his daughter, presumed taken against her will by forces unknown. The smuggler had provided them with good information, and necessary resources for many years. Losing that connection because they failed to retrieve his daughter in an acceptable condition would be unfortunate.

"And the secondary?" Reaper asked, not expecting to hear any better news.

Mateo hesitated. "Conscious. Physically, she's been through some stuff. Medical testing of some kind, maybe. She's Talented, and…" Mateo stopped, looking nervous. Whatever it was, he was reluctant to voice it. Reaper's interest sharpened.

"She's what?"

"I feel this pull," Mateo said finally. He looked at Reaper. "I haven't felt anything like it since I was a kid. Since Lilith."

Everyone in the compartment went still. Reaper was pretty sure some of them stopped breathing. Lilith, the pirate's last Queen. Power hungry. Ruthless. Callous to the point of cruelty. For forty years, she ruled the pirates with a jackboot at their throats. When the virus swept through their ranks eleven years ago, taking Lilith with it, no one shed a tear at her death. But it left a void that filled with violence and chaos, until her grandson Cannon stepped over the bodies of his cousins and took control, kept them in line, stopped the senseless fights and sudden eruptions of violence. It wasn't perfect, but it was working. For now.

"How old is she?" asked Reaper. His voice sounded distant to his own ears. He was going to that cold, familiar place of quiet inside. The stillness before death.

"What?" Mateo was clearly startled by the question.

Reaper just looked at him. He knew his eyes had chilled to pale chips of white blue.

"Um, hard to say in her current condition," Mateo said nervously. "I'd guess somewhere in her twenties, maybe early thirties."

Young, then. Too young to be Lilith's missing daughter. Not too young to be her granddaughter. A flash of memory hit Reaper, of standing on a spaceport dock staring at a young girl as she begged him to let her go. To this day, he didn't know why he'd done it. He was a Killer, not one to be moved by emotional pleas. But she'd stared at him with green eyes wide with terror, and he'd been powerless to refuse her.

He'd asked himself countless times since, why? Why had he allowed her to leave? Why had he distracted his brother Dem, a Hunter on his first hunt, to give her time to escape? The only answer he could come up with chilled him to the bone. Because that girl was a queen. And her influence, even as a child, had been so great he'd been powerless to refuse her.

Now it was possible their paths had crossed once again. More than possible. Queens were the rarest of Talented, and Reaper had never seen or heard of another. For a small, frozen eternity, he considered killing her. Seriously weighed it. The pirates were doing all right with Cannon at the helm. Another queen was a risk; one he wasn't sure he was willing to take.

Dispassionately, he looked at all the possibilities. And realized that a queen's abilities were more than just about calming the populace. A queen, a true queen, like Lilith, could hold the key to their survival. Or she could finish what the virus had started eleven years ago and destroy what remained of them.

Part of him wanted to kill her, regardless. Lilith had targeted his family more than once. Tried to assassinate his mother. Arranged to have his father killed. If the virus hadn't ended her, Reaper would have. But too much was at stake. When the virus swept through, moving from ship to ship and colony to colony, attacking female Talented minds young and old, it wiped out nearly half their population before they managed to get it under control. In the decade since, they had made little ground toward recovery.

Like it or not, they needed another queen and what her Talents could do for them. For now, they needed her. If she became another Lilith, Reaper would reevaluate. For a moment, that young girl in his memory looked at him with pleading eyes once again. Would he still be so susceptible to her now, as an adult? He pushed the thought aside. There would time to wonder about that later. Right now, they had a mission.

"That woman is now our primary," he said finally.

Everyone stared at him. He felt the weight of their eyes, their questions. It said something about their training, or perhaps their fear of him in this moment, that no one voiced those questions out loud.

"We retrieve her at all costs. Alive."

CHAPTER FIVE

I will kill her. Willem Frain's mental voice was cool and matter of fact. He thought the words with no inflection, his expression smooth and calm. Mercy believed him. She was also terrified that the only choices she had were to watch Atrea die, or damage her irrevocably in trying to prevent it.

Because she'd found it. That infinitesimal hint of Talent in Atrea's mind. Barely visible, it was more of a feeling than anything, a suggestion of that familiar warmth so prevalent in the Talented minds around them. Mercy had stumbled across it while drifting without any sense of purpose or direction in Atrea's mind, letting the thoughts and memories filter past her without paying attention to any of them.

Unfortunately, Willem knew she'd found it. He was, she realized, in her head, a phantom presence in the background, watching and patiently waiting for precisely this moment. Just so he would know, and could threaten Atrea one more time in a bid to force Mercy to do what he wanted. She was really getting tired of that. She fought the sudden, irrational urge to attack him in the only way she could, here in her own mind. The only thing that stopped her was what he might do to Atrea. Mercy was pretty certain that while she had no real notion of how to kill someone with her mind, Willem Frain was some kind of expert. He wasn't holding a disrupter to Atrea's head, but Mercy could sense something, a coiled tension to his presence that let her know he was prepared to do…something.

Mercy. Stop wasting time. Do it now.

Do what? She wanted to scream the words at him. She had no idea what she was doing, didn't he understand that? She didn't want to damage her friend's mind.

Instinct will lead you, he told her implacably. *If you don't take that hint of Talent and make it real and viable, she is useless. I will do more than damage her, and my patience is officially at an end. Do it now, or not at all.*

If Atrea dies, I have no reason left to cooperate with you, Mercy told him desperately. *You will have nothing to hold over me.*

I see. Remember, Mercy, you chose this. Before she could react, she felt the tension in his mind release. Something with the appearance of black smoke moved like quicksilver from his mind to Atrea's. It left a miasma of oily sickness in its wake, hitting Mercy with waves of disorientation and nausea. She choked on it, struggling to hold onto her thoughts even as she screamed at him.

Stop! Atrea, Atrea!

Mercy…what's happening? Something… Atrea's

thoughts dissolved into incoherence. Nightmare images and gibberish words made a chaos of noise without sound. Mercy had to fight to keep them out, to separate her own mind enough to stay clear.

In a moment, the waves of turmoil and nausea lessened and stopped, and Mercy could think clearly again. Panic seized her as she saw the black smoke settling in the crevices of Atrea's mind, sliding between thoughts and memories until it filled all of the spaces between.

What have you done? She raged at Willem Frain. *I will kill you for this.*

There is still a chance for your friend. Give her Talent, Mercy, and I will save her from the lethal poison I just unleashed inside her mind.

He'd given Atrea some kind of poison? How was that even possible?

She has little time, Mercy. Do it.

I don't know how! If she could have, Mercy would have pounded her fists against something in sheer frustration. Preferably against Willem Frain's skull. Unfortunately, she sat immobilized to a chair by gravity bindings. She couldn't move her fists beyond clenching the fingers more tightly together.

If you fail, she will be dead within the hour. An excruciating hour.

Desperate, Mercy scrambled back to where she'd felt that hint of warmth, searching through the chaos her friend's mind had become, sliding past the nightmares and black smoke. She ignored images of Wolfgang Hades dying a horrible death in the cold of space, shut out the sound of Atrea screaming as she watched an image of Mercy being cut apart in some kind of lab. These were distractions, ghostly images trying to pull Atrea down into insanity. Mercy had no time to think about them now.

She found it then, burning more brightly in this new darkness. Without stopping to think it through, Mercy grabbed that hint of warmth and yanked on it as hard as she could, using the strength of her own mind to build it into something bigger, something more. It occurred to her that the glow seemed to be beating back the black smoke, and she redoubled her efforts, pouring her own energy into that speck of light until it grew, blinding in its brilliance. Just when she thought she'd run to the end of her own ability, when she had nothing left to give, it burst outward in a wash of spectacular colors: purple, blue, gold and green, a display as awe-inspiring as it was powerful. The shockwave threw Mercy out of Atrea's mind, and Willem Frain out of hers.

Bright spots of light danced in front of her eyes, her own mind feeling heavy and distant. Her ears were ringing, and something warm and wet dripped from her nose and over her lips, tasting metallic and strange. Blood. Mercy tried to speak, and found she couldn't make her lips move, couldn't make her tongue obey her commands. For a moment, she was grateful for the gravitational field holding her bound to the chair. She was pretty sure it was the only thing keeping her upright.

Then the world lurched and came into focus. The ringing in her ears had either stopped or faded, because she could suddenly hear noise all around her. People were talking all at once, something about an airlock and a ship. A woman's voice said she had the samples, asked Willem what he wanted to do. And Willem? He was laughing, sounding just a little bit drunk and a lot crazy. But over all of that, one sound had Mercy's blood running cold, adrenaline chasing the last of the muddled feeling from her system.

Atrea was screaming. Screaming like someone in untold amounts of pain, like the sound was being ripped from her forcibly, raw and keening. Someone lifted the scanner away from her, and it just made the screaming louder. A man rushed in and jabbed a capsulet into her leg. Atrea slumped into her bonds, all the tension leaving her body at once.

"What are you doing? Help her!" Mercy found her voice, forced her mouth to shape the words. They came out much weaker than she intended, barely audible even to her own ears. She was afraid that using telepathy right now would send her spiraling into burn out, and she couldn't afford that. She strained against her bonds, her vision still colored with spots, painting people as shadows outlined in light.

"Willem." She focused on him, said his name louder. "Willem! Help her, damn you."

He leaned against one of the tables, his expression a strange mixture of triumph and something like fear. A woman grabbed his arm, shouting at him. Three other people were running to the door, disrupters in hand. A man moved with them, no weapon in his hands, his body moving with a strange, stiff gait that looked unnatural. He was athletic, arms and back corded with muscle that he must have worked to build. More than anything, that identified him as some kind of soldier, one who didn't rely purely on his Talent. He wore supple, armored clothing that wouldn't do much more than slow down a knife blade. Then Mercy realized she could see a faint shimmer around him, a shield of some kind surrounding his body.

It occurred to her that something more was happening, that something beyond what she had just done to Atrea was behind this chaos. She didn't care. Whatever it was didn't matter right now. Only Atrea.

"Can you take them both, Octavia?" Mercy heard Willem ask the woman beside him. Focusing back on them, she was startled to realize the woman was no more than a young girl, maybe seventeen at most. Her eyes were wide and frightened. She shook her head.

"I can take the samples, and you. Unless you want to stay behind, sir."

Willem's eyes narrowed, his mouth tightening. Mercy had seen the expression often enough to recognize when an answer displeased him. So did the girl, apparently, because she flinched before she caught herself, the smooth pallor of her ebony skin taking on the ashen undertone of fear.

"I—I could try, but if I'm not strong enough, we will all be lost. Sir."

Willem appeared to consider before shaking his head.

"No, that is too great a risk." He cursed softly.

Over by the door, the man with the strange

walk had stopped. The others moved to either side, waiting, but he stood directly in front of the hatch. A sudden blast of heat washed from him over Mercy, and she realized he was doing something with his Talent, something big. It built inside of him until he outshone everyone else in the room, a beacon that called to her and made gooseflesh raise along her arms at the same time. Then the pool of power burst out of him in a bubble she could see. It filled the doorway, a shimmering wall of telekinetics, giving a pearlescent sheen to the empty doorway. It was more than just a shield. Mercy could tell by the way those nearest edged away from it, fear etched onto their faces. The man smiled and stepped back, hands loose at his sides, an expectant bounce to his feet. He didn't look afraid. He looked eager.

Mercy's heart pounded as adrenaline hit her. Someone was here. Someone had found them. She looked over at Atrea's unconscious form, and felt a rush of tears. Someone who was too damn late.

Willem Frain moved into her line of sight.

"We could have learned so much more," he said. "It is a tragedy, but a possibility we prepared for."

Mercy glared at him, saying nothing.

"I am truly sorry, Mercy," he said. "I had hoped to continue our experiments for some time longer. I'm afraid that will no longer be possible."

"You said you would help Atrea." Mercy had never hated anyone as much as she did Willem Frain in this moment. "You fucking killed her."

"Yes. I'm afraid she will die. You can take small

comfort. She won't live long enough to go mad from you've done to her."

"What *you* have done."

He favored her with a small smile, kneeling in front of her while the girl huddled behind him, casting anxious glances toward the door, and gripped a temperature-controlled travel case tightly.

"Yes, I suppose we are equally responsible. It is too bad that Octavia's Talent is not stronger. I would have enjoyed watching you awaken Talent in someone again, Mercy." Willem reached up a hand and wiped away the blood still dripping from her nose. "Although it does appear to take its toll on you to do so. Something else to note into the log, I suppose."

"Fuck you," she bit out.

His smile faded. "I will not miss your vocabulary, however."

He reached up a hand and cupped her face, the action much like a lover's, but the touch impersonal and cold. His mind touched hers, and Mercy was horrified to see that same coil of black smoke he'd unleashed on Atrea. It gathered like a storm, roiling and spinning in the cage of his mind as he poised to release it.

"I *am* sorry, Mercy," he said. "It is an unspeakable loss to end your life. However. If we can't have you, and all that."

Mercy felt his shields open, and tried with everything she had to strengthen her own, already shredded and weakened as they were. She flinched away, waiting for the inevitable impact of sickness and turmoil to hit her mind with the black smoke.

Nothing happened. She stared at him, saw him narrow dark eyes that sparked with sudden irritation. His shields opened wider, and still the coils of smoke didn't move. She saw his jaw work with effort, his whole body tense. Something was wrong. The mental poison stayed where it was, deadly and waiting within his mind. Her shields were not keeping it out; it simply did not move toward her.

Mercy felt the sudden presence of more Talented minds at the same moment that one of Willem's people by the door called out, "They're here."

With a curse, he stood. He pulled a disrupter free and pointed it at Mercy. He pressed it to her head, a lethal range for a weapon that normally stunned its targets. She stared at him while he stared back. She could feel the tension in his body, but by now was starting to realize that something was happening, something outside Willem's control. His finger poised on the trigger, and didn't move.

"Sir." Octavia sounded nervous behind him. "Sir, we should go."

Willem stared at Mercy, not moving. Dimly, she was aware of what was happening by the hatch. The man in the center took one step forward, and *pushed* with his mind. The telekinetic wall he'd built suddenly exploded outward, an iridescent tangle flying down the hallway like shrapnel, the shards like jagged knives of psychic energy. Mercy felt them hit some kind of wall, the impact jarring. Suddenly, the man was no longer smiling. A strange look crossed his face, and then his entire body went limp, and he collapsed into a boneless heap, a puppet with its strings cut. The light of his Talent snuffed out as suddenly as a candle flame in a gust of wind. Willem's head whipped toward the movement, his eyes wide.

They have a Killer, one of Frain's people broadcast this news in a mental voice laced with pure panic. *They have—*

The voice cut off abruptly, and another mind went dark.

"Sir!" Octavia's voice had risen. She grabbed his arm, the one holding the disrupter. "We have to go *now, now, now! Please!*"

Willem's arm lowered. The two other minds by the door went dark, bodies falling bloodlessly to the floor.

"Do it," he said grimly. In the next instant, he and Octavia disappeared in a flash of Talent that literally blinded Mercy.

When she blinked her eyes to clear them, people she didn't know were moving into the room from the hallway, stepping over bodies with the precision and care of professional soldiers. They all wore armored clothing, and it looked like some kind of uniform. Black, with pale blue piping at the collar. Their minds glowed with the familiar warmth she had come to associate with Talent. Yet Willem had run from them.

She stared blankly at the bodies on the ground, men and women responsible for kidnapping and imprisoning her. Responsible, ultimately, for whatever fate had in store for Atrea. She couldn't drum up an ounce of guilt or sympathy for their deaths. If she felt anything at all, it was regret that

Willem Frain wasn't among them. That somehow, he'd escaped.

Teleported.

It didn't seem possible. Mercy hadn't known it *was* possible.

"Boss," said one of the men now in the room, "looks like two of them jumped out. Had to be somewhere close. Maybe the surface of the moon. Maybe a ship."

The only one of them not wearing some kind of uniform nodded his head, and then, without warning, looked directly at Mercy. Blue eyes so pale they were chips of winter ice met hers with an impact that was as shocking as it was powerful. She was caught, unable to look away. Lean and athletic like the others, he radiated an intensity that set him apart from them. His dark hair was cut short to his skull, and there was a shade of swarthiness to his skin that intensified the paleness of his blue eyes, made them seem colder. Emotion swept her, the same feeling she had watching a solar storm erupt on the surface of a star, as though she was looking at something as terrifyingly beautiful as it was powerful and deadly. For an eternal moment, their gazes held.

"Titus says a ship is breaking atmosphere on that moon, boss. Must be our missing two. You want him to intercept?"

"No." The man with pale blue eyes looked away. "If the ship is armed and he chooses to attack the station, we'll all be dead. We need to leave. Now."

Mercy took a shuddering breath, the rest of the room moving into focus again. One of the men knelt by Atrea's chair. He was reaching a hand out to touch her, the glow of his Talent moving with it.

"Don't!" The word tore from her throat with the force of fear behind it. "Do not touch her with your mind."

He froze, looked first at Mercy, and then flicked his gaze up behind her, to the man Mercy knew stood there. She could feel his presence in the warmth of his Talent, blazing brighter than anyone else's in the room.

"Why?" The voice came from over her shoulder. His voice gave nothing away, the single word completely neutral.

"They did something to her, released some kind of poison into her mind that's killing her. I don't know if it's safe to touch her, mentally." A sudden hope filled Mercy. These people were Talented; maybe they knew something, could do something to save her. "Can you help her? He said it would kill her in under an hour."

The man kneeling beside Atrea frowned. His brown hair hung in a shaggy mess around his face, obscuring the rest of his expression. His Talent stayed contained to his mind, but he reached out with a hand and turned off the gravity bindings holding Atrea. When her body would have tumbled forward out of the chair, he caught her and lifted her easily, setting her gently onto the floor. He ripped open a compartment on his pant leg and pulled out a medi-pack. He attached the sensor pad to the skin of her throat, then positioned another device over her chest. He let it go, and a blue light flared from the tech, enveloping

Atrea. A rigid cocoon formed around her, its surface reflective blue and shining.

A stasis field. Relief flooded Mercy. Atrea was, for all intents and purposes, snowed. The stasis field suspended the passage of time, holding living things inside of it in a kind of frozen, infinite moment for as long as the field remained in effect. Slang referred to it as the Snow White effect, something from an old story.

The man behind Mercy moved to her side and turned off the gravity bindings holding her. She stayed seated in her chair, her hands gripping the arm rests tightly. This was the man in charge, she knew. The one who would decide their fate. She forced herself to meet his eyes again, but this time she was prepared, lifting her chin in a deliberate gesture of defiance against the intensity that radiated from him. *I wasn't afraid of Willem Frain. I won't be afraid of you, either.*

She might have imagined it, but she was pretty sure his mouth moved in the hint of a smile.

"You don't need to fear us," he said evenly, and Mercy's stomach twisted. Was he reading her thoughts as easily as Willem Frain had done? Had she and Atrea simply exchanged captors?

"I don't know you," she said. "I have no reason to trust you."

"Boss," called one of the others. "Titus says we need to move our asses."

Irritation flickered across his face. He didn't look away from Mercy, and it took her a second to realize he'd extended his hand in an antiquated greeting.

"I am Reaper. You might not remember me, but we know who you are."

Mercy hesitated. His words sparked something, a memory on the edge of her awareness. She reached for it, but she was too tired, her mind still sluggish from what she'd done. She knew one thing: she was getting very tired of everyone knowing who she was, while she didn't know anyone.

"Stay out of my head," she snapped, ignoring his hand. "What kind of name is that, Reaper? Not exactly filling me with confidence." She pushed to her feet, praying she wouldn't wobble too much. She could just imagine falling flat on her face.

"I'm not in your head," he said mildly. "I don't need to be, to recognize you. Mercy, daughter of Pallas, granddaughter of Lilith, the last pirate Queen. We've been looking for you for twenty-five years." He paused to allow the words to sink in. "We are here to take you home."

CHAPTER SIX

ercy flinched. *Home* was not a comforting word in her vocabulary. Not since she was three, and her mother explained to her that if they ever went home, Grandmother would kill them. The way she'd killed Mercy's father. It took every ounce of will she had not to fall back a step. It helped that she had nowhere to run. Her legs shook, reminding her how physically weak she'd become over the course of her captivity. Running right now was not an option, even if she had somewhere to go, even if she was willing to abandon Atrea.

Her gaze went to the stasis field, her friend's face a pale smear beneath the translucent blue shell. The man with the shaggy hair was standing next to it, and as Mercy watched, Atrea rose into the air beside him, hovering like a load of cargo about to be moved with anti-gravity boosters.

"Her father is waiting to see her."

The quiet words drew Mercy's gaze back to Reaper. She stared at him, her brain sluggish to process and respond.

"The old Wolf?" Hope was a fragile thing in her chest. Her fists clenched at her sides. She didn't want to trust these people, didn't want to place herself in their hands. At the same time, she ached to trust someone, to believe even for a moment that the nightmare could be over and Atrea might be saved.

"Captain Hades, yes," said Reaper. He paused. "Further explanations must wait. We are not safe here."

He gave a nod to the man with Atrea, then turned on his heel and made for the door. Everyone else watched Mercy, waiting. No one made a move toward her, not physically, and not with Talent. In that, at least, they were a step above Willem Frain and his friends. *They* would have picked her up and forced her to go with them. She let out a breath, realizing that no one needed to resort to that now. If she didn't go with them, she'd be trapped on this station with no way to leave it. She had no choice. Whether it meant marching home to her Grandmother, taking Atrea back to Wolfgang Hades, or both.

She followed Reaper. The others fell into step behind her. Mercy felt the weight of their stares, and was suddenly self-conscious, too aware of her weakened state, the short bristle of hair she'd begun to grow, and the way her wrinkled synth-cloth clothing hung on her too-thin frame. She had given up feeling awareness of her vulnerability while with Frain, unable to spend energy on something that had become a constant state of being. Now it came rushing back, and she hated it.

She turned her head and glared at the nearest

of Reaper's soldiers. His face was startlingly handsome, with sharp, chiseled features and bronze tinted skin, slightly darker than her own. His eyes were a deeper blue than Reaper's, and he radiated a similar intensity. Dark, nearly black eyebrows rose in surprise at the fierceness of her look, and he raised a hand as if to placate her.

"None of us here are your enemy," he said, in a voice meant to be soothing.

"We'll see," she said grimly.

They moved quickly through the hallways of the station, a sense of urgency dogging their heels. Mercy knew better than any of them how much Willem Frain wanted her dead. There was, however, the peculiar way he couldn't seem to follow through and actually kill her. She wondered if that odd reluctance would extend to blowing the station to pieces. It wasn't something she wanted to find out.

When they finally reached the airlock, Mercy wasn't surprised to see bodies strewn across the hallway, plasma shields lying spent and inert beside them. Reaper's group didn't even pause, stepping quickly over the fallen and into the airlock. Mercy hesitated, then stooped and picked up a disrupter pistol. Just the weight of the weapon in her hand made her feel a little less like a captive. No one stopped her.

It took an extra few minutes to maneuver Atrea through the hatch and docking seal, but Mercy refused to step through until her friend was safely on board. Some part of her feared they would decide to leave Atrea behind.

"Strap in," Reaper said as she crossed the

threshold onto his ship. A quick glance around told her it was a smaller vessel, probably a corvette or a frigate not unlike Captain Hades' *Dauntless*. They were already breaking the seal with the station airlock, so she found a seat in the crew compartment and strapped herself in. The man with the shaggy hair was securing Atrea with cargo ties.

She could hear a conversation drifting from the cockpit. Something about another ship getting ready to jump, did they want to try and intercept it?

"No," said Reaper. "Our priority is the woman." Not *women*, but *woman*, singular. Mercy's stomach tightened with worry.

With nowhere else to put it on her person, Mercy held her new pistol in her lap. She wasn't quite willing to let it go by storing it in the webbing beneath her seat. The too-handsome man sat next to her. He tried a smile, but somehow it looked a bit forced, despite the feeling she got that he was really trying to be charming. That intensity she'd sensed before had faded a bit, and he seemed a little more relaxed.

"I'm Zion," he said. When she said nothing, he continued on, introducing the others. "That's Mateo, Knox, and Jaxon is over there securing your friend. Up in the cockpit is Titus, and you already know Reaper." He paused, then continued in a gentle tone. "You don't need to be afraid. No one here will harm you."

She ignored him, only looking up when Reaper sat across from her. She watched as he secured his safety harness.

"You said I've been missing for twenty-five

years," she said evenly. The ship disengaged from the space station with a sharp dip that jostled them in their seats. Mercy's hands tightened on her pistol. "Do you work for my grandmother?" She was pleased when her voice didn't tremble over the words.

Reaper looked up and met her eyes, the impact less shocking this time, but still there, thrumming through her blood like a jolt of adrenaline. She couldn't figure out if her response to him was a reaction to the power of his Talent, fear, or something else. He was attractive enough beneath all of that cold intensity, but the idea was ludicrous given the situation. She couldn't fathom that her response was purely physical. There had to be something more to it. Again she felt that sense of familiarity, that brush of memory she couldn't quite grasp.

"No," he said. "Your grandmother is dead."

Shocked, Mercy stared at him mutely. Of all the possibilities, that one had never occurred to her. She remembered Lilith as this towering, powerful figure, dynamic and imposing in both her demeanor and her Talent. In Mercy's mind, she'd never aged, never weakened. Her memory had dimmed with the passage of time, but she would never forget the sheer presence that had been her grandmother. Lilith had seemed eternal.

"When?"

"Eleven years ago," said Reaper. "A sickness took her."

It seemed even more improbable. Lilith succumbing to something so mundane as an illness just didn't fit the image Mercy had carried for the past twenty-five years. She sat silently for a few moments, processing.

She could feel the ship's engines spooling up to jump. Wherever they were going, she would find out soon enough what it all meant. For now, exhaustion pulled at her. It was like finding out the news of Lilith's death had finally drained her of the adrenaline keeping her going, and everything she'd endured and experienced was now a heavy weight bearing down upon her.

Maybe he was lying, but she didn't think so.

"My grandmother wanted to kill me," Mercy heard herself say. She forced her eyes up to meet Reaper's again. "Do you?"

That faint smile tugged at his mouth. She wondered if he ever just smiled, like a normal person. "No," he said. "If I had, you wouldn't have left the station."

No, she supposed that much was true. Her eyelids drooped, and she forced them up again.

"Go to sleep, Mercy." Reaper leaned forward, and the winter pale of his eyes had somehow warmed to a deeper blue. "You are safe, for now. No one here will hurt you, or your friend. There will be plenty of time for more questions, later."

"I don't trust you."

"I'd be disappointed if you did." Reaper shrugged. "I could point out that we just saved your life. That we have no reason to wish you harm, after going to such lengths to retrieve you. But I'm sure your instincts are telling you that despite that disrupter you now carry, you are anything but safe. Your instincts are correct. I could kill everyone on this ship, almost before you took another breath. Certainly before you could use that weapon. I have no intention of doing so. Get some sleep."

Oddly, Mercy found his words comforting. He was right. Her instincts were telling her that he – that all of them – were dangerous. By not trying to downplay that, by being blatantly honest about it, Reaper had somehow diffused the nerves trying to keep her from lowering her guard. She found herself relaxing into her seat, her eyes drifting closed. She felt the odd, endless stretch of time as the ship made its first jump, and the familiarity of that soothed her as well.

Wherever they were going, for the first time since her capture she knew she wouldn't be dying on that cold, hellhole of a space station. It was the last thought she had before she finally allowed herself to drift into sleep.

✦

REAPER IGNORED the astonished look Zion was giving him. The speech he'd just delivered to Mercy was a great deal more discourse than any of them were used to hearing from him, but he'd been unable to stop the words from tumbling out. His desire to reassure her was too strong. The look on his face must have been dark, because Zion suddenly blanched and found something else to occupy his attention.

Whatever else she might be, it was clear that Mercy was a queen. Her ability to influence the minds around her made that apparent. It made him wonder how her captors, Talented who should have felt the effects, had managed to hold her prisoner for so long. An image surfaced in his mind. A child, small and slight, begging him to let her go. He should have turned her in, but he hadn't. If he'd harbored any doubts Mercy was that child, he didn't any longer.

Reaper contemplated Mercy as she slept. The stamp of Lilith's line was unmistakable, even in her exhausted and maltreated condition. The bone structure that was usually so striking, often referred to as arresting in both men and women, stood out starkly in a face grown too thin. Even her bronze tinted skin, which usually glowed with a robust sense of vigor, had a pale, unhealthy pallor. Often, the women of Lilith's line were shorter, but Mercy must have inherited her height from her long dead father. A stubble of dark hair covered her head, but this did little to soften her features. The brilliant, green-gold eyes were currently closed in sleep, but Reaper remembered their impact well. If he'd had any doubt as to her lineage, that alone would have erased it. In Lilith, those eyes had often held the spark of rage, tinged with a kind of madness. In Mercy, they held a strength of spirit that glowed all the brighter, juxtaposed with her current physical weakness.

Reaper wondered if their impact would increase when she regained her health. It was an uncomfortable thought. So far, she had not displayed any of Lilith's famous cruelty, but much could change when she realized her power.

"Boss." Mateo sounded reluctant to speak. "Shouldn't we send a message, letting them know we're bringing…" He trailed off, and gestured to Mercy.

Reaper considered this. Returning to the fleet with a queen was going to create a storm of chaos, no matter how it was handled. Not everyone would be supportive. Dead for over a decade, the memory of Lilith was still too strong. Like Reaper, some would question whether a new queen was worth the risk. Others might look at Mercy and see someone ignorant enough to be used.

He frowned. She was going to need to build her power base quickly. He wasn't used to feeling uneasy. It took him a few moments to identify the feeling that slid through him as he tried to pin-point who would ally themselves alongside her and who might try to worm their way into her inner circle before she established herself.

A subspace message was too risky.

"No," he said finally. "I'll contact Cannon my-self as soon as we're within range."

Telepathy was by far the safest choice. Reaper was one of the rare Killers with a strong telepathic Talent. His range was greater than most. He was able to reach out to the pirates' current king the instant they completed the final jump.

Cannon.

There was always a sense of wariness when he spoke with Cannon telepathically. Although the two had grown up together, they'd never exactly been friends. It was difficult to build the kind of trust necessary for friendship when everyone knew your Talent could kill them with a thought.

Reaper, said Cannon, his mental voice decep-tively laconic. Cannon liked to make people underestimate him with a charming and lazy demeanor. Reaper never made that mistake. *Tell me you have Atrea Hades. Her father is not the easiest guest, and I'm sorry to say that even my patience is wearing thin.*

We have her. But her condition is grave. She is currently in stasis.

What the fuck happened?

She was being held by Talented. One of them released a lethal mental poison into her mind.

Reaper waited out the string of profanity from Cannon. Wolfgang Hades was a valuable contact for the pirates. This meant he was privy to more of their secrets than was strictly comfortable, and making an enemy of him could be problematic.

If it becomes an issue, said Reaper evenly, *I will remove him.*

Don't you think I've already thought of that? I'm not worried about what to do with Wolfgang if his daughter dies. I'm worried about losing one of our primary sources of intel inside of the Commonwealth. One we need now more than ever. Why was his daughter targeted? Does Veritas know of our connection to him?

Cannon was referring to the organization of Talented working from within the Commonwealth of Sovereign Planets. Unlike the pirates, who turned outlaw in order to survive the order prohibiting Talent, Veritas remained within the core, civilized worlds, hiding in plain sight. Although they functioned in secret, they could move throughout the Commonwealth freely. This allowed them privileges unknown to the pirates. They could, for example, hunt and find Talented people trying to live unknown and undiscovered, recruiting them to their organization. They used their gifts to manipulate the nulls around them, up to and including planetary representatives, and rumor had it, even the monarchy itself. They also saw their pirate brethren as a threat and had, over the years, taken increasingly bold steps to remove them.

I don't think she was the target, Reaper said.

Cannon was silent for a moment. *The friend taken with her, you're referring to her?*

Reaper looked across at Mercy. Once he took this step, there could be no going back. No last minute reversal of his decision to let her live. Not without consequences he would be forced to endure. For better or worse, everything was about to change.

Reaper?

I have found Pallas's daughter, he said at last. *Her name is Mercy. She is Atrea Hades' friend, and she is Talented.*

Reaper was no empath, but he didn't need to feel Cannon's shock radiating across the link to hear it in the silence that stretched on and on. It was not just a matter of finding one of their own who had been lost for so long. Cannon was also of Lilith's line, his mother, Nemain, having been a sister to Pallas. Mercy would be his cousin.

You're certain? There was nothing lazy in Cannon's voice now.

Very. As you will be, when you see her.

Ah. The genes breed true, as ever. A touch of amusement softened his tone. *We are all of us a bit alike, however hard we try to deny it. And she is Talented, you say? Not a surprise, given her parentage.*

This is good news, indeed. The pirates had grave need of Talented people, particularly women, to bolster their population. *How does she strike you? It's hard to imagine one of us growing up outside of this backbiting and charmingly vicious family.*

Reaper thought back to his first meeting with Mercy, the one he'd never spoken of to anyone, the one he kept buried so deep even his brother Treon would have trouble digging it out. A child, terrified and alone, she'd stared at him across that spaceport and asked him to let her go. And he'd done it.

Strong. Her captors subjected her to rigorous testing and experimentation, for weeks. Yet she picked up a disrupter with the intention of shooting us if she felt the need.

Shooting you? Cannon laughed. *All of you? Strong, and I would say either brave, or extremely ignorant.*

Both.

Well, ignorance we can cure. She'll be needing that bravery. Where do you see her fitting into the hierarchy?

Lilith had had several children, each with children of their own, and, in addition to strong Talent, nearly all harbored a hunger for power. This led to a sprawling family, constantly battling one another for position and influence. As king, Cannon stood above them all, but he had been forced to kill several of his own cousins over the years. Many waited hungrily for him to make a mistake they could use to topple him. Mercy, Reaper knew, would be the equivalent of a bomb going off in the midst of all that, simply due to her existence. There was no way to soften that for Cannon.

She is a queen. It remains to be seen if she will be another Lilith.

For the second time, Reaper heard the shock in Cannon's silence. It lasted for so long, he began to question whether the link had severed. In the end, Cannon's response came so softly, Reaper had to strain to hear it.

Mother help us all.

Mercy woke slowly. The bunk beneath her was familiar, too hard, and for a despairing, confused second she thought she was waking from a cruel dream and she would find herself still captive on the space station. Then unfamiliar sounds assailed her, voices she didn't know, and an odd electronic hum she couldn't immediately place. She realized her bunk was covered in soft linens, lying against her skin like fluffy clouds that felt so luxurious, it nearly brought tears to her eyes. A familiar antiseptic smell hit her nose, and she stiffened. The scent was unmistakable. She was in a medical facility.

Memory returned in a rush. Reaper, the ship, falling asleep.

She froze, not moving, doing her best to keep her muscles from tensing, wanting a few solitary moments to get her bearings before anyone realized she was conscious. The stupid machines betrayed her.

"Her heartbeat's picked up. She's awake." The voice sounded young and female, like a teenager's.

"Good. Right on schedule." Male, older, with a faint accent Mercy couldn't immediately identify.

"It's about time." This was said with a sniff of disdain, the voice female, and somehow more mature than the other two.

"I told you," said the male voice with more than a hint of clipped impatience. "I don't think it's a good idea for you to be here, Vashti."

"Too bad. If you think I'm leaving now, you can think again, Hikaru Jiro. I've already waited for nearly three days. I'm not waiting any longer."

"Doc," the male voice muttered. "*Everyone* calls me Doc."

"*Everyone* clearly doesn't remember when you tried to be captain of your own ship, marauding across the galaxy. I do." A pause. "Bet you didn't know that, did you girl? Even *Doc* has his secrets."

The young girl laughed. The man muttered something in a language Mercy didn't know. It didn't sound complimentary. She gave up the sham and opened her eyes.

A woman sat beside the bed, her long, silver hair streaked with black. She held a walking stick in one hand, elegant fingers lined with age curved around the knob. She wore a long blue robe wrapped around her slim frame, the waist belted with an elaborately embroidered length of fabric. Her skin was a few shades darker than Mercy's, but when she turned her head, familiar green eyes looked back at Mercy. Her own eyes.

She stiffened, and the old woman smiled gently.

"Yes, I know, I look a great deal like my sister. But Lilith is long dead, my dear. You have nothing to fear from me." She reached one wizened hand over, and squeezed Mercy's fingers. "I'm sure you don't remember, being so young. I helped the two of you escape, you know. You and your mother. My name is Vashti." She paused, and then continued on when Mercy said nothing. "I suppose something untoward has happened to Pallas, if she isn't with you."

A trace of hope laced the statement, almost turning it into a question. Mercy spent a long moment searching the other woman's face, noting the lines that seemed given to smiles. That didn't mean she trusted her, or believed a word she said.

"She's dead," Mercy said at last, the word heavy with her own sense of loss. After so long, it was hard not to believe the statement herself. She didn't imagine the sadness that clouded the other woman's eyes.

"I see. Well, she would be pleased that you've returned to us, after all this time."

"Would she?" Mercy couldn't quite stop the challenge from leaving her lips. "She spent my entire life leading me away from you, training me how to remain lost."

Vashti sighed. "I see trust will take time. She did all of that because her mother, my sister, wanted to kill you. *Lilith* wanted you dead, Mercy. Not me. Not the rest of us." That hand squeezed her fingers again, a gesture meant to comfort. "For now, know that I am personally delighted to see my great-niece again. For so long, I feared I never would." Vashti turned, gesturing behind her.

"The taciturn man looming over us is Hikaru

Jiro, but as I'm sure you heard, he prefers to be called Doc."

At this, the man pushed forward, brushing by Vashti with his dark eyes focused on the datapad in his hand. His black hair was lightly salted with grey, and combed as ruthlessly straight as his clothing. He glanced at Mercy, a frown fixed across his face.

"Your red blood cell count has improved, and your muscle tone has increased, thanks to neuro-muscular stimulation. You have Nayla to thank for that." He nodded toward the girl, who Mercy saw wasn't as young as she'd first perceived. Some-where between eighteen and twenty-one. She had long, dark hair pulled back into an efficient braid, mesmerizing eyes that were pools of clear blue, and a scattering of freckles across her nose. In contrast to Doc's stark expression, Nayla gave Mercy a huge smile.

"I'm so happy you're doing better. I tried to fix your hair for you, too, but I'm afraid I didn't get as far as I'd hoped."

Mercy put a hand reflexively to her head, and was surprised to run her fingers through three to four inches of new, soft hair. Doc scowled even more.

"I told you, growing hair is an absolute waste of your Talent." He sounded furious. "Purely cosmetic!"

Nayla just shrugged, seemingly unmoved by his disapproval. "If someone shaved my head, I'd probably cry," she confided to Mercy. "I thought you might feel better if you had at least a little hair when you woke up."

"Thank you." Mercy didn't know what else to say, given Doc's obvious agitation. She was certainly glad to have more than a short, prickly stubble covering her head. "It was kind of you."

"*Bakana onna no ko*," muttered Doc. His tone made it clear he didn't approve, whatever the words meant. He glared a Mercy as though he blamed her. "Now, you. How do you feel? Headache?"

Mercy took a moment to take stock. The edge of exhaustion that had been with her for so long was gone. She felt rested, hungry, and strangely anxious. An uneasy feeling hovered over her, and it took a moment to pinpoint why.

"Where's Reaper?" she asked.

Doc started in surprise. He exchanged a look with Vashti, so quick Mercy couldn't identify his expression.

"Reaper has many duties," he said. "None of them in the infirmary. Did you need him for something?"

Mercy didn't know what to think of the odd disappointment she experienced. What did it matter where the man was? She'd met him for all of five minutes. Annoyed with herself, she shoved the anxious feeling aside.

"No," she said. "Just curious."

"It would be best to avoid curiosity where Reaper is concerned," Doc told her. Mercy had the feeling he meant every word, as though warning her to keep her distance was a kindness. "Now, how are you feeling?"

"No headache," she told him. "I'm hungry,

though." She said this last a little warily, hoping they wouldn't hand her a nutritional bar.

"Yes, yes." Doc waved this away as inconsequential. "A meal is already being prepared. Sit up slowly, and tell me if you experience any dizziness, nausea, or discomfort."

Mercy did as instructed, and noticed the shape of the room as she shifted upright, the limited space and nano-graph paneling, conducting light to panels inlaid into the ceiling. Now that she thought about it, she could feel the low vibration of engines.

"We're on a ship," she said aloud. A really big ship, given the distance of the engines and the space allocated for an infirmary.

"Yes, brilliant deduction," Doc said. "Your head?"

"It's fine. I feel great, actually."

Nayla beamed happily at Mercy. The girl was so earnest and genuine, she couldn't help but smile back. Then she glimpsed something sitting across the room that wiped away all of her tentative good feelings. A blue stasis field, about the length of a person, hovered in an empty suite. In an instant, all of Mercy's concerns for herself were swallowed by worry for her friend. It became easy to box up her fears and put them away.

"Atrea!" Mercy moved to push herself down from the medical bunk she was sitting on, and a steely grip closed around her arm.

"No," said Doc. "You leave when I say you're finished."

Maybe it was the way she'd been constantly moved and handled by Willem Frain and his people, but the sudden surge of anger that swept through Mercy shocked her. She was actually shaking, the realization distant behind the haze of emotion.

"Oh dear," said Vashti, eyeing the two of them.

"Get your hand off me." Mercy enunciated each word.

Doc let her go, but did not back away. He was crowding the table too closely for Mercy to jump down without shoving into him. "You won't do your friend any good if you collapse halfway across the room. She's stable, for the moment."

Mercy stared at him incredulously. "She's in stasis."

"Yes, which means her condition isn't changing anytime soon." Doc scowled at her. "Yours, on the other hand..."

"Is that a threat?"

Doc threw his hands into the air, one still holding the datapad.

"*Bakana yatsura kara, sukutte kure!*"

Mercy was pretty sure whatever he'd said was some kind of insult. "Listen, you piece of—"

"Let's everyone take a moment and calm down." Vashti's voice was cool and collected. "Mercy, I assure you, everything that can be done for Atrea is being done. Her father would never settle for anything less. Doc, you must understand that Mercy has been through quite an ordeal. She has no real reason to trust us."

"Yes," snapped Doc, "saving her life and returning her to health is certainly not enough of a reason."

"*Reaper* saved my life." Mercy glared at him. "I

don't know what you've been doing. I've been unconscious for three days." The words were out of her mouth before she realized that was part of her problem; she didn't know what had happened to her here, or back on that space station. Not knowing was a weight in her chest that hurt, like a physical sense of pressure. She rubbed at it with one hand, but it did nothing to ease it. "I'm tired of not knowing what the hell is happening to me."

Doc eyed her, and something in his expression softened. "I assure you, we took no samples, did nothing beyond treating your injuries and overall condition. I would never violate any of my patients." He eased back a step to give her more space. "You have my word as a physician."

Mercy wished she could believe that, but she just didn't know what to trust, or who. These were the very people her mother had spent years hiding from. Then something Vashti had said penetrated, and Mercy looked around the room. "Wolfgang is here?"

Vashti smiled, tilted her head slightly. "Of course. Where else would he be?"

"Where—where is he, then?" Mercy couldn't imagine why he wouldn't be here, ordering someone to do *something* to help Atrea. Some of that pressure in her chest eased. Wolfgang would never have let them do anything to hurt her. That much she was certain of.

Vashti waved a hand in the air. "I made him go and eat something. He's barely left either of you in three days. You were clearly recovering, and no one knows quite what to do for Atrea yet, poor dear. There was really no point in his constant hovering." She gave Mercy's hand a quick pat. "Now that you're awake, I'm sure he'll be here very soon."

"You *made* Wolfgang Hades get something to eat?" No one ordered the old Wolf around.

"Of course."

Mercy stared at this old woman, with her easy expression and fond smile. "You pressured him, didn't you? With Talent?"

Vashti gave a careless shrug. "For his own good. The man had barely eaten since you went missing. With you finally safe, it was time he did."

"May I finish my examination now?" Doc framed it as a question, but there was no mistaking the stiff irritation in his tone, or the fact that it wasn't really a request.

Calmer now, Mercy gave him an amused look. "Has anyone ever told you that you have the worst bedside manner?"

"Oh yes, dear," said Vashti. "Everyone says that."

Doc cast her an irritated look. "I've had about enough of you—"

"Doc."

The word was spoken with such quiet authority, it arrested the attention of everyone in the room. Mercy turned her head to see a man standing in the doorway of the hatch, tall, with wide shoulders. He took up the entire space, and not just physically. He wore a casual white shirt tucked into a worn pair of armored pants. The sleeves were rolled up to the elbows, showing muscular forearms. His dark hair hung loose around his shoulders, and the stubble of beard marking his face made it seem like he hadn't cared enough to shave in a day or two. He could have been anything. A smuggler, a deck hand, a dock worker. The sheer presence that came with him when he stepped into the room said he was something more.

Subdued, Doc ducked his head and muttered to himself under his breath. Vashti sat down as if she just didn't have the strength to stand any longer. She favored the newcomer with a smile that radiated innocence, and he looked back with a raised eyebrow that said he didn't buy it for an instant.

"Cannon!" Only Nayla seemed unaffected, crossing the room to give him a quick hug, which he returned briefly before turning his attention to Mercy.

He had the same green eyes as Vashti.

"Let me guess," Mercy said, feeling an odd sense of the surreal. "We're family." For so long, she'd been alone. Now suddenly she was related to everyone she met. It was disconcerting.

"Cousins," Cannon confirmed. "My mother was Pallas's older sister, Nemain."

Mercy shrugged. She knew the family tree. Pallas had drilled the names into her, so she knew her mother had three sisters: Nemain, Athena, and Macha. Just like she knew Vashti was really her great-Aunt.

"And your name is Cannon?" she asked drily.

He gave her a lazy smile, his teeth a flash of white against the golden bronze of his skin. It transformed his face from merely good looking to wielding a wicked sensuality. *Wow*, she thought. Charming didn't begin to cover it, and she had a feeling he was only half trying. *I bet women throw themselves at his feet.*

"Our family tends toward unconventional names." He paused, his grin widening. "Mercy."

"Point taken." She couldn't help but smile back, amused and appalled despite herself. She spared a moment to be thankful he was a relative. Maybe that would provide her some form of armor against what she suspected was a lethal charisma.

Cannon glanced around the room, then jerked his head toward the door. "Walk with me? I've taken the liberty of preparing a meal. I imagine you're starving."

Mercy thought once more of the nutritional bars she'd been surviving on for who knew how long. She might not know or trust these people yet, but real food went a long way in winning her over.

"You have no idea," she said feelingly, and jumped off the bunk.

"I haven't finished my examination," Doc said, irritation in every word.

Cannon paused. For some reason, Mercy expected him to neatly ignore the implied request. Instead, he gave the doctor his full attention.

"You have concerns?" he asked.

"Physically, she's made a good recovery. However, she is still underweight, and likely to experience periods of weakness and exhaustion. Her mental state is more difficult to measure. Her Talent was severely overtaxed, over a long and continuous period of time. The trauma she has endured is also a concern."

"Doc." Cannon managed to infuse the single

word with layers of meaning. The doctor frowned, eyeing Mercy critically.

"She should be fine," he said reluctantly. "Provided she doesn't push things too fast, either physically or psychically. I recommend keeping a close eye on her for at least a few days."

"I'm standing right here," Mercy muttered.

"So you are." Cannon looked at her. "So, would you be comfortable with a babysitter for a few days?"

"Are we pretending I have a choice?"

He smiled. "Let me ask it a different way – would you rather we watch you from a distance, letting you fumble your way around an unfamiliar ship full of people you don't trust? Or do you want a guide? One who will pull double duty by keeping an eye on your welfare."

"When you put it that way, it's not much of a choice."

He shrugged. "A guide will be useful. You also need help rebuilding your shields. I'm afraid whatever happened to you on that space station has left them in a very vulnerable condition. You're going to need extensive retraining from someone very skilled before you'll be safe around nulls again. Here, everyone shields their own thoughts, so you're relatively safe. Not so much, out there." He gestured vaguely with a sweeping motion of his hand.

"Are you planning on keeping me prisoner here?" This was the question she'd most wanted to ask since waking up, the biggest concern hovering in the back of her mind. Had she traded one jailer for another?

"No," he said. "No, we are not. You are free to come and go as you wish. But your friend Atrea is going to have to stay until we can figure out how to cure her of whatever infects her mind. I believe she and her father are staying for the foreseeable future." He paused. "Did you wish for me to arrange transport for you?"

Mercy was aware of a strange silence in the room, as if every person there literally held their breath, waiting for her answer. It was odd, and uncomfortable. But of course she couldn't leave Atrea. She closed her eyes, suddenly weary of it all. Of her own emotions, and this horrible unease that filled her whenever she thought of her family. She couldn't afford to run anymore, that much was clear.

"No," she heard herself say. "Of course not. I just...I don't know what I'm feeling. I'm tired of being at everyone else's whim but my own."

"I don't doubt it. From what I've heard, you had a very harrowing few weeks." Cannon leaned a hip against one of Doc's infirmary beds, his arms crossed over his chest. "What can I do to help you feel more comfortable? I realize you don't trust us yet. You have little reason to, other than Wolfgang's good opinion, and you haven't had the opportunity to speak with him."

"I don't know," said Mercy quietly. She shrugged. "I don't know you. Any of you. My mother used to tell me if we ever came home, Grandmother would kill me. Well, here I am, and I'm supposed to let all of that go because Lilith is dead and gone. I'm supposed to assume that none of you have that same agenda."

"I understand why family might be the most difficult for you to trust, at least at first," Cannon conceded. "That doesn't change the fact that you need training, and someone to keep an eye on you as you recover."

"Reaper." Mercy leaped on the name, so fast it startled even her.

Cannon stared at her. He couldn't have looked more shocked if she'd pulled out a disrupter and stunned him. He looked over at Doc and Vashti. The latter shrugged.

"She trusts him."

"He could have left me on that station to die." Mercy said. "He didn't have to free us, but he did. If he wanted me dead, I already would be. I don't trust him, exactly, but let's just say I trust him more than I do you."

It took Cannon a moment to find his voice. "A first for everything, I suppose." He stroked a hand over his chin. "Well, if you want Reaper to train you, so be it." He straightened, sweeping a hand to the door. "Now, can we go and eat that meal before it grows cold?"

Feeling she'd established some small measure of control, Mercy nodded, and stepped out of the room ahead of him. She felt shaky, and light headed. She had the feeling she'd just committed to much more than just someone to retrain her Talent. Somehow, between waking up and getting something to eat, she'd decided to stay.

Like it or not, she'd just thrown her lot in with the very family who once tried to kill her. It was a sobering realization. She wondered what her mother would say. *It doesn't matter*, she told herself firmly. She'd spent the last fifteen years living by her mother's rules. In the end, it hadn't been enough to keep her safe. The choice had been taken from her, and maybe it was time. Time to embrace change. Time to let Pallas go.

CHAPTER EIGHT

They'd barely stepped out of the infirmary when Mercy stopped, placing a supporting hand against the smooth, nano-graph wall of the corridor. A diagram lit up in blues and greens under the touch of her hand, looking like a map. Mercy barely glanced at it. The sheer number of Talented minds around her was staggering. They blazed like individual stars, lighting the darkness with warmth and energy. It was at once comforting, familiar, and frightening.

"Mercy?" Cannon's voice held concern. "Should I get Doc...?"

"No." She definitely didn't want a return to that medical bunk. "No, I just need a minute. I've never felt so many Talented minds before, all at once."

"Ah." Cannon leaned against the opposite wall, giving her as much space as the small hallway permitted. "I see. I imagine it's a bit disconcerting. Doc has inhibitors up that shield the medical bay, so you wouldn't have felt it until now."

The idea of some kind of tech capable of

blocking Talent was a new and intriguing concept. One she set aside to ask about later.

"I guess it's different for you, having lived with it your whole life," she said.

He hesitated. "It is different for me. Very different. Not all of us can sense the Talent in others, Mercy. It's…an extremely rare gift."

"Oh." She closed her eyes. "Lucky me." When she opened them again, Cannon was watching her with an odd look on his face, an expression she couldn't quite identify that made her uneasy. "What?"

"Nothing. I just keep forgetting that you know basically nothing about us. I'm wondering how to explain it all without overwhelming you."

Mercy laughed. She shook her head as she straightened away from the wall. "I'm already overwhelmed. But I'll get over it. I've always been a quick learner." Now she eyed the diagram, noting that it only covered a single deck, but one that contained a confounding amount of space. She frowned. "What class of ship is this?"

Cannon smiled, crossing over to stand beside her. He swiped a hand over the diagram, and it expanded and shrank at the same time, new lines of light tracing over the wall too fast to follow, until the entire ship was outlined. Mercy's jaw dropped. There was only one class of ship with that silhouette, or that sheer size.

"A Monarch." She stared at it, then looked at him. "We're on a Monarch? That's a military vessel." The biggest class, the flagships of the Commonwealth Navy.

"I know." Pride radiated from him. "We stole it."

Mercy laughed, in disbelief for the first few seconds, then in realization.

"You're serious," she said.

"Two decades ago, this ship was the first Monarch off the production line out of the Ivaldi Shipyards."

Mercy stared at the diagram. "The first military vessels to be built using nano-graph."

"Yes. Taking her was an enormous victory for us." He placed his hand against the wall, and the diagram disappeared. "Lilith was a young Queen at the time, and she immediately transferred her transponder flag and made this the flagship of our fleet. The Commonwealth was so embarrassed to have *misplaced* their prototype, they hushed up the whole thing. They said *Nemesis* had to be returned to Ivaldi and overhauled for design flaws that didn't work with military needs."

Mercy frowned. She vaguely remembered reading something about that when she was studying *A History of Shipbuilding* under the direction of Captain Hades. He'd insisted on a staggering amount of database learning, on top of the much more engaging lessons on piloting, navigation, and gunnery both Mercy and Atrea delighted in.

"Ivaldi couldn't have been pleased by that." She remembered the shipyard had taken a brief hit to their reputation over the whole debacle.

"No. We suspect a government payoff was involved, not to mention the exclusive contract with the Commonwealth Navy that Ivaldi has enjoyed for the last two decades. Then the *CSS Phoenix* came off the line as the first officially recognized Monarch-class ship. *Nemesis* was forgotten, and Ivaldi went into the history logs as the most influential innovator of spaceship technology in a century."

Mercy shook her head, amazed. "We're standing in a piece of history right now."

Cannon grinned. "Yes. The Commonwealth's, and our own. Now, if you're finished admiring antiquity, let's get that lunch I promised you. This way."

Mercy couldn't help but look everywhere as she followed Cannon. He led her down one corridor and another, into a lift, and down two decks before they reached the ship's galley. Now that she knew what to look for, she thought she could see some of the changes made to what had been intended as a military vessel. The hallways and hatches were on the narrow side, as one might expect from a military ship. But the lift they used was spacious enough to allow for cargo, if necessary, and some of the walls contained a variety of artwork, very much not to military regulations. When they entered the galley, it didn't have the narrow columns of tables a typical mess employed, but instead round or oblong tables throughout the room. It made for a more relaxed, conversational area.

Mercy didn't have time to notice anything more, because in the next moment Wolfgang Hades was suddenly in front of her, a familiar, tall figure in a battered flight jacket. She had time to notice the uncharacteristic growth of white beard over his usually clean-shaven face, and then she was engulfed in a bone-crushing hug. She was struck speechless. Through the shredded remnants of her shields, his thoughts were disturbingly clear.

Still too damn thin. Thank the Mother she's awake at last. At least one of them is awake and well. My girls.

To her shock, Mercy could feel a fine tremble in his arms. She was horrified to realize tears were prickling behind her own eyes, and fought them off. Wolfgang was the closest thing she had to a father, but she'd never realized how deeply her own emotions ran, or that he considered her in the same light as Atrea, his actual daughter.

What the hell were they doing on Yuan-Ki?

He finally pushed back from her, and Mercy was grateful her eyes were dry. Cannon, she noticed, had stepped aside to give them at least the illusion of privacy.

"What the hell were you doing on Yuan-Ki?" the old Wolf asked aloud, his voice gruff, unaware that his thought had already been heard.

"I...Atrea found information. A tip. My mother." Appalled, Mercy closed her mouth. She'd just stumbled over words she never intended to say, reduced to babbling incoherently, explaining something she knew was bound to piss him off. She felt like she was thirteen years old again and he'd caught her doing something she wasn't supposed to.

Eyes the same dark blue as Atrea's narrowed, and Mercy knew with a sinking feeling that she hadn't been as incoherent as she'd hoped.

"Your mother! I told the two of you to give up

that nonsense, that it was too damn dangerous." He studied her face for a moment. "I see. You never gave it up, did you? I suppose Atrea never did, either. Damn it, Mercy."

Mercy suddenly found her feelings of guilt giving way beneath a surge of her own frustration and anger. She glared at him.

"Don't," she said. "Just don't. You knew I wanted to find my mother. You always knew from that first day. When did you figure out the rest?"

He stood there in that stupid, scarred flight jacket three decades old, all of the military patches painstakingly removed so long ago you could no longer make out where they'd been. The lines of age usually marking his face were hidden beneath that growth of beard, and he just stared at her in infuriating silence.

"When?" she insisted. Mercy flung a hand toward the galley and the handful of curious people seated there. "You obviously know these people. *My family*. You sent them to find us and bring us back. *You know them*. When did you figure out who I was?"

"Mercy." He said just that, her name, in this voice so weary it hurt to hear it. His shoulders, always so strong, slumped at her words, but he shook his head, saying nothing.

"*When?*" Mercy shoved at him as she said the word, hands against his shoulders, then immediately stepped back, dismayed. She curled her hands into fists at her sides. "Damn you, answer me."

"I suspected that first day," he said finally. "You look so much like the Bitch Queen. Later, I put together little things you did, and knew I was right. Remember that crate that fell on Atrea? It should have crushed her. It didn't even leave a bruise."

Because Mercy caught it with her Talent. Atrea had been fifteen, and some lazy dock worker had stacked the damn crates wrong. She wrestled with this revelation for a moment, filled with conflicting emotion at his words. She was still angry, but also sad that he could have known for so long who she was, and never said a thing. There was also an unexpected spurt of amusement, as well, at the title.

"My grandmother?" She phrased it that way on purpose, had the satisfaction of seeing him wince.

"Lilith, yes." His voice held a surprising amount of bitterness. The kind only someone who had known her personally could possibly feel. Mercy stared at him as coldness swept through her. How much, she wondered, did she not know? The sense of betrayal was acute.

"You knew her." The words were barely a whisper.

He sighed. "Not really. Tess did. Atrea's mother. Mercy, none of it matters. Yes, I've known the pirates for years, worked with them now and then, done small jobs, passed information their way. Yes, I knew they were your family, but you were so afraid, so obviously running from something. I never would have told them. Never. I knew you were safe with me, or safer than you would be on your own. So no, I didn't tell you I knew. I was afraid you would run if I did."

Mercy stared at him for so long, his brow finally furrowed in irritation. The old Wolf wasn't used to being questioned.

"Damn it," he said, "I was protecting you. You're like my own daughter, Mercy. I would have done the same for Atrea."

"You mean if she had Talent?" A sick kind of guilt spiraled up through Mercy. She tried to hold onto her anger, and couldn't. *Oh, Mother. Atrea.* How was she going to tell Wolfgang she'd as good as gotten his daughter killed?

"Of course. If she'd been born with Talent, if she didn't want to be brought to her mother's people, I wouldn't have. I'd have kept it a secret." He shrugged, a jerky movement. "She wasn't, so the point became moot. But I would have."

"Nice to know our partnership was so equitable," said Cannon dryly, ruining the illusion of privacy. Mercy abruptly became aware of all the stares and attention being directed their way, and her cheeks burned.

Wolfgang glared at Cannon. "You know I don't agree with everything you do, Cannon. I *especially* didn't agree when Lilith was in charge. You tell me things have changed, but how do I know that until I see it with my own eyes?"

"Enough." Mercy closed her eyes. "Go to the infirmary, Wolfgang. Be with Atrea. I'll come by later, and we can talk." She hesitated. "Please."

He stared at her for another minute, then dipped his head stiffly, spun on his heel and marched out of the galley.

"Well," said Cannon. "That was an enlightening conversation."

Mercy gave him a sharp look. "Don't start.

Where is that food you promised me? I don't think I can take much more enlightenment until I've eaten something."

"This way." He guided her to a table, set apart from the others. Mercy avoided looking at anyone as she followed him over, but she could feel the curious stares.

As Cannon gestured for her to sit, a figure darted around him, dancing back a few steps to avoid running into Mercy. It was a boy, maybe fifteen, with messy dark hair and familiar green eyes. *Family*, she thought automatically. The resemblance to Cannon was unmistakable. And, she supposed, to herself. He wore a flight suit that had seen better days, the top half open and tied haphazardly around his waist. Dirt of some kind streaked his chin and smudged the undershirt he wore. No small feat with self-cleaning fabric.

"Sorry," he muttered, throwing her a shy smile and ducking his head.

"Max." Cannon said the name with a frown, but his voice held an infinite patience that made Mercy smile. "Aren't you supposed to be working for Bruzer today?"

"I am." Max sounded defensive. "Just wanted to grab something quick. I was up three hours before shift start this morning."

"Working on your secret project again." It wasn't a question. Cannon picked up two trays and set them on the table while Max stood and fidgeted. He was a gangly youth, thin and awkward with it. But Mercy could see the flex of muscle in his arms, and the suggestion of the man he would become in the stubborn set of his jaw.

Cannon eyed him. No hint of a smile softened his expression. "I told you that project could only go forward if it didn't interfere with your duty station."

Max's chin lifted, his green eyes sparking with a familiar hint of temper. "It doesn't!"

Cannon lifted an eyebrow.

"Sir." Max looked away. "I just missed breakfast."

Cannon held a chair out for Mercy, then took a seat himself. Max cast a longing look toward the trays, but made no move toward them. Even without telepathy, Mercy could almost hear his thoughts. She hid a smile.

"If it wasn't clear before, I am making it clear now," Cannon said as he picked up a fork. "Skipping meals isn't acceptable. Even if it means you're eating a ration bar."

Mercy winced, thinking of her own recent experience. Max grimaced, evidently familiar with the bars as well. But he heaved a sigh.

"Yes, sir."

"And you better get back before Bruzer misses you. If he reports any delinquency to me..." Cannon left the threat unfinished, but clearly Max understood.

"That's why I was running." He muttered the words under his breath, but stopped when Cannon narrowed his eyes.

Mercy hid a smile as her cousin made the boy wait, watching as he fidgeted restlessly from foot to foot for an agonizing stretch of time. When Cannon finally lifted a hand in dismissal, Max darted away as quickly as he'd arrived.

The savory aroma from her tray made Mercy's mouth water, but she glanced at Cannon as she picked up her fork. "Secret project?"

He flashed a quick grin. "If I told you, it wouldn't be secret."

Mercy huffed a laugh, and focused her attention fully on her tray. To her surprise, it wasn't a rehydrated s-meal, though even that would have been delicious at this point. A colorful array of fresh greens and chunks of some kind of fish filled the plate. They were covered in a dark sauce, the source of that savory scent, and so appetizing her stomach growled.

It had been so long since she had real, actual food, she could have wept. Eagerly, she took a bite and then closed her eyes, relishing the savory, lightly herbed flavor that filled her mouth. She'd taken three bites before she could tear enough of her attention away from the food to speak.

"Where," she said, picking up the cup Cannon placed in front of her, "did you get *real food*?" She took a drink, and was shocked by the wash of refreshing, hoppy liquid across her tongue. She stared at the cup in amazement.

Cannon looked amused. "We do have our own colonies, you know. Farms, and the like." He grimaced. "Those deep space nutritional bars are enough to survive on, but who wants to just survive? We do, of course, stock a variety of s-meals to be rehydrated and eaten if the need arises, but we always stock our stores with fresh ingredients whenever we make port."

She took another drink, eyes closed. "I think this is the best meal I've eaten in my entire life."

For the moment, it was true. She tapped a finger on the rim of her cup as she set it down. "This beer, it tastes like Thalian ale."

It was arguably the most popular ale in the Commonwealth, with limited batches brewed each year via a secret recipe out of Thalia, a colony world that started out as just another mining operation. It quickly rose to much greater prominence for its beer.

Cannon smiled. "Does it?"

Mercy leaned forward. "It really does. What did you do, steal a shipment?"

"Stole the recipe."

Her mouth dropped open. "Seriously?"

Cannon shrugged. "We enjoy good things. Several years ago, one of the ships we took happened to be carrying one of their brewers as a passenger. He bartered the recipe and process in exchange for his freedom."

Thalia never produced enough beer to meet the demand. Mercy gestured to her cup again. "You could be selling this and making a nice profit."

"Who says we aren't?"

Mercy shook her head, returning her attention to her meal. "I'm getting the feeling that you people are a lot more than just pirates."

"Oh, make no mistake. We *are* pirates." He eyed her. "How much do you know about our history?"

She shrugged. "What everyone does, I guess. Talent started out as a military thing. Then, when the government united under the banner of the Commonwealth of Sovereign Planets, they didn't need Talented people anymore."

"That is true, to a point. The reality is, Talent was engineered by scientists in a lab, centuries ago. They created telepaths, telekinetics, people with highly specialized gifts rooted in both. We were made to be soldiers, spies, and assassins, and yes, the government did decide they didn't need us anymore. More to the point, they decided we were far too dangerous to keep around. They spread that idea among the populace with that Mori Shinjo farce."

"The Admiral who killed his entire crew, right? Mass suicide?" The images were still broadcast throughout the Commonwealth. The Talented Admiral responsible for many of the victories that led to a united Commonwealth, a decorated war hero. He went mad and killed himself, his gift inspiring his entire crew of more than three hundred people to do the same thing, at the same moment. It was the catalyst the Commonwealth used to finally outlaw Talent and sweep up the Talented, to either imprison in some remote location or, more likely, execute.

"Yes. But it wasn't suicide so much as murder. Nothing like it has happened before or since, and the timing was extremely convenient for a government that wanted us all dead." Cannon shrugged. "The way I understand it, the Commonwealth executed hundreds under the guise of preserving public safety. Talented people, realizing they were facing genocide, stole whatever ships they could get their hands on and escaped. The location – in fringe space, and thus outside the reach of the core worlds – was broadcast telepathically until enough of them had gathered to make some kind of life."

"And then they turned to piracy?"

"It was the only way to survive. They needed supplies. Terraforming equipment, food, medicine, clothing."

Mercy could picture it all too clearly.

"We still do. We may have colonies now – I grew up in one. But everything we have, we gained by taking from the Commonwealth, and then pooling our resources and building on them." He smiled. "I'm sure it really pisses them off that we have not only survived, but thrived out here. Now, we take Commonwealth ships not just because we have to, but because it's fun to remind them we're still here."

Mercy looked down at her empty tray regretfully. She would have liked to ask for more, but at the same time, having gone so long without meant her stomach probably couldn't take much more. She pushed the tray aside.

"But the Commonwealth has a Navy. Surely they've tried to retaliate."

"Oh, they've tried several times. Early on, before we were organized, they nearly succeeded. But they did create us to be the very best soldiers and assassins government money could make. Every time they've come against us, they've lost ships and people. We added to our fleet, and became stronger as a result. The media glamorized the conflict, so every loss became bad PR for the government. It became cost prohibitive for them a long time ago."

Mercy couldn't imagine the Commonwealth

giving up so easily. "Are you saying they've left you in relative peace?"

Cannon's easy smile faded, and a look came into his eyes, one that spoke of old pain and bitter anger.

"No," he said. "They turned to other, less direct methods." He took a breath, let it out. She realized he was about to talk about something that was deeply, personally difficult for him.

"Eleven years ago, they devised a way to deal with us that didn't involve a messy war in the media headlines. They sent the trade ship *Hermes* on a shipping lane we'd hit before. She was a fat target – a heavy transport filled with medical supplies and, most irresistible of all, a group of Talented prisoners, rumored to be on their way to a scientific outpost for use as experimental subjects. We had to take it. It was armed and escorted, but we handled it with minimal losses. We took the ship, distributed the take among half our ships and colonies by the time we were done, and welcomed the newly-freed Talented among us."

He paused, looking down at his hands, fingers laced together.

"We didn't know those Talented people we freed had already been the subject of experimentation. They were carriers. According to our own doctors, the Commonwealth developed the Matera-D virus to attack the portion of our minds associated with Talent. It was quite effective. It spread quickly, invisibly, and killed indiscriminately. It yielded to none of our attempts to treat it. It should have meant our extinction, but something went wrong. It didn't work quite as intended. Only our women died. Infants, children, mothers and grandmothers – it didn't matter to the virus. We lost over eighty percent of our female population before we got the victims effectively quarantined and sent the unaffected safely away. The death toll was in the tens of thousands."

Mercy felt the meal she'd just eaten congeal in her stomach. Eleven years ago…so this would have been well after she and her mother left. After they fled to the Commonwealth. If they hadn't, if they'd still been here… Words failed her. She had no idea what to say in the face of such massive losses.

"By the time the virus was done with us, our population was nearly cut in half. And when you get down to the level of basic survival, we had perhaps one woman to every eight men, and that figure is generous. We had to adapt to survive, again."

"I don't…what does that mean?"

A humorless smile ghosted across his face, there and then gone again.

"It means women are precious to us. You could even say revered. And it means we don't have enough of them."

$\mathcal{M}$ercy's head spun with the implications of everything Cannon had shared. She couldn't imagine what that must have been like, how helpless people must have felt watching loved ones sicken and die, knowing someone had created that sickness to do exactly that.

"Is that what killed Lilith?"

Cannon nodded, and there was something in his eyes, an echo of old pain and grief, but underscored with such an intense, cold fury that she could practically feel it radiating from him.

"Yes. Lilith, my mother, my sister, cousins, nieces…too many others to count." His voice was stiff, and Mercy realized he must not speak of this very often. That he was doing so now to share the experience with her because he felt strongly that she needed to understand it. But doing so dredged up memories that still hurt him on a profound level.

"I'm sorry." Slowly, she became aware of a hushed silence in the room, where before there had been the low hum of voices, private conversations filling the background as people chatted over their meals. Now, no one spoke. There was a quality to the silence, a reverence, and Mercy felt acutely that everyone was aware of the subject of their conversation, and responding to it. The emotions she saw in Cannon were not limited to him, but shared by all of the pirates. Everyone had lost someone. Everyone mourned.

Cannon looked down at his drink.

"A few years back, we found out something that made it even worse, if you can imagine that."

Mercy tried to imagine what could make it worse, and failed.

"The people responsible for creating Matera-D and sending it to us, the people who tried to wipe out our existence, were not the Planetary Representatives and the monarchy as we know it." He took a breath. "They were not nulls who hate or fear us. There is a group within the Commonwealth. A group of Talented, like us. Who, instead of fleeing the persecution, went underground. They disappeared within the core worlds, creating a network of Talented people who became very adept at hiding. We suspect very strongly that they have infiltrated the government. That, in fact, they are the power behind the monarchy, one that the nulls do not even suspect exists."

He looked at Mercy, his eyes flicking up to the mop of recently grown hair just brushing her ears. Something in her chilled.

Willem Frain, she thought. "The people who held me. The people who hurt Atrea." In her lap, her hands curled into fists. *The people who took my mother*. She was still making a big leap there, since she had no proof. But it was so easy to imagine Willem and his people being responsible.

"Yes. Nulls may have driven us from civilized space, may have made us turn pirate to survive. But our own people tried to destroy us. Talented people."

"Why?"

He gave her a bitter smile. "That's the question, isn't it? We found out this information because we have those among us who escaped this group and found their way here. Unfortunately, these people were not deep enough within the organization to understand all of their motives. I suspect that it's a matter of power." He shrugged. "Clearly, we represent some kind of threat to them, to what they've built. They have made an enormous effort to destroy us." Remembered pain still lurked in his eyes when he said, "It is not an act we can allow to go unanswered."

"I understand," Mercy said very softly.

For a moment, the two of them stared at one another in perfect empathy. Mercy would never be able to ignore the disappearance or death of her mother. She imagined how much worse she would feel if she'd actually watched her mother die, murdered by a virus engineered to take her life. She could see the resolve in Cannon's face, in his eyes and the tension of his body. He would never let this go, never forget what had been done, or who had done it.

A loud crash sounded nearby. It startled them both, but Mercy jumped so badly she spilled half her beer onto the table. She didn't realize she'd grabbed at the cutlery from her tray until the knife was fisted in her hand, her chair knocked to the floor because she stood up so fast. Adrenaline made her shake, her heart pounding as she took in food splattered over the floor a couple of tables away. Another chair was overturned, and two teenagers stood facing off over the dropped tray. Max, and another boy.

The second boy was considerably larger, but it was Max who threw a punch. It hit the larger boy in the face with enough force to throw him back into another table and chairs. The occupants jumped up and out of the way with hurled curses, none moving to intervene. The boy landed with a crash that took out three chairs and rocked the table.

Not just a punch then, but one backed by telekinesis. Mercy understood the principle, though she'd never had the time to practice her own Talent to perfect it. What she didn't understand was why the larger boy had simply stood there and done nothing to defend himself. Two or three other boys hung back, grouped together in that way unique to packs of teenagers. One flashed a malevolent grin at Max, and Mercy's eyes narrowed. Though he appeared to be the aggressor, it was clear to her that Max was somehow the victim.

A touch on her arm brought her attention back to Cannon. He'd moved around the table to stand beside her, his eyes flicking down to the knife she held so firmly. She let out a breath. It was just two boys fighting. She forced her fingers to unlock and dropped the knife back onto the table.

"Shouldn't you do something?" Her voice came out with a faint tremble, and she blew out a frustrated breath. She didn't like being this jumpy. The question was, was she just being paranoid because of her recent experience? Or did it go deeper, because she was finally back home, where it all began? Where she started running? Both, probably.

"I could. But we have a plan." Cannon inclined his head, and Mercy felt the familiar brush of his presence a breath before she turned and saw Reaper walking across the floor. Unlike Cannon, Reaper didn't wear armored clothing. His shirt was thin gray cotton, the real stuff by the look of it, tucked into casual synth-cloth pants just like those Wolfgang and a thousand other spacers wore, self-mending, self-cleaning, and utilitarian black in color.

He'd just entered the room, and he crossed over to the boys with a smooth, unhurried stride. The larger boy lay crumpled on the ground, moaning in apparent pain. Max stood with his fists clenched, hair hanging in his eyes, breathing heavily. A look was beginning to dawn on his face, one of horror that only increased when Reaper stepped into his line of sight. His face went dead white. He glanced around at the other people in the room, but no one moved to intervene. It was a little disturbing, actually, how no one had even stirred when the fight erupted.

Reaper arched an eyebrow. He glanced back at the boy still moaning. When he spoke out loud, Mercy knew it was a deliberate choice, so everyone could hear. "Kator, shut up. If you were really hurt, I'd see it."

The boy stopped his moaning instantly. He sat up, and his face, too, had paled. His hair was cut close to his head, and he wore an old flight suit like Max's. Mercy wondered if he hadn't thought this whole event through, because there was no doubt in her mind that somehow, he'd set Max up. He looked around, but his friends had melted away from Reaper's presence, backing up like they meant to escape from the room. A couple of Reaper's dogs blocked the doorway. Mercy recognized the shaggy haired one, Jaxon, and Zion with his too-charming smile. He didn't look charming now, but crossed his arms and gave the boys a flat look. They edged away from the doorway, but made no move to go back and help their friend.

Kator looked around, and Mercy glimpsed real fear on his face a second before he gathered himself and flung a hand toward his opponent. "Sir, Max attacked me!" He rubbed at a bruise and winced. "He hit me because I bumped into him."

Head bowed, Max stared at the ground. His fists were still clenched, and Mercy could see his jaw was tight as well. From the crowd, another voice spoke up.

"It's true. Kator knocked into him, spilled his tray. It looked like an accident. But Max here threw the first punch." The tone of the speaker was reluctant, as though he didn't like incriminating Max.

Reaper's face remained impassive. Mercy saw his dogs move into the room. They leaned casually against the far wall, but their eyes moved over the area, vigilant and watchful.

"Max."

"Sir?" The boy's eyes darted up to Reaper's face, and dropped back down again. Like he couldn't stand to look him in the eye.

"You know what the law says about disagreements."

Max swallowed. "Yes, sir." The words were spoken so softly, Mercy had to strain to hear them.

"Unless the two of you can settle this now?"

"He attacked me!" Kator's voice was full of outrage. "Everyone saw. Sir."

Reaper turned his head and favored him with a cool look. He stared at him until Kator dropped his eyes. "I take it that an apology will not satisfy you?"

Kator didn't look up from the floor. "No, sir. I want my day in the arena."

Ah. So that was his game. Whatever this arena was. Mercy glanced at Cannon, but his face was as impassive as Reaper's. Maybe some kind of tribunal? Over boys fighting?

No. Cannon's voice was resigned in her mind. *If we don't allow them to settle it, this will continue to escalate. It's already been escalating, for months now.*

Why haven't you done something?

He glanced at her. *We are.*

"Very well." Reaper never looked at Cannon, but Mercy realized the two of them knew exactly what was happening here, and there was more to it than she knew. "You can settle this once and for all this afternoon."

"Today? But—"

A look from Reaper had Kator swallowing his protest. "You wanted your day, boy. This is the only chance you get." His gaze flicked to his dogs, so fast Mercy wouldn't have seen it if she hadn't been watching so closely. Jaxon moved to where Max still stood, while Zion went over to Kator. He nudged the boy with a boot.

"Get up."

Kator scrambled to his feet, and a few minutes later both boys were escorted out. Max cast a look back at Cannon, but went willingly with Jaxon. Kator's friends slunk out after them.

"What happens now?" Mercy asked as Cannon picked up her chair and set it back where it belonged.

"Now the boys will settle their dispute, and this bullying nonsense will end."

"Right," Mercy said as she retook her seat. She glanced up at Reaper as he approached the table. "I got that part. But how? Do they each make their case to you, or what?"

Cannon gave a crooked half-smile. "Our system of justice is a bit more…"

"Direct," said Reaper. He sat, no hint of expression on his face as he looked at Cannon. "You haven't told her."

"Told me what?"

Cannon sighed. "I was getting to it."

Anxiety was a swirl of unease in Mercy's stomach as she looked back and forth between them. "Whatever it is, somebody better tell me."

Cannon folded his hands on the table before him, shifting his attention from Reaper to her. "It's why we put up with Lilith for so many years, despite her many cruelties. You are important to us, Mercy, far beyond being family."

Mercy wasn't sure what she'd expected, but the

apparent shift in topic wasn't it. The anxiety sharpened, making her nauseous.

"Important? Like I was important to Willem Frain? You are not going to hold me prisoner." The fear cut through her, not entirely rational. No one had made any attempt to lock her away. Wolfgang was here, and so was Atrea. Mercy had decided to stay of her own free will, but Cannon's words sounded so close to what Frain had said, she couldn't stop her reaction.

Control it. Don't let it control you. Reaper's voice in her head, calm and even, somehow anchored her. She took a deep breath and moved past her fear.

"I'm sorry," she said to Cannon. Her fingers laced together in her lap. "Please, whatever it is, just tell me. I have to know what this is all about."

"Fair enough," said Cannon. "Do you re-member what Lilith was to us?"

"Sure." Mercy shrugged. "Queen Lilith. She was in charge of everything."

"Yes. It wasn't just a title, though. Being a queen is who and what Lilith was." Cannon drummed his fingers on the table. "We were, as I said, created to be soldiers and assassins. The Tal-ented have always been a violent race, and those responsible for creating us knew we could turn on them. They built in a genetic fail-safe."

"Okay," said Mercy cautiously.

"We are a matriarchal people. There is a…call it a psychic pheromone, if you want. All Talented women are born with it. It connects us. Makes us feel whole. But alone, this isn't enough. Especially for some of our more specialized Talents, like Reaper's."

"Meaning what, exactly?"

"Lilith," said Cannon, "was a queen. A living embodiment of that fail-safe. A woman like her was created by the scientists who made Talent. The psychic pheromone all women have existed a hundred times over in her. It was designed to connect us all together. To lead us. To control us if we rebelled. To keep us from killing one another. Lilith was a descendant of that first queen."

Cannon and Reaper exchanged a look. It settled the fear in Mercy, but another worry crept in. A thousand different half-conversations and moments with her mother cascaded through her mind. Things Pallas had refused to talk about, or alluded to without explaining. It made sense. A terrible kind of sense.

"Wait." Mercy lifted her glass and swallowed what was left of her beer, the cold wash of liquid wetting a mouth and throat gone suddenly dry. "Are you saying...?"

"Yes," said Cannon. "Your grandmother was a queen. And so are you."

CHAPTER TEN

*M*ercy laughed. She had to. For a few precious moments, she clung to denial. Her grandmother had been a cold-hearted bitch capable of murdering her own grandchild. Mercy also suspected Lilith was responsible for her father's death, though her mother had never explicitly said the words. Not to mention, there were aspects of this that truly were unbelievable.

"Let me get this right. The two of you think I can control people with Talent? You couldn't be more wrong." She never would have been trapped on that space station if that were true.

"That's not quite how it works," said Cannon.

Reaper gave him flat look. "I told you showing her would be more effective."

"Fine." Cannon spread his hands. "By all means, if you think you can do better."

Reaper stood up. "Come with me."

"That's it?" She looked from him to Cannon. "No more explanations, just go with Reaper?" She had a strong urge to refuse.

"Oh, yes." Cannon shot Reaper an amused smile. "You've already won her over, clearly."

Reaper ignored him.

I'm told, he said to Mercy mentally, *that you've chosen me to retrain you in using your Talent. Is this true?*

Get out of my head, she sent back, irritated.

Make me.

She stared at him. Was he serious?

Your shields are pathetic. A child could breach them. Until you rebuild them, they present a very real danger to you. Anyone could attack you mentally. I could kill you right now.

She glared at him. She'd given him a certain amount of trust, and he repaid that by threatening her?

I'm not threatening you. I'm telling you the truth. If you want to work with someone who will hold your hand and tell you pretty lies, pick someone else.

Cannon, evidently reading her expression, stood up and leaned over the table toward her. "This would be why everyone was shocked when you picked Reaper," he told her. "Let me know if you decide to retract that." Shaking his head, he left the galley.

Mercy watched him go, then took a deep breath and let it out slowly. She needed to fix her shields. She needed someone who could make sure people like Willem Frain would never be able to use her again. She didn't much care if that process was pleasant.

She looked at Reaper. "Can you fix my shields?"

"Yes."

"So that even you can't breach them?"

He thought about it, seeming to weigh his answer. "Probably. My telepathy is strong, but so is yours."

"Okay then. I don't need someone to hold my hand. I need someone who can teach me as quickly as possible."

He nodded. *Then let's go.*

Mercy suppressed a sigh. "You're going to keep doing that until I can keep you out, aren't you?"

At least you learn quickly, he said to her, and she could feel the thread of amusement that accompanied the words.

"That's just great," she muttered, and pushed to her feet. "Where are we going?"

First, to your new quarters. He looked her up and down, and she was suddenly conscious of the plain, infirmary issue tunic and pants she wore. Thin, synth-cotton, and completely unflattering. *I thought you might want to change. Then, I'm going to show you the arena.* He paused. *It relates to what Cannon tried to explain.*

"This queen stuff." She wanted to see the arena anyway, after witnessing Max's altercation with Kator.

Mercy followed Reaper without further attempts at conversation. She might not like the idea that she, like her grandmother, was a queen, but she didn't entirely disbelieve it. Clearly, Willem Frain and his group had taken her for a reason. Frain had been sure there was something unique about Mercy and her Talent. Something that let her take a null like Atrea, and make her Talented. Mercy hadn't believed him initially, either, but in the end he'd been proven right. Mercy's disbelief was fueled by fear. Fear that they were right, fear at what would be expected of her if she really *was* like Lilith. Fear at what she could do, and who she would become in this place.

Mercy walked with Reaper down multiple corridors, lost in her own brooding thoughts. She should have been paying attention to where they were going, but a Monarch-class ship was as big as a small city, and it came equipped with maps and directions accessible at every wall. Finding her way was the least of her worries at this point.

If Reaper was in her head, eavesdropping, he didn't comment. She couldn't feel him, but that didn't necessarily mean he wasn't there, hovering just on the periphery of her mind.

"Why do they call you that?" she asked finally, curious, as she followed him into a lift, and Reaper selected a deck.

Call me what? Now his presence was there, distinct. Reaper's mind had a particular feel. Like everyone Talented, his mind was strangely familiar to her. But where most people radiated a soft, golden warmth that was tinged with their unique personality, Reaper's was like a cold flame. The light was there, the familiarity, but there was nothing warm to it. It was actually kind of refreshing. The press of so many Talented minds around her felt claustrophobic.

"Reaper. Or are you going to tell me that's actually your name, like Mercy or Cannon?"

He considered her for a long moment. "My name is Nikolos. But most people call me Reaper.

That's been my…common name for years. Since I was a child."

She could understand someone, especially in this place, earning a nickname like that as an adult, but as child? It didn't fit. "Why?"

Reaper held her gaze for a long moment before replying. Like he was measuring her.

I am part of a unique subset of Talented. His words were back inside her mind, intimate in a way she still wasn't used to. *Yes, I have telepathy and even some telekinesis, but my primary Talent is…different. I look at someone, and see all of the ways in which to kill them. For example, your shields are so poor that a mental assault could stop brain function in 1.3 seconds. However, your body is also not in peak shape. You are malnourished and weaker, physically, that you should be. You wear no armor. I am taller, I outweigh you significantly, and I am trained. I could snap your neck in 2.6 seconds. Those are only the two most efficient methods.* His voice was casual throughout the explanation. He looked completely relaxed, as if discussing how he would kill her was as normal to him as discussing what to eat for breakfast.

Mercy stared at him. The lift suddenly felt claustrophobic, and small spaces didn't typically bother her. She realized she'd backed away from him while he was talking, and now stood pressed against the wall as far from him as she could get. There was literally nowhere to go, trapped inside this small box. The hairs on the back of her neck prickled. He was already inside her mind. That coldness to his presence was no longer something soothing.

Yes. I could kill you instantly, more or less. But as we previously discussed, I have no reason to.

The lift stopped, the door opened, and he walked out. Mercy stayed where she was, remembering how to breathe. Unbidden, a memory surfaced from the space station, when Reaper's team had assaulted it. *They have a Killer,* someone had said. The words had sparked a near frenzy of fear in the young girl with Willem Frain, and had spurred him to teleport out, abandoning his plan to kill Mercy.

This was why.

She forced herself to step out of the lift and into the corridor with him. It was like that time she and Atrea had gone zero-g jumping together. It was one of the attractions at Windfall, a vertical shaft through the center of one of the station modules that ran the entire length of the station, approximately eight kilometers. People stood on a tiny ledge looking down a hole so deep you couldn't see where it ended, and jumped off. Somewhere in the middle of that adrenaline-inducing fall, an operator turned off the gravity generators, and bam, you were weightless, floating. You got to play around for about twenty minutes before they fished you out, and then it was someone else's turn. But there was that fear, right at the beginning. If something went wrong, you'd hit the bottom.

Mercy felt the same sense of fear now, stepping out of that lift to stand beside Reaper. Taking that step felt exactly like that jump. Free-fall.

He studied her face.

Are you rethinking your choice? There are others on

this ship who could teach you. People who are not like me.

She probably should have stopped to seriously consider his words, but Mercy found herself smiling wryly. Now that she'd made the jump, her fear faded.

"They're pirates. Are you telling me these people aren't violent? That they have never killed anyone?"

No. He looked at her. *But it is different for them.*

"Maybe. Maybe not." She lengthened her stride to keep up with him as they walked. "Look, nothing has changed. Out of everyone on this ship, you've had ample opportunity to kill me, if that's what you wanted to do. You haven't, so I believe that makes you the safest person for me to be around right now." She paused, then shrugged. "Safer than family, anyway."

He gave her an odd look, and stopped beside a door.

"What?" she asked.

No one has ever called me "safe" before.

Mercy met his gaze for a long moment before answering. "I've spent my entire life running from things. When I was four, I had nightmares about my grandmother trying to kill me. I used to look at every stranger as a potential threat. When you live like that, you learn pretty quickly not to let fear control you. I can be hyper-aware of danger without giving in to being afraid." She switched to speaking telepathically. *What you are is frightening, but I'm used to viewing everyone that way. You have control of it. That control makes you safe.*

Reaper smiled, and Mercy caught her breath.

He was a striking man, with hard, masculine features and pale blue eyes that seemed to hit her with adrenaline every time he looked at her. But the smile softened his face and added a hint of warmth that made him suddenly approachable. It took striking features and made them compelling. She had the sudden, irrational urge to lean into him, to reach out and touch him. Watching his mouth, she found herself wondering what it would be like to kiss him. His smile widened as he watched her, and Mercy remembered that he could hear every thought.

Don't let it go to your head, she told him, ignoring the way her face heated. *I just spent weeks thinking I was a dead woman. It's natural to think of sex after coming back from the brink of death.*

Were you thinking of sex? Reaper shocked her by reaching out and taking her hand. The second his fingers brushed her skin, her stomach tightened, and warmth bloomed down the back of her hand, seeming to spread over her entire body in an instant. He pressed her fingers to the door panel. *I thought it was just a kiss.*

He dropped her hand as the door slid open, and Mercy cradled it against her like it was burned. She glared at him.

"Don't look so smug. It isn't attractive."

He laughed softly, and it was a startling sound coming from someone who usually showed very little emotion.

"Liar," he told her out loud, watching her with amusement as he leaned against the door jam. It was odd, the way his eyes didn't quite reflect the laughter, but she could still see his mood in his posture, in his expression, and hear it in his voice. He was actually teasing her, and she wondered briefly if Cannon or Vashti would be shocked to know it. She had the impression that people didn't often see things like that from Reaper.

She grinned, her own amusement eclipsing whatever embarrassment she felt.

"Let me have my illusions," she told him.

As you wish.

Still smiling, he gestured through the doorway.

"Your new quarters," he told her. "Already keyed to your biometrics, obviously."

Mercy moved past him into the room. She'd been expecting the same kind of standard closet common for most shipboard bunks. Space enough for a bed, maybe a private head if you were lucky, enough room to stand and change clothes, with a couple of drawers in the wall to store your belongings.

This was nothing like that.

The door opened into a spacious living area with actual furniture. Two chairs and a table, all bolted to the floor. They weren't even utilitarian, as one would expect from a military vessel. The chairs were plush, with high end, self-cleaning fabric manufactured in a comfortable micro-velvet. Along one wall was a length of counter with an attached cold unit for refrigeration, a nano-replicator, a sonic cleaner and an entire bay of storage drawers.

And that was just the first room. Off to the left was a doorway, and when Mercy stepped through it she found a bedroom, with an actual, full sized bed. Bunks on board most ships were narrow affairs affixed to the wall, barely large enough to accommodate a single person. This was in an alcove in the wall, much like her old bunk on Captain Hades' *Dauntless*. But there the similarity ended. The alcove could comfortably sleep two, and it was long enough to fit someone much taller than her, and she wasn't exactly short. The mattress fit inside the alcove, with nano-graph coming up from the floor to shape around it, holding it securely in place. The bedding that lay on it looked like real linen, and when she ran her fingers over it, the fabric was smooth and soft, with none of the stiffness that came from synth-cotton.

Drawers lined the adjacent wall, and on the opposite side of the room a doorway led into a bathroom, complete with a sonic shower that could be, Mercy noted with interest, switched to water when it was available. Not many ships wasted water for bathing, but it was a luxury many people enjoyed when they could. It wouldn't have been standard on a military ship, so this was another alteration to *Nemesis* made by the pirates.

"You'll find the drawers are already stocked with clothing," Reaper said from the doorway. "I'll wait outside."

It was on the tip of her tongue to ask how that was possible, when the door shut. Then Mercy remembered she didn't need to speak the words aloud. Irritated with herself, she reached out to him mentally. It was going to take time for her to get accustomed to using Talent as a matter of course; she'd spent too much of her life avoiding it.

How are they already stocked with clothes? I just got here.

You were kept in a medically-induced coma for three days while Doc assessed and treated you, Reaper told her. *More than enough time to provide you with anything you might need.*

Mercy opened a drawer and found it stuffed with multiple shirts, everything from simple cotton undershirts, to fully lined armored clothing. She ran her fingers over the armored clothing. It was the expensive stuff, too, made from nanograph, like the ship's walls and hull, but smaller, more flexible honeycombs that produced a supple, cloth-like finish. It wouldn't stop an armor piercing round, but it would take the impact from a disrupter, or turn aside a knife blade. It was nearly as light and flexible as normal fabric, which is what made it so damn expensive. Mercy had noticed Cannon and others wearing it, but she had to wonder how something that cost so much could be so commonplace to them. The pirates seemed to have a penchant for expensive things.

Physical weapons were perhaps the least dangerous thing Mercy faced on this ship, but she pulled the armored shirt from the drawer anyway, knowing it would make her feel more secure. She found armored pants in the drawer below, as well as a variety of underthings. Everything, she noted, looked and felt new. It also fit her, for the most part. She did have to cinch the waist of the pants tighter, and she wondered if that was intentional. She knew she'd lost weight during her captivity.

Touching one of the panels on the far wall, she selected the option for a flat, mirrored surface. It was the first time she'd really looked at herself closely since before she and Atrea were kidnapped. Taking stock of everything done to her body was one thing. Seeing it reflected starkly back at her in one whole picture had her inhaling sharply in shock.

She hadn't lost just a little weight. Body shaping and toning had never been an issue for her. She wasn't someone who needed a body regulator implant to maintain her ideal health. Her life required the ability to pick up and run at a moment's notice, and she'd kept herself in reasonable shape to accomplish that. But her face had a hollow look now, the cheekbones sharp slashes, the skin around her eyes almost bruised looking. Her arms were too thin, the muscle tone achieved from hauling crates across the galaxy all but gone. Her bronze skin did not have a healthy glow, but an ashen undertone. Her newly-grown hair hung in a messy cap, the dark strands bedraggled and uneven. It hung down to her eyebrows and barely brushed the tops of her ears on the side, looking like she'd chopped it off with a dull blade. The armored clothing she'd chosen was a dark burgundy, with a decorative scroll in gold down each sleeve and at the throat, a color that would normally have showcased her complexion. Now, it only served to look oddly bold and out of place, like a child playing dress up.

She had a sudden, inexplicable urge to cry, and choked it back ruthlessly. She was not a vain person, and normally didn't care much for her appearance beyond whether or not she looked basically presentable. She'd spent so many years trying to be invisible to everyone, she just didn't bother with enhancements and cosmetics. But looking at herself now, she didn't see how Cannon, Vashti, Reaper…how any of them could look at her and think she was something special. She looked nothing like the vibrant, striking woman her mother had been, or the intimidating presence she vaguely recalled of Lilith.

She looked weak.

Mercy?

Reaper's voice in her head was like a slap in the face. Mercy flinched.

Can I have one damn moment of peace? Is that too much to fucking ask? She thought the words at him viciously, suddenly so tired of it all. She just wanted him, all of them, to stay out of her head and leave her the hell alone. Turning away from the mirror, Mercy swiped a hand to change it back to an unreflective wall. She didn't want to look at herself anymore. She sank onto the bed, not even bothering to fight the hot rush of angry tears now. Maybe Reaper realized she needed a minute without being pushed, because she couldn't feel him in her head anymore. She curled up on her new bed and buried her head in her arms, trying to shut out the world. It was a lot harder than it used to be.

Mercy lay there for a long time. It was easier than trying to face everything. The silence of her room, the black emptiness of space, cold and free of all those Talented minds, pressed against the outer wall of her room, just on the other side of the bulkheads that protected her from a hull breach. She'd never found that comforting before,

but she did now. She wanted to stay like that forever, but that proved impossible.

It could have been minutes, or hours, before
her own thoughts proved too much, crowding her
illusion of peace until she had no choice but to
deal with them. She would give anything to have
Atrea here. Someone who couldn't read her mind,
who would pull her into a hug, and shake her two
seconds later, telling her to stop being an idiot.
But Atrea was in stasis, maybe dying. *Because of me.*
That was the crux of it. Mercy had been weak, and
it was Atrea who would pay the price.

Not that she would blame Mercy for it. Atrea
wasn't like that, had never been like that. Mercy,
on the other hand, could blame herself without
any help from her best friend.

"I'd trade places with you, if I could," Mercy
said to the empty room. She tried to imagine what
Atrea would say in response, and almost laughed,
despite everything.

Get over yourself, Kincaid. That's what Atrea
would say. Mercy could practically hear it. *It was a
bad situation. One we never would have been in, if I
hadn't walked us into that dive on Yuan-Ki. So stop
crying and figure out how to fix me.*

"Yes, ma'am."

Mercy wiped at her face with a sleeve. The armored clothing was, among other things, self-
cleaning and self-mending. It absorbed the moisture instantly. With an effort, she stopped her
tears. She didn't have time for self-pity. She had to
figure out everything she possibly could about her
Talent, everything she'd never known, if she was
going to help Atrea.

When she left her new quarters a few moments later, she was carefully composed, all trace of tears gone. Reaper waited for her, leaning against the wall in the corridor like he had all of the time in the universe. He straightened when she stepped outside the door, but she didn't meet his eyes.

"You're still here."

He considered her carefully. Mercy was pretty sure her efforts to erase the evidence of her tears had not been good enough to escape his notice, but he said nothing.

Where else would I be?

She decided the safest thing was to ignore that. The last thing she wanted to think about was Reaper's whole day revolving around her for the foreseeable future.

"This Queen thing," she said. "Is it the reason I was able to…make Atrea Talented?"

From the corner of her eye, she saw him visibly react to her words, going absolutely still. "Is that what you did?" he asked, his voice without inflection. She noticed that he spoke out loud, instead of in her mind. She nodded.

"Yes. What Frain did…it might kill her. But what I did could kill her, too. Her mother was Talented, but Atrea was born a null. Somehow, I found that potential inside of her, and I…I made it real." Mercy looked down at her hands, realized she was holding them clenched together, so hard it hurt. She forced them to relax, holding them loosely at her sides.

"Yes," said Reaper. "Lilith used to make certain Talents stronger when she found it useful. It is something unique to being a Queen. The ability to sense Talent in someone, and manipulate it."

Mercy nodded, almost to herself.

"So, if I learn how to use it, maybe I could change what I did."

Reaper didn't answer right away. Mercy had the impression he was weighing his words. She suddenly wished she could be inside his head, listening to his thoughts. She wanted the truth, however stark or unforgiving it might be.

"Don't lie to me," she told him, looking directly at him for the first time. She met his eyes without flinching. "Don't ever lie to me. Not to make me feel better, or protect me, or for any reason." She took a breath. "Can I fix Atrea?"

"I don't know."

"But maybe." If he wasn't sure, that didn't mean it couldn't be done.

Reaper watched her carefully. "It's possible."

"Okay, then." Dry eyed, and more determined than she'd ever felt in her life, Mercy lifted her chin. "I want to get started. Show me this arena."

CHAPTER ELEVEN

In most spaceports, especially those with a smuggling presence, underground fights were a mainstay. They went hand in hand with the more accepted and legal gambling dens and bordellos. Jump jockeys lined up to spend their credits in places like that, anxious for anything to relieve the monotony of one long jump after another. Mercy could never understand why the Commonwealth lawmakers thought a bunch of bored and isolated men and women could indulge in alcohol, drugs, and sex, but stop short at violence. Losing their pay to dice or cards was just not as viscerally satisfying as betting against one human being's ability to beat the shit out of another.

Mercy figured the government saw it as wasteful. Spaceships didn't fly without pilots and navigators. People broken and stuck in a med ward weren't doing their jobs. No matter how often a spaceport authority found out where a match was taking place and shut it down, another would spring up, almost before the writ of arrest had finished being issued. And people with credits or hard currency to spend could always find them.

Just after Atrea's sixteenth birthday, the old Wolf had taken them to a match. Atrea's birthday was a mere nine days after Mercy's, so both of them had been feeling full of themselves. Old enough to drink in most systems, old enough to take and pass the exams to complete their primary education certificate. Adult.

Wolfgang offering to take them to a fight had seemed like an official acknowledgement of this truth. Looking back, Mercy should have known it was nothing of the sort, but at the time she felt a secret thrill and no small sense of pride, one she knew Atrea shared.

That feeling had only lasted to the end of the first fight. The combatants looked like a good match, both of them being about the same size, with the kind of muscled build that said they probably did more than just flying cargo. Any smuggling crew worth its salt had a few beaters in the ranks. Captain Hades didn't, but he stuck to soft goods. No drugs, no weapons, no slaves, no illegal tech. He smuggled agriculture past checkpoints to desperate colonists. People left him alone because he didn't offer competition, and most smugglers had colony ties. Wolfgang Hades helped feed their families.

Plus, Mercy suspected he was a bit of a beater himself. Not that he ever talked about it, but she knew he'd been in the military at some point. He moved like someone who had implants.

So did one of the fighters. The other did not. When the first punch landed, Mercy knew it would be over quickly. But that wasn't how it played out. Later, Wolfgang explained that the losing fighter had probably owed a lot of money to someone, and the fight had been a set up. The question of whether or not he could win was answered very quickly. The beating went on, and on. Until there was nothing recognizable left.

As a message, it was effective. The crowd knew what happened to people who didn't pay their debts. So did Mercy and Atrea. It was the last fight either of them ever attended.

Even given that limited experience, however, Mercy knew what the arena was the moment she and Reaper stepped inside the room. Hard to say what the space was originally intended for. A cargo hold, maybe. But the pirates had long ago converted it to something else. One of the things that made nano-graph such a valuable ship material was its fluid nature, without sacrificing strength. It was built to self-repair, but this was only the beginning of what it was capable of. Reprogram the nanobots built into the graphene, and they would restructure the material into a different form or shape. Evidence of this already existed in the way her room had been arranged, or the size of the lifts.

Here, it could be seen in a much more spectacular fashion. The arena was exactly what it sounded like. An eight-meter-square space was marked off in the center of the room, with seating sprawled around it. The seats were structured in rows of benches around the outside edges of the room, and were already half-filled with people when Reaper and Mercy arrived. Two men stood in the center square and faced off against one another, stripped to the waist, skin gleaming beneath the lights. Both were young men, in their twenties, one darker, the other the unnatural pale pallor of someone who spent much more time on ships than walking the dirt of any world. Both were lean with well-defined muscle, holding themselves with a confidence that said each expected to win. A third man, this one fully clothed, stood between them, speaking in a low voice.

Mercy stopped just inside the room, remembering that long ago lesson with Wolfgang. She tried to ignore the way people were turning to stare.

"What is it this is supposed to prove to me, exactly?" she asked Reaper stiffly. She didn't care to watch two men beat the crap out of each other for fun, especially not while on display to a crowd of people she didn't know. Then she thought about Max and Kator. "Wait, is *this* what you're going to have those boys do?"

Reaper touched a hand to her shoulder briefly, and she knew it was meant to reassure her.

Be patient, and you will see, he said. *Hopefully, you will understand.*

"I see we're back to speaking telepathically," she muttered.

Reaper arched an eyebrow.

One of us is. The other could use some practice.

The best response to that, Mercy decided, was to ignore it. Not that he was wrong. She just didn't like having it pointed out. It didn't escape her that he hadn't answered her question, either.

Patience, Reaper said. Mercy's teeth ground together. She was going to get really tired of hearing that.

Looking around at the crowd, she suddenly became aware of a familiar presence hovering just outside her shields. She was starting to be able to differentiate between individual minds, although it would have been difficult with this many people, had this person not made a point of being noticed. Mercy hesitated, and Reaper gave her a look. He didn't need to say anything for her to interpret it. He clearly thought she was being a poor student if she continued to avoid actually *using* her gifts. Remembering her vow to learn as much as she could, Mercy sighed and squared her shoulders. She reached out with her mind, feeling horribly vulnerable in this crowded place.

Vashti?

Yes, dear. Please do come and sit with me. Over here.

Mercy felt a tug at her attention, and turned her head to see the older woman lifting a hand and waving in their direction from across the room. She was sitting right in front of the arena, her bench center to the action. Mercy hoped none of the surprise she felt leaked through her shields. From the little she knew, she never would have pictured Vashti as a fight fan.

She and Reaper made their way around the room. Mercy steadfastly kept her gaze pointed straight ahead, ignoring the countless curious eyes on her, and the whispers, both vocal and telepathic, that followed in her wake. It was with a wave of relief that she finally reached Vashti and took the empty seat next to the old woman.

Reaper sat on her other side, so that Mercy was between them. That helped, too. She'd been afraid she would end up with a stranger next to her, and right now she was already feeling overwhelmed.

When Reaper sat down, the people on the other side of him got up and moved, giving up their good seats for worse ones, much further away. Mercy quirked a brow at Reaper, but he just smiled. It was the kind of smile that was more sharp than amused. He wasn't the least bit bothered by the discomfort others experienced around him. In fact, Mercy suspected he rather enjoyed it.

Beside her, Vashti let out a low laugh. Two men were seated on the other side of her, one in his mid-thirties, the other clearly younger. The older of the two gave Vashti a brief, unreadable look, while the younger looked uncomfortable. Both had the same familial stamp to their features that Vashti, Mercy and Cannon shared, with skin a burnished bronze shade, angular cheekbones and jawlines, and the dark hair and green eyes that seemed universal. Mercy found herself going tense.

"Ever the popular one, eh, Nikolos?" Vashti asked easily, seeming to ignore the byplay around her. Reaper shrugged in response, and Mercy wondered if Vashti usually used his given name, or whether she did so now to provoke him. That made her wonder a bit more about Vashti. Intentionally provoking someone like Reaper seemed like a bad idea.

Mercy had to force herself to relax, concentrating on her muscles and keeping her breathing even. She reminded herself that, with Lilith dead, her family no longer wanted to kill her. Or so they said.

Vashti gave her a warm smile. "Griffin and Cage are my nephews. Lilith had four daughters. Pallas, Macha, Nemain and Athena. Your mother, you obviously know. Nemain was Cannon's mother. Athena was Griffin and Cage's. They are my great-nephews, and like me, mean you no harm. Quite the opposite, in fact."

"I'm sure I'll start to believe that eventually," Mercy said with a stiff smile. She leaned forward slightly, and gave them a nod of greeting, while making sure her shields were still in place, bolstered by Reaper. The older of the two nodded back.

Griffin, Reaper told her, so softly she barely heard it. *His younger brother is Cage. Neither will try anything while I am here. They fear me.*

Good, she sent back. Maybe it was wrong of her to feel pleased that Reaper inspired such fear in others, but if it helped make her feel safe, she didn't care.

"Such a pleasure to have everyone together," Vashti said aloud. "The family, and Nikolos, of course." She gave Reaper a chastising shake of her head. "I keep telling you to visit me more, boy."

And how many people, Mercy asked him in amazement, *call you "boy"?*

He gave her a flat look. *Only Vashti.*

Interesting. So, if Vashti *was* provoking Reaper, it was something she did regularly. On purpose. Mercy studied her great-aunt, making no attempt to hide the fact. A sparkle lit the old woman's green eyes, and she seemed anything but worried or intimidated. Her hair was braided back, and some of the dark strands still untouched by time framed her face and wound through the braid like a black ribbon against the white.

"You aren't afraid of him." It wasn't a question. Mercy recognized fear pretty easily, and Vashti displayed none. She sat easily, relaxed, with no tightness around her eyes, or stiffness to her lean frame.

"When you reach my age," Vashti said with a shrug, "you realize you have nothing left to fear from death."

It wasn't quite a lie, but somehow Mercy knew it wasn't the whole truth, either.

She smiled at Vashti, eyeing her carefully. The old woman smiled back, for all the world looking like someone's harmless, innocent grandmother. *Sure.* Mercy reached out to Reaper mentally.

She's never been afraid of you.

No, he said. *She hasn't.*

Why? Mercy had a feeling there was more to Vashti. If she wasn't afraid of someone like Reaper, there would be a reason. A good one.

Reaper glanced at her.

When I was a child, Vashti was one of my teachers.

In...telepathy? Telekinesis?

No. Most Killers train together. They grow up apart from the rest of the pirates, in their own colony, and they don't mix with the rest of our population much. Accidents happen, otherwise. He paused, letting her absorb that. *They get very specialized training in using their Talents. My childhood was different. My mother wasn't a Killer. She was a telepath and tele-kinetic. I was raised by her on Ardon, our primary colony world. My father wasn't always around, but when he was, he provided the specialized training in using my Talent, and in physical and mental combat. Vashti provided the rest.*

The rest?

Interpreting what my Talent showed me. Understanding someone's vulnerabilities, how to exploit them, and which method is best for which situation.

Mercy wrestled with that for a moment.

She taught you the intellectual part of assassination?

Yes.

Mercy looked back at her great-aunt. The easy smile hadn't changed, but now it felt a lot more dangerous. An old children's story surfaced in her memory, something about a wolf pretending to be a harmless old woman. *What large teeth you have, grandmother.* Mercy no longer wondered why Vashti would be here, watching the fights. Her aunt leaned over and patted her hand.

"Now you understand us a little bit better," she said softly. "We might not all be Killers, like Nikolos. But we are all dangerous, Mercy. Best that you learn that now."

In the center of the room, the fight started. It was nothing like the shows broadcast across the Commonwealth for entertainment. It wasn't even much like that long ago fight she and Atrea had witnessed. This was short, fast, and brutal. The two men circled one another briefly, then the distance between them closed, a flurry of blows leaving the pale one on the floor, curled protectively around his ribcage. The snap of bone had happened so quickly, he was down almost before Mercy registered the sound.

No one stepped between the two men to stop the fight. The watching crowd didn't cheer, but Mercy saw hard currency exchanged between more than a few hands, a low murmur sweeping the benches. A moment passed while the dark skinned man contemplated the one on the ground. The hair rose on the back of Mercy's neck. He was considering killing the other man. She didn't know how she was so certain of the thought, but she was. She held her breath, hoping she wasn't about to watch one man murder another. After an endless moment, he suddenly nodded to himself and stepped back. This time, the whispers that swept the crowd had the feel of surprise. No. It was shock, and people began talking all over the room, low, intense voices and thoughts layering and overlapping.

"Interesting," said Vashti beside her. She glanced at Mercy. "They were here to settle a grievance. Fights for position or rivalry don't necessarily end in death, but those where a disagreement has escalated to the arena always do."

"Always?" Mercy was stunned. "Aren't you trying to rebuild your population?"

Vashti shrugged. "We don't believe in leaving an enemy at our backs when it can be avoided. Fights to the death were a practice Lilith encouraged and rewarded. The old Queen's ways are extremely difficult to throw aside." She gave Mercy a long, penetrating stare. "You don't approve?"

"I…not like this, no."

"Hmm," said Vashti. "This will be an interesting

day." She turned back to watch as two men finally came out and picked up the fallen fighter, carrying him from the room.

Two more men were already walking out to the center ring. Mercy was startled to realize that she knew one of them.

Zion, Reaper said in in her mind. *One of my dogs.*

Yes. Mercy remembered. He was classically handsome, with blue eyes a darker shade than Reaper's. He moved now with an easy confidence, stepping casually into the arena, and waiting calmly as his opponent, looking far more nervous, stood on the opposite side.

"Do they—" She caught herself a second before Reaper's disapproving look. *Do they have a disagreement?*

No. Shane is applying to become a dog. Candidates have to prove themselves against a current dog. They can challenge any they choose, since Dem trains them all. The fights are a test, not to the death.

Dem? Mercy didn't recognize the name.

Reaper took a long time to answer. *My brother,* he said reluctantly. *Also, the Chief of Security aboard the Nemesis, and a member of the Core.*

Mercy's mind spun, thrown by the sudden flood of information. She focused on the most personal, first. *You have a brother?*

*I have two. Technically, we are half-brothers, but the separation of blood is of little consequence. Regardless of the number of parents we have in common, we are siblings. Dem is the most like me. His father, though different from my own, was also a Killer. Treon is...*Reaper hesitated. *Treon is different. Unique.*

Intrigued, Mercy filed the names away for further investigation, later. Reaper's tone wasn't exactly closed, but she could tell he wasn't eager to answer more questions about his family right now.

And the Core? What is that?

It's supposed to be the balance to our monarch. A council, of sorts. The goal is to keep in mind what is best for our people as a whole, and vote on laws and practices to best support and aid them. Theoretically, we can also overrule the monarch if we disagree with something unanimously. In practice, though, that has not always proven possible. His tone was dark, making Mercy think of everything she'd heard regarding her grandmother's reign.

I'm guessing that's another reference to what an understanding and fair Queen Lilith was?

That is correct.

And Cannon? Has the Core tried to overrule him?

No. So far, there hasn't been a need. But Cannon sits in on Core meetings, and generally he and the majority tend to agree.

You said "we" before. Are you a part of this Core?

I am.

Mercy was silent for a moment, thinking. She watched as the fight started, this one taking more time than the previous bout. She was no beater, but from what she could see, Zion was deliberately testing the other man, giving him openings and analyzing his defenses.

So, she said finally, *you guys left the Commonwealth, but you created a system of government that mirrors the Council of Sovereign Planets, and the monarchy.* She wondered if the irony came through with her telepathic words.

We are the product of our experiences. Reaper shrugged.

How do you decide who becomes a member of the Core? Voting?

Reaper laughed in her mind. He looked at her, clearly amused.

"Please," he said aloud. "We are pirates, Mercy. Core members are decided by power and position. Who can take it, and who can keep it."

In the center ring, the tone of the fight abruptly changed. Zion, having taken a few hits up until now, became untouchable. His opponent, a passable fighter who probably could have gained employment as a beater on many a smuggling ship, could no longer land any punches. In the space of a few moments he took jabs to the kidneys, ribs, and solar plexus, before finally being thrown roughly to the floor. He lay gasping, pained grunts escaping as he struggled for air, holding his hands close to his head in a futile attempt at protecting himself. Zion dropped his hands and left the ring. Beside Mercy, Reaper shook his head, his mouth turned down.

"He lost." Mercy glanced at him. "Does that mean he won't become a dog?"

Reaper moved one shoulder in a shrug.

"He was expected to lose. It's a matter of how he lost, and how he responds to it, that will ultimately decide whether Dem accepts him."

Two men came, helped Shane stand and moved him out of the ring.

"Dogs are often a stepping stone to greater

things," Reaper added. "Most Core members once served someone in that capacity. I don't believe Shane is capable of taking power. Even with training, he may never become more than he is now." He tilted his head. "Zion? That is another story entirely."

Hmm, Mercy thought, a little darkly. *The charming one.* She didn't realize she'd broadcast it until Reaper switched back to telepathy.

You don't like Zion because he is charming? She could hear the underlying ripple of Reaper's amusement. *Not the usual response people have to him.*

No. I don't like Zion because he isn't what he appears. He pretends to be whatever will get him what he wants.

Most people do that.

Mercy hesitated, struggling to put her feelings into words.

Maybe. Not like Zion. I don't know how to explain it. I just feel like underneath he is someone entirely different. His charm is a lie. His pretty smile is a lie. I don't like liars.

"Oh!" Vashti suddenly grasped Mercy's arm, fingers tugging at her for attention, seemingly oblivious that she was interrupting. "Here he is. My boy." There was no mistaking the pride in her voice. On the other side of her, Griffin and Cage both sat straighter, their attention intensely focused on the center ring. It was enough to intrigue Mercy, until she saw the youth walking out to the arena.

Max.

"You have got to be kidding me," she said

aloud. She looked at Reaper. *You told me to be patient. I have been, and now I have to watch these two boys beat the shit out of each other?*

He lifted an eyebrow. *Hopefully not.*

What the hell does that mean?

Reaper didn't answer, and Vashti's fingers tightening on her arm pulled Mercy's attention back to the ring.

Max had that awkward, gangly gate inherent to teenage boys who gained height quickly, too fast for their muscle control and physical command to keep up with. Although his skin tone was the burnished bronze of family, he looked starkly pale under the lights. His dark hair was messy, and hung in his eyes. He made his way to the center and stood, looking uncomfortable and, Mercy thought, scared.

"Griffin and Cage's brother," Vashti said, smiling. "My youngest nephew, Max."

For a moment, Mercy was startled out of her observation of the boy enough to look at Vashti.

"Griffin, Cage, and…Max?"

Vashti shrugged. "You'll get used to the odd naming conventions we have. Most of us shorten Max's name. Maximum can get a bit caught in the mouth. Too many M's, you know."

Mercy blinked at her, then looked back at Max. By this time, his opponent had come to stand with him, and Mercy felt herself go cold. Under the harsh lighting, the difference between the two boys was highlighted even more starkly than before. Kator looked impossibly large. He was clearly older by a couple of years and a hulking figure, with wide shoulders, huge, meaty hands, and a breadth of muscle that didn't seem to fit with his apparent youth.

"He must outweigh him by nearly double," she said.

"Almost," muttered Griffin, but Mercy heard it.

"That's not a fair fight," she said, looking from Vashti to Reaper, and back again.

Vashti frowned at her. "It is. Talent makes the smallest boys strong. This is how disputes are settled." The old woman gave a sharp nod. "Here, there are rules. A one-on-one combat gives Max an opportunity."

"At what, getting beaten or killed in front of everyone?"

Cage leaned forward to glare at Mercy. "At earning his place," he said. "Stay out of it."

This is insane, Mercy told Reaper. *That boy doesn't stand a chance, and you know it.*

Reaper gave her a look empty of emotion. *If he wants it badly enough, if he's prepared, he can win. There are ways to beat a physically stronger opponent, and Max knows some of them. He demonstrated that this morning.*

In a confrontation Kator clearly engineered. He didn't even fight back, because he was waiting to do it here! If that bully wasn't absolutely sure he could win, he never would have made this happen.

True. Reaper's implacable calm grated on Mercy's nerves.

Then you can't let this happen.

It's our way. They have a dispute. Let's call it a long, ongoing conflict. This will end it.

This is what you and Cannon call dealing with the situation?

Reaper didn't answer, and she found herself wanted to smack that impassive look right off his face. His eyes paled, and a deep, instinctive caution kept her still. *Mother take you,* she fumed, feeling more impotent than she had since the space station. She thought about Max's shy smile this morning, and hated everyone.

Mercy stared at the two boys as they took positions opposite one another. Now that she was watching for it, she could see that Max wasn't just awkward from his height and gangly limbs. He was favoring his right side. She couldn't remember if he'd already been doing that this morning, or if this was something new.

"This boy has been beating on Max for awhile?" she asked Vashti, keeping her voice even.

"Since they were small," Vashti said. "Children often establish a hierarchy in such ways. Max comes from a powerful family, but hates conflict. His Talent developed late as well. It made him a target." She nodded to the arena. "This is his opportunity to turn things around and put Kator in his place."

Mercy sat stunned for a moment. That even Vashti, who clearly loved the boy, condoned this was unfathomable. *I thought children were precious to you. I thought you would protect them above all else.*

Reaper regarded her thoughtfully. *We would never permit an adult to abuse a child. However, ours is a hard and difficult life. They must be permitted to settle their own issues amongst peers.*

You are letting children fight, she said to Reaper.

He looked at her, and his lack of response just stirred her own emotions more.

You are letting them beat each other for position. Coldness settled in her gut as she remembered Vashti's earlier words. *Does this count as a disagreement? Or is this just a fight to say who is who in the pecking order?*

Why?

I want to know if this fight will stop when someone goes down.

Reaper took his time answering, seeming to weigh her question.

Kator and his friends have spent the past several years bullying Max. They attempted to kill him at least once that I am aware of. I doubt it will stop when one of them goes down.

Mercy stared at him. She looked at Vashti again, still hoping she would see some of her own incredulity reflected there. Instead, she saw pride, worry, and hope. She looked beyond her to Griffin and Cage, but they sat with identical, grimly stoic expressions.

"He's your brother." Mercy said, her chest tight. "You're just going to let this happen?"

Griffin glanced at her, a flash of anger in his green eyes. "If we try to intervene, it will make things worse."

"How?"

"No matter the outcome, it will look like we're protecting him. It will make him look weaker, more of a target. Even if we killed Kator for him, it would still make others believe Max to be weak. It's as good as a death sentence."

In the ring, a man stepped between the boys, clearly explaining whatever the rules were. If they even had any. Max nodded stiffly, his face grim and determined. Kator just nodded sharply. He was anticipating winning already. It made Mercy's stomach turn.

"This is insane," Mercy said aloud. "You are all insane."

She glared at Reaper.

Is this what you brought me here for? To watch boys kill each other?

No.

Then, why?

In the ring, the boys started moving. Kator lunged in, hands going for a grab, and Max danced out of the way.

You needed to see this. We are a people fighting for survival. Every day is a battle to that end.

Then why kill each other? She gestured to the arena, wincing as Max didn't move quite fast enough, and one of Kator's fists caught a glancing blow to his shoulder, staggering him.

Because Lilith wanted it. Because she spent her reign making things like this happen. It entertained her.

Kator took Max down with an arm wrapped around the other boy's waist. Max got in a punch, but the bigger boy just grunted and held on. In a minute, he'd have Max in a choke.

"Lilith is fucking dead," Mercy said aloud, fists clenched at her sides. "You don't have to do what she wanted anymore."

"A Queen's influence is not so easy to throw off," said Vashti quietly. Her hands gripped tightly together in her lap as her eyes never left the arena. Kator gave a sudden yelp and Max regained his feet, breathing hard. The bigger boy was back up in the same instant, removing any chance for Max to hurt him while he was down. Blood ran freely down Kator's face, his nose swollen, but Max was bleeding, too, red rivulets running down the side of his neck from long, deep scratches.

"Cannon is your King now, right? He can stop this." Mercy looked around, trying to spot him in the stands.

In the arena, Max and Kator were grappling again, each boy trying to gain purchase against the other. Max was slippery and wiry, but he wasn't strong enough to gain and keep a hold on Kator. Their movements were odd, stilted and halting, not fluid like most fights. Each boy kept gasping like a fish, pulling in a great gulp of air at irregular intervals. She realized it had to be Talent. The boys were using telekinesis to try and kill each other.

Vashti gave a small, sad smile.

"No. He can't. Cannon is not a queen. He can work around the deepest pieces of our culture ingrained by Lilith, but he cannot overrule them."

"That makes no sense." Mercy couldn't see how that was possible.

Vashti met her eyes.

"We have had many years to test it, and have come to this conclusion: only a true Queen can undo what another Queen has wrought."

Mercy stared back at her, her stomach twisting into painful knots. Realization crashed over her in a wave.

This is why you brought me here, she said to Reaper. *You want me to stop it.*

We have been killing each other for decades. Our population continues to dwindle each year, each day that goes by. We are violent by nature, and Lilith took that trait and made it worse.

Vashti reached over and took Mercy's hands between her own. Her green eyes were hopeful, and pleading.

"Save my nephew," she said. "Please, Your Majesty."

CHAPTER TWELVE

*P*anic fluttered through Mercy. Her new armored clothing was suddenly suffocatingly warm, the collar half strangling her. Her fingers, by contrast, went icy cold, her throat closing. She couldn't seem to tear her eyes away from Vashti. The lines in the older woman's face had deepened, highlighting her age and making her look less the dangerous trainer of assassins, and more an aunt who loved her nephew, and was desperate to save him.

"What can I do?" She had to force the words past frozen lips. Cannon was the King, known and respected by these people for his entire life. If his voice couldn't stop this, she didn't see how hers would be heeded.

"Just as Lilith once made these fights to the death compulsory, my Queen, you can stop them," said Vashti.

A huge crash drew their eyes back to the center ring. Kator and Max had hit the floor, locked together as each boy used Talent and body to try and choke the life from the other. This wasn't just

Max's life in the balance. Kator, too, might not survive. In a worst-case scenario, Mercy could see them killing one another, snuffing out two young Talents in the space of a breath.

"How?" she asked. "How do I stop this?" She looked at Reaper, then at Vashti. Her aunt squeezed her hands, having not let go of them.

"Your presence is clearly having an effect," said Vashti gravely. "The first fight ending without a death is proof of that. Already your wants, likes and dislikes are beginning to countermand Lilith's. But it isn't enough yet. These boys are young and driven by their emotions. For Max, this is a matter of survival. For Kator, it is the culmination of years. They will not stop just because they may have a choice now. You will have to intervene directly."

"I just tell them to stop?" Mercy realized neither boy had gasped for breath in the past twenty seconds. Her heartbeat kicked up, adrenaline pounding in her ears. They were out of time.

"That would be an excellent start, Your Majesty," said Vashti.

"Don't call me that." Mercy stood up, pulling her hands away.

No one paid her any attention at first, not until she'd taken the first ten steps or so. Then she felt it. The prickling awareness of notice swinging her way, of eyes watching her. First it was just a few, most people still focused on the fight. Sensing that it was reaching a culmination, a few people even rose to their feet, gaining a better vantage point. The idea that watching children kill each other was thrilling to some of these people made Mercy's stomach turn. She quickened her pace, but did not run. She had the sense that appearing to run at them in a panic would send the wrong message. She had to do this, but in a way that projected strength.

You learn quickly, said Reaper in her mind. *Any perceived weakness here will give an opening to those who don't want another Queen. The boys are evenly matched in telekinesis. Neither can quite get a crushing grip on the other. Instead, they will slowly suffocate. You have less than two minutes.*

No pressure, she sent back. *I don't even know what I'm doing.*

You are a Queen, Mercy. You have instincts. Let them guide you.

Mercy felt tension flood her body. Reaper's words were so reminiscent of the things Frain had said to her. But she brushed that aside. She couldn't focus on that now.

By this time she had almost reached the arena. Enough eyes were upon her now that she felt the attention of the whole room. A silence had fallen, one weighted with more than expectation. There was a heaviness here, one of judgment, and of threat. Mercy had a sense that what she was about to do would start a cascade, one action leading to others, a building, unstoppable force that would determine her future, or her death.

She took a deep breath. She couldn't walk away, knowing that doing so would doom these boys, who could not save themselves.

"Stop." She used the same voice she'd learned from Captain Hades at fifteen, spoken from her diaphragm and meant to project across the length of a spaceport dock filled with loud machinery and ship engines. It commanded respect from dock workers and cargo officials, carried the sort of confidence that kept them from questioning the ship and its cargo.

There was a brief hitch in the desperate battle between the boys, a quick suck of air that lasted barely a second before they went right back to their stalemate of imminent death.

It didn't work. Panic tried to well up.

Don't think. Listen to your instincts, said Reaper calmly.

Mercy didn't pause to consider his words or what they meant. As soon as she heard them, something clicked inside of her, something that felt this was the right path.

"Stop!"

This time, she spoke the word and projected it with her mind at the same time. It left her body and carried with it all of the emotion pouring through her. It emptied her of desperation, fear, anger, disgust, and determination, all of those feelings tangling together in a powerful wave of feeling that gave her voice, both mental and vocal, power.

Everything froze.

The boys stopped moving. The crowd went still and silent. For a second, or a nano-second, everything simply fixed in place like a stasis field had activated in the whole room. Mercy felt not just the weight of attention from every pirate in this room, but from every pirate aboard the ship. It held for an endless, eternal second, like when a ship jumped through otherspace, traveling light years in the moments that existed between time. Then the boys fell apart, both of them gasping and breathing huge gulps of air, chests rising and falling desperately as they lay a few feet apart, neither one able to move enough to continue the fight as they struggled to get precious oxygen back inside their bodies.

A low roar of mental sound rose up as the crowd responded to what it had just seen. Voices threatened to overwhelm Mercy a hairsbreadth before her shields tightened, shoving them out. *Reaper.*

Very good. Everyone here sees a woman who thinks herself a Queen. Now, make them believe it.

Mercy fisted her hands at her sides.

I am not my Grandmother. I don't want to be.

Then tell them.

I don't want to be your Queen!

Cannon's voice was suddenly in her mind, resonating, deep. *Don't think about that now. You've opened a door, and you must continue walking through it if you want to minimize the impact. Don't talk about being Queen; just talk about why you did this. Do it now, and be as truthful as you can. Enough of us can sense lies that you must be honest, above all else.*

Mercy took a breath, lifting her chin.

Not a problem, she sent back.

Before she spoke, she gestured a hand to both boys. A tremor shook it, one she hoped no one else could see.

"Is this what you want?" she asked, sweeping her eyes around the room. She turned a circle, so as not to miss any one section. "I have been here, awake, for less than a day. I have heard the story of the virus that decimated your population. And the first thing I see of your culture is children, killing each other for sport." Her eyes narrowed, and she let her personal sense of outrage color her words. "You—"

We, said Cannon in her mind. *Make this about all of us.*

"—*we* are a people dying, more each day. We are desperate to have more children, to raise our population and *not let them win*. Yet here you are, helping our enemies to gain more ground. The Commonwealth. The people who sent the virus. Those who kidnapped me. Do we not have enough enemies, without turning on each other?"

She stepped over to where Max and Kato struggled to sit up.

"No more." Leaning down, Mercy helped first Max, and then Kator, to stand. She nearly staggered trying to aid Kator, and then she felt his weight lighten and knew someone was helping with telekinesis. Probably Reaper, or Vashti. Both youths blinked at her, confused. Perhaps unknowing, they stood and swayed close together in an unconscious seeking of support, for this one moment united in their bewilderment.

Finish it, said Cannon. *Make your will clear.*

"From this moment, there will be no more fighting to the death in the arena, for any reason."

They must have an outlet, Cannon said. *Something to focus on. And we must be able to kill when we need to.*

"Save your thirst for blood to serve our enemies." She was suddenly grateful for the brief glimpse Reaper had given her into their politics.

"For now, only your King and the Core will sentence any pirate to death. If you must kill one of our own in self-defense, be prepared to prove the necessity. The virus is still killing us. Every life we have is precious. Every life must be protected and nurtured if we are to survive."

For the first time since she stepped into the arena, a voice challenged her.

"Who are you to dictate to us?" It was just one in the crowd, but Mercy *felt* the agreement of many.

She hesitated.

Own it, said Cannon.

She scowled, suddenly angry at him, at all of them. *I don't want to be your Queen.*

He said nothing, the silence its own answer. To her annoyance, Reaper too remained silent, though she could feel his presence.

Fine. She glared at the crowd.

"I am Mercy Kincaid. Pallas was my mother. Lilith was my grandmother. I may not know all of you, but you know me. Don't insult us both by pretending otherwise."

She turned her back to them all and walked, not back to Vashti and Reaper, but in the opposite direction, to the door. She walked right out into the hallway beyond, and kept going. Until the minds behind her faded from her awareness. Until she was alone enough to realize that she was well and truly lost, and had no idea what part of the ship she was on, much less where she was going. She'd bite her own tongue before she asked Reaper or Cannon right now.

Stepping up to the wall, she touched it, and a

blue and green diagram lit up beneath her fingers. She studied it for a few seconds. It was only the deck she was on, and it didn't tell her things like where her quarters were. But some ships, particularly military vessels, had voice activated AIs that could help with that.

She hesitated. The question was, where did she want to go? She didn't actually want to be alone, she realized. She wanted her family. The only family she'd ever really had.

Mercy cleared her throat.

"Nemesis, show me how to get to the infirmary."

*

"It's a start," said Vashti, clearly pleased. "And it went quite well."

Reaper gave her a long look, one she returned with an arched eyebrow.

"Oh, don't think to intimidate me, boy," she said. "It's many years too late for that." She stood up and moved in her unhurried way across the floor to Max's side, her robes swishing around her. Griffin and Cage followed dutifully in her wake, as ever.

Reaper stayed where he was, his own thoughts more complex than he'd anticipated. He'd played his own role in what had just happened. Convincing Mercy to come here was only part of it. From the moment they entered the arena, his actions and words had helped to create this moment. He'd even been the one to suggest it to Cannon. *If you want the fights to change, there is only one person who can accomplish that, and she just came aboard this ship.* His words.

So why did he feel uncomfortable with the outcome? It was an odd feeling for him. A kind of disquiet. He could kill with no feeling, no regard for his actions or the results. Yet it bothered him that Mercy had shut him out.

He could force his way past her shields. They were still fledgling things in need of strengthening, but to do so would destroy whatever fragile trust existed between them. No, there was nothing to do but wait. Wait for Mercy to be ready to talk.

Reaper was not accustomed to waiting on others and their comfort.

How the mighty have fallen.

The words and the voice that went with them were an instant irritant, like a fleck of dust caught in his eye. Reaper stood, and began making his way out of the arena. One never knew how conversations with his youngest brother would go, and he preferred not to have them surrounded by people who could get caught in the mental crossfire.

Treon, he said, his mental voice utterly neutral. Reaper had learned long ago not to give his brother the smallest morsel of inflection to respond to. Treon might not have been a Killer, but in his own way he was just as dangerous.

Back when the Talented were created, Commonwealth scientists had their own way of classifying Talent and rating individuals' power on a scale. The pirates had thrown aside such classifications when they went into exile. They knew, better than any null scientist could understand, that the lowest level of Talent was still capable of miraculous things, and no one should be discounted. Some Talents didn't need raw power to have a devastating effect, Reaper's being one such.

In the time since the virus, however, the pirates had begun developing their own system, purely for categorizing Talent in family lines. It was all Doc's brainchild, a way of planning what bloodlines would beget the best results in the next generation. He and a few other scientists developed a series of tests to measure Talent. It was controversial, and not everyone had embraced this new classification system. Doc forged ahead, determined, until he tried the test on Treon.

Treon's telepathy test produced the impossible: a perfect score. The test was designed to be adaptive, gaining in difficulty based on the individual's response. It used an algorithm designed to go to infinity. In Doc's words, the test did not have an end, and therefore it wasn't possible to achieve a perfect score. It could not be beaten.

And yet, Treon had done so.

Doc was convinced he'd cheated somehow, in protest. Reaper, having grown up with Treon, wasn't so sure. Either way, Treon's results had put Doc's program on temporary hold, something that had delighted more than a few pirates. Reaper was pretty sure his brother hadn't needed to buy his own drinks since.

What do you want? Reaper moved through the crowd beginning to spill into the hallway with little effort. People moved out of his way, always afraid to let a Killer touch them. When he moved into the lift, no one stepped inside it with him.

He remembered Mercy standing in the lift with him earlier, how she wrestled with, and overcame, her fear of him in the time it took to move from one deck to the next. Extraordinary.

I must admit, I wasn't at all sure it was true.

Reaper frowned, his attention once again pulled to his brother. He leaned against the lift wall, crossing his arms.

That I found Pallas' daughter? He asked the question more to irritate Treon than anything. Reaper knew what he was really saying.

That you found a new queen. More, that you would find a queen and bring her back. I believe you once vowed to kill any such person.

Do you have a point, Treon?

Yes, I believe I am making it. I knew she had to be extraordinary if you let her live. What we just witnessed confirms it.

It was no coincidence that his brother used the very word Reaper had been thinking of only a moment ago in relation to Mercy. Those thoughts had been beneath his inner shields, hidden below the surface conversation they were sharing. Not that Treon respected such things. Reaper sighed.

You get more annoying with each conversation we have, he said. *Go away, Treon.*

I want an answer first.

Reaper sighed as the lift came to a halt, and he stepped out. A man wearing the overalls of an engineer was waiting in the hallway. He blanched when he saw Reaper, and nearly tripped over his own feet stumbling back.

You haven't asked me a question yet, Reaper told Treon resignedly, ignoring the man's reaction.

Do you think she can do it?

There was a sudden seriousness to Treon's voice that had been lacking until now. Reaper realized then that his brother had not simply contacted him in order to peck and goad. He knew what Treon was asking, but he held his silence as he weighed his answer. Long enough that his brother spoke again.

Do you think she can save us?

Yes, Reaper said at last, turning into the doorway to his own quarters. *If she decides to stay, and embrace what she is. If she wants it badly enough.*

He was somehow not surprised to see his brother already inside, standing at the bar and pouring two glasses of whiskey. He'd long ago given up on keeping either of his brothers out of his private space. In the end, they were the only two people who ever invaded it, and not so often as to be inconvenient.

They looked nothing alike, the three of them. Treon least of all.

Though not as dark as Dem, Reaper's skin was still more brown than pale, his eyes the cold blue of a Killer, his dark hair cut almost military short. Treon was pale, his skin almost alabaster white, a fact emphasized by the sweep of black hair that brushed the neck of his shirt. His angular face held arrogance, but also an empathy and emotion that Reaper lacked. His eyes were their mother's: a liquid, golden brown not unlike the whiskey in the glass he held. He was beautiful where Reaper was terrifying.

For the first time in his life, Reaper almost envied Treon that. It was not a feeling he wanted to analyze closely. When his brother offered him a glass, he accepted, taking a cautious sip. One never knew what to expect with Treon. He did so enjoy his little games and jokes. But only the clean burn of alcohol hit his mouth and throat, a soft and rolling flavor with it.

Treon lifted his own glass in a kind of salute.

"Then we just have to ensure it," he said, drinking.

Reaper frowned at him.

"Ensure what?"

Sometimes Treon liked to talk in riddles. Or maybe Reaper just didn't care enough to pay him close attention.

His brother smiled.

"That your little Queen will want to save us. Very badly, indeed."

CHAPTER THIRTEEN

$\mathcal{A}$trea was alone when Mercy reached the infirmary. She lay, still encased in the blue stasis field, on a bunk at the far end of the room. Wolfgang wasn't here, and Mercy had to shove aside an acute sense of disappointment. Privacy screens were engaged, giving the illusion of a private room with their distortion field, but Doc's young assistant Nayla gave Mercy the code. She slipped inside to sit with her friend.

She sat with her for a long time.

Atrea looked like she belonged in the infirmary. Her eyes were closed in peaceful sleep, thanks to whatever drug had been used to knock her out, but the stasis field kept her body, her cells frozen in exactly the condition she'd been in. Her blond hair was mussed from her struggles, and dark circles around her eyes and hollow cheeks gave her face a gaunt, unhealthy cast. She was thin, her time as a captive with Willem Frain a visible stamp on her body's condition. Doc could do nothing to help or improve it while she was in stasis. The flip side, of course, being that she couldn't worsen and die, either.

After a time, the silence was too much, too sad. So Mercy started telling Atrea everything that had happened. She started with the escape from the space station, moved on to waking up on the *Nemesis*, and ended with the arena. It took a surprisingly long time.

"I feel like, since the moment you and I walked into that stupid bar on Yuan-Ki, I've been dancing to someone else's tune, and I'm just so tired." Mercy stared down at her friend, wishing more than anything that she could really talk to her.

Atrea always knew what to say.

Of course, being Atrea, Mercy could well-imagine what her friend would say. Atrea never did have time for things like self-pity and regret. She was someone who took action and *did* things.

Then stop dancing. Do what you *want, not what* they *want.*

"But doing what *they* wanted saved the lives of two teenage boys," Mercy said aloud. She leaned one elbow on the arm of her chair, and rested her chin in her hand, so she could stare into the stasis field. "I'm not against that."

Then what are you against?

"Being manipulated. Feeling like I was maneuvered into having no choice. They want me to be their Queen, and I just want to be me."

So why do those two things have to be exclusive? Maybe you don't want to be Queen because you're afraid of what it will mean.

Since her own subconscious was creating this conversation, the thought gave Mercy a moment's pause, and she turned it over in her mind, really thinking about it.

What *would* it mean?

Staying here, probably forever. Becoming more like her grandmother – who everyone seemed to despise. Never returning to the smuggler's life she'd lived for the past fifteen years. Never getting into another adventure with Atrea, sure to turn the old Wolf's hair even grayer.

Never finding out what really happened to her mother.

Don't be ridiculous. Phantom Atrea's voice was just as dry as real Atrea's would be. Mercy could almost see her rolling her eyes. *You would never be like that murderous old bitch. I'm not sure you remember, but the smuggler's life isn't exactly living the dream. Spaceport security is* always *a pain in the ass. Who says a Queen can't have adventures, anyway? And we will* never *give up on finding your mother. Remember?*

Mercy stared down at the wrist of her left hand, at the faint shimmer of the lemniscate imprinted on her flesh with holographic ink, matching the same figure eight symbol on Atrea's left wrist. They'd snuck out and had them done at the same time when they were fourteen. Atrea said it was a promise, a vow to keep looking for Pallas together, forever. Captain Hades had tried to interfere with that vow many times in the years since. He ordered them to drop it, kept them too busy to indulge in the search, and kept tabs on their movements. Which, since it had ultimately led to getting them off that damn space station, Mercy couldn't be too upset about.

Wolfgang said the search was too dangerous. He wasn't wrong, but Mercy could not turn her back on her mother. Atrea, who never had the chance to know hers, was determined to help Mercy reunite with Pallas if she still lived. Nothing Wolfgang said or did had ever made a dent in that determination.

"Right," said Mercy softly. Something unfurled in her belly, a tension that had been filling her with anxiety since first being told what she was.

Besides, if you're Queen, you can order them to help us, right? Atrea would say that with a cocky half smile, hands on her hips. Mercy almost laughed.

"Maybe," she said, smiling at the stasis field. She reached out a hand and splayed it against the surface of the field. It was cool to the touch and smooth like glass. But Mercy knew it was a million times stronger, stronger than the hardest plasteel. Nothing could penetrate a stasis field once it was created, so long as power kept feeding it.

As quickly as it had come, her amusement suddenly vanished, morphed into a crushing sadness that had her blinking back tears.

"Damn it, Atrea," she said softly. "You better wake up and get better. I don't think I can do this without you."

This time, only stark silence answered her. No imaginary quips or assurances forthcoming. Maybe because deep down, Mercy's greatest fear was that Atrea would never wake up again.

With the privacy screen open, she could hear the low thrum of the various medical machines in the background behind her, Nayla's voice speaking softly when Doc entered the infirmary, no doubt explaining to him that Mercy was here. He better not try to examine her. Mercy was in no mood for poking and prodding, especially from a pirate. After several minutes went by and the irritable doctor didn't try to invade the sanctity of the privacy screens, she relaxed again.

She stayed for a long time, long enough to lie against the stasis field and cradle her head in her arms, and drift half asleep. If she waited long enough, Wolfgang was sure to come back. He would never leave his daughter's side for any prolonged length of time.

But when a voice jarred her to wakefulness, it wasn't the low, reassuring rumble of the old Wolf. It was unfamiliar, high pitched and melodic in the way of the very young. A child's voice.

Mercy opened her eyes to a strange sight. A small figure wearing a pink ruffled dress and barefoot, perched precariously next to her. Her arms were stretched to balance against the stasis field, and her feet stood on...nothing. Mercy's heart leapt into her throat as she watched those tiny toes curl, dangling in the empty air. No, not dangling exactly. Her feet were flat, as though they stood on a solid surface, except there wasn't anything for them to stand *on*.

Telekinesis. This child was using telekinesis to levitate herself as easily as most adults walked across a room.

She had creamy brown skin and a wild head of gold-touched dark curls. A purple ribbon lay askew against the curls, having clearly lost the battle to keep them contained. She was singing, her voice clear and pretty as she stumbled her way through the words of a lullaby. The melody sent a shiver of recognition through Mercy; she knew it.

Memory surfaced, faint and distant. Her mother's voice, singing the same song. It made her throat ache.

Abruptly, the child stopped. She broke off between one word and the next, and turned to stare at Mercy. Her eyes were brightly blue and seemed familiar. She couldn't have been older than three or four. Mercy sent a covert look over her shoulder, but no adults lingered nearby. Even Doc and Nayla weren't in the immediate vicinity, though she could hear the low murmur of voices from the far side of the room.

"Don't be sad." The little girl regarded her with wide, innocent eyes. "Rasa says singing made Mercy sad." She gave a guilty shrug. "Sorry."

Mercy stared at her, wrestling with where to start dissecting that statement. "How do you know my name?"

The child's mouth dropped open and a giggle escaped. "*Everyone* knows." She leaned over and touched Mercy's hand with a finger. "Queen." The word held a kind of reverent respect that was almost awe.

Mercy's heart pounded. It sent a surge of adrenaline through her to know that everyone on this ship, down to the smallest child, knew who she was. She felt vulnerable in a way that scared her to her bones. She closed her eyes and forced it away, spending a few seconds to concentrate on her breathing and remind herself that she wasn't in hiding anymore. Her heartbeat slowed and the fear faded.

Habits formed for more than two decades were hard to break.

When she opened her eyes, the little girl was staring at her with a fascinated expression. She had plopped herself down into a sitting position. She swung her legs in the open air as though she was perched on a seat or a ledge. One arm clutched a stuffed animal that had seen better days, the fabric ragged and the mottled, brown and white fur rubbed smooth in a few spots. It was missing a nose and one ear, but Mercy was pretty sure it was supposed to be a cat. She was also pretty sure it hadn't been there a moment ago.

Who *was* this little girl? And who was Rasa? She cast a quick look around, but it was just the two of them, and Atrea.

The child put a hand against her own chest. "I'm Tama." She pointed at Mercy. "Queen Mercy." She turned and looked at the stasis field, placing a gentle hand against it. "Lady. Tama help the Lady."

"You want to help Atrea?"

To her surprise, Mercy felt a brush against her shields, the equivalent of a light knock. She struggled with herself for a moment, reluctant to expose herself in any way, but she sensed no threat in the presence. She opened her shields a crack.

Talking out loud is hard. The petulant look on Tama's face convinced Mercy who she was talking to as much as the sing-song sound of the voice in her head.

I think talking like this is hard, she admitted. Another giggle from the girl made her smile.

That's silly!

Not to me.

Tama studied her face for a long moment. It was an odd sensation. Mercy felt like she was being weighed and judged in some way.

Help you. There was such conviction in the mental statement that Mercy couldn't bear to argue. Despite her mood, this strange little girl brought a smile to her face. One Tama returned, looking happy. *We already help.*

I suppose you did. Her mood had definitely lightened in the past few moments. *Who is "we"?*

Another of those musical laughs made Mercy smile. Tama grinned at her. *Me and Rasa. You can't see him 'cause he likes to be divisible.*

Invisible?

That's what I said. Tama swung her legs harder. *Maybe later you can see him. When he knows you better.*

Mercy relaxed. It wasn't unusual for a child Tama's age to have an imaginary friend. She turned and spread her fingers over the stasis field. *Why do you want to help Atrea?*

Tama bit her lip, looking down as her fingers plucked at her cat's remaining ear. *Wolf is sad. Queen is sad. Aunt Nayla is sad. Everyone is sad about the lady. Tama can help.*

It should have surprised her that the little girl apparently knew Wolfgang, but it didn't. Mercy had the impression this child had been here before, many times. Singing lullabies and visiting.

"You don't need to call me Queen," she told her. "I'm just Mercy."

Mercy. Tama peered up from between dark lashes, giving a shy smile.

"Tamari?" The sound of Nayla's voice had the little girl ducking her head and peering around Mercy. The privacy shields were open just enough to give a glimpse of the rest of the infirmary, to where Nayla stood with her hands on her hips, looking straight at them. "What did I say about giving people privacy?"

Tama fiddled with her stuffed cat again. Mercy was beginning to see why it was so bedraggled in appearance.

I just sing to the lady.

Looking unimpressed with this excuse, Nayla marched past infirmary beds toward them. In that moment, Mercy could see the influence of Doc's caustic nature on the young woman. There was a glint in her eyes that said her niece was about to be in trouble. Tama looked at Mercy with those wide blue eyes, pleading, and her heart melted a little.

"It's okay," she said aloud. "Tama was just keeping me company."

Nayla hesitated mid-stride. "You sure?"

Mercy smiled conspiratorially at Tama, who giggled, hiding her face against her cat's head. "I'm sure. It's no bother."

Nayla's mouth twitched, and Mercy had the impression she was fighting a smile. "All right, then. But Tamari, what did I say about you coming to visit me? Or *anyone* in the infirmary?"

Tama swung her legs harder, not looking up at her aunt. She mumbled a word so quietly, Mercy almost didn't hear it. It sounded like "mission".

"That's right, you ask permission. Does your Mama know where you are? Or Papa? Or any of the dogs?"

A reluctant shrug.

"I'll take that as a no." Nayla shook her head. "They're probably all looking for you. You stay with Mercy, all right? I'm going to let them know where you are, and you *better* not run off!"

Mercy eyed the girl as Nayla moved away. She had to wonder who her Mama and Papa were. She didn't look like family, so at least there was that.

She'd met enough of them for one day.

After a moment, Tamari stopped kicking her legs and looked up at Mercy with another of those shy smiles. *Friends?*

Charmed, Mercy returned the smile. *I don't know. I expect a lot out of my friends.*

Tamari cocked her head. *Like what?*

Honesty. Partnership. No sneaking around behind my back. Letting me know what you plan to do so I can have fun with you, or help you. Or keep her out of trouble. But Mercy let that part remain unsaid. *Telling me when you're in trouble or scared.*

Tamari considered her for a long time. She glanced down at Atrea, and then out where Nayla was. *Will you tell Mama and Papa?*

Only if it you're in danger of being hurt.

Okay. Tamari gave her a smile so brilliant, it dazzled.

"Tamari?" Mercy recognized the gruff voice that spoke behind her. Evidently, so did Tama, because the little girl jumped to her feet with an excited squeal.

"Wolf!" The name was spoken both aloud and

telepathically. Tama launched herself from her telekinetic platform straight at Wolfgang. Luckily, if there was one thing the old Wolf had experience with, it was raising daughters. He caught her easily, and tucked her against his side so smoothly it was like he'd done it every day of his life.

Well, maybe Atrea hadn't been born with Talent, but Mercy was well acquainted with her best friend's daredevil ways. He probably had.

Since the last time she'd seen him, he'd cleaned himself up and shaved. His face was smooth, his gray hair dark and damp from a shower. She could see the tension around his mouth and eyes, though, and knew he had one of his headaches. A lot of the old soldiers with cybernetic implants got them. Wolfgang's had been getting steadily worse in recent years. Enough that Atrea had started researching what might happen if he had the implants removed, particularly the control circuit implanted in his brain. Unfortunately, the survival rate was not good.

His eyes met Mercy's for a moment, and he flashed her a brief, tired smile before he turned his attention back to the little girl in his arms.

He tweaked Tama's nose and made her giggle. "Have you been singing to Atrea again?"

"Singing helps." Tama said this so seriously, Mercy couldn't help but smile a little sadly. Nothing penetrated a stasis field. Just like a ship jumping through otherspace, Atrea was removed from time, frozen within a single instant and untouchable by anything happening around her – or to her. Which was the point, of course.

"I'm sure it does," Wolfgang said, equally grave.

His eyes met Mercy's over Tama's head. "I see you brought company."

"I've been here for awhile." Mercy glanced back at Atrea. "No change?"

"No." Wolfgang cast a look over his shoulder. "They're working on it. I know that much. But no one seems to understand what was done to her." His voice was so bleak, Mercy felt her throat constrict.

This was it. She had to tell him she was the one responsible for his daughter's condition. She opened her mouth, but before she could actually form the words, Tama started singing again.

It was the same lullaby, and the little girl leaned her head against Wolfgang's chest as she sang, the ribbon in her hair even more askew now, her eyes closed. One hand with its tiny fingers reached up and stroked the side of Wolfgang's face, a gesture clearly meant to sooth. A transformation occurred before Mercy's eyes. All of the worry and tension drained from Wolfgang's features. His shoulders relaxed, and the lines of pain around his eyes and mouth faded. He blinked in surprise, sharing an incredulous look with Mercy.

"Tamari!" This time Nayla disengaged the privacy screens completely. There wasn't enough room for her to storm past them with Wolfgang taking up the doorway. Her mouth was set in a firm line and her hands were on her hips. Tamari stopped singing and hid her face in Wolfgang's jacket. "What are you supposed to do before using your Talent on someone else?"

Curious, Mercy eyed the little girl. What Talent had she been using?

Tama said something out loud, but it was so muffled no one could understand it. Wolfgang lifted her away from him and gave her a look Mercy knew well. *Uh-oh.* He set Tama gently but firmly on the floor, crouching so he was at her level.

"Tamari. Answer your Aunt Nayla."

The girl was back to fidgeting with her stuffed cat's ears and not looking anyone in the eye.

"Tama." Wolf's voice was soft, but unyielding.

"Ask 'mission," she said in a very small voice.

"And did you ask my permission?"

She shook her head.

"Do you understand why you need to?"

Those tiny shoulders hunched, but as Mercy knew well, no one escaped the old Wolf's interrogations. He had endless patience. When Nayla made to move forward, Wolfgang just shook his head slightly. "It's better if she understands why. Tama, why do you need to ask permission?"

"Privacy."

"And what else?"

A shrug.

"Did you know that nulls like me don't have shields like you?"

Startled, the girl looked up at him. She shook her head, eyes wide.

"That means it's easier to hurt us, even unintentionally. I know you wanted to help me, but it really is important to ask first. Next time, we can have someone who knows how monitor what you're doing. It's safer for me and you."

"Okay." She reached out a tentative hand and touched his face. "Wolf hurt?"

Wolfgang smiled. "No. You helped me. Thank you. Just be sure and follow the rules from now on."

She gave a tremulous smile. "Okay." Then her gaze focused on something beyond him, and the moment was forgotten. "Papa!" Joy filled her face.

In the next moment, Tamari was gone. There was the snap of air rushing into the space she'd occupied a moment ago, and then she was across the room and in the arms of a huge, dark-skinned man who made Wolfgang look small. He wore an expensive suit and had a serious face, with close-cropped black hair and cold blue eyes that sent a shiver through Mercy.

That was why Tamari's eyes had seemed so familiar – they were the same color as Reaper's eyes. An icy, pale blue that verged on colorless. Except Tama's eyes held a warmth Reaper's lacked.

A warmth her father's eyes lacked, as well. Tamari's father was a Killer, like Reaper.

Mercy stood up slowly. She had the urge to place herself between Wolfgang and this man in case this went badly. She had the sense that she was standing in the same room as a very dangerous weapon, a hair's trigger from going off. The man's blue eyes focused on her, and it wasn't nearly as comfortable a look as Reaper's gaze. For the first time, Mercy understood why everyone had such a reaction to Reaper.

She cleared her throat. "Apparently your daughter likes to visit Atrea," she said cautiously.

"Yes, I know." The man's voice was deep and calm. He didn't sound angry. He sounded...flat.

Unaffected. "Tamari, are you supposed to be teleporting without supervision?"

No, Papa. The mental voice sounded so chastised Mercy had to choke back a laugh. She was starting to see a theme with this little girl. Then Tamari tilted her head, and there was a crafty look to her. *But you were here! And Rasa. That's superized.*

"No, it is not. I need to know *before* you teleport. As you well know, Rasa does not count as supervision. If you do it again, I will have Uncle Treon lock down your Talent until I believe you can follow my directive."

Her lower lip quivered, but Tama didn't try to bargain further. Considering her interaction with the girl, Mercy supposed Tama knew such tactics didn't work against her formidable father.

"Okay, Papa." Her voice sounded exactly like it had when she'd agreed with Wolfgang: resigned.

The man looked back at Mercy and the others, and gave a single nod. "Thank you for watching her. Nayla, thanks for the heads up."

"Anytime, Dem. Have you met Mercy?"

"Not yet." He inclined his head, and Mercy returned the nod. "I'm the Chief of Security aboard *Nemesis*. I hear Reaper is taking care of your security."

That was true enough. Then she thought about the arena and frowned. "For now, anyway."

Dem studied her for a long moment. "I see. I have no doubt in my brother's abilities, but perhaps you do."

Mercy wanted to argue that she didn't doubt Reaper's abilities, just his intentions. But then she thought better of it. Whatever manipulation had happened today was between her and Reaper.

"Wolfgang, when she's ready, perhaps you would escort Mercy to her quarters?"

Mercy bit back the urge to argue with him. It was clear that no one was comfortable yet letting her run around the ship unattended. If she had to have someone with her, better it was Wolfgang than someone she didn't know. Besides, she wanted a chance to talk to him.

"You don't trust that she's safe on this ship?" There was a challenge in the old Wolf's voice.

Dem simply raised one black brow. "Do you?"

Wolfgang barked a laugh. "Point taken."

"Now." Dem studied his small daughter, and Mercy was surprised to see his lips curve into a smile. "Why don't I give you a lesson on teleporting, *halla*? And you can explain to your mother where you've been all afternoon."

Okay! Bye Mercy! Bye Wolf! Bye Auntie!

The two of them were gone between one blink and the next, with only a snap of air to show they'd ever been there.

"I thought the ability to teleport was extremely rare," Mercy said aloud. She was thinking not just of Tamari and Dem, but also of the young girl who'd facilitated Willem Frain's escape from the space station.

"It is," said Nayla with a sigh. "That's what makes keeping track of Tamari so hard. People aren't used to an active, curious child who can teleport."

"That's not all she can do." Mercy glanced at Wolfgang.

"No." Nayla smiled. "Tamari's mother is my sister, Sanah. An empath. We're still learning how that gift has manifested in Tama, but it's clear she has some form of it."

A teleporting empath, who was also the daughter of a Killer. "That must make for some interesting family time."

Nayla laughed. "You have no idea." She shook her head, then went back to whatever task Tamari had interrupted.

Wolfgang touched her shoulder. "When was the last time you ate?"

"Not long ago. Cannon fed me right after I woke."

"Hmm. Probably couldn't manage much after so long with so little. You're too thin. You should eat small amounts at regular, short intervals, until you're back up to fighting weight."

Mercy barely managed not to roll her eyes. Wolfgang didn't miss it, the corner of his mouth twitching as he suppressed a smile.

"If you won't do it for yourself, do it for this old man. I can only pester one of you right now, so you get the brunt of it."

Mercy saw his gaze go to Atrea, saw the raw worry and pain that moved through his steely eyes and grizzled face. Her heart twisted.

"Okay, fine. I'll eat." She grabbed his hand and squeezed it. "Come sit with me?"

His attention switched back to her, and he smiled. Tired, but genuine.

"I would love to."

With one last look at Atrea and a silent promise to return, Mercy led the way out of the infirmary. Nayla waved, and Doc didn't look up from the datapad he was muttering over in the back. He hadn't even stirred with all of the coming and going from the infirmary, and Mercy figured he must be used to Tama's unscheduled visits. That was just fine as far as she was concerned. Mercy planned to avoid the good doctor for as long as possible.

"You know," said Wolfgang conversationally as they moved down the corridor together, "Doc keeping tabs on you isn't the worst thing, given the condition you were in when you arrived."

Ha! Mercy didn't dignify that with an answer. She hated doctors at the best of times, always too worried about what they might discover about her to relax around them. Doc's abrasive personality just made it easy for her to distrust him.

Wolfgang signaled for the lift as they reached the end of the hall, smiling at Mercy sardonically. He knew exactly how much she hated medical facilities and doctors poking their noses anywhere around her.

"You don't need to worry about being discovered here," he pointed out. As if she didn't know that.

The lift arrived, and the doors began to open.

"Look," she said, "just because—"

The tremor of *something wrong* hit her a second before Reaper's voice burst into her head. An awareness that had her eyes widening, adrenaline flooding her limbs.

MERCY, DOWN!

She moved, shoving into Wolfgang with her entire body.

Stupid. It shouldn't have worked. His implants should have kept him solidly on his feet. But the two of them stumbled to the side, hitting the wall just as the doors to the lift opened and a blast of heat and flame belched out.

CHAPTER FOURTEEN

*R*eaper waited, unfettered by emotion. The cold dark had driven away distractions like worry and anger beneath an implacable wave of endless quiet. Relaxed and alone, he closed his eyes. The cold stilled his body, suffused his bones, and sharpened his mind with a clarity of thought only attainable in times like this, when the killer washed away everything else, weaving an emptiness around him so vast he might have been suspended in space like the ship that carried him.

A faint awareness glimmered within his mind like a distant star, the knowledge that he wasn't safe to be around any living person. So he waited for his dogs to report their findings from the scene of the explosion. He sent only two: Titus and Jaxon. The object reader and the Hunter. The two had worked together often in the past. Titus's gift for reading residual mental impressions from objects worked well in tandem with Jaxon's ability to track.

Boss, Jaxon told him only moments after arriving on the scene. *Your brother is here.*

Reaper didn't need to ask which brother. As the chief of security, Dem would have been the first to arrive.

He won't interfere, Reaper told Jaxon.

If you say so. Doubt came through loud and clear in the Hunter's tone, but Reaper remained unconcerned. Dem was the only one of his kind, both Hunter and Killer. He also knew Reaper better than anyone else alive.

This is a mess. Titus sent Reaper a visualization of the scene. The blast radius had warped the corridor, twisting metal bulkheads and rupturing the walls and floor. The lift shaft was a smoking black hole. The gravity generators woven into the floor had clearly been compromised. The damage radius could be seen in the floating debris that crowded what was left of the lift and corridor. Larger pieces of shrapnel, blackened and twisted, floated weightlessly among scattered metal shavings that slowly spun, glittering like stars where emergency lighting cut through the black. Where the damage stopped, so too did the weightless zone, as though an invisible wall separated the unmarred corridor from the damaged section.

It wasn't a wall, exactly. It was where the working gravity generators and the field they created bumped up against the weightless carnage of the blast zone. A few scattered pieces of shrapnel flung further down the hallway littered the floor, but if Titus wanted to get his hands on something the bomb maker had touched, he was going to have to find it inside the floating mess.

We're damn lucky the hull didn't breach, Titus said. *This could be a slow process.*

However long it takes. It didn't matter. The ship was locked down. No one was leaving.

I see Treon did not exaggerate. Dem's voice in Reaper's mind was not unexpected. Deep and familiar, it was even welcome, in its way. Dem had trained Reaper when they were young. His voice had been the one to teach Reaper how to manage the cold, how to control it instead of allowing it to dictate his actions.

Since Dem had spoken the words as a statement, Reaper saw no reason to respond. He didn't care what Treon said about him.

He told me you'd developed an attachment to the new queen, Dem continued. *I thought surely he must be mistaken. After Lilith, no queen would ever command you again.*

That elicited a response.

Mercy does not command me.

She does. Finding her attackers and punishing them is my job. Yet, here you send your dogs.

Everyone knows I stood beside her. It was exactly why Reaper had taken her to the arena. Not just to show Mercy who the pirates were, and what she was capable of, but to show everyone he had allied himself with her. Word would have spread quickly.

Dem didn't answer immediately. When he did, the words were measured. *You once swore, very publicly, that you would kill another queen like Lilith.*

Mercy is no Lilith.

That remains to be seen. There are those who be-

lieve she will be, just by what she is. Can you blame them?

For the first time in their adult lives, the Killer within Reaper focused intently on his brother. For a long breath, neither of them spoke, the telepathic connection between them weighted with wordless things.

The next time you say Mercy does not command you, Dem said softly, *remember this moment, brother.*

Reaper said nothing. He weighed the threat Dem represented to Mercy. If anyone could kill a queen, it would be a Killer. And only two of those existed aboard *Nemesis.*

I will not stand in your way, Dem said at last. *Whoever is responsible for this could have killed many others. Could have killed us all.*

Even now, Mercy and Wolfgang were in the infirmary, where Doc and Nayla fought to keep them among the living. It was a genetic imperative hardwired into the Talented not to attack or harm a queen. This inelegant violence had been someone's attempt to get around that imperative. It might have killed anyone so unlucky as to use that lift at that time. Doc. Nayla. Anyone.

His brother's words reassured him that for now, at least, Dem was no direct threat. Reaper went back to waiting.

Be wary how much closer you get to this queen, brother, Dem said. *If she survives.*

She is strong. She will survive. Reaper did not allow himself to consider the alternative. *Our people need her. Mercy could be the key to our survival.*

Or our destruction. You are no longer objective in

this matter, Nikolos. Emotion has clouded your perception.

Suspended within the void, Reaper could give the thought no credence. *That is not possible,* he said.

You forget, brother, we are but half Killer. Both of us feel emotion. We are just more adept at choosing not to than others.

No. Reaper paused, considering. Dem had never before voiced such things. *Your wife is an empath. She does not understand us.* Sanah had to be the reason behind Dem's sudden belief in the impossible.

She understands me more clearly than anyone ever has, said Dem. *Make no mistake, Nikolos. You are compromised.*

Dem was the one compromised. Reaper chose to end the discussion by changing its focus. *Keep my path clear.* They both knew what would happen if Dem didn't.

I will. It looks as though your man has found something.

Titus?

Yeah, boss. The dog's mental voice sounded distant, distracted. *I think this whole area was painted with plas-charge, and activated by a thermal sensor. I'm double-checking with Knox, now.*

A small eternity passed while Titus consulted with the dog who specialized in demolitions. Finally, his voice came back.

I'm right. We aren't going to find the detonator. Plas-charge probably disintegrated it into nano-particles.

Reaper considered. *Someone had to paint it.*

Yeah. They were careful. Used telekinesis. I can't quite get an image, and Jax can't get a psychic trail. Not enough plas-charge left for me to see who mixed the stuff.

So careful. Whoever had done this expected to be hunted.

There are few people with the fine control necessary to telekinetically paint plas-charge, Dem said suddenly. *Less than twenty on this ship.*

The Killer wanted to end them all, just to be certain. Reaper choked back the urge. Once, perhaps he could have indulged in such excess, but not now.

Fewer still, said Dem, *with the expertise to mix it. Give me an hour, and I'll have a list of suspects. Give me two, and I can narrow it down significantly.*

I will wait.

Boss, said Titus. *I can pick up vague impressions. Perpetrators are male...and Mercy was definitely the target.*

Of that, Reaper had never doubted.

I am patient, he told his brother. *There is nowhere for them to run.*

* * *

MERCY FLOATED IN A BLACK VOID, an abyss so deep she could sense nothing outside of it. No minds pressed against hers. For the first time since the space station, she was truly, utterly alone.

It was peaceful. She had no sense of time, so it was impossible to say how long she spent floating, letting her mind drift. She could feel nothing of her body. In this place, she was weightless. Giving herself to the dark was calming, serene in ways she lacked the words to describe. No worries penetrated her thoughts here. Nothing disturbed her. It was like the endless quiet of space. Or the calm tranquility of a still pond. It felt safe, and comforting. She couldn't remember a time in her life to match it.

"Why are you so difficult to kill?"

The familiar voice sent serrated shards of adrenaline through her, destroying the tranquility like waves crashing against jagged rocks. Fear and anger followed in equal measure.

"What the hell are you doing here?" She didn't speak the words either physically or mentally. In this place they just existed as though already spoken and waiting to be acknowledged.

It felt like an abomination to have him here.

"I keep trying to kill you." Willem Frain's voice was bitter. "Why won't you just die?"

Mercy laughed. "Maybe I am dead. This feels a lot like I imagine death."

Except for him, of course. Sharing the afterlife with Willem would be a nightmare.

He ignored her.

"I won't let you destroy everything I have built. No matter what it takes, I will kill you, Mercy."

"Keep trying. I'm right here."

"I killed your bitch of a grandmother, and I will succeed with you."

Wait, what?

Mercy struggled to focus on him, but Willem was just as lacking in a corporeal presence as she was. "What about my mother, you bastard? Did you kill her, too?"

"I'm a scientist. When one experiment fails, I begin another. I will find a way."

"Answer me!" Mercy struggled to move closer, to find him, but now the weightlessness worked against her. She couldn't move, couldn't even begin to direct herself in this void. She just was. The more she tried, the more her thoughts seemed to circle. She struggled harder, and chaos twisted the abyss around her, faster and faster.

Dizziness swamped her, chasing away whatever vestiges of peace and calm remained, dragging her down in a suffocating whirlwind. It closed around her like the jaws of some terrible creature until she felt her awareness fading. Even Willem's voice dulled to white noise. Her struggles slowly ceased.

She'd lost him. And with him, any chance at finding her mother.

It was the last, bitter thought she had before the jaws of oblivion closed around her.

**

REAPER MOVED SWIFTLY AND SILENTLY. As promised, the hallways he walked were empty, the path between decks deserted of crew. Not that he couldn't control himself, but the wrong word, the wrong posture, or tone…it would take very little to draw his focus.

So Dem ordered the path from Reaper's quarters to the engineering deck cleared, and people were either smart or frightened enough to listen. Even a ship as large as *Nemesis* felt small when nothing obstructed movement from one deck to the next. Not even the whispered presence of a mind brushed his as Reaper made his way down the corridor and opened the panel to access the narrow crawlspace housing the emergency ladders that spanned between decks. He wanted no lift to signal his arrival.

When he came out in engineering, Reaper startled a sleeping man who either hadn't heard the message, or didn't take it seriously. Slouched against the bulkhead across from the emergency hatch, he wore the brightly colored, battered and stained uniform of a deck mechanic. He had a rough, scarred visage that spoke of many hard-fought battles. Catching the movement of the hatch opening, his hand closed over the grip of a needlegun. The weapon's flechette ammunition was deadly to soft targets, but unable to penetrate the hardened nanograph walls of a ship. He had the weapon half drawn when his hard eyes finally focused on Reaper's face.

He froze. Reaper knew what he saw, knew the Killer had leeched the color from his eyes until they burned a cold, wintry blue so pale they might have been chips of ice. He held a telekinetic grip around the man's mind, his shields pathetically easy to bypass. He was a low level telekinetic, and an even lower-level telepath. He relied largely on his physical stature, which was beefy and strong. His thoughts beat frantically against Reaper's grip like the panicked fluttering of a trapped bird's wings, slowly settling as he realized there was no escape.

Carefully, one finger at a time, the man opened

his grip on the needlegun until it clattered to the floor.

Reaper tilted his head, eyeing the man dispassionately. He was not on the list, but he was here, between Reaper and his prey. He'd raised a weapon.

I didn't see it was you...those others you're looking for, they're down that way. The man jerked his head toward the end of the corridor.

The words meant nothing, less than nothing. But Reaper found himself intrigued. The man's mind had quieted. The terror had receded, and he met Reaper's eyes without fear.

I've stared at death before. The man's thoughts were strangely calm. *If it's my time, so be it.*

Nikolos. Dem's voice was a whisper in his mind. *You promised to kill no one who wasn't involved in the bomb. Our numbers are few.*

True.

With a final, long look, Reaper released his grip on the mechanic's mind. Tension drained from the man's body and he scrambled back. Reaper walked on without a backward glance. As an afterthought, he lifted the needlegun and floated it down the hallway after him, until it came to rest in the palm of his hand.

The corridor was short, with only a handful of doors. Reaper passed by them all, for none held his quarry. It ended at an enormous door designed to cut off this section of the ship and contain a drive breach during a catastrophic engine failure. The door was several inches thick, spanned the length and height of the hall, and was secured by support beams that came out several feet on either side. It was closed.

Reaper could feel a dozen minds behind the door. Five had shields raised high, their minds tightly closed. Seven were less frightened, or perhaps had less reason to be. They were huddled closely together, sharing a conversation. The careless holes in one shield allowed Reaper to slip past all seven, connected as they were. He could have killed them then, but their words gave him pause.

...how is holding us hostage going to help? No Killer will give two fucks about our lives.

They ain't thinking clearly.

Doors won't stop him. Hostages won't either.

Quiet! You want them to kill us before Reaper ever gets here?

We're dead either way. Ain't no way out of this room alive. I heard they attacked the Queen. If the Killer don't kill 'em, Cannon will. We're caught in the middle.

Wrong place, wrong damn time.

Because he'd promised his brother not to waste lives, Reaper eased back from their minds without killing them as he could have. Just as he was leaving the conversation, a wisp of stray thought caught his attention.

...maybe the door will take him out. Lotta plas-charge on that thing.

Idiot! It's a fucking blast door.

Idiots indeed. These doors were designed to contain an explosion many times more powerful than plas-charge, even if it was coated in a layer of the stuff an inch thick. If it was designed to go off when the door began to open, most of the blast would be reflected back into engineering…right onto the people inside, not to mention the propulsion engine and jump drive.

In their zeal to kill him, they might have doomed the entire ship. How had such minds conceived of the plan to kill a queen? Simple answer: they hadn't. Someone much more capable had used them. They were pawns.

He could kill them from this side of the door. It would take time to work his way past their shields. Two of the five, in particular, were more powerful than the rest combined. They had to be the ones who handled the plas-charge.

Reaper considered his options. These men were foolish enough, or perhaps terrified enough, they could panic and blow the door in an ill-conceived attempt to kill him in the time it took to overcome their mental shields. The door had to be neutralized.

Sebastian? Reaper reached out to the man who acted as Cannon's first mate. In reality, Sebastian was the Captain of the *Nemesis* in every real way. Cannon just appropriated the title because he felt more comfortable being called *Captain* than *King*.

It took Sebastian a moment to answer after Reaper brushed up against his mind. An intelligent man, he was probably debating the wisdom of allowing a Killer in full-on hunting mode past his shields.

Reaper. The word was spoken cautiously.

I need to get past the blast door in engineering. It is covered in plas-charge. I am going to use telekinesis to remove it. At which time you will open the door.

Sebastian's Talent gave him absolute control of

the ship's systems. It was a rare gift, the ability to mentally interface with the complicated, energy-driven pathways of machines like the brain of a ship. Sebastian had spent so much time learning every pathway, every nano-bot of the Nemesis, he often seemed connected to the ship like a living organism. Opening the blast doors was a simple matter.

They covered the blast door in plas-charge? Sebastian's shock was palpable.

Apparently hoping I would walk through it and set it off.

And what, kill you, them, and Nemesis herself? Creating a drive breach and killing us all?

Reaper shrugged. *They are desperate men, and not thinking clearly. I could open the door myself, but it would be a risk while handling the plas-charge.*

No, I've got it. You make sure my ship doesn't blow up today.

Sebastian went silent, and Reaper began the painstaking task of slowly scraping the plas-charge from the surface of the door with his telekinesis, effectively creating a thin layer of space between the explosive and the ship. He also surrounded the volatile mixture with a telekinetic shield as he worked, to hopefully contain it if something went awry and the charge detonated.

They used a thermal mix for the detonator, I see, Sebastian observed. *Smart, since it mixes in with the explosive and effectively disintegrates when it goes off. Untraceable.*

Almost, corrected Reaper. He had, after all, found them despite all their precautions.

Perhaps three inches of the door had been

scraped clean. That was the problem with finely controlled work like this. It took time. But he was nothing if not patient. They had made a mistake holing up in a place where there was nowhere to run. Not that they could escape anywhere on the ship. Cannon and Dem had the flight deck locked down, as well as the escape pods, and guards at every airlock as an added precaution.

Reaper stood pressed against the blast door as though listening for sounds on the other side. The needlegun floated in the air beside him. The metallic surface was smooth and cold beneath his hands. He was using the physical contact as an anchor from which to work. His telekinesis was not as powerful as either of his brothers'. Dem, in particular, could have had the plas-charge removed in easily half the time, but Reaper had to feel for it through six inches of door. Working from sense rather than sight added a layer of difficulty.

A thought occurred to him suddenly.

Sensing it, Sebastian tensed.

What is it? What's happening?

Nothing, yet. But be ready.

Reaper focused on the blast door, on the miniscule imperfections in its form, crevices so small as to be considered insignificant. He sought them out with his Talent until he had suffused every infinitesimal scar or crack. In other circumstances, he might have used his telekinesis to widen them, to literally rip the blast door apart. It would take a herculean effort, but he thought he could do it. Not with the plas-charge, though. It *probably* wouldn't go off just from such movement, requiring the thermal heat of a human form passing closely by it, but just to be safe…

Instead, he *tapped* the door with his gift, like a hammer taken to steel. It reverberated, subtle vibrations spreading out from each imperfection. Reaper rode them with his mind, right through the door to the plas-charge. It, too, moved, though so subtly as to be imperceptible…except he was counting on that movement. Reaper used it as his leverage, riding the vibration with his Talent and pealing the plas-charge from the door in one swift measure.

The startled oath from Sebastian was almost admiring.

Clever, the other man said as Reaper moved the plas-charge away from the door, choosing to push it off to one side, carefully contained within a telekinetic shield. Once he built the box, it took very little concentration to maintain it. Hopefully none of the five he was hunting happened to look closely in this direction.

Not that it mattered much if they did.

Sebastian, if you please.

Right.

The locks that held the door securely in place disengaged with a hiss of released air, and it began to slide open. There was no disguising that, but if they still believed it to be rigged with explosives…

A flurry of panicked thoughts rose from the hostages. Nothing came from their captors, still safe behind their shields. No shots came toward the door, either. They still believed it to be a risk. Reaper sought out their minds and mapped their positions in the room.

He retrieved the needlegun by raising it into the air with his gift. With his focus no longer on the plas-charge, his Talent was free for other uses. When the opening was big enough, he stepped through, sending the needlegun arching up sharply and to the left. Before he fully entered the room, he pulled the trigger twice. Two minds went silent, their thoughts simply ceasing to exist between one breath and the next.

He took another step, adjusting the needlegun's angle further forward as he did so. He pulled the trigger, emptying the cartridge. Another mind went silent. Reaper tossed the useless weapon aside. The two strongest were left. They'd begun to realize their clever plan for the door wasn't working. Panic beat at their shields, creating weak spots where their concentration and focus slipped.

A disruptor went off. The fools didn't stop to ponder why the plas-charge had failed, actually using energy weapons when a heat discharge could easily blow them all to pieces. It bounced harmlessly off the telekinetic buffer Reaper had encased himself in seconds before. Their panic spiked. Cracks formed in their shields. Reaper arrowed through one, lethal and fast.

He dove past surface thoughts, rifling through thoughts and memories until he reached the time and place he was looking for. Nothing. Empty blackness.

For the first time, he frowned. Emotion touched him, even in the cold dark. Frustration. They had no memory of whoever had helped them attack Mercy. Just missing time, and the outline of what they were to do.

Someone, a telepath with the skill to do so, had altered their memories. He closed a mental fist around the man's mind, and gave a sharp, vicious twist. He fell like a rag doll, his mind empty.

One left.

The man came scrabbling out of his hiding place on hands and knees. Crying. Shaking. Pleading with his thoughts and his words.

"Please, please don't kill me. We didn't know you was protecting her." He stopped, curled into a pathetic huddle in the middle of the floor. He was unwashed and unshaven, his clothing old, threadbare, and dirty. For someone of his telekinetic ability to be so low was unusual. Reaper could see it in his mind, his dependence on drugs that skewed his Talent and made it worthless. He sobered up long enough to earn the coin for his next fix, never longer.

The man stretched a hand up toward him, pleading.

"I'm sorry, I swear. I can tell you things. Please!"

Reaper stared down at him with cold eyes.

"You know nothing I haven't already taken," he said. It was barely a thought to kill him, to crush his mind into paste.

It's done, he told his brother a moment later. He left the hostages to Sebastian's mercy, knowing it to be kinder than his.

You could have left one for questioning, Dem admonished.

Ever the critic. They knew nothing. Someone altered their memories.

Dem took a moment, processing that. *So, we know whoever arranged this is a powerful telepath.*

Yes.

He felt Dem give him an evaluating sweep.

I'm fine, brother.

You don't feel it.

I am in control. Reaper suppressed a flash of irritation; the cold dark was beginning to fade.

Good, his brother said. *You're going to need to be.*

Reaper sent him a questing thought, asking an unspoken question.

Mercy just woke up. She wants to see you.

CHAPTER FIFTEEN

*R*eaper didn't relax until he walked through the infirmary door and saw Mercy sitting up on an infirmary bed, a scowl on her face. Somehow, the knowledge of her survival had failed to quiet the tension within him the way actually seeing her did. As he watched, she swatted away Doc's hand and the scanner he held.

"How many times do I have to say it?" she asked, clearly not for the first time. "I'm fine! You should be working on Wolfgang, not me."

A dark bruise marred her temple, disappearing into the unruly mop of dark hair now long enough it fell past her ears. He wondered if Nayla had made it grow again. The bruise was the only visible sign of injury, but he knew all too well that some injuries were not immediately apparent.

"Kono onshirazu me!" Doc met her scowl with one of his own. Reaper recognized one of his favorite phrases to hurl at patients who didn't listen. He'd just called Mercy ungrateful. "Captain Hades has implants that protected him from the worst of

the blast. The same cannot be said for you. You almost died, Your Majesty."

"Stop calling me that," Mercy muttered.

Doc gave her a thin smile in response.

Reaper stopped just inside the door, taking a moment as an unfamiliar feeling swept his body, leaving his hands tingling and his mind confused.

That would be relief, Cannon informed him from where he sat against the far wall, his expression tight with worry. *Something we are all feeling right now.*

No, Reaper disagreed. *Not all of us.* Whoever had ordered that bomb to go off had to be feeling a lot of things right now. Relief would not be one of them.

"Reaper!" Mercy's face lit up when she saw him. He gave her a reserved nod, but did not cross the room to her. Experience taught him to stay out of Doc's way until he'd released his patient. *Let Doc see to you.*

He already has, Mercy sent back with an edge to her tone. *I keep telling him, I'm fine.* "He needs to see to Wolf," she continued aloud, with a meaningful look at Doc.

Wolfgang sat on the bed to the right of Mercy's, a nano-skin patch covering his right temple, his left arm suspended and immobilized.

"I'm fine, Mercy," the older man said. She twisted to get a better look at him.

"Your arm is broken."

Doc picked up a capsulet. The fact that he had to inject a nano-solution instead of using a standard bone knitter spoke volumes about the complexity of the break. The bone wasn't just broken, but shattered. Reaper gained a new respect for Wolfgang's pain tolerance.

"It won't be, shortly," Doc said, jabbing the capsulet unceremoniously into Wolfgang's injured arm. The older man winced, but didn't complain.

"Your implants could cause interference with the bone knitting." Doc's voice held more annoyance than usual. "You'll need to stay absolutely still until the process finishes."

"I'm not going anywhere until I know Mercy is all right," said Wolfgang. Doc muttered something under his breath in his own language, his tone acerbic.

"I *said*—" Mercy began.

"*Iie!* Enough!" Doc snapped, throwing his hand through the air in a sharp, decisive motion. Along the far wall, an assortment of vials and containers vibrated in warning. They stopped again almost immediately, but silence blanketed the room. Reaper couldn't remember the last time Doc's temper resulted in a loss of control over his Talent. As he watched, the doctor took a deep breath, and exhaled slowly.

"A few hours ago, someone nearly blasted a hole in the side of this ship with an explosive device that destroyed the lift to this infirmary," Doc said stiffly. "They managed to nearly kill two people, one of them the new queen. If things had gone differently, it could have been much worse. All I ask, is for my patients to *listen* when I tell them what they need. *Wakatta?*"

After a tense moment, Mercy's expression softened. She nodded. Some of the stiffness eased from Doc's face, but his dark eyes still glittered when he looked at Nayla, motioning with his head for her to take over with Wolfgang.

"What are Mercy's injuries?" Reaper asked, stepping fully into the room.

Doc glanced at him, one black brow raised in surprise, and Reaper stared back with a patience he did not feel. The other man frowned, turning back to Mercy and resolutely picking up his datapad again.

"A telekinetic shield safeguarded them from the worst of the blast—the explosion itself, fragments and shrapnel. She must have thrown one up in the last instant." Doc glanced at Reaper as he said this, an unspoken question on his face.

"We've been working on her telepathy," Reaper told him, shaking his head. "I haven't even tested her telekinesis yet."

"Well, sometimes instinct kicks in," said Doc. "It saved them both from being burned, even killed instantly. But the blast energy was extreme. Captain Hades' implants granted him a level of protection, hence the superficial nature of his injuries. Mercy, however, was not so fortunate. She suffered contusions to ears, stomach, and lungs. The most serious of these was the buildup of blood in her lungs that took Nayla several hours to correct."

"But she is recovered." Reaper wasn't sure if it was a statement or a question, even as he said it.

"Yes, the worst of her injuries have been dealt with," said Doc stiffly. "It was only when she woke that she became a difficult patient." He gave Mercy a severe look. "Fortunately, the incident took place very close to the infirmary. We were able to get to her quickly." He looked away from Mercy, who had the wisdom to stay silent, though a frown hovered at her mouth. "She is very lucky. We all are."

"Are you sure this was an attack aimed at Mercy?" asked Wolfgang, wincing. Bone knitting was an uncomfortable process at best, Reaper knew from personal experience. Those with cybernetic implants often complained that discomfort upgraded to pain, as metal parts interfered with the organic healing of the body. Nayla was watching the process intently. Reaper assumed she was monitoring it with her Talent. The girl's dark hair was tied back in a messy ponytail and her brow wrinkled as she concentrated on her task.

"The method points to it," said Cannon. "Blowing up any part of a ship is dangerous at best. If something goes wrong with the charge or the blast radius, if a hull breach occurs—"

"Everyone on board is at risk," Wolfgang mused. "Including the bomber." He looked from Cannon to Reaper, and back again. "Then why do it? Surely, there are safer ways to kill someone."

"To kill *someone*, yes," said Cannon. "But not if the intended target was Mercy."

Wolfgang frowned. "What am I missing?"

"Yeah, what are we missing?" asked Mercy.

"You are a Queen," said Reaper. "Killing a Queen is a genetic impossibility for most of us."

"Most of you?" Mercy asked. "What the hell does that mean?"

Reaper shrugged.

"It means a Killer like myself can probably get around the genetic imperative. We are designed for one thing: taking life, any life, in the most efficient way possible."

Despite their conversation in the elevator earlier, Reaper expected her to recoil at his words. Instead, she stared at him for a heartbeat, then threw back her head and laughed. It was a light, genuinely amused sound, and Reaper found himself relaxing, though he hadn't realized he was tense.

Cannon stared at Mercy like she was crazy. So did Doc.

She eventually stopped, but her smile was huge and her green eyes danced with mirth. "You're telling me, the only man actually capable of killing me on this ship is *you*?"

"And my brother, Dem," Reaper said cautiously. "He is also a Killer."

"So you, and your brother."

"Yes."

Mercy shook her head. "You guys really should have led with that when I came on board."

Doc looked at Cannon. "She should be a lot more worried. Shouldn't she?"

Cannon gave a laconic shrug. "Queens are a breed unto themselves, Doc. Never forget that."

It was, Reaper, thought, a truer statement than Cannon knew. As Mercy, still amused, looked at him with a complete absence of fear, he felt something odd, a shift inside of him that he couldn't explain. She trusted him. Every time something happened that made him expect that trust to waver or break, she surprised him. It drew upon him in a wholly unexpected way. He realized suddenly that he never wanted to disappoint her, and that made him begin to understand something else.

He no longer wondered how Lilith had inspired such loyalty in so many, despite her cruelty. If she looked at them with such absolute faith, how could they dare to let her down? It dawned on him that Mercy's true power lay not in her Talent, but in her ability to inspire. He didn't know for certain if this was a queen thing, or just something unique to Mercy herself.

"Reaper?" A faint frown furrowed her brow, and then her telepathic voice spoke softly to him. *You're staring at me. Is everything okay?*

He hesitated.

I just killed the men who set the bomb. Not the architect who told them to do it, but those who actually handled the explosive.

She gave a little shrug. *I'm not surprised to hear it.*

I shot three of them. The other two, I crushed their minds to pulp with my Talent.

Mercy frowned. *Normally I'd have expected some kind of incarceration and a trial, but given where we are...you're certain they were involved?*

Yes. Someone erased their memories, but they had more of the plas-charge, and attempted to use it again.

Mercy looked across the room to Cannon. Doc still buzzed around her with a datapad, muttering to himself, but he seemed satisfied enough with her healing because his anger had lessened. One could usually measure the seriousness of someone's injuries by the shortness of Doc's temper.

"What's the process for handling attempted murder on this ship?" she asked. "You know, say, if someone tried to blow someone else up, what would the appropriate punishment be?"

Cannon raised an eyebrow. He looked from her, to Reaper, and back. Then he shook his head.

"I assume you're asking due to recent events. They endangered more than ten thousand lives. Women and children among them. There is only one sentence for such a crime."

Mercy looked back at Reaper. *Then I don't see a problem. Thank you for stopping them from blowing up the ship.*

She was thanking him. For killing people.

She wasn't scared. He'd told her the worst thing he'd done today, and she wasn't afraid. He didn't know how to assimilate that.

"Mercy," Cannon leaned forward, steepling his hands in front him, his elbows propped on his knees. "This isn't over. Reaper killed the perpetrators, yes, but whoever directed this to happen, whoever wiped their memories clean, that person is still somewhere aboard this ship."

She sobered instantly, and Wolfgang shifted closer to her, though Nayla hissed in a breath and whispered an admonishment to hold still.

"They could try again."

Cannon nodded gravely.

"The probability is strong. I'm not sure you understand the level of animosity Lilith left as her legacy. Everyone here living only has that experience by which to judge life ruled by a queen. Well…" He lifted a shoulder. "Everyone but Vashti, perhaps. Kiana, their mother, was queen before Lilith. She died when Lilith was only seventeen. There are very few still living who knew her well."

Mercy digested this with a thoughtful look.

"Kiana, my great-grandmother. I should ask Vashti about her."

Reaper moved away from the door a breath before Vashti stepped through it.

"Did I hear my name?" Mercy's great-aunt hobbled into the room using her cane, flanked by her ever-present escorts, Cage and Griffin. When they would have followed her in, she lifted a hand and waved them back into the hallway. *It's crowded enough in here,* she told them, not bothering to keep the thought contained.

Why are they always with her, Mercy asked Reaper privately.

Vashti likes to appear as old and fragile as possible. The cane isn't necessary. She could easily use telekinesis to support any weak knees or arthritic joints, but that wouldn't give people the visual impression she wants. Griffin and Cage act as her bodyguards for the same reason. Don't let her harmless old-woman act fool you. She is the only one of her siblings to survive Lilith's reign. She is brilliant, and dangerous.

Hmm, said Mercy thoughtfully. *I saw that at the arena. Thanks for the heads up.* Then she met Vashti's warm smile with one of her own.

"I'm so glad you're all right, dear," said the old woman. "I would have been here sooner, but you understand with the lift not functioning, the emergency ladders are a challenge for me."

Mercy met Reaper's eyes over Vashti's shoulder as her aunt came to stand beside her. "I understand," she said.

There was genuine warmth in her gaze as Vashti patted Mercy's shoulder. Whatever her machinations, Vashti at least admired her great-niece, and was perhaps even growing fond of her. It was hard for Reaper to judge; emotions were far from his specialty. He glanced over, and found Cannon watching them as he stroked a hand over his jaw, speculation in his eyes.

"I hear you heroically pushed Wolfgang to safety," Vashti said, tilting her head close as though sharing a confidence. "I'm sure it was well-meant, my dear, but you should know his cybernetic implants give him much more durability to survive than you have."

"I'll keep that in mind the next time someone tries to blow me to pieces," Mercy said with no sincerity at all.

Reaper had no doubt she'd sacrifice herself in an instant for those she loved. His brow furrowed at the thought. An unfamiliar tightness filled his chest. What the hell was wrong with him?

That would be worry, said Cannon.

Empathy, Reaper decided in that moment, was a particularly annoying Talent. Vashti was still talking to Mercy. He took advantage of the distraction to duck back out into the hall, taking a deep breath once he got there.

"That's not something you see every day."

He'd forgotten he wasn't alone. Reaper sent a cold look to Griffin, but they'd grown up together. The other man wasn't intimidated; he knew too well what Reaper's eyes looked like in the grip of a killing mood. His younger brother, Cage, drew a bit further away.

"Look, Cage," continued Griffin, nudging him

with a shoulder. "Probably the only time we'll ever see Reaper run from a room."

He hadn't been running. Just…taking a moment. Reaper's eyes narrowed. He'd forgotten how irritating Griffin could be, always quick with a joke at someone else's expense. Normally it didn't bother him. Now, he found himself studying them both with a killer's eyes. Mentally running through all of the most efficient ways to kill them calmed his nerves, and the annoyance faded. Reaper favored them with a cold smile. Griffin grinned back, an unperturbed as usual, but Cage's complexion whitened.

The two of them stood in the hallway waiting for Vashti, as alike as brothers could be. They both sported the family line's signature green eyes, nebula bright. Griffin was an inch taller, and slightly heavier, but Cage was the dangerous one. Griffin's Talent was the more powerful, but he had a carefully strategic mind and was generally, annoyingly, good-natured. Cage was unpredictable, and he'd never recovered from the loss of their sister several years past. Although unsure around Reaper, the younger man was normally quick to anger. And he reacted with brutal, callous efficiency.

Reaper had once seen him beat a man to death in the arena. The insult had been slight, and the man's skill poor. Cage could have knocked him unconscious and left it at that. Instead, he'd beaten him with a methodical, cold competence that had been as impressive as it was deliberate. Reaper marked the moment and never forgot.

"Griffin." Reaper nodded in greeting. "Still dogging Vashti's heels, I see."

The insult wasn't subtle. Griffin was a member of the Core, the ruling body that helped govern the pirates. Reaper knew Dem had offered Vashti her own set of dogs and she'd politely refused, saying she needed none with her nephews around. When Griffin wasn't personally with her, his own dogs were, including his brother Cage. Reaper wondered how much of their protectiveness was in response to Vashti's demands, and how much revolved around protecting the few women left in their immediate family.

Griffin just smiled, as Reaper had known he would.

"You know me, always looking to get out of meetings. Besides, she's always where the really important action is."

That was true enough. Vashti had her nose in everyone's business, from Cannon to each member of the Core.

Sobering, Griffin said, "Someone must really want Mercy dead."

"They must, yes."

"She's family," said Cage with a frown.

"She is." Griffin looked back at Reaper. "Anything we can do to help?"

Reaper debated for a moment, but Griffin was Core. He would know soon enough, whether Reaper was the one to tell him or not.

"Those who set the bomb are dead. The one who directed them to do it wiped their memories."

Cage and Griffin exchanged a look.

"That's a pretty crude way of covering his tracks."

"But effective." Reaper thought it interesting that Griffin assumed the perpetrator was a man. The population being what it was, chance weighed heavy in that direction, but there were women aboard *Nemesis* who were more than capable. He had certainly not discounted any of them, including Vashti.

"I thought she'd be here much sooner to see Mercy," Reaper said, testing the waters.

"She went to check on the children first," said Cage. "That explosion was felt six decks away. People were scared. Especially the little ones."

"Cannon kept in touch," Griffin commented. "We knew what was going on."

Good enough for now. With the family history of back stabbing and assassination, Reaper wasn't ready to cross them off the list yet, but truthfully, Vashti was low in the pool of suspects. He couldn't see a real advantage to her in Mercy's death, and the warmth in her eyes just now when she'd entered the infirmary had not been feigned.

"You should have left one of them alive," said Griffin, leaning back against the wall with his hands at his belt. "I bet Treon could have pulled something from them, memory wipe or not."

Possible. But a moot point, since they were all dead. Reaper almost scowled. No doubt he would hear about that later from Treon.

"Hey."

All three of them turned to the door as Mercy stepped through it. The bruise was still a livid mark against her temple, but her hair hid most of it now. It hung almost to her jaw in a disheveled wave that managed to flatter and highlight the slash of her cheekbones and narrow features. Nayla had definitely made it grow. Griffin straightened from the wall, his trademark grin in place.

"Glad to see you survived, cousin. But then, we're hard to kill."

If he was trying to win some kind of approval from Mercy, he failed miserably. As she always did with family, she eyed him warily, and stepped closer to Reaper as she navigated the hallway.

"Not from what I remember," she disagreed in a mutter. Her eyes cut to Reaper and she lowered her voice. "Can we go somewhere and talk?"

Of course.

She winced. *Damn it, I keep forgetting I can just talk in your mind.*

It will take time to become second nature.

Yeah.

Oblivious to their mental conversation, Griffin was holding out his hand and trying to invite her to dinner. He really was charming, but Mercy did not appear swayed.

"No thanks," she said, and brushed by him to move down the hall.

Reaper met Griffin's eyes, and allowed himself a small smile as he followed her.

"So, we have to go the long way, right? And use emergency ladders?" Her voice floated back over her shoulder.

Indeed. I'll show you how to glide down with telekinesis. Reaper didn't examine too closely why he felt such a surge of…something, at Mercy's indifference to Griffin.

Thankfully, Cannon didn't sense it and tell him what it was. At this point, Reaper would rather not know.

"Great," said Mercy with false enthusiasm. "That doesn't sound dangerous at all. You know, I think I'll just watch, and then climb down the old-fashioned way."

If you like. Until whoever was behind this is caught, I'm going to assign one of my dogs to you. If I'm not with you, one of them will be.

Mercy didn't answer him, but he caught her frown at they reached the end of the corridor. Reaper grabbed her arm, and she stopped and looked up at him. Her eyes were shadowed with unhappiness.

"All right?" he said softly, aloud. He didn't want to force the issue, but he also wasn't going to let it go. Mercy's survival had somehow become extremely important in a very short time.

"All right," she said, reluctantly. "For now."

He could live with that.

CHAPTER SIXTEEN

They ended up back at Mercy's quarters. It was a small space, but ten times bigger than the bunk she'd grown up with on Wolfgang's ship, *Defiant*. As private spaces aboard a ship went, her new room was positively luxurious.

But it wasn't home. Not yet.

It will be, Reaper told her, from where he sat on one of the cushioned chairs covered in velvety fabric. Mercy was too wired to sit in the other, choosing to pace the confines of the room instead. It didn't take long to cross from the bedroom doorway to the counter with the cold unit, and back again.

She glanced over at him with a frown. *That was a private thought.*

He shrugged, clasping his hands in front of him. *Then keep it private.*

Easy for you to say.

Yes, he said with an amused tone. *It is.* His head tilted back and he stared up at her ceiling, as though it held some particular entertainment for him.

She decided to ignore his attempt at humor. Her mind kept turning over that weird dream she'd had with Willem Frain. Had it merely been a dream? Or something more? And if he was the one responsible for the explosion, how? Either way, someone on this ship had acted, had got to those men Reaper killed, and used them. Unless Willem could reach out across star systems to affect minds, he couldn't have done it himself.

"So, who do you think was behind it?" She finally voiced the question that had been burning through her thoughts since the moment she'd woken in the infirmary, her ears still ringing and her body so full of aches she was afraid to move. "Cannon?"

The noise from Reaper startled her so much she stopped pacing. At first, she wasn't sure what it was. Then she realized – the bark of sound was laughter. Reaper was *laughing*. She stared at him. What was this strange mood of his?

"I'm glad you think it's funny," she said stiffly, arms crossed. "I'm afraid I find it difficult to laugh when someone tries to kill me."

The laughter stopped, but an amused smile lingered around his mouth as he looked across the room at her. She wished his eyes weren't such a brilliant blue. It felt like a punch to the gut every time she met his gaze. Unnerving and…just unnerving. She squelched the thought before it could complete, reminding herself that clearly, Reaper could hear every damn thought in her head. Stupid shields.

If you don't like it, fix them. Make them stronger. Keep me out.

I'm working on it. She sent him a glare before resuming her pacing.

"Cannon would never try to kill you," Reaper said, his tone so laconic Mercy couldn't mistake his complete faith that what he said was true.

"But he's the king, right?" She argued, unwilling to let the idea go. "He has the most the lose by me being here."

"Not at all. Cannon never wanted to be king. He hates it. He's probably counting the days even now before you wrest power from him and take control."

"Wait, what?" She stopped again, hesitated, and finally sat in the other chair. It took her weight, and the gel cushion formed around her in perfect support, the velvety micro-fiber so soft beneath her hands she couldn't help but marvel and pet it with her fingers. The ships she'd grown up in and around didn't have this level of luxury. Utilitarian was more the word. Reaper's voice pulled her back from the brief distraction.

"Cannon doesn't want to be king," Reaper said again. "After Lilith died, he stepped into the void because anarchy was killing what was left of us. We had hundreds of deaths every day as Captains squabbled for power, each trying to lay claim to the empty throne. What remained of our women were quarantined away on a colony world to keep them safe from the virus. Without the influence of a queen, we were an undisciplined rabble. Lilith spent years pitting us against one another to prove who was strong enough to stand beside her. We were primed to destroy ourselves."

"What happened?"

Reaper lifted his shoulder in a shrug.

"Cannon. His Talent wasn't as good as another queen, but empathy is a powerful gift, often underestimated. He used his abilities to beat back the blood lust and hunger for power until a semblance of peace reigned. And he had to keep using it, every day, year after year, until we'd managed to piece ourselves back into some kind of functioning society."

Mercy struggled to imagine it, hordes of pirates killing each other, with only Cannon's force of will keeping them alive and going. She didn't trust him yet, but she couldn't deny the surge of respect she felt, listening to Reaper's story.

"Wow," she said softly.

"Yes," Reaper agreed. "There are those of us who are significantly more powerful than Cannon. Myself, Treon, even Griffin, to name only a few. Many have wondered why one of us doesn't just kill him and take the throne."

"Because if you did, it would go right back to what it was before."

"It would. Without Cannon and his Talent, the virus might well have succeeded in destroying us. But he would happily turn that power over to you in a heartbeat." He leveled his gaze at her, and Mercy's heart jumped into her throat. Honestly, she wasn't sure if it was just the usual impact he had, or the idea that Cannon desperately wanted her to actually be the queen in truth.

She cleared her throat, and looked away. "So, Cannon's not a suspect." She could agree with that, now that she understood where he was coming from. "Vashti?"

Reaper's silence forced her gaze back to him. His face was expressionless, but somehow she knew he was surprised.

She lifted an eyebrow. "What? You're the one who told me not to trust her."

"True." He frowned, thoughtful. "I've already considered her. I don't see a motive. She gains nothing if you're dead. But if you do ascend to power and she manages to make herself your indispensable dear aunt…"

"Then she gains position, has the ear of the new queen."

Reaper gave a single nod.

"Okay." Mercy tried to take a step back and look at everything objectively. "I admit I lean toward family first as suspects. But maybe that's just old fear talking."

Reaper said nothing, letting her think. Mercy brushed her fingers over the arm of her chair, watching the microfiber change color slightly beneath her hand, reacting to her body heat. Her nails were short, programmed with nanobots to stay that way. She knew a smuggler who had hers strengthened and sharpened to razor sharpness, but Mercy had always thought that a dangerous affectation. What if you cut yourself with them in your sleep?

But it made her think. Anyone could have a hidden set of claws. She couldn't trust them. Except for Reaper. The one person who could kill her whenever he wanted. The irony in that wasn't lost on her.

"Who do you think it is?" she asked finally.

He shrugged, not the response she was

hoping for.

"There are too many suspects for now. We know whoever it is has telepathy powerful enough for a memory wipe."

"How many people can do that?"

"On board *Nemesis?*" He thought about it. "Maybe one in every twenty telepaths. It's an unsophisticated method of covering his trail, but maybe that's why he chose it. It takes little finesse, so almost anyone with the raw power could do it."

"Great." Mercy leaned her head back against the chair. "And how many telepaths are there?"

"Nearly everyone has at least low level telepathy. *Nemesis* has a standing crew of over ten thousand souls."

"So our suspect pool is five hundred people." A trickle of unease went through Mercy.

"Five hundred and twelve. Approximately."

"And they're perfectly willing to risk blowing up the ship."

"That is a concern, yes."

She lifted her head to stare at him. "Can you find out if any more of that explosive is aboard?"

A smile tugged at Reaper's mouth again. "We are a pirate ship, Mercy. Of course there is more. We keep it locked away in the armory. Sebastian and Dem are investigating that thread now, but we are not hopeful."

"You think the bomber covered his tracks."

"That is a certainty."

Damn. Frustration was a living thing within her, making her restless and angry all at once. "Then what the hell do we do?"

Reaper lifted a brow. "Right now? There is

nothing more that *we* can offer to aid the investigation. Dem is extremely thorough, and he will not stop until the threat has been eliminated. So we concentrate on what we *can* control."

"Which is?"

"You."

Mercy lifted her head. "Me?"

"As I've stated before, you need training. As fast as possible. The more you embrace your gifts, the harder it will be to kill you."

Mercy couldn't help the sigh that escaped her. She'd much rather be out there, trying to find whoever had attacked her. Training her Talent was all well and good, but it felt passive.

Only because you have no idea what you are capable of. I assure you, Lilith was the least passive person I have ever known.

"Fine." She sat forward in her chair. "Let's do this."

The first thing you're going to need is patience. You aren't going to succeed overnight.

I can be patient.

The look he gave her could best be described as incredulous. She scowled at him. *What? You don't know me.*

Amusement settled around his mouth. *I believe I am beginning to.*

Right. Because we've known each other for so long. She gave him a look, in case the sarcasm of her answer escaped him.

A challenge, then. You wear a brusque demeanor like armor. You use it to push everyone away. But in truth you do this for their protection, not yours. You are self-sacrificing, and always think of others first. In a fight, you would do whatever it takes to survive, including run away if the opportunity presented itself.

Are you saying I'm a coward?

A survivor. And an idealist. Two things that normally have no place together.

Mercy barked out a startled laugh. "So, I'm a coward and naïve?"

Reaper contemplated her for such a long time, Mercy had to fight the urge to fidget.

"It would be easier if you were either of those things. A coward would cringe away from danger. Someone truly innocent would listen to me and be easier to protect. You are neither. You also can't take a compliment."

"Funny, it didn't sound all that complimentary."

Reaper leaned forward, resting his hands on his knees. His face was still, coldness creeping into his eyes. "Lilith cared for no one but herself. She willingly sacrificed her own family—be they her consorts, her siblings, or her children—to get what she wanted. This made her a powerful queen, one able to hold us together by sheer force of will." He relaxed fractionally. "I expected you to be the same. But you aren't." Reaper looked away, his voice so quiet she almost didn't hear him. "You are nothing like Lilith."

Stung, Mercy glared at him. "Sorry to disappoint."

His gaze swung back to her, and the look that came into his eyes rocked her with its intensity. She sucked in a sharp breath, unable to look away.

You mistake my meaning. His presence in her mind took on a more intimate feel, his words softer and more laden with unspoken things. The tension between them increased to such a degree that Mercy found each breath difficult. Warmth spiraled through her, unlooked for and unwelcome.

Stop it.

His shoulders lifted. *Am I doing something?*

You damn well know you are. Mercy couldn't tear her eyes from the way the thin cloth of his shirt clung to every muscular line of his torso. He folded his hands across the flatness of his abdomen, and for some reason the simple movement made her mouth go dry. *If this is a game, knock it off. Toying with my emotions isn't training.*

If I could *do that, it would be excellent training. But I am no empath.*

Mercy swallowed. *You are Mother-damned doing something, and you know it.*

He smiled faintly, and it drew her gaze—and her thoughts—to his mouth. *I never said I wasn't. Just not with your emotions.*

Then what? The image of kissing Reaper was a vivid thing in her head, and it made her want to punch him.

Soft laughter echoed through her mind. *Reacting to attraction with violence—I've only encountered that in other Killers.*

It isn't the attraction; it's that I know you are using it to screw with me.

All I can do is plant the suggestion. What your mind does with it is entirely on you.

Fuck you.

Is that an invitation?

Mercy stood up too fast, nearly losing her balance as her head spun and the gel foam of the chair didn't quite want to let her go. She grabbed the edge of the armrest to steady herself. Damn. The work Doc had done on her muscles might have kept them from atrophying, but she still felt weaker than she had since she was thirteen, trying to master the fitness regime Wolfgang insisted on. Atrea had made her look like a day-old kitten on that stupid holo routine, and she hated feeling the same way now.

Having a bomb detonate mere feet from her probably didn't help either. Her head still felt a bit wobbly, taking a moment to settle from her sudden surge upwards. How long was this going to go on? How long was she going to feel this vulnerable?

Your physical limitations are nothing to your mental vulnerabilities. No trace of humor touched Reaper's tone. *You're easily targeted, easily distracted, and—*

If you say easily manipulated, I will stab you.

Reaper went silent, and Mercy closed her eyes. *Great.* Nothing like an ineffectual threat to make her feel completely humiliated.

"You are not ineffectual." Hearing his voice aloud surprised her into opening her eyes and looking at him. Reaper wasn't laughing at her, and he didn't look offended or condescending. His eyes were steady, his expression serious. "You are a queen, Mercy. You may have no idea yet what you are capable of, but I do. So does everyone else on this ship. Do you know why someone tried to kill you today?"

Her brow furrowed. "We don't know their motive."

"Fear." Reaper's eyes took on a distant, faraway look. "You don't know what Lilith did with her gifts. The things she forced us to do. My mother had three consorts. Three. Two of them were Killers. One was the most powerful telepath of his age. Only Lilith boasted a coterie as powerful, and she resented the hell out of our family because of it."

Slowly, Mercy sat back down. Multiple consort partnerships were not rare on certain worlds. Many people preferred relationships limited to two people, and some worlds had their own laws regarding the number of consorts one could legally have, but plenty of others allowed as many as three or four to pair together. It didn't surprise her that the pirates allowed multiple partners, particularly given their population problems.

But that wasn't why Reaper was talking about this.

"Go on," she said.

"I'm not talking love matches. My mother chose her consorts carefully. My grandmother was a contemporary of Lilith's. They were both from family lines that had produced queens in the past. They grew up in the same colony. Went to the same classes, had the same trainers. Our family knew what Lilith was capable of. My mother chose her consorts accordingly."

Mercy watched him, digesting both his words and what he left unsaid. "You're saying your mother chose the most dangerous men she could to make sure her family was protected."

"Yes. And it was still only partially successful."

"Partially?"

His eyes chilled until they verged on that pale blue she had come to associate with Reaper at his most dangerous. "Dem's father died when I was six. He was on a mission for the Queen. Treon's father died less than a year later. A malfunction with the life support on a ship he was commanding. My father lived the longest, but he was eventually killed by one of our own."

"Another Killer? Why?"

Reaper shrugged. "Because he was told to. We never did find out who, but very few people can order a Killer to do anything."

"Why did she target your mother's consorts? Why not target your mother?"

"Until our fathers were removed, it was too dangerous. What would a Killer do if he suspected his consort had been assassinated?" Reaper shrugged. "A few years after my father's death, Matera-D happened. Lilith died. So did our mother."

"I'm so sorry."

Reaper didn't react to her words of sympathy. "My mother was a threat to Lilith as long as she was capable of bearing children. If she'd had daughters—"

"One might have been a queen." Mercy drummed her fingers on the arm of her chair. "Like me. That's why my mother took me and left. Because she knew what I was, and she knew Lilith would kill me. Why? Didn't she need an heir?"

Reaper shook his head. "Lilith was seventeen when her mother died and she became Queen." He paused. "It has often been speculated exactly what killed her. A powerful queen in the prime of her life."

"You're saying she murdered her own mother to take power."

"Why else would she view you, a child, as a threat?"

A thousand conversations with her mother ran through Mercy's head. The number of times Pallas had told her how dangerous her grandmother was, how she couldn't trust anyone from their family, or anyone with Talent. Lilith would send people after them, and anyone could be a threat. One conversation in particular floated to the surface. It was a few months into their stay on an agricultural ship, working in a biodome. Mercy had liked it there because most of the people were nice, and everything around them was green and growing, fragrant with the scents of flowers and herbs. Dirt was everywhere, but it was cleaner than any place they'd stayed before. Mercy was six. She loved learning all of the names of the plants, watching fragile stems burst through their little pods of earth, misted with water and bathed in the light of a nearby sun during every day cycle.

What was the name of the girl she'd spent most of her days beside? She was older, ag-born, and she knew *everything*. She'd shown Mercy the orchards and given her peaches right off the branch as they worked, the succulent fruit impossible to get on a hundred worlds. The name wouldn't come to her. Not that it mattered. She'd had dark hair, and freckles.

Everything had seemed perfect. Until the day a

new group of workers arrived, and a new man was assigned to their plot. Mercy knew right away that he was different. Talented. It was the first time they'd run across someone else with Talent, and terror had rooted her to the spot. When she could move again, she ran to her mother as fast as she could, desperate to get away.

Pallas didn't waste any time. They were on a ship, but one that stayed in orbit, shuffling workers to and from the colony on the world below them on a daily basis. Certainly, it sent harvests that often. Mercy's mother had grabbed the bags they always kept packed and ready, and ushered them to the next shuttle down, where they could get to the spaceport and flee. She'd only stopped long enough to ask a single question.

"What color were his eyes?"

Mercy couldn't remember what she'd said. But she remembered him.

Blue. His eyes had been blue. Like Reaper's.

CHAPTER SEVENTEEN

*R*eaper crossed the room before Mercy completely processed that he'd left his chair. He gripped her arm, his fingers painfully tight. He was standing so close she could feel the heat radiating from his body. It was a distinct contrast from the intense cold of his eyes, so pale they took her breath. Her heartbeat thrummed loudly in her ears as her body responded instinctively with a wash of adrenaline.

Reaper was gone. In his place, an implacable Killer stood before her, the bones of her arm grinding together in the grip of his hand.

"Reaper." Her voice trembled over his name, and she stiffened her spine and cleared her throat. "You're hurting me." She glared at him, refusing to be intimidated.

The fingers around her arm relented fractionally, but he didn't move away. "You're sure you saw another Killer?"

"Um…pretty sure." Mercy remembered those eyes. They'd looked exactly like Reaper's did now. Or was that her memory playing tricks with the present and the past? "But how many people have blue eyes?"

The corner of his mouth twitched. "The shade is distinctive. *Are you certain?*"

"I was six!"

His hand flexed, like he was thinking about shaking her.

She winced. *Okay, that's going to bruise, and I'm done.*

Mercy didn't stop to think about what she did. They were already standing so close, and Reaper was only slightly taller. His head was tilted down as he stared into her eyes. All Mercy had to do was lean forward to brush her lips against his. It was feather-light, barely a kiss at all.

Reaper froze. Mercy was no empath, but she could feel the shock course through him. He stood stone-still, tension in every line of his body. She pressed closer, placing a hand against his chest and sliding it up to his neck. He hadn't responded yet, but he hadn't killed her, either. That was something.

She brushed against his lips again, using more pressure. His hand on her arm loosened. The bruising grip relaxed. She could have pulled away then, but she'd come this far. Why not take it further? She flicked her tongue out, teasing. This time his lips parted, his mouth moving against hers.

Reaper kissed her back, and everything changed from light and teasing to something much more intense. It had been a long time since Mercy kissed anyone. That was the fleeting thought she had to explain the sudden spike of lust rushing heat through her veins. Her fingers curved around his shoulder as his tongue slid over hers, his mouth more sensuous than she ever would have imagined from a man as controlled as Reaper.

Maybe that was the attraction.

He broke the kiss an eternal moment later, letting her go and stepping back. It was so abrupt she almost stumbled, left standing there like an idiot with her arm still raised in the air. She lowered it quickly.

Color had come back into his eyes, a darker circle of blue bleeding back into the irises.

"Why did you do that?" His head tilted, and she knew he was confused.

"It seemed like the safest option." She shrugged, running nervous fingers through her hair. "Besides, I've been thinking about it for a while. Practically since the day we...met..." Mercy heard her own words trail off as she stared at him, stared at his eyes as they darkened. Something in the tilt of his head, the confusion that tugged his mouth into a frown.

Nik, what are you doing?

Nikolos.

The boy on the dock. Verath 6.

"Mercy?"

"It's you. You're him." Feeling a little shaky – from realizing who he was, not from the kiss – Mercy sat in one of the chairs. "The boy from the docks."

It made so much sense. Why she'd felt such an instant connection to Reaper. Why she'd trusted him on an instinctive level, even when everyone else clearly thought she was crazy for doing so.

She looked up at him. "I'm right, aren't I? You were on Verath 6 all those years ago. Looking for my mother. And me."

"Yes."

"Why?" She'd always wondered why a boy would be sent on such a mission.

"You and Pallas were Dem's first assignment as a Hunter." Reaper hesitated. "You might not remember, because you were so young. But he knew your family. We both did. Or at least, we'd met you. Dem was the only Hunter who ever had."

Mercy shook her head. "I don't remember. I was only three when we ran."

"I know. Dem and I were trained together in those days. I was brought along so our training as Killers wasn't interrupted."

Mercy remembered the moment clearly, standing frozen, knowing her life was over. Reaper staring at her from two docking spaces away. The others had been grouped behind him. Oblivious.

"Why didn't he find me? If he tracked me that far…"

"Not you. Pallas. Dem didn't remember your psychic imprint well enough, and it changes a little as we grow. After ten years, he couldn't get a fix on you. He tracked Pallas to Verath 6, but we lost her there."

Mercy's throat closed. She stared down at her folded hands. *I lost her, too.*

I know. I'm sorry. Reaper knelt in front of her. *Do you want to talk about it? What happened to her?*

Mercy looked anywhere but at him. "I don't know, exactly. She just...didn't come home one day. Only two things could keep my mother from me. Death or capture." Mercy closed her eyes. "She always told me not to use my Talent to try and find her if she ever disappeared. That it might lead people to me. But I couldn't...I had to look for her. On the third day, I searched for her mind."

"What did you find?"

"She wasn't dead. I felt the connection, her presence. But it felt...different."

Run Mercy! The command had been so powerful, Mercy had been compelled to follow it. She didn't remember leaving their tiny apartment or grabbing her go bag. She only remembered walking down the street to catch a transpo to the spaceport.

"I knew she'd been discovered. Taken. I thought, at first, by you. Well, by people working for Lilith." She opened her eyes and gave him a shaky smile. "But then you arrived on world, and I knew I'd been wrong. That someone else had her. Someone worse."

"Why worse?"

Mercy shrugged.

"This is important, Mercy. You thought Lilith would kill you both. What is worse than that?"

She stood up fast, moving away from him. She realized she was rubbing her hands on her thighs, and stopped. Her throat was dry and her heart was beating too fast. She'd never told anyone this, not even Atrea.

Reaper waited silently. Patient.

"It was just an impression," Mercy said. "A

feeling when I connected with her. I think she was trying to shield, to keep me from knowing what was happening to her. But I know she was being held. She was lying on a cold surface, and there was the sound of a heartbeat, the hum of technology. The smell of cleaning agents and…it was faint, but I could smell blood."

"A medical facility. Or lab." Reaper's tone was thoughtful.

Mercy swallowed, trying to keep control of her emotions. Her fear. Her anger. "Like the one Willem Frain had on that space station."

She felt Reaper's eyes on her.

"You think Frain's people had something to do with your mother's disappearance?"

"Yes." She turned to face him. "Maybe not Frain himself. He isn't much older than you. But whoever he works for."

"It's possible. Why? What do you think they want?"

"I don't know. They invaded my mind, examined me physically and mentally. Took samples." Mercy had to swallow bile at the memory. "I think he knew I was a…queen. Maybe that has something to do with it."

"Pallas was no queen."

"But she produced one. Me."

Reaper stared at her for a long time. Mercy sat down, and then stood back up, too nervous to sit still. It felt so strange, finally telling someone everything she remembered.

"There's something else," she said into the silence. "I think…I think Willem had something to do with the bomb." Saying the words out loud made it real.

Reaper shook his head. "There is no way he could have boarded our ship, even if he could find us. Why do you think that?"

"Maybe he's not here physically, but I had a dream…or a vision maybe? Like a conversation with him, before I woke in the infirmary. I don't think my mind made it up. He said things. I'm telling you, whoever planted it was being influenced or ordered or…I don't know. But he's responsible for that bomb."

Reaper said nothing for so long that Mercy had paced the confines of the room twice. She made herself stop and face him.

"You believe me, don't you?"

"I believe it's worth looking into. I think others need to hear this. All of it. My brother Dem, Cannon."

Mercy hesitated, but now that she'd told it once, what did it matter if she did so again? Thinking about it now, she wasn't sure why she'd felt so compelled to keep silent all these years. Absently, she rubbed at her forehead. It surprised her when she felt fingers close around hers, and realized Reaper had taken her hand. He didn't squeeze it the way someone else might have, but just stood in front of her, holding her hand in his own.

I will find whoever threatens your life, he said in her mind. It went unspoken what would happen then.

Mercy stared at him. This was Reaper being reassuring, she realized. It occurred to her that he used wording not just addressing *this* moment, *this* threat, but any threat. Ever.

"What are you going to do? Kill anyone who looks at me wrong?"

Don't be absurd. I will limit my response to those with the intent to harm you.

It was on the tip of her mind to ask him just how he meant to discern what anyone intended, when she realized he was quite capable of reading that, if not in their body language, then in their thoughts.

"You can't kill everyone who wishes I was dead."

Reaper raised an eyebrow. His eyes weren't that icy cold color yet, but they held enough chill to assure her he was serious.

"Reaper, seriously. People think things they don't mean all of the time."

Trust me to know the difference. No one understands the intent to kill better than a Killer.

That was probably true. But the idea of Reaper killing just anyone who threatened her still made her queasy. On the other hand, she was tired. Tired of looking over her shoulder, of wondering who she could trust, of never trusting *anyone*. Outside of Wolfgang and Atrea, of course.

Reaper was watching her intently.

"What?"

"I have contacted Dem. We'll have dinner with his family this week, and after, you can tell him what you told me."

The abrupt change in subject left Mercy groping for an appropriate response. She didn't want to have dinner with people she didn't know and trust. She didn't want to talk to Reaper's brother, who had spent part of his youth hunting her.

Then she thought about Tamari, the little girl she'd met in the infirmary. Dem's daughter. She sighed.

"All right." She had to start making connections with these people. Connections beyond Reaper and Vashti. She'd decided to stay, but along with that came making a life here. It would be fun to see Tamari again. And informative to watch how Dem interacted with the little girl and his wife.

Mercy shied away from looking too closely at why she found that prospect interesting.

And who knew? Maybe these people would be able to help her do what she had failed to accomplish. Maybe they could help find her mother.

$\mathcal{M}$ercy spent the next few days training her Talent with Reaper, and following doctor's orders. That meant when she wasn't training, she was resting, eating a strictly directed diet, and a visit from Wolfgang to make sure that's exactly what she was doing. When she opened the door to her quarters for him on the fourth day, she caught a glimpse of Zion leaning against the opposite wall. He flashed her one of his too-charming smiles, and she had to resist the urge to scowl back.

She wasn't surprised Reaper had followed through on having his dogs shadow her when he wasn't around. She just wished he'd chosen someone else to do it. Now, even with the door closed again, she was uneasily aware of Zion's presence right outside.

Which she'd have already known if she'd bothered to do the most cursory mental sweep. *Damn.* She could almost hear Reaper's voice admonishing her lack of attention. Training had been going well; her old lessons with her mother had, according to Reaper, laid an excellent foundation. But Mercy struggled most with using her Talent as a normal routine. She'd spent her entire life practicing *not* to use it.

"What's this about?" Wolfgang gestured to her face, and she realized she must be scowling after all.

"Nothing," she muttered. "Trust issues, I guess." She swept him with her gaze, but he appeared fit and whole. No evidence of his injuries in how he held himself or moved.

"You look good," he said. Some of the tension eased from his face, and she realized he'd been taking a similar inventory of her.

The two of them stood awkwardly for a moment, until Mercy decided *what the hell*, threw awkwardness aside, and gave the old Wolf a hug.

"I'm so sorry," she whispered as his arms squeezed her. Her voice wobbled a bit, and she cleared her throat, stepping away. No way was she going to cry again.

He frowned at her. "What are you sorry about?"

To give herself something to do, Mercy crossed to the tiny kitchen area and poured them both glasses of whiskey. Wolfgang liked coffee, but after the day they'd had, she figured something stronger was called for. It surprised her at first to find her kitchen fully stocked with not only food, but nearly a full bar of alcohol. Then she remembered these were pirates, probably even more given to vice than smugglers.

"This," she said. "All of it. I've dragged you and Atrea into my mess." She crossed the room and handed him a glass. She had to work to keep her voice steady. "I have to tell you something, and it isn't going to be easy for either of us."

"Let me stop you right there," said Wolfgang as he accepted the glass. "One, no one has ever 'dragged' Atrea into anything that girl didn't want to be a part of. Me included. Two, if you're going to tell me Atrea's in that stasis cocoon because of you, I'm going to be angry."

Mercy took a deep breath. "But she *is* in that stasis field because of me."

"No, she isn't. The people who kidnapped you put her there." Wolfgang set his drink aside. He had his serious face on, the one that usually made Mercy' stomach drop into her boots. Still, he didn't know everything that had happened, and she couldn't let him continue in ignorance. Her own fingers were pressed so hard against her glass, she was surprised it didn't shatter.

"You don't understand. Yes, we were kidnapped by Frain and his people. But *I'm* the one who hurt Atrea." It burned her to say those words, guilt eating her from the inside out.

Wolfgang regarded her for a long moment. He didn't say anything, so Mercy soldiered forward.

"Willem forced me to use my Talent on her, to…" She still struggled with this part. "To unlock the latent Talent in her genes, somehow." She couldn't look at him, and stared down into her glass. "It hurt her."

Wolfgang could move silently when he chose to. Mercy didn't realize he'd crossed the room to stand right in front of her until he was gently prying the glass from her fingers and setting it down. When she still didn't look up at him, he put a hand under her chin and forced it up. His blue-gray eyes were flat. Implacable, but not condemning.

"Did you put that poison inside her mind?"

"No, but—"

"It's a yes or no question, Mercy. I've spent a lot of time in the infirmary. I've talked to Doc and Nayla. What's killing my girl is a poison, an agent that will, according to Doc, attack her brain and consume it until nothing is left. That stasis field is the only thing keeping it from happening. Did you poison her?"

"No." The word was barely a whisper.

"Then I'll hear no more of how this is all your fault. I think you have enough to worry about without shouldering responsibilities that aren't yours."

The sick feeling in her gut slowly evaporated, but Mercy didn't feel the relief she expected. Because no matter what Wolfgang said, she couldn't absolve herself of Atrea's fate. She swallowed, and forced herself to nod, knowing if she didn't agree the old Wolf would just keep at her about it.

He gave a wry grin and shook his head. "You think I don't know you're only agreeing to shut me up? I've known you for half your life, girl. I can read you almost as well as Atrea."

"I can't change how I feel."

"No, I don't suppose you can. At least, not until we find a way to help Atrea. Once that happens, maybe you can let this go." He picked up his whiskey glass. "Just know that I don't blame you. I may not be able to stop you from blaming yourself, but I sure as hell don't need to pile on any more guilt." He drained the glass in one long drink, dragging a reluctant smile from Mercy.

She'd forgotten. Wolfgang never could sit around for long, not even to play a hand of cards or sip a glass of something nice.

He grabbed her shoulder in a gruff half-hug. "Why don't you come and have some dinner with me?"

"I wish I could, but I have plans."

"Do you, now?" The look he gave her was far too perceptive. "With Reaper?"

Mercy fought to keep embarrassment from flushing her cheeks. Wolfgang had never judged her for any of the connections or liaisons she'd had in various spaceports. Her life hadn't been conducive to anything long term, and the old Wolf never seemed to have any illusions about what two young women might get up to when most of the people around them were smugglers, thieves and mercenaries. He gave them one lecture about being safe and careful, showed them the contraceptive and health treatments stowed with the rest of the medical supplies, and never asked any more questions. Mercy had always been grateful for that.

And truly, the one time she'd tried for something more had ended in disaster. She forced her thoughts away from that and gave a casual shrug.

"With his family. His brother's the head of security on this ship. Reaper wants me to talk to him about the bombing."

"Yes, I've met Dem a few times now. He seems competent." Wolfgang crossed his arms. "Be careful, Mercy." This was said so softly, Mercy knew it had nothing to do with Dem or security.

She glanced at him. "I am. I will."

He said nothing else, just brushed his lips across her forehead in farewell, and showed himself out. Mercy heard Zion greet him before the door slid shut.

With the upcoming dinner on her mind, Mercy made quick use of the shower, taking a little longer than necessary as she reveled in using the water option. Her room actually had a full size tub, something she'd never seen aboard a ship outside of expensive luxury liners only the wealthy elite could afford. She hadn't noticed it on her first inspection as it was hidden behind a clever panel that made the bathing room look smaller than it really was.

A bath sounded like heaven, but she didn't have time now. She looked at the nano-graph tub fashioned to look like pale grey marble shot with gold, and ran a mournful finger along one edge. *Later*, she promised herself.

Turning one wall into a mirror again, Mercy did the best she could with her hair. It was longer now, not quite brushing her shoulders so not long enough to tie back. Unfortunately, Nayla's growing spells didn't mean it looked nice. The hair fell in uneven dark waves, ending up with tufts that stuck out funny and didn't lay nicely. Still, it was much preferable to the shaved look Willem Frain had left her with. She'd have to get some nano-bots and clean it up. For now, though, she combed it as best she could and divided it into two sections, twisting them into braids and using a sealer she found in one of the drawers to tuck the ends in. She looked like a grown woman wearing the hairstyle of a five-year-old, but it was something.

Mercy decided wearing armored clothing to dinner might not set the right tone. Especially given Dem's title. She had just finished pulling on a casual cotton shirt – the real stuff, so soft beneath her fingers she lost a few moments playing with it before she pulled it on – when a chime at her door sounded. She stood up, hastily tugging the deep purple shirt straight, and did a mental sweep to see who it was. She was expecting Reaper.

But it wasn't him.

She was so shocked she opened the door to verify with her eyes what her mind was telling her. Sure enough, Max and Kator stood side by side outside her door, neither one looking comfortable.

Both boys were dressed in plain, serviceable synth-fabric clothes. Their bruises were still spectacular, even a few days later. Apparently, no one had treated their minor injuries, probably as a deliberate lesson. Half of Max's face was covered in a mottled purple bruise beginning to yellow in places, that started at his left eye, extending down to his jaw. It looked painful. Kator's nose was still a little swollen, and thin red scratches extended down one side of his neck. He kept giving Zion nervous looks over his shoulder, and that one wasn't helping with the grim look he wore. He stood up straight, looming over them with silent menace like he'd as soon pound them into the deck as allow them to see Mercy.

She glared at him. *Do you have a problem?*

Nope.

She gritted her teeth.

"S-sorry to bother you, Your Majesty." Max stuttered out the words, looking ready to bolt at any second.

"Don't call me that." The words came out sharper than she intended, thanks to her irritation with Zion. Max's face went white beneath the bruising. To her utter mortification, both boys dropped to the floor, heads bowed like she was some kind of idol. Or tyrannical monarch.

"Please forgive me, Your—I mean ma'am."

Seriously?

But Mercy could see Max's whole body quake as he knelt before her. He was definitely, ridiculously, serious. If anything, Kator was worse. He huddled in as small a mass as he could bend his large frame into, like he hoped to disappear into the deck.

Mercy looked at Zion. *What the hell is wrong with them?*

He shrugged. *They might be too young to remember Lilith, but they've grown up hearing the stories.*

She looked down at the boys again. *So they're terrified of me.*

Pretty much.

She sighed. "It's Mercy. You can just call me Mercy."

Neither boy moved, and she got the feeling her words did little to reassure them.

By the Mother. "Would you stop that? Get up." She reached down and took each boy by an arm, hauling them up until they scrambled to their feet. "I'm just Mercy. You don't need to be afraid of me, and you don't need to bow or call me anything but my given name. Got it?"

"As you wish, M-Mercy." Max stuttered over saying her name, and it was everything Mercy could do not to roll her eyes.

"Let's get straight to the point." Better to get this conversation over with and put everyone out of this misery. "Why are you here?"

The boys exchanged a look. Mercy found it interesting that these two had come here together. There was no sign of Kator's group of friends anywhere in the corridor. Folding her arms across her chest, she leaned against the door frame and waited.

"We came to apologize," said Max. He was staring down at his toes.

"For what?"

"For what happened at the arena. F-for making you personally intervene in our disagreement."

Mercy raised an eyebrow. "Is that what happened?"

Kator had crossed his arms in a defensive posture. He was twisting the material of one sleeve so hard she was surprised the fabric didn't rip. Max kept staring at the deck. Mercy eyed them for another long minute.

"Bullshit," she said, and both boys flinched. "Why are you really here?"

"I—I—"

"The apology might be part of your strategy,

but it isn't why you came to see me." She was sure of that. Spending half her life dealing with swindlers and thieves had given her a healthy meter for falsehoods. "The two of you are the opposite of friends, yet something made you come here together."

"We want to swear ourselves to your service," Kator blurted out, the words so fast they almost ran into one another.

Mercy felt her jaw drop. "What?" She looked at Zion. *They want to* what?

He smiled, and for the first time it felt genuine. *It means they're declaring their loyalty. They might want to be trained as future dogs, or you could assign them specialized training and tasks. For example, you might want to give one of them command of a ship that answers directly to you.* He eyed both boys with a speculative look. *When they've proven themselves, of course. In the meantime, their focus of study would change to what you direct, and they'd do odd jobs for you when required.*

So, what? They'd be servants?

Zion gave her a disapproving look. *No. It means you would become responsible for their training, for... mentoring them. And they would gain the advantage of having that mentorship. And your favor.*

She stared at both boys, who fidgeted and waited. They almost seemed to be holding their breath. The very last thing Mercy wanted was to be responsible for anyone else. What the hell was she supposed to do with two teenagers?

It would crush them if you refused, Zion said. The bastard's eyes were twinkling. *They won't be the last, either. You'd better decide now if you plan to refuse everyone who asks.*

Mercy thought a lot of colorful swear words. She could hear Zion chuckle mentally, and gave him one last glare. She could also hear the thoughts of both boys, they were thinking so hard. They badly wanted her to say yes.

What happens if I tell them no?

Zion sobered.

This is the first thing I have ever seen the two of them united on. Your refusal could very well send them back to being at odds.

Are you just saying that to manipulate me?

Now he gave her a flat, cool look. *Do you think I don't give a shit about their lives? Don't think you know me, lady.*

"Fine," Mercy said the word aloud. Both to him, and to the boys. "I guess I accept." She held up a hand to forestall the tumble of words she knew was coming. "But I'm still learning all of this. You're going to need to be patient while I figure out what the hell I'm doing."

"No problem, You—I mean Mercy." Max bobbed his head in something between a nod and a bow. "Thank you. You won't regret it."

"No more fights. *Especially* to the death. If I hear about it, you're both out –got it?"

"Absolutely." Kator was nodding like a fool.

"But if you have to fight to protect yourselves, I mean, definitely do that." Mercy wanted to rake a hand through her hair, but couldn't because she'd braided the stuff. Damn, she was already messing this up. "If anyone is giving you trouble, I expect to hear about it. Hopefully before it becomes physical."

They both continued their vigorous nodding. Exasperated, she waved a hand. "Unless there's something else, I have a dinner to get to."

"Yes, I mean no. Mercy." Max gave her a fervent grin as the boys backed away. "We'll report to you first thing in the morning."

She winced. "Let's go for a couple of days from now."

She could tell from their expressions that the delay was disappointing, but neither boy argued. Apparently they knew the value of not pushing their luck. The two of them ran down the corridor, jubilant in their body language and smiles. They passed Reaper on the way, who gave them a long look as they hurried by.

"You mean I only have a few days to figure out what to do with them?" she asked Zion.

"Come on, it's not that bad."

Mercy sighed, watching Reaper approach. "That's a matter of opinion."

CHAPTER NINETEEN

Mercy was anxious. Reaper could see it in the way she kept smoothing her hands down her thighs, or how her brow furrowed when she ducked her head. She'd been nervous before, when he'd taken her to the arena. But not like this.

Part of him wondered why dinner with his family could possibly be a more stressful prospect than facing a few hundred pirates, some of whom had every reason to want her dead. He could look into her thoughts to find out, but she'd actually been bolstering her shields. They'd finally reached a level of strength where forcing his way past them felt like cheating. So he didn't.

"What?" She looked at him warily, and he realized they'd been standing outside the door to Dem's quarters for too long while he watched her.

He shook his head in answer, and brushed against his brother's shields with his mind. He bit back an oath a moment later, but not soon enough to stop Mercy from shooting him an alarmed look.

"What's wrong?" The tension in her body reached new heights, and Reaper huffed a frustrated breath as he felt Dem acknowledge his presence.

"My brother is here," he said, keeping his voice low.

"Isn't that the point?"

"Not *that* brother."

He could say no more before the hatch opened, framing the exact person he'd been hoping not to see tonight. Treon blocked the doorway with his body, a move as intentional as it was provoking. Reaper already wanted to throttle him, and he hadn't even spoken yet.

His youngest brother looked nothing like him. All three of them had sharp differences in their physical characteristics due to their different fathers. But Treon was somehow even more removed, because unlike Reaper and Dem, Treon was no Killer. His eyes were the golden brown of their mother's. They reminded Reaper of her every time he saw them. His skin was fair, his features beautiful in a way Reaper's or Dem's would never be. Treon put even Zion's looks to shame. Only in the dark fall of his hair, and the masculine lines of his jaw, did he resemble his brothers.

"Well, well." Treon crossed his arms. "I've been looking forward to this moment."

Reaper cast a look Mercy's way. If anything, her wariness had increased, the furrow in her brow deeper.

Treon gave her a long, penetrating look.

Don't. Reaper kept the thought on a tight mental thread, reserved just for his brother.

Oh, come, Nik. Don't tell me you haven't been inside her head.

To train her. Not to take whatever I wanted.

So scrupulous. How unlike you. Aloud, Treon said "Your Majesty, it is an honor to finally meet you." He even tilted his head in a kind of bow.

"Don't call me that." Reaper saw Mercy take a moment to rally after snapping the words. When she spoke again, her tone was lighter. "It's just Mercy."

Prickly, isn't she?

But Reaper saw something behind the glint in his brother's eyes. He wasn't just here to provoke. He wanted to see this new queen for himself. He didn't yet trust that she wasn't another Lilith, despite what Reaper told him.

Move aside, Treon.

His brother opened his mouth, probably to say something else obnoxious, but he was forestalled by the sudden presence of a small whirlwind. Tamari appeared between them, dressed in a yellow frock with red flowers and fat ladybugs. Her curls were bound in pigtails on either side of her head. She was so excited she danced in place, each step moving her up through the air until she stood at eye level with them.

Uncle Nik! Mercy! Uncle Treon, Momma says to stop being you. What does that mean?

Treon softened instantly, reaching out to tweak her nose. "It means she wants me to stop poking at Uncle Nik and let them in the door."

Tamari giggled. *You weren't poking him.*

With my words, halla. With my words.

Tamari wrinkled her nose. *That doesn't make*

any sense. Mercy, come see my room! Uncle Nik, Papa wants to talk to you.

Tamari grabbed Mercy's hand and tugged her right past Treon, who had no choice but to move. Reaper gave his brother a small smile as he followed. There was a simple satisfaction in watching his brother's arrogance punctured so easily by a child.

That child makes mighty Killers back down, Treon said. *What chance do I have?*

Reaper gave him a cool look. *Humility doesn't suit you, Treon.*

I am merely speaking the truth, brother.

Stop it, both of you. This is a no-sniping zone. Treon, I know that will be especially difficult for you. Sanah, Dem's wife, inserted herself between them to give Reaper a hug. After more than four Galactic Standard years, it was still a practice that startled him. People just didn't hug Killers voluntarily.

Unless you happened to be married to one, it seemed.

And *that* was still a shock to Reaper. Killers didn't marry. On rare occasions they became consorts, but in those situations, there were always other men in the coterie who could provide the emotional resonance a woman needed. In nearly all other circumstances, Killers formed short-term contracts with other Killers to produce children. Men and women who weren't themselves Killers rarely sought more than a single night's thrill when sharing a bed with one. The physical act of sex could be mutually satisfying without emotional resonance, but rarely in a long term arrangement.

Reaper had often wondered since meeting Sanah how Dem managed it. Maybe the fact that she was an empath had something to do with it.

As Sanah let him go, Reaper studied her. She was short, pretty, with wild red curls, pale skin, and a dusting of freckles. Her blue-green eyes sparkled with a warmth that was at once fascinating and alien, largely because she directed that warmth at him. As though she cared for him.

Oh, Nikolos. I do care. When I married Dem, you became my brother. Sanah linked her arm through his and pulled him further into the room. He could see they'd expanded the kitchen counter into a full table, suitable for seating several people. It was already set for dinner.

Very few people would have dared to breach his shields so casually, and Reaper had known all of them for much longer than Sanah. But she'd never seemed afraid of him. Wary at times, but not afraid.

How do you make it work? Even he was surprised at the boldness of his own question. As much as he had wondered, Reaper had never before asked Sanah about her relationship with his brother. She gave him a long, searching look.

You and Dem had more than Killers for fathers, Nik. Sanah never called him by the name everyone else used. It reminded him of his mother, and something inside him softened, thinking about her. *Yes*, said Sanah. *You are half the genes of your mother. I wish I could have met her.*

She would have liked you. Reaper wasn't sure

what prompted him to speak the words, but the radiant smile Sanah turned on him was both unsettling and pleasing.

She squeezed his arm. *Thank you for that. Now, to answer your question more fully. Dem has emotions other Killers I've met lack. No, that's not quite right. Dem is able to connect with his emotions in a way other Killers can't. The same is true for you, though it seems more difficult. Perhaps because Dem is only a quarter Killer, where you are fully half.* She gave him a sober look. *It will be a long and difficult journey. But if you want to build a loving relationship with her, it can be done.*

He raised an eyebrow.

Oh, don't look at me like that. I felt the connection between you and Mercy the instant Treon answered the door. Don't worry, wanting to strangle him is perfectly natural. Dem felt the same way when I entered his life.

Amused, Reaper gave her a faint smile. *I've wanted to strangle Treon since childhood. Mercy has nothing to do with it.*

Sanah gave him a pitying look. *As Cannon likes to say, don't argue emotion with an empath.* She gave his hand a pat, and stepped away. *I'll go rescue Mercy from Tama while you speak with Dem.*

As Sanah slipped away, Dem entered the room, dressed more casually than Reaper could remember seeing his brother. Instead of his usual suit, Dem wore slacks and a long sleeved shirt in pale blue, a simple clasp holding the collar closed at his throat. For any other pirate, this would have been formal wear. On Dem, it made Reaper stop and nearly gape. His brother ignored him, adjusting his shirt sleeve and looking faintly uncomfortable. Although he was large-framed and taller than either of his brothers, somehow Dem looked smaller than normal without his suit. Reaper wondered if he knew that, and this was part of why he wore them. His black hair was still cut ruthlessly short to his skull, dark skin gleaming beneath the lights. The shirt made his Killer's eyes stand out even more, something Reaper would have thought he wanted to avoid.

Sanah likes the color. A hand descended on his shoulder. Treon, his mind brushing Reaper's before the hand touched down. More than anyone, Treon knew better than to startle him. *He looks dashing, don't you think? Almost like a real pirate.*

Smiling, Reaper folded his arm across his chest. *Sanah's influence, then.*

Oh, no. This is a concession Dem started making after Tamari was born. Apparently constantly cleaning all of those suit jackets was just too much trouble, and having a small child smear food and...other things...all over his clothing was driving Dem mad.

Reaper could imagine it well enough. Dem's perfectly-pressed attire was part of the control he asserted over everything around him. Having that control challenged must have been an experience.

But then, you'd know all of that if you came around more.

Reaper's smile disappeared as Treon continued past him to pour them each a drink. Wine was already on the table, so he appropriated three glasses and made use of it.

"Treon," Dem's voice rumbled. "Leave Reaper be. I understand why he has stayed away, even if you don't."

Treon handed Dem a glass. "As you wish. You are the eldest, after all." He gave a mock bow, prompting Dem to give him one those steady stares that normally made men quake. Treon merely chuckled.

"We were too easy on him in childhood," Dem said. Reaper made a noise of agreement, accepting his own glass of wine.

Without any sort of segue, Dem switched to telepathic conversation. *Treon and I have each given the ship a thorough search in our own ways. There is no evidence of Willem Frain or any other Veritas agent on board.*

And I found no hint of telepathic possession, Treon added, referring to the kind of mind control the strongest of telepaths could sometimes do. A Veritas agent had come aboard *Nemesis* in this way once before, and Treon had taken steps to insure it never happened again. *None of my traps have been triggered.*

Mercy is certain Willem and Veritas are involved. Reaper frowned down at his glass. He didn't doubt his brothers' abilities, but it worried him. The whole thing worried him; the bomb, the fact that another Killer had been hunting her, Veritas.

Dem and Treon exchanged a look.

Mercy went through an ordeal, said Dem carefully. *It's possible the stress of that is making her see shadows where none exist.*

Reaper felt a familiar chill wash through him. He set his wine glass down. *A queen's instincts are telling her something. Are you suggesting we ignore that?*

I'm saying we need to be careful and consider all possibilities.

Treon made a subtle movement. It drew their attention to him, and Reaper knew in that instant that he'd done it on purpose. *We will remain vigilant,* Treon said. *But thus far, there is nothing to indicate Veritas has breached this ship.*

Nothing but Mercy's vision.

Yes.

Before Reaper could say anything else, the others walked back into the room, Sanah and Mercy chatting together. Tamari disappeared from beside them and reappeared next to Treon, giggling.

"Tamari." Dem's voice was even. "No more teleporting."

"But Papa—"

"No. It is time for dinner."

Treon tweaked one of her pigtails. "You can sit next to me, *halla.*"

Mercy sat beside Reaper, across from Tamari and Treon. As Sanah and Dem sat at each end of the table, slots appeared in the center and steaming dishes rose up from within in serving bowls. A platter of steaks, a chilled mix of greens and vegetables, and several side dishes filled the air with savory smells.

Tamari wrinkled her nose. *I don't want steak.*

Sanah eyed her daughter. "You don't have to eat it, Tama. But you will eat some of the Berax tubers I fried up. You need the protein."

I don't like tubers. Papa!

Tamari. Dem's mental voice was flat and implacable. *You will choose one or the other. Steak, or tubers.*

Tama heaved a huge sigh. *Fine.*

Reaper could feel Mercy's amusement at the exchange, her body relaxed as she leaned back in her chair.

"I never liked Berax tubers, either." Mercy's voice was light, conversational. "But Wolfgang used to fry them up in this special sauce that made them actually taste good. Your Mom's smell pretty similar." She speared a tuber and put it on her plate, cutting a generous bite and making a big show of chewing and tasting it. "Mmm." She looked over at Sanah, narrowing her eyes. "Did the old Wolf give you his recipe?"

Sanah gave a light shrug. "He might have mentioned you liked them cooked this way. I wanted to be sure and offer things you would enjoy."

"And he gave you tubers! Of course." She shook her head, laughing. "Well they *are* really good. You should try them, Tama."

Intrigued, Tamari made no protest when her mother put one onto her plate.

You're good with her. Reaper kept the words private, just between himself and Mercy as he filled his own plate.

She's adorable. Mercy sipped her wine. *So, are you going to tell me what Dem and Treon had to say? Don't look so surprised. I know it was about the investigation.*

Reaper hesitated. *They found no evidence of Willem Frain or Veritas aboard this ship.*

That's not unexpected. She cut a piece of steak,

juices flowing from the meat. *You did tell Dem they have access to a teleporter, right?*

He is aware.

I can't explain how, but I know I'm right about this, Reaper.

I don't doubt you.

Mercy went rigid beside him, dropping her fork and knife with a clatter. "What the hell was that?"

Everyone looked around, though Reaper wasn't too concerned. He had a suspicion of what had startled her.

What is wrong?

"Something just brushed against my leg! Something…" Mercy paused, struggling, and Reaper was intrigued to see a flush of embarrassment color her cheeks. "…something with fur."

"Oh." Everyone relaxed again, Sanah smiling as she spoke. "That's just Rasa. Tama's *kith.* You get used to it."

Mercy didn't relax. She looked under the table, then around the room. "Ah, no offense, but where I come from imaginary friends do *not* feel real."

"Rasa is not imaginary." Dem gave a heavy sigh. "Show yourself, Rasalas. It is rude to remain camouflaged if you are going to interact with our guests."

Reaper had seen Rasa before, so he was prepared when the large furry shape materialized beside Mercy. She, on the other hand, leapt out of her chair swearing viciously. The great cat looked back at her, calmly blinking green-gold eyes. He'd grown since the last time Reaper saw him, standing nearly as tall as Mercy's chair. His white fur shimmered with a faint luminescence in the light, broken up by coppery-brown whorls that formed a striking pattern. His long tail flicked back and forth, and a faint sound rumbled in his throat.

"Mother protect us." Mercy put a hand to her throat. "I-I'm so sorry for my language. I don't normally swear in front of children."

Tamari was giggling into her napkin.

"That's all right," said Sanah. "We've all been given a fright once or twice by Rasa."

"Not all of us." The words were a faint growl from Dem's end of the table. Sanah gave him a *look.*

"Is…is it purring?" asked Mercy, her shock fading as fascination took hold.

"He is." Sanah sighed, taking a drink of wine.

"He likes you!" Tamari sounded positively joyous. "He's never met a queen before. He says you feel different."

"Thanks?" Mercy cautiously retook her seat, keeping one eye on Rasa, who hadn't moved beyond the flicking tail.

Tamari leaned toward her mother. *Rasa says he'll have my steak, Mama.*

Sanah raised an eyebrow. "Rasa had his own steak before everyone arrived."

Tama's lower lip came out as she pouted. "But he's hungry."

Rasa chose that moment to yawn, displaying wicked fangs. Mercy flinched. "Maybe he could have another."

Sanah narrowed her eyes at the cat as his rumbling purr grew louder. "Only because the queen asks."

She placed a hunk of steak on a small plate and set it on the floor. Mercy tensed as the cat languidly stretched and moved closer. Reaper could tell it would take time for her to trust that Rasalas wasn't truly a danger. It was amusing how she found the cat's predatory nature unsettling, but was so accepting of his own.

You don't have fangs longer than my thumbs.

It startled him. He hadn't realized he'd been projecting that particular thought. Mercy turned her green eyes on him, smiling. *Now you know what it feels like.*

What?

Having someone in your head when you didn't give them permission to be there.

Reaper raised an eyebrow. *Mercy, you gave me permission the moment you requested I teach you. I gave you access past my shields not long after. This is just the first time you've used it.*

Oh. Her smile widened. *I still surprised you.*

He had to concede that. *True enough.* In more ways than one.

"So, what are *kith*?" Mercy asked out loud. She looked around the table as she spoke. "Obviously they have some…abilities."

"They are Talented in their own way, as we are." Dem answered her question. "On their home planet they form psychic bonds. Symbiotic pairings across species. When we colonized it – when Hunters colonized it, they found humans made excellent partners. Tamari is Rasa's bond-mate."

You are an interesting species. You have strengths

we do not. And weaknesses we can balance. The voice was resonant, male, and had an odd burr to it. Reaper saw Mercy's eyes widen.

"Did he just talk?" She stared at Rasa. "You can speak telepathically?"

The cat inclined his head, and then began industriously rubbing at his whiskered cheeks with a paw. Mercy watched this with almost hypnotic intensity. Then again, the paws were huge. Easily bigger than the plate Sanah had used to serve his steak.

"Like Killers," said Treon, "Hunters have a Talent unique to them. They can track someone psychically."

"I know." Mercy forced her gaze away from Rasa. She glanced down the table at Dem, then away. "I've been tracked by one before. Well, technically he was tracking my mother."

An awkward silence descended on the dinner. Dem lifted his wine glass, staring at it with a frown. "A Hunter never loses a mental signature once he has it." He took a drink as Mercy's head came up.

Reaper could practically feel her tension as she vibrated in the chair next to him.

"You mean you could still track her? Find her?"

"No." Dem set the glass back down. His face was so still it might have been carved from stone. But something like regret gleamed briefly in his eyes. "Pallas is gone, Mercy." His voice was as gentle as Reaper had ever heard it, outside of when he spoke of Sanah, or Tamari.

Mercy stared at him. The rest of the table remained silent. Tamari looked from one adult to the next, her eyes wide. Sanah brushed a hand across her daughter's head, and Reaper saw the little girl's lip tremble.

Finally, Mercy released a breath that shuddered. "If she's dead, just say that. Don't use a euphemism. Be blunt. Be honest."

"When a Hunter tracks someone dead, there is nothing." Dem spoke the words slowly, as though he was choosing each one with care. "No hint of a trail to follow. No presence in the universe that can be felt. I only met Pallas a few times, when I was a child. My sense of her was never particularly strong. But it led me to Verath 6. I *felt* her there." He hesitated. "And then I felt her vanish."

Mercy swallowed. "You felt her die?"

"No. *Vanish*. When I think of her now, when I have thought of her every time since, I don't feel the sense of *nothing* I should. I feel a void."

Mercy's brow furrowed in confusion. She looked at Reaper, but he had no answers for her. He could only shake his head, just as confused as she was.

"Isn't a void and nothing the same thing?"

Dem looked frustrated. "It is difficult to explain. The Hunter who led me on my Hunt could not understand it either. No one has ever experienced anything like it as far as I have been able to determine. But no, the void is not nothing. It is simply…as though her trail is swallowed by emptiness."

"You're saying she's in some kind of limbo."

"I don't know where she is, whether she lives, or not." Dem paused. "And no one else can answer that question, either."

CHAPTER TWENTY

$\mathcal{M}$ercy made the walk back to her own quarters lost in a mental fog. She didn't remember much of the meal's end, or the wonderful dessert Sanah had provided. The soft, rich cake might as well have been made from sand, instead of whatever sweet concoction it had actually been. Mercy hadn't tasted it. Hadn't heard even half of the conversation around her. Her mind kept turning back to what Dem had said.

After all this time, she still had no idea if her mother lived or died. But it almost didn't matter anymore. Because she was gone. And it was more clear than ever before that whatever had befallen Pallas, she was not coming back.

Mercy would never find her.

Gradually, she became aware that Reaper was still with her. When they reached her quarters, one of his dogs stood outside. She couldn't remember his name. The one with the shaggy hair.

It didn't matter. She said good night, opened the door and walked inside mechanically, expecting Reaper to leave. He didn't.

"Mercy." He said her name out loud. She realized he'd already said it mentally more than once, but it had sounded distant. Separate from her thoughts. She turned and looked at him as he stood in the doorway. It felt like she was moving under heavy gravity, each movement painfully slow and ponderous.

"What?"

"I'm not leaving you like this." He walked into her quarters without waiting for permission, but she couldn't bring herself to care. He crossed to the bottle of whiskey she'd left sitting out from Wolfgang's visit, and poured some into a glass.

Mercy just stood in the middle of the room, feeling at a loss until Reaper grabbed her hand and forced her fingers around the glass.

"Drink this. I think you might be in shock."

She almost laughed. But it bubbled up her throat and then faded to nothing. "I can't be. Mom's been missing for fifteen years. It's hardly a surprise anymore."

Reaper frowned at her. He looked really grim, but his eyes were still bright blue, not the pale winter color that would have been a warning. Because it seemed like he was going to loom over her until she drank, she lifted the glass to her lips and swallowed. Fire burned its way from the back of her mouth, down her throat. It burned away the numbness, flooding her with warmth. She inhaled sharply, and promptly choked on the lingering fumes. After a short coughing fit, she took another long swallow.

The burn gave her something to focus on that wasn't her mother.

"All of that is true." Reaper watched her closely. "But I think you've been holding on to the possibility of finding her for all these years."

Mercy turned sharply away from him, unable to bear seeing herself reflected in his eyes. She raised the glass to her lips and drank it dry, gulping down the whiskey like it was water, welcoming the burn that brought tears to her eyes and closed her throat, making speech impossible.

But Reaper was relentless. *That is no terrible thing, Mercy.* His mental voice was soft, but still inescapable.

She closed her eyes. *Isn't it?*

Then tell me why. Explain this response you're having. I don't understand.

She shook her head. The whiskey had accomplished one thing. It had steadied her. She was able to cross the room easily, without feeling that heavy weight. She moved to the bottle and poured more into her glass.

I'm not going to leave until you talk to me.

"Then I guess you're in for a long night."

You're angry.

"Guess again."

He cocked his head, considering her. She did her best to ignore him, looking anywhere else, pacing the room as she sipped the whiskey more slowly this time. Getting drunk sounded like a great idea.

"You are. You're angry. But also sad."

Sad was too tame a word for what she was feeling. Reaper stood silent for a few minutes, long enough that Mercy began to hope he would leave her alone. She stopped her pacing and rested her head against the wall, her eyes closed. *Please, just leave me alone.*

"No. But I can leave. I'll ask Wolfgang to come—"

Mercy's eyes flew open. "No!" She pushed away from the wall, alarm making her voice rise. "Not the Wolf. I can't—I can't face him right now."

"Why not? He's your family. He should be with you."

Mercy rounded on him. The words burst out of her of their own volition. "Because I got his daughter poisoned, maybe killed, and it was all for nothing!"

Suddenly so furious she couldn't contain the emotion, her free hand curled into a fist. She threw the glass with so much force it shattered against the nano-graph wall, spilling onto a plush hand-woven rug that probably cost more than three smuggling runs put together.

Reaper didn't react to her fit of rage. He just stood in the middle of the room, stoic and silent. He didn't look reproving, or sympathetic, or raise an eyebrow at her to ask why. He just stood there. Mercy couldn't decide if that was infuriating or an enormous relief. Maybe both, as odd as that was.

She covered her face with her hands, sitting heavily in one of the chairs. She took a long, shuddering breath, then another. Calmer, she let her hands drop.

"She told me not to look for her. It was a directive. An order. Above all else, if she ever disappeared I was supposed to do two things: run, and never look back. Never look for her. It was too dangerous." The words sounded leaden and dull leaving her lips. "But I ignored that order from the very beginning. I never stopped looking for her. Not when it risked my own capture. No even when it put my only friend in jeopardy."

"You were a child."

She shrugged. "Like that's an excuse."

Reaper knelt beside her. "That's your guilt talking. But it isn't the real reason you're unhappy."

It forced her to look at him. So she glared. "No? I'm listening. Go ahead and tell me what I'm really unhappy about. This ought to be good coming from a guy who doesn't feel."

If she hoped to get a reaction from him by lashing out, she was doomed to disappointment. His body language didn't change, his face didn't so much as twitch, and his eyes remained bright blue.

"You're finally accepting the loss of your mother. You've spent the last fifteen years in denial, and hearing Dem tonight made you understand that you can't deny it anymore."

Mercy didn't answer right away. She looked away again, down at her hands, linked together in her lap. Finally, she cleared her throat. "That's really perceptive for a guy who doesn't feel." She spoke the words softly, not intending to hurt this time.

"Just because I don't feel as connected doesn't mean I don't understand loss. I grieved when my mother died."

This time she met his eyes willingly. The anger was draining away, leaving sadness and shame in its wake. "I'm sorry."

He shrugged. "An advantage of *not feeling* is not taking things personally."

Mercy winced. "Yeah, I didn't mean that." She reached over and took one of his hands. "I know you feel things. I'm just...looking for someone to take it out on."

"I know."

"I'm sorry it was you."

"I'm not." His hand closed around her fingers. He stretched his legs out and sat on the floor. It couldn't have been entirely comfortable, but Mercy was glad he didn't move away to sit in the other chair. "Sanah told me you'd need me tonight. She could feel what was happening."

Mercy gave a short laugh. "Well, that's embarrassing."

"Why?"

"Because you don't have dinner with someone to show them all of your most private emotions."

Now Reaper raised an eyebrow. "Keeping secrets on this ship is very difficult. I would think you'd know that by now."

"I guess I'm still getting used to it." Tears blurred her vision, and she blinked them back. She was too tired to cry. "I miss her so much. I don't know how to let her go."

For the first time, Reaper looked uncomfortable. A frown pulled at his mouth. "I don't know how to help with that. For me, my mother's death was final. One day she was alive, and the next she was not. There was no in between. There is no such thing, with death. It just is."

"I will probably never know what really happened to her. I'll never have closure in that way."

Reaper was silent for a long time. When he

spoke, his tone was thoughtful. "Maybe not, but you can be assured of one thing."

"What's that?"

"Your mother loved you enough to leave everything behind. To take you away from the rest of your family and into the territory of our enemies to protect you. She loved you very much."

Mercy leaned her head back against the chair. "She did. But she was grieving, too, when she made that choice. My father had just died."

"An accident?" Reaper's tone made it clear he didn't believe that any more than she did.

Mercy shook her head. "She never talked about it, or him. Eventually I stopped asking because she would only tell me he'd died to protect us. It was too painful for her, I think. But reading between the lines, I think Lilith had him killed."

"A strong possibility. Your mother didn't have consorts. She chose a husband. With him gone, she wouldn't be producing more children anytime soon."

Mercy tilted her head to look at him. "Do you remember him at all?"

"A little. I know Lilith didn't approve of the marriage. Your father wasn't a Core member. He was just a pilot with a fairly strong telekinetic gift. No one of consequence, in the Queen's eyes." Reaper was stroking the back of her hand with his thumb. It felt nice. Between the warmth of the whiskey in her stomach and the heat of his hand stroking hers, Mercy almost felt relaxed. "I don't think Lilith was expecting the match to produce a queen."

"What, she wanted my mother matched with

someone powerful, but she didn't want powerful grandchildren?" Mercy couldn't keep the sarcasm from her tone.

"Oh, she did. Lilith had plans for all the members of her family, the more powerful the better. She just didn't want any rivals."

How did someone become like that? Was it the way Lilith was raised? The society she grew up in? Or something else, something she was born with?

"Do you think I'll ever be like her?" Mercy voiced one of her greatest fears; that in embracing being a queen, she would grow to be like her grandmother.

Reaper gave her the ghost of a smile. "If I thought that, you'd be dead by now."

This time she did laugh. It came out a little breathless. She blamed the whiskey. Or maybe there was something wrong with her that she found Reaper so attractive, even when he discussed the possibility of killing her. No, of *not* killing her.

She focused on his face, staring into his eyes. Her heartbeat increased. "Sanah told me something, too." She sat up in her chair, leaning dangerously close to Reaper. He remained still, watching her. "She said if I wanted things to move forward, I was going to have to move them. That you don't believe yet."

"Believe what?"

"That you can be more than what you are."

She leaned forward and kissed him. This time he accepted it right away, his mouth pliable and responsive. Heat flared between them immediately, combining with the whiskey in her gut to spread throughout her body like a flame. That didn't stop Mercy from shivering with a sudden chill as Reaper broke the kiss.

"I think you might be a little bit drunk." His face was still very close to hers. She could feel the warmth of his breath against her skin.

She laughed. "Clearly you've never seen me drink before. I drink hardened smugglers under the table when I want to." She reached out and threaded her fingers through the hair at the back of his neck. "I have a choice here. Either I can get drunk enough to forget everything I'm feeling tonight."

She didn't need to voice the other option. It hung in the air between them.

"You might regret this later."

"Why? Because you're a Killer? Please. We just had dinner with your brother and his family. Don't hide behind what you are, Nik."

He gave a small jerk of surprise at her use of his real name.

"For fifteen years I haven't been able to forget you. I'm pretty sure the same is true for you. Don't sit here and tell me I'm making a mistake."

ercy didn't give him another chance to argue. She kissed him again. She didn't hold back, pouring everything she had into it. She'd never had to convince someone to go to bed with her before. For the most part, smugglers took their pleasure when and where they felt like it. She imagined most of the pirates were much the same. Even Killers like Reaper.

But Sanah had warned her while they were alone. *Nik doesn't know what to do with what he feels for you yet. Dem had me to help him understand his emotions. You're not an empath, so you'll have to help him understand another way. He's going to be reluctant. He believes he can't give you what you need, the emotional connection you deserve. He's wrong.*

Mercy kissed Reaper with wild abandon, using tongue and lips and teeth to coax him into an equally passionate response. His hands went to either side of her head, holding her in place while he stood up. He made a sound, and in the next moment everything flipped, and instead of Mercy being the aggressor, Reaper was.

He pressed her back against the chair. One hand fisted in her cotton shirt as he leaned over her, straddling either side of her legs. The other was in her hair, tangling in her braids and unraveling the seals so they came undone. Or maybe he'd already undone them with telekinesis. She couldn't be sure, as heat swept through her, chasing away the last of her chill, his mouth moving over hers with an intensity that left her breathless.

He smelled clean. The faint scent of soap clung to his skin, in his hair, and his mouth tasted of the wine from dinner. The scruff along his jaw scraped her skin, but it didn't hurt. It just added to the keen-edged need spiraling between them. Who knew that a man so emotionally removed could kiss with such feeling?

His hands slipped under her shirt, splayed over her ribs, trailing up to palm her breasts. They were warm and a little rough. Heat stabbed her gut, quick and sharp as a knife blade, and she gasped into his mouth.

"Reaper," she managed, pulling her head back. *No, that wasn't his name.* "Nikolos."

He stared into her eyes, and she saw with a shudder that the color of his had deepened. Not the cold of the Killer, but more like the heat in the center of a blue star.

If you want to end this, do it now. His voice in her head was careful and controlled, and reflected none of the desire she knew was making his breath short and his heart race.

I started it. Why would I want to end it? To make her point, she pushed up his shirt, running her hands up the hard lines of his abdomen. He was tense beneath her touch, holding himself perfectly still.

I am not what you need. I could send someone else to you. One of my dogs.

Shocked, she stared at him, her mouth hanging open. "You did *not* just say that!"

Stubborn, he soldiered forward. *You need someone to be with you tonight. You're choosing me because I'm here, but there are better options—*

Keep talking and I will *fucking end this.*

Wisely, he went silent. She took a deep breath, forcing aside her anger. This is what Sanah had warned her about. She could get angry, yell at him, destroy whatever progress they'd made. Or she could convince him he was being an idiot.

"I'm not choosing you because you're convenient, Nik. I'm choosing *you*. I want *you* with me tonight, not just a warm body." She gentled her tone, reaching up to cup the side of his face with one hand. She kept the other pressed against his side. "I know you feel it. This pull between us. The moment I saw you on that space station, before I knew who you were, that we'd met before. I felt it hit like a damn freighter crashing into me. It's only gotten stronger the more I've come to know you."

He struggled. She could feel it in the whirl of his thoughts, see it in the indecision on his face.

I'm not my brother. Dem is only a quarter Killer.

And Sanah is an empath. I know. We aren't them. We can never be them, because we're different people. She hesitated. *I've never had a real relationship before. I tried once, but it wasn't possible living the kind of life I had, keeping so many secrets, preparing to run at any moment. Sex was just sex. I don't want that with you.*

It's all I have to offer.

I don't believe that.

She stretched up and kissed him again. Leaned forward until she was pressed against him, feeling his heartbeat against her as she played with his mouth, coaxing once again.

I'll hurt you. He was still holding back, stubborn man.

The very fact that you care about that possibility proves my point. Now stop talking.

She stood up, forcing him back. She was almost as tall as Reaper. Standing, she had the leverage she needed to press herself fully against him, her hands once again running over the hard planes of his chest until she'd pushed his shirt all the way up. His breath hitched when she bent her head and followed the path of her hands with her mouth.

It wasn't until cold air hit her back that she realized her shirt was being cut from her body. With an icy precision of Talent that made the hair stand up on the back of her neck, sending a chill down her spine far colder than the temperature in the room warranted.

She looked up at Reaper through half-lidded eyes. "I liked that shirt."

I'll get you another.

Stepping away for a moment, she shimmied out of her pants before he could destroy them as well. "I don't see you cutting *your* clothes free. Maybe I should try?"

He lifted his shirt from his head and threw it

aside. The rest of his clothing followed quickly. *I don't yet trust your control for such work.* Amusement lifted the corners of his mouth.

He stepped close and captured her hands before she could finish removing every scrap of clothing. "Hey—" His mouth covered hers, and he used that kiss ruthlessly, his tongue teasing, his stubble a scrape against her skin. Everything narrowed to that contact until she wasn't aware of anything else. Until, her hands still held by him, she felt a phantom touch stroke down her back, and cup her hard against him. The length of his cock pressed against the juncture of her thighs and she gasped. The thin barrier of her underwear was at once frustrating and erotic.

You are a lot more playful than I ever would have guessed.

I'm not playing. He moved against her slowly, his chest a hard wall pressed against her breasts while he tortured her with his hips. It turned her legs to water, and she was pretty sure she'd have fallen if he hadn't been holding her up.

He lifted her up, and her legs went around his waist automatically. He continued kissing her as he walked them to the alcove with her bed. They sank down among the linens and pillows, her legs still locked around him. His cock continued to tease her, each slide becoming more excruciating until the small triangle of cloth between them was torture instead of a tease. Before Mercy could say anything, the material parted and fell away. She gasped as his warm flesh connected with her own. Her arousal made the next slide so smooth, it was as if he was already inside her.

The first glimmer of an orgasm sparked within her center, and she leaned her head against his shoulder, panting. He knew. He took her head in his hands and kissed her deeply, slowing the thrust of his hips until the spark built so slowly she wanted to scream. Her legs trembled and she tried to thrust against him harder. Something held her hips still.

Reaper, damn you.

Just wait.

A long, slow thrust, then another. The tension built, coiling tighter, the pleasure increasing. Mercy moaned into his mouth. Abruptly he changed the tempo, thrusting hard and fast, his skin scraping against her clit. She did scream then, the pleasure cresting over her in a wave.

Reaper barely gave her time to recover, her limbs just turning languid when he lifted her hips and thrust into her. Her skin was already sensitive from the orgasm. She gritted her teeth as he slid inside, sparks dancing behind her eyes. Perspiration dotted his skin beneath her hands, the only evidence of what his control cost him.

You are an evil man.

Killers can see where you're most vulnerable. One of the easiest times to kill anyone is while they're distracted with sex and pleasure.

His hips began to move, a steady, fast rhythm this time. Tension coiled in her center again, more intense the second time. Mercy couldn't remember the last time she'd had more than one orgasm during sex. Most of her liaisons were short and fast by necessity. This was something entirely different. She could feel a level of intimacy she'd never known in the connection of their minds and bodies.

Are you saying your Talent shows you how best to pleasure me?

Something like that.

He propped himself above her, his arms bracketing her. His eyes were darker than she'd ever seen them. She reached up a hand to trace his face as his hips thrust against her, lifting her own to match his rhythm. This time, no phantom hands held her still.

Why are women not lining up to take you to bed?

You know the answer to that.

The pleasure coiled tighter, spiraled higher, and she bit her lip, arching against him. She could feel it in the way he moved, the tension in his body, his mind. He was close. He shuddered, and in the next instant the pleasure broke over them both. Mercy pressed her mouth to his shoulder, letting the waves wash through her. It lasted long enough that when her muscles finally relaxed, it was a relief.

She lay still, breathing hard, listening as Reaper's breathing slowed in her ear. He was a heavy weight for another minute or so, before he rolled away to settle comfortably beside her.

Those women are all idiots.

Which women?

The ones too frightened to be with you. Their loss. My gain. She felt adrift, lazy, content. "That was intense." She spoke the words aloud while Reaper stroked lazy fingers over her shoulder. It was pleasant, comforting. Her eyes drifted shut. *Exactly what I needed.*

Good. You should sleep while you can.

Her eyes flew open. "What does that mean?"

"Only that it's a long night, and I'm not finished."

"Promises, promises."

He grinned at her, and the simple laughter in his eyes made something in her chest go tight. She barely caught a gasp before it left her lips. She'd been the one to point out the connection between them, so why was she so surprised that sex had created one more bond, one more intimacy?

Mercy? Reaper's smile had faded. He watched her now with serious eyes.

That sent a wave of sadness through her. She shoved it aside, curving her lips into a mischievous smile.

I'm just wondering how many times you'll be able to do that.

An eyebrow lifted. *Is that a challenge?*

Well, women don't have the same physical limitations men do.

He rolled on top of her, pressed her into the mattress. "Definitely a challenge. We'll see which of us reaches our limit first then, shall we?"

She just grinned, and kissed him.

CHAPTER TWENTY-TWO

*W*atching Reaper prepare breakfast was surreal. Mostly because she'd never imagined him as someone who spent time cooking. On the other hand, Mercy wasn't entirely sure he hadn't just ordered up from the galley. Either way, she wasn't going to complain when he handed her a plate of real eggs and some kind of hash that smelled divine. Not to mention the cup of genuine coffee. She sat savoring that first sip, and knew if she hadn't already committed herself to staying here, the coffee would have convinced her. How could she ever go back to the bitter, ashy taste of the synthetic stuff again?

"How many ships do you guys take just to keep supplied in coffee?"

Reaper sipped from his own cup, his expression amused. "We don't have to steal coffee anymore. Did you know it can grow on any world with the right climate and environmental conditions?"

She sat up in her chair. "Are you telling me you have a colony for growing coffee?"

"Several, in fact."

"But it's supposed to be so difficult. Just the right climate and altitude, the right seasonal temperatures and rainfall."

He lifted his shoulders, taking another sip. "It is specific, but possible on multiple worlds. The D'veen conglomerate just doesn't want anyone to know that, so they keep a tight regulation on the plants and crush anyone with the means and temerity to try and grow their own."

"Those bastards!" She meant it, thinking of all the times she'd choked down the synthetic crap sold throughout the Commonwealth. Real coffee was so expensive, only the wealthy could afford it.

She eyed her cup speculatively. "So, between this and the Thalian beer, are you guys making a killing selling on the black market?"

Reaper leaned against her kitchen counter. "We have a few other investments, as well. There is a certain satisfaction in making profit off the people who exiled us and tried to wipe out our population."

"Do you even need to take ships anymore?"

His eyes glinted dangerously. "Need? Maybe not. But there is also satisfaction in making sure the Commonwealth never forgets us."

"I bet." Mercy was hungry. She sat at the counter and devoured her plate. She was starting to eat larger portions. Her face was beginning to fill out as well. She'd noticed it this morning after soaking away her aches and pains in a bath full of gloriously hot water.

Her body was slowly putting weight back on, and she could recognize her own face in the mirror now. Amazing what a difference even a few short days of regular food and rest could make. Of course, Nayla's healings probably helped, too. Even her hair looked better now. Sanah had taken the opportunity the night before to give her some nanites to regulate the length. She was almost tempted to color it too, but staring at the dark swing of hair that actually looked stylish now instead of ragged, she couldn't bring herself to do it. She'd spent so many years altering the color so she could look like someone else, it was strange to look in the mirror and just see herself. Strange, but good.

They ate in companionable silence. Reaper wasn't the most talkative at the best of times, but Mercy didn't mind. It was good, just sharing a meal together. Not talking about her abilities, how to make them stronger, or who might be trying to kill her. It felt like all of that was distant, separate from the happiness making her smile as she swallowed more coffee. Right now, Reaper was the man she'd shared a bed with the night before. This wasn't the first time she'd stayed with someone long enough to share breakfast, but it was close. Who knew how much fun that could be?

But as though thinking about it had allowed anxiety to pierce the bubble of optimism, Mercy felt the first doubts creep in. What happened now? Was this the start of something more? What the hell did she know about relationships? The one time she'd tried for more than just sex, it had ended disastrously. Smugglers didn't make the best partners, especially when they had a different woman at every port, and didn't know one of them was a telepath who could feel their lies and see their thoughts.

This situation was completely different. Reaper was different, and for the first time in her life, Mercy was able to just be herself with someone. No lies, secrets, or pretending to be someone she wasn't. Surely that would make a difference. Assuming he even wanted this to continue.

"You're thinking very hard." Reaper's voice brought the real world even closer.

Mercy fiddled with her fork. "I'm surprised you didn't just look in my mind."

"Your shields have improved. It would be rude to force my way past now. But if you think with enough intention, your thoughts can escape your shields. Something you should be aware of."

"Really?" The idea that she might be making actual progress on her Talent was a bright spot. "But you could still break them?"

He considered her for a long time. Finally, he shook his head. "I might, but it would be my strength versus yours. A contest that would become painful and perhaps cause one of us injury. It isn't worth the risk to test it."

She cocked her head at him as she swallowed a bite of hash. "When do you think that happened? Last time we worked on it, it felt like such a failure."

"Failure is a harsh word. Shields are something instinctive. Something you don't have to actively think about. Most children learn how to do them as one of their first exercises in Talent. Your mother probably taught you the basics, but wasn't able to reinforce them as you grew older. Once you learn how to maintain them, your subconscious does all of the heavy lifting for you. When we were done actively training, your mind continued to work the problem. Evidently, you figured it out."

"That's fantastic."

He arched an eyebrow, sipping his coffee. *Of course, now the hard work begins. With your shields in place, we can start working on your Talent.*

Mercy sighed, some of her triumph deflated. Then she frowned at him. "Wait. If my shields are working, why can I still hear you?"

"Your shields guard your inner thoughts. Those you direct outward can still be heard, although you can choose who you direct them to. I can also still direct thoughts at you. You can hear them without the risk of lowering your shields."

Now that she thought about it, she'd always been able to hear her mother, no matter how tightly shielded she was. Something inside her relaxed, as she realized she'd be able to have conversations without opening her innermost thoughts to people.

"I suddenly feel so much better about being surrounded by a bunch of mind readers."

I can't have you getting complacent. I heard enough of your thoughts earlier to wonder if you regret last night.

What? She froze with her fork halfway to her mouth, then put it down. "That's not it at all. I was just wondering what the plan is."

"Plan?"

"For us."

Reaper leaned back. His face was as expressionless as ever, giving her no hint of what he might be thinking. *Not fair.*

"Maybe it was just sex." His tone had no inflection, either. She was starting to get irritated.

"Was it? Do you really believe that after everything we said?"

He took his time answering. Good. Maybe he was actually thinking it through.

"Most women wouldn't want to be tied to someone like me."

The anger drained away. She realized he was being careful to protect her, to give her an out.

"I'm not most women. I'm a queen, as everyone likes to remind me. And if your mother could handle two Killers as consorts, I think I can handle one half-Killer."

He stood very still. She had to double check his eyes to make sure they weren't leeching of color.

"Are you saying you're choosing me as your first consort?" He studied her face as he spoke.

Was she? *Wait.* "*First* consort?"

"You're a queen, Mercy. You are going to need the protection and power multiple consorts can give you."

"I think we're getting a little ahead of ourselves—"

A knock on her door interrupted them, followed by the brush of a familiar mind. Mercy stiffened. "What is he doing here?"

Reaper eyed her. "Still don't trust him?"

She gave him a pointed look. "He's family."

But she opened the door for Cannon anyway. He was the king, after all.

He strode in smiling. He was dressed casually,

in a dark green cotton shirt that fit him like a second skin, and the armored pants a lot of pirates wore. His hair was tied neatly back, and for once he was clean-shaven.

"Good morning." He paused, and his smile widened. "I'm interrupting, I see. I'd apologize, but it's important."

Reaper handed him a cup of coffee without being asked, and Cannon took it with an appreciative nod. The pirate king glanced at Mercy over the rim as he took his first sip. *There are many who won't agree, but allow me to be the first to congratulate you on your choice.*

My choice? She hadn't relaxed since he walked into the room, and she remained tense as she watched him lean casually against her counter, making himself at home.

"Please," Cannon said aloud. "I'm an empath, Mercy. Give me some credit. Reaper is a bold choice for your first consort. No one will expect it. Some will be threatened by it. But others will change whatever plans they had to target you, whether that means physically, psychically, or politically." He shrugged broad shoulders, muscles flexing in his biceps. "Good move."

Mercy set down her own empty cup with a twinge of regret. "Let me be clear: Reaper and I haven't finished discussing where we are, and when we do, I'm sure as hell not including the rest of this ship, or the rest of the family, or anyone else, in my choices."

Cannon chuckled, completely unrepentant. "By all means. I'm just saying perhaps you're more politically savvy than some people have given you credit for."

"People like you?"

"Oh, no. I wasn't rushing to any judgments."

Mercy glanced at Reaper, and a thread of anxiety wound through her. *I didn't sleep with you for political reasons.*

I know.

Do you?

"I apologize." Cannon's humor had fled, and he regarded them with a serious expression. "I appear to have given you both the wrong impression. Regardless of your reasons for being together, the move will have political ramifications." He gave Reaper a pointed look. "As you well know."

"I have never cared about politics, Cannon." Reaper's voice was glacier cool. "As *you* know."

"I hate to be the bearer of bad tidings, but anyone who is with Mercy better learn to care. She's the queen."

Mercy threw her hands in the air. "Enough." She glared at Cannon. "Whatever I choose to do with Reaper is my own damn business. Everyone else can just go float themselves if they think they get a vote, or even an opinion."

"Of course, Your Majesty."

"Don't fucking call me that." Mercy crossed her arms. "You're the king. I'm not stepping up to replace you."

Cannon gave her a smile tinged with regret. "You may not have a choice."

"What the hell does that mean?"

He sighed. "I'm sorry, but I think that's a conversation for another time. I came because I need to speak with Reaper, and I didn't want to risk a telepathic conversation across the length of the ship."

Reaper went still, and Mercy felt her anxiety increase. "What's wrong?" She looked back and forth between them.

"I'd prefer to keep this conversation quiet. We've found a derelict."

"An abandoned vessel?" Mercy didn't see why that was a problem. Salvage rights gave anyone who came across one the right to explore a derelict and even take the ship for their own, if it was more than space junk.

But Cannon's voice was grave, and Reaper's stillness echoed that concern.

"It's a scientific vessel, marked and bearing the appropriate colors. It's just inside the boundaries of the Commonwealth, bordering the shipping lanes that run closest to fringe space."

"A tempting target," Reaper said.

"Exactly."

"You think it's a trap?" Mercy asked.

"The last time such a fat target wandered our direction so easily, it contained a virus that almost killed us all." Cannon's voice was bleak. "So yes, I'm suspicious."

Reaper looked thoughtful. "Salvage is usually Mason's operation."

"True. But I want a larger team on this. Doc is going, as well as Sanah."

"Dem isn't going to like that."

"No, which is just one of the reasons I want you to go. Having his brother along will ease some of Dem's concerns. Having a Killer present will ease some of mine."

Reaper nodded. "Mason's people?"

"We're meeting up with the *Revenant* in a couple of hours. Mason's agreed to wait and go in with you. Sanah and Doc will be under your command."

Reaper looked at Mercy. "Jaxon will stay here. And Dem will need to assign one of his dogs."

"He said if you agreed to go, he would put Haggerty on Mercy's detail."

"Just how long is this going to take?" Mercy felt uneasy, thinking of Reaper being gone.

"We're pretty deep into our territory here." Cannon finished off his coffee, handing the cup back to Reaper. "A day, maybe two for travel. At least another for exploring the derelict."

"Probably two or three," Reaper said. "If we're being cautious."

"Which you will be."

"So a week." The Galactic Standard week was six days long. Mercy was surprised at the depth of disappointment she felt. A week wasn't a particularly long time, yet she felt a chill go through her at the thought of being separated from Reaper. He made her feel safe in a way no one else did.

"I realize the timing is less than ideal." Cannon sounded almost apologetic.

An idea occurred to Mercy. "I've done salvage ops before. With Wolfgang. Maybe I could—"

"Absolutely not."

"No."

Wow, she sent to Reaper on a private thought thread. *You didn't even let me finish.*

I am not taking you back into Commonwealth space, where Veritas might be waiting. Especially given that this derelict might be no more than bait.

But you'll risk Sanah? She told me she used to work for them. They might want her back.

They might. But we know *they want you dead. My answer remains unchanged. You are safer here.*

With a bomber still running around the ship?

Even with an assassin here, yes. Dem is here. Treon is here. Both of them are vigilant. You will have guards.

Angry, she pushed away from the counter. Breakfast no longer held any appeal. Even another cup of coffee wasn't tempting.

"Mercy." Reaper said her name aloud, drawing her gaze to him. His face was still without expression, but there was a glimmer of something in his eyes. *Please.*

Her anger softened to annoyance. *I suppose that's not a word you use often.*

No, it isn't.

She huffed out a breath, looking away. "Fine."

Cannon clapped his hands together. "I'm glad that's settled. Mercy, once Reaper is gone, I believe two young men are waiting eagerly to meet with you."

It was on the tip of her tongue to protest she wasn't in the mood to meet with anyone, when she remembered Max and Kator. She groaned, closing her eyes. *Do I have to?*

They are excited for direction from their new mentor. It isn't really fair to keep them waiting long.

Reaper came around the counter. He leaned in and brushed his lips over hers in an overt show of affection that felt uncharacteristic for him.

Stunned, it took Mercy a minute to rally her scattered thoughts.

You'll be fine, Reaper told her. Amusement tugged at his mouth. "Stay busy. Stay with others. I'll be back soon."

She had never been one of those needy women who couldn't function without someone else around. Her reliance on Reaper to feel secure might not be a good thing. She forced a smile. Time to pick up her independence again. "We can finish our conversation then."

I look forward to it.

To her surprise, so did she.

CHAPTER TWENTY-THREE

*D*espite possible security risks, there was a part of Reaper that looked forward to the separation from Mercy. An uneasy feeling had plagued him from the moment he found her on that space station, and it had only intensified since spending the night with her. A question nagged at him. One he didn't know how to answer.

Sanah said he had feelings for Mercy. She was an empath, and clearly one who understood Killers. But she'd never met a queen before. What if she was wrong? What if he only felt something because of the draw all queens inflicted on the Talented?

He'd been a teenager when Lilith died. He remembered her influence well enough, but his mother had shielded them from more personal contact with the queen. He'd never stood beside her, one on one, and felt the effect of her power. He couldn't shake the idea that Mercy, however compelling he found her, was simply a queen unconsciously exerting her will over him.

It would be the simplest explanation for how

he felt. For the fact that he *felt* anything at all. No queen should have a Killer for a consort. He knew this to his bones, and yet he'd been powerless to resist temptation. A first for him.

Sex was just sex. The physical needs of the body being met. At least, it always had been, before. This time felt different. The connection between them was stronger now, and he found himself thinking things he never had. Imagining a future that had never before been a possibility.

But he couldn't shake the thought of what a queen could do with a man like him. The lives she could destroy. Taking lives was not something he lost sleep over, but Reaper had no desire to be an instrument of punishment or a tool to harm the future of his people.

Mercy isn't like that. The voice whispering in his mind was his own. He scowled. *I can't be sure. She's a queen. When she comes to understand her power, anything could happen.*

You know her better than that. This time, the voice was definitely not his. He glanced over at Sanah, belted into a jumpseat a few spaces down. She was watching him with a knowing look. *Mercy cares for you. She would never abuse her abilities to hurt you.*

Hurting me isn't what I'm concerned about.

Isn't it?

"Boss, you okay?"

Reaper glanced over at Mateo, realizing that either some of his thoughts had leaked through his shields, or the scowl on his face was dark enough to warrant comment. He pushed aside his concerns. There was no place for them here.

"Fine." He glanced again at Sanah. *Leave it alone.*

Her lips thinned as she pressed them into an unhappy line, but she didn't argue with him. Instead, she turned her attention back to whatever conversation she and Doc had been engaged in. Something tedious and scientific that Reaper had been ignoring for most of the trip.

Coming out of the final jump. Titus' voice came just as the stars solidified around them and the ship dropped from otherspace. A welcome chill washed through Reaper, numbing all other emotion. He could see a hunk of metal marring the endless black of space outside the viewport.

Get us closer, he told Titus.

On it, boss.

Reaper felt an odd sense of déjà vu as Titus brought the corvette near the huge frigate. It looked nothing like the space station where they'd recovered Mercy, and there were no signs of life to be felt or seen from the vessel, dead and adrift in space. A Nova-class research frigate, it bore no obvious damage. Nor did he feel the buzz of distant minds. It was, to all appearances, lifeless. So how had it come to be here?

He couldn't shake the sense that somehow, there was a connection.

A Killer's Talent was part of the cognition family of gifts, a kind of prescience that showed him the possibilities of how to kill at any given moment. He'd occasionally experienced other forms of precognition. Rare glimpses of future possibilities that manifested more as feelings than anything more direct. He'd learned to listen to them.

He looked over at his dogs. Titus was in the cockpit, but Zion, Mateo, and Knox waited in the crew compartment. Mateo slouched in one of the jumpseats, his feet stretched across the aisle and propped in the seat across the way. Zion stood beside him, arms crossed. Knox was fiddling with one of his toys. He'd spent the trip prepping several small explosive packets, "just in case".

"Be ready." Reaper nodded to Mateo and Zion. Zion looked down at the other man, his trademark grin in place. He clapped a hand on his shoulder. No doubt he was relieved to be duplicating Mateo's Talent this time out instead of becoming a Killer.

Mason. Reaper reached out to the man commanding *Revenant*, a cruiser with more guns and a much bigger crew. It had made the jump with them, and come out of otherspace beside them. Mason and his people handled salvage for the pirates. By rights, this was his territory and Reaper was the interloper. But no one refused an order from the King. Still, Mason had made it clear he wasn't pleased with the inclusion of Reaper and his dogs.

What do you want, Reaper?

Because he was aware of the other man's resentment, Reaper chose his words carefully. *Ghost should scout the vessel before you board.*

You're here because Cannon ordered it, but I'm in charge. Your dogs don't have my crews' experience with salvage.

No. But I don't believe this is just any dead vessel.

I'm aware of Cannon's concerns. Mason's irritation made the words clipped. *And it isn't anything we don't deal with every fucking day. You do realize that each ship we salvage carries the same risks?* When Reaper didn't reply, he continued. *Besides, we aren't picking up any signs of life. Not with our instruments, and not with Talent. There's no one over there to kill, so what use are you?*

Reaper didn't negotiate or play politics. He was a Core member because he chose to be, and he had the strength and power to hold the position. So did Mason, and apparently he found Reaper's presence a threat to that. It was clear Mason wasn't inclined to listen to him, so he saw no point in continuing the discussion.

You will do as you must.

What the hell does that mean?

Reaper pushed his shields to shut the other man out. Mason was a powerful telepath, but he didn't rival Treon's strength. And blocking Treon had been a game for all of Reaper's life.

He looked at Mateo. "Go."

The other man nodded, his dark eyes serious. Reaper had allowed the conversation to take place openly, so everyone heard it. He didn't need to explain that right now, Mason was launching a shuttle with a boarding team toward the derelict.

But no shuttle could move as quickly as Ghost. Or two Ghosts, since now two spectral duplicates of Zion and Mateo stood side by side. A moment later, they vanished through the hull of the ship, moving towards the derelict. Reaper could have mentally ventured onto the ship himself, but what Ghost's Talent did was different. It allowed him to literally project himself aboard the vessel. He would be able to move and act as if physically there, with all his senses engaged, not just his mind.

"Titus, what have you found?" Reaper had asked his pilot to dig up whatever he could on the Kynerath Corporation, the company which owned the dead ship.

Lots of public information, boss. They're a big time research company in the fields of cloning and new-growth organs and limbs. Word has it they're experimenting with some new anti-aging tech.

Such as?

They want to grow clones and freeze them in stasis. Something about transplanting consciousness from the original body to the clone's. There's a whole spiel on the net designed to get them investors. I guess a hundred and fifty years isn't enough.

It was how long the wealthy could extend their lives through organ transplant and the expensive anti-aging treatments that kept the body youthful. Unfortunately, even those could only be effective for so long.

All of that meant it was very likely this vessel had expensive equipment on board. Cloning equipment that was difficult to procure, and might prove invaluable to the population research Sanah and Doc were doing.

"Kynerath Corp." Doc's mouth twisted into a frown as he said the words. He stood from his seat, peering out the viewport to stare at the slowly drifting ship. "I've been trying to get someone inside one of their research facilities for years, but they have more security than a military base." He gave Reaper a knowing look. "Quite the lucky coincidence that one of their research ships should find its way out here to the fringes."

Exactly.

"I don't believe in coincidence or luck." Doc said this stiffly, as though expecting an argument.

Reaper gave him a long look. "Neither do I."

Both of them watched as Mason's shuttle launched from *Revenant,* making its way across to the derelict.

"*Damashimasu,*" Doc whispered. "Too many of the Core are threatened by what you are. They fail to listen to what you say, too caught up in what you can do."

"Mason is no fool."

"He is right now." Doc wore a flat, serious expression on his best days. Today was worse. "If you think it will get better once they realize the new queen is choosing you as her first consort, you would be wrong." Something moved through his eyes. An emotion Reaper couldn't hope to identify. "Be very careful, Nikolos."

"No one has said Mercy is choosing me to be her anything."

Doc snapped a glare his way. "I have eyes, don't I? Ears to listen with?" He gestured back to where Sanah sat. She'd been giving them space, quietly speaking with Knox. "I may not be an empath, but I am quite observant."

Reaper didn't know what to say to that. He considered and discarded several options he might have used with anyone else. But it wasn't wise to make an enemy of the man most likely to treat him if he were injured. Silence was best.

They watched as Mason's shuttle formed a seal with the ship's airlock.

"She could do worse," Doc said grudgingly.

"Ghost, update," Reaper said, ignoring him.

"It's all quiet, boss." Ghost spoke aloud from behind him. His eyes were closed as he reported back what his projected self observed. "No bodies so far. The ship does have power, but only to emergency systems. Basic life support, evac pods, and the infirmary. Pods are all accounted for, so no one left the ship that way. Everything else is down. No propulsion."

"Down why?"

"Not sure. Zion's trying to access logs now."

By now Mason's men would be boarding the ship.

"You are about to have company."

"Copy."

Reaper frowned. The feeling that something was wrong intensified. It was premature of Mason to have boarded the vessel before they had confirmation of exactly what they would be walking into. Why was the ship without power? Where was the crew?

"Ghost, check the labs."

"I'm there now. No power."

Moving around Ghost and Zion carefully, Sanah came to stand beside Doc. "No power to the labs could be dangerous," she said in a low voice. "Some things need to be kept in stasis for the safety of anyone working with them."

Before Reaper could pass this on to Ghost, his dog spoke again. "Nothing here, boss. I mean *nothing*. It looks like this place has never been used. Just a bunch of brand new equipment and empty shelves. It's creepy."

"I've accessed the logbooks," Zion said. "According to this, they were on their way from Charon to Ocium."

That made no sense. Uneasy, Reaper tried to remember the last time he'd looked at a Commonwealth star chart. "Ocium is in the Trillium Cluster, isn't it?"

"It is," Doc agreed.

On the far side of the Commonwealth. As far in the opposite direction as it was possible to get. There was no reason for this ship to be here. None at all, except to lure the pirates to it. How it had come to be here and why it didn't have power, propulsion, or a crew became irrelevant.

Reaper reached out to Mason.

Get your people out. He was expecting an argument, but Mason took a long time to answer.

I can't raise them. Not with comms or Talent. What the hell is going on?

I don't know. Nothing good. Reaper looked back at Ghost and Zion. "Mason's lost contact with his people. Find them."

When neither man responded, Reaper turned and walked to them. "Zion. Mateo."

Both men stood still and silent, eyes closed. If not for the fact that they were standing, they might have been sleeping peacefully. He brushed against their minds and felt…nothing. It was as if they were empty shells.

"Doc."

The doctor was already moving, pulling a portable scanner from his pocket.

"What's happening?" Sanah asked.

"Do you feel anything from either of them?" Emotions weren't the same as thoughts. Maybe an empath would pick up something he couldn't.

"Conflict." Sanah looked at Reaper. "I feel a sense of peace from both of them, but also fear. It doesn't make sense."

"None of this makes sense."

"Physically, they're fine." Doc studied the results of his scan. "Slightly elevated blood pressure and heart rate, but that could be a physical response to the strain of using Mateo's Talent. I've never scanned him before while he's used it."

Reaper. Reaper didn't need Sanah's empathy to hear the anger in Mason's voice. *What is on that ship?*

I don't know, but I am going to find out. Can your AI disengage that shuttle from the airlock? Ships as large as *Revenant* almost always employed an AI to manage and connect ship systems. Usually they could maintain remote control of shuttles and dropships in emergency situations.

Yes. What do you want me to do?

There's only one airlock, and I need it. Reaper gripped Sanah's arm. "You and Doc stay here and monitor them."

She searched his face. "You're going over there? Are you sure that's a good idea?"

"It's why I'm here. Very little in this universe can truly threaten a Killer." He glanced at Knox. "If you lose contact with me for longer than a few minutes, get everyone out of here."

As he'd expected, his dog wasn't happy with

this order. "Boss, you can't go over there alone. Let me go with you. Titus can stay here."

You are both staying here. Reaper took a moment to make sure his words were on a tight thread, just between him and Knox. *My brother's wife is here. I will not leave her unprotected. Titus is piloting the ship. You will guard Sanah, Doc, and the others.*

Boss...

Reaper didn't bother responding. *Titus, get the dropship prepped.*

He wasn't going to risk everyone on board by connecting the corvette directly to the derelict. A Viking dropship was connected to the ship's undercarriage for planetfall when the corvette remained in orbit. It would work just as well as a shuttle.

"Nik," Sanah said softly. "Be careful."

He spared her a glance. "I'm getting our people back.

CHAPTER TWENTY-FOUR

By the time the dropship docked with the derelict, any feelings of worry Reaper had over his dogs or Sanah were distant, meaningless emotion. It was comfortable, being the unfeeling Killer. Far preferable to experiencing emotions he had no idea how to process. Cannon would probably have some typically annoying observation about that, but fortunately the king was not here.

He pushed ahead with his mind, mentally searching the ship. He found no trace of his dogs, or Mason's men. It was as though they'd ceased to exist. Like the crew that had so mysteriously disappeared. Reaper no longer believed that. Someone, or something, was aboard this vessel.

As with the space station weeks ago, surprise was not on his side. There was no way to quietly dock with the ship, to wait for the airlock to pressurize. He half expected something to happen when he boarded, but nothing did. Stepping out of the airlock, it looked exactly like the dead ship it pretended to be. The barest hint of light reflected from the ceiling, a permanent, natural illumination built into the nano-graph of the structure. Reaper passed his hand over one wall to be sure, but no map lit up beneath the touch. Power was still off. But the air remained breathable, circulating through filters. The temperature, while low, was warm enough to support life. Gravity was working.

Convenient for whoever was here.

Reaper didn't plan to search deck by deck and room by room. He made his way directly to the command deck. He was done with games. With no engines or propulsion, the stabilizers also appeared to be out, which meant the ship tilted at an awkward slant. It wouldn't have been a problem without the gravity generators, but it made for a challenge with them. It was nothing he couldn't handle, but in a fight it would add a challenging environmental element.

The command deck was empty. He could see both his corvette and *Revenant* through the viewport, reminding him to send Knox and Titus an update as he looked over the frigate's controls. He'd never been aboard a *Nova*-class ship before, but it wasn't too difficult to find the basics.

He sent a quick mental probe out, but still found nothing. No sign of either his men or Mason's. There was one entrance to the command deck, and an emergency hatch. He sealed it with a portable gravitational generator exactly like the one that had held Mercy captive when he'd found her. With only one way in or out, he triggered the ship's start up sequence. It didn't surprise him at all when it actually worked.

The engines spooling up made the deck vibrate beneath his feet. Basic propulsion came back on-line, and the ship righted itself, a dizzying tilt that put everything back as it should be.

It wouldn't be long now. Reaper stood in the center of the room, and waited.

He felt her before he saw her. He knew it would be someone powerful, perhaps even as powerful as Treon, to pull off such a large scale mental illusion. Making a ship of this size appear empty when it wasn't, both physically and mentally, was no small trick. He let the ice take him until his inner self reflected the cold vacuum of space. So deeply into the Killer that not even surprise registered when the hatch opened, and a small figure stepped through. A girl.

She wore a basic flight suit, the kind that could offer a short period of protection if a pilot ended up adrift in space without power. But no helmet covered her head, and her face was young. Reaper placed her at barely fifteen. Perhaps even younger. Curiosity filled her face as she eased into the room, enhancing the child-like impression.

Watching the girl approach, Reaper was struck by two things. One, how closely she resembled Mercy. The bone structure, bronze skin, dark hair and green eyes were a striking and familiar combination. Two, the power that exuded from her was so strong it washed heat through him, chasing away the chill that was as much a part of him as breathing. He felt it leech away, was powerless to stop it. The harder he tried, the faster it seemed to leave him.

For the first time in his life, he could not call

upon his Talent. He couldn't see how to kill her. He realized he didn't *want* to kill her. He felt an instant desire to please her. If she didn't desire him to kill, he wouldn't. It was that simple.

She came close enough to invade his personal space, a daunting move for most people, but especially for someone as young as she appeared. She didn't flinch, didn't seem afraid at all. She frowned as she studied him, and a sudden desire to do whatever it took to make her happy flooded him. Reaper clenched his teeth, fighting the pull he felt.

There was no doubt in his mind. This girl was a queen.

He fought to access his Talent, the exertion breaking a cold sweat over his skin.

The girl glanced to the side, and the moment her regard left him, he felt the faintest sense of control returning. But it wasn't enough.

"I was expecting more," she said, sounding confused.

More what? Reaper followed her gaze and saw a familiar scarred face. The face that haunted Mercy's dreams. Willem Frain stepped through the hatch and fully into the room. Reaper waited for the expected wash of cold, but it never came. Frain had a permanent place on his mental kill list. Seeing him should have brought his Talent to the surface, but nothing happened.

"Even the vaunted Killers are powerless before a true queen," Frain said. He favored Reaper with a mocking smile as he crossed to stand beside the girl. "What do you think?" This question he directed at Reaper. He lifted a strand of her hair, fingering it lightly. "An improvement, wouldn't you say? It took some doing, overwriting her DNA with Mercy's, but we couldn't wait around for a new clone to grow. We needed a functioning queen now. Yesterday."

Reaper was no scientist, but something about that wasn't right. It made no sense.

"You cannot create a queen." He knew this; the pirates' own scientists had been trying for years to make Talented children in a lab, but Talent required the mental connection of child to mother – which developed in the womb – to nurture and grow. Well, with the rare exception of whatever Mercy had done to her friend that had awakened latent Talent. He knew Doc and Sanah were studying that closely, but they had no answers yet.

Willem raised an eyebrow. "True. But you *can* clone one. That is, cloning was the basis for what we did. We already had a queen, you see. One created and cloned from various genetic samples, implanted in a Talented mother until birth. But the samples were old, degraded. Everything eventually degrades over centuries, and not all of the old stasis units were intact when we found them. We did the best we could, but the queen we produced was unstable." He favored the girl with a look that Reaper could only describe as possessive. "It became more obvious as she grew. We had to put her in stasis until we could find a solution. New genetic material to use." He smiled, looking back at Reaper. "How fortunate that we found Mercy."

Not the word Reaper would have chosen. It was odd, but being in the girl's presence seemed to split his thoughts from his desires. He could think for himself, but he could not seem to act on those thoughts. Every tiny inflection from her inspired an answering emotion within him, and those emotions dictated what he could and could not do. He wondered if what he was afforded him some protection, or if all people experienced this dichotomy when a queen unleashed her full presence.

Perhaps that was why only a Killer had a chance to truly kill a queen. If he could just figure out how to override his emotions, he might be able to act. He didn't need his Talent to kill. Something that others often forgot.

The girl sat in one of the empty chairs. "Are we done here? Can we finally leave?" She sounded like a bored teenager.

Willem stroked a hand over her hair. "Yes, Rani. We are finally done here. I think we have everything we need." He paused, favoring Reaper with a cutting smile. "Well, we do have one more thing we must do, but then we are free to leave."

Reaper stared back at Frain without wavering. He imagined severing his spine. There were quicker ways to kill him, surely, but that one held a particular satisfaction. And without his Talent, he was free to imagine whatever he wished.

Frain's smile faded. "Rani, perhaps it would be best if you told this man your expectations. Reaper, is it? Supposed to strike fear in the hearts of your enemies, I suppose?"

"No. It's just a name they gave me." Reaper tried to reach out to Titus and Knox, to tell them to leave and take *Revenant* with them. He found he could not do even that much. It was as though an impenetrable wall separated him from his Talent.

The girl frowned at him. "That's a funny name. Who gave it to you?"

Reaper switched his gaze to her. When her face paled and fear crept into her eyes, he knew that his expression reflected what he wanted to do, whether he was the Killer right now or not.

"Everyone," he said.

"Enough." Frain's hand fell onto Rani's shoulder and tightened there. "Rani, tell him."

She had to take a deep breath before she spoke. "You will only access your Talent or act violently if I order it." Her voice was infused with more than words. Her Talent and will reached inside of Reaper until his subconscious mind agreed with her. His body relaxed.

"Excellent," Frain said, sounding insufferably pleased. "Let's get the rest of our visitors under your influence, my dear, and then we can be done with this façade and go."

Words still came easily to Reaper despite everything. "Where?"

Frain's smile grew again. "Home," he said. "We're taking you home. You should be pleased, Reaper. Veritas is finally done fighting against you pirates. We're going to accept you into the fold."

ercy spent the first few days of Reaper's absence learning about the administrative side of pirate society. It seemed impossible, but the pirates had their own government and economy, like any other system. Cannon spoke with her for hours, explaining exactly what he did as King, and what the Core did as the balance to that. He went deeper into the power hierarchy, trying to tell her how a King could never replace what a Queen did for them. But Mercy avoided that subject with the skill of someone who'd managed to keep her own secrets for years. She asked what it meant to be sponsoring two boys on the cusp of adulthood, and ignored any references to taking power as queen. Cannon seemed to understand that she wasn't ready for that yet, so he didn't push. Thank the Mother.

She'd barely finished her conversation with Cannon when Treon stopped by for a visit that seemed impromptu at first, but definitely wasn't. She had to admit to a certain wariness where both of Reaper's brothers were concerned. Dem unnerved her on a primal level. She still didn't understand why he frightened her so much, when Reaper didn't. Maybe because she knew he'd hunted her once.

But Treon bothered her in a way that was more difficult to pinpoint. Was it his arrogance? Maybe, but she didn't think so. She'd known plenty of arrogant smugglers in her time.

"Treon," she said after she let him in and he still hadn't admitted the reason for his visit. "What can I do for you?"

He gave her a self-deprecating smile she didn't believe for an instant. "It is more what I can do for you, I think. We should talk."

"About?" She couldn't help but be wary.

"My brother, and consorts."

Surprised and a little appalled, Mercy laughed. "What? Does everyone know we slept together?"

"Secrets don't stay secret for long on this ship." Treon waved a dismissive hand. He sat in one of her chairs, making himself comfortable. "For all that he is my brother, Reaper is not good relationship material, particularly for a queen."

"Because he's a Killer."

"Yes." Treon sighed. "Has anyone explained consorts to you yet?"

"I know what they are. I can't remember what world started the practice, but consorts are basically when a relationship has multiple husbands and wives."

"I think the strictest definition depends on the world or colony, and their laws. But our society has embraced this practice whole heartedly. It has only become more prevalent in the time since the virus."

Mercy thought about that for a minute.

"You don't have enough women. I'm guessing at least some women will end up with consorts instead of a single husband or wife."

He inclined his head. "Exactly. It is a practice encouraged since we lost so many, though we still have those who prefer single pairings. But consorts have another layer here: power."

She frowned.

"Allow me to explain," said Treon. "Our hierarchy is largely decided by power. Who has it and wields it most effectively. It is how positions are won and kept. Carefully chosen alliances can help propel one much further than one could otherwise manage alone."

"I know all of this." Mercy waved an impatient hand. He was just repeating things she and Cannon talked about.

"Consorts," Treon said, emphasizing the word and ignoring her protest, "are a part of that. It is a contract of commitment, and all who look at, say, a woman and her consorts, will look at the power each of them hold as a whole."

Ah. That went beyond what Cannon had shared with her. Mercy sat down. "You're saying if this hypothetical woman surrounded herself with powerful consorts, people would look at her as being more dangerous than if she were alone."

"Just so. Our mother used this strategy quite effectively. For her consorts, she chose two Killers and a powerful telepath. Collectively, our family was one of the few largely safe from Lilith's machinations and threats, because even the Queen had reason to fear what they could accomplish."

"I see." Mercy's brow furrowed as she thought this over. She had never seriously considered a multiple partner arrangement. If she was being honest, she'd never considered *any* arrangement, ever. Her life staying low and largely on the run was not conducive to trust and romantic partners.

She'd had exactly one semi-serious relationship, when she was twenty-one. He was a smuggler – no real surprise there – and their runs often overlapped. It was fun, at first. Hadrian loved adventure. He loved the romantic aspects of defying Commonwealth law and helping out colonists at the same time. Young, good looking, he'd been something of a thrill seeker, and for a while Mercy had thought she loved him.

But then they'd happened to be in dock at Befarr together, enjoying a little down time between runs. It was a remote water system that exported water to half the Commonwealth, sporting a few resorts on its islands for weary space jockeys. It started out idyllic. Sun, sand, swimming, and sex. On the third day, a news bulletin hit the waves about a local man suspected of being Talented. Hadrian spent half an hour ranting about what a threat people like that were, how he couldn't understand why they wouldn't just turn themselves in rather than live with being a danger to everyone around them. What had been the best vacation Mercy ever had turned into an excruciating nightmare. She couldn't run right after his outburst. She'd had to go on, pretending everything was fine to allay any suspicions. Letting him touch her, even though she couldn't stand being in the same room with him.

Finding out he'd been cheating with several other women just gave her the excuse she needed to break things off. After that, Mercy had avoided entanglements.

Since being with Reaper, she'd allowed herself to think about the possibility of a future. She was both anxious and excited to see him again, to talk. Maybe she was jumping into things, but she didn't think so. It felt like she'd known Reaper for much longer than just a few weeks. And she'd never felt so close to anyone, not even Atrea. Sharing her thoughts with Reaper added a level of intimacy level she'd only experienced with her mother, though with Reaper it was an entirely different experience.

"Okay," she said after a long silence. Treon had patiently waited while she worked everything through, saying nothing. "I still don't get it. It sounds to me like a smart woman chooses her consorts carefully, not just for how she feels about them, but so the family will be protected and safe."

"True," said Treon.

"Not everyone is going to be happy to have a queen around, after Lilith."

"Also true."

"So, whether I have a husband or consorts, I'm going to want to make sure we are a really strong and powerful unit together."

"Again," Treon said, "true."

"So what's the problem? Everyone here is afraid of Reaper. It's clear he's respected, and I know he's a member of the Core. Why wouldn't he be a good choice?"

"Because, as a queen, you need consorts, not a single husband. Unless you are absolutely opposed to the idea of having multiple partners, in which case I fear for your future."

Mercy drummed her fingers on the arm of her chair.

"I haven't really thought about it yet," she said. "Consorts, that is. I mean, Reaper's discussed it a little, and we're supposed to talk when he gets back. But I didn't really seriously think about multiple partners."

"Well, trust me," said Treon. "You need consorts. They will solidify your position, and make you and any children you have safe. Particularly any young girls who may or may not inherit what you are."

She shook her head. "Even if that's all true, I'm still not seeing why Reaper is a bad choice."

Treon sighed. "Because Reaper wanted to kill me when I suggested seducing you, and you weren't even sleeping together yet. I am also his brother, arguably one of the few people in his life normally safe from his instincts to kill."

Mercy stared at him, pretty sure she'd just figured out what bothered her about him so much, and it did have to do with his arrogance. "You were going to try and seduce me?"

He waved a hand as if it didn't matter. "As a way of coercing your connection to us as a people. For a moment I thought he might kill *me*. Do you know he hasn't looked at me like that since I was six years old, and he was eight?" Treon looked away from her for the first time, his gaze distant. "He used to practice his Talent on me, until our mother realized what was happening and told him one didn't stalk family. Or plan out how best to murder them."

Mercy could honestly say she was struck speechless. She wasn't sure if she was horrified, or horribly amused, or both. It felt a bit inappropriate, given how genuinely distressed Treon seemed. He leaned forward.

"I dislike knowing my brother actively wants to kill me, so I withdrew the suggestion immediately. I do wonder, though, if you have any idea what you're getting yourself into."

"You think Reaper will kill any other consorts I choose."

"I think it is a very strong possibility. It is why Dem and Sanah married and chose to remain a closed unit."

"That's why you came here," she said. "To tell me this."

Treon inclined his head.

Mercy didn't know what to say. Reaper was the one to tell her she needed consorts. She hadn't given it a lot of thought yet, but she was now. Why would he suggest it, if what Treon said was true? Honestly, she wasn't at all sure a multiple-partner relationship was for her, anyway. Hell, she had yet to succeed at a single partner relationship. Wouldn't more people make it even more complicated?

To get a woman's perspective, she visited Vashti. Of course, that was with a certain amount of wariness. Mercy was growing fonder of her aunt every day, but she couldn't say that she entirely trusted her yet.

Vashti invited her inside quarters more spacious than Mercy's own, and served tea to drink. It was good, but Mercy was too restless to make small talk. She got right to the point, setting aside the pretty cup with flowers embossed along the rim.

"What do you think of consorts?"

Vashti raised one elegant brow. "For you?"

"Is this the part where you tell me I need them to solidify my power base and keep my future family safe?"

"I see you've been speaking to someone. Cannon?"

"Treon."

"How interesting. He doesn't normally concern himself with the interpersonal relationships of others. Or at least, others outside his family."

Mercy huffed a laugh. "Please. Don't bother pretending you don't know I slept with Reaper."

"Are you choosing him for your first consort?"

"I don't know what I'm doing." And if that wasn't the understatement of the millennium, she didn't know what was. "Did you have consorts?"

"Yes. Three."

"And?"

Vashti set down her tea. "What are you really asking me, Mercy?"

"I don't know. Was it hard? Do you regret it?" Mercy took a deep breath. "I never even thought I'd get married, much less have consorts. Treon thinks Reaper will kill anyone else I choose."

"And Reaper?"

"He's the one who first told me I should have multiple consorts." Mercy still wasn't sure how to feel about that.

Vashti stared at her with penetrating green eyes that saw far too keenly. Mercy picked up her tea again and sipped it for something to do.

"You wonder if he really cares for you, to have suggested such a thing."

"I don't know what I wonder right now. It's all too new." She looked away, her face burning. She fiddled with the warming feature on her cup. "I think I'm in love with him." Mercy said this very softly.

"That's lovely, dear." Vashti smiled, huge and genuine. "I would want nothing less for you. Love is one of the most magical experiences the universe has to offer."

"But?"

"No." Vashti reached across the table and grabbed one of Mercy's hands, squeezing it. "Don't put qualifiers on it. Don't let others fill you with fear. I have never seen Reaper act with anyone as he does with you. Never. I've known him all his life. He loved his mother. In his way, he loves his brothers and his niece. But he has no idea what romantic love is, or what it means." Vashti patted her hand. "You'll need to be patient with him. It's going to take a long time for him to embrace it fully and incorporate it into who he is."

"So, you agree with Treon? That he'll kill anyone else I choose?"

"I didn't say that." Vashti's eyes took on a calculating look. "For all their similarities, Reaper and Dem are two very different people. And Nikolos is very self-aware. He knows himself well enough to understand that it will be a long time before he's able to be the other half of your relationship."

"I'm not sure I follow."

"Reaper loves you, Mercy, but he doesn't understand it yet. I wish you had more time, but that isn't how our society works. We are an immediate people. We take what we want, when we want it. We are desperate to have more children. We are desperate for a Queen who will lead us away from the violent traditions of the past so we might survive long enough to have those children. At the same time, many of us are afraid of what that will mean." Vashti gave a heavy sigh. "Change is hard, and always a risk. Some will do anything to try and prevent it. Reaper is right. You will need multiple consorts. He knows this. He knows you will need them not just for politics, but on a personal level."

Mercy just shook her head. "I don't need consorts to keep me safe. Reaper has dogs."

"Listen to me for a moment. I had three consorts." Vashti looked down at her hands. Pain etched lines deeply into her face. "I loved each of them. Darius was my first consort. He was a powerful precog. His gift of foresight was so strong, he won every battle he fought and never lost a single ship or man. My sister wanted him for herself, but he only saw me." A soft smile lit her face. "We loved each other deeply. But that love and his Talent were not enough to save his life. He made an enemy of Lilith when he rejected her, and she had him killed."

"I'm sorry."

Vashti shook her head. "It was nothing I could prove, of course. But I knew. I had two other consorts, both powerful men. Leaders in their day. One died in an accident. His ship went into otherspace and never came out. The other was killed in the arena. A fight that was supposed to end at first blood went to the death. I watched it happen. Lilith worked the crowd into a frenzy, knowing what it would do."

"What a bitch."

Vashti gave her a sad smile. "I loved all of my consorts, Mercy. I couldn't have loved them more deeply if I'd loved them each in their own time or turn, instead of all at once. We never had any children. I had five pregnancies, and each ended in miscarriage. After the last, I was barren."

"Consorts didn't save you."

"Oh yes, they did. Lilith couldn't stand what she thought of as competition. I was her sister, and no queen, but she still feared me. She feared the children I might have. And she resented me for Darius and a hundred other little sibling rivalries. By my count, she tried to have me killed at least six times. My consorts protected me. It was the real reason she killed Darius. And that ship that disappeared into otherspace? I was supposed to be commanding it. I wasn't on it because we suspected the trip was a trap of some kind and Arturo insisted he be the one to go in my place. When I refused, he used his Talent to put me to sleep and went anyway."

Vashti took a moment to pour them each more tea, though Mercy's cup wasn't yet empty. Her hand was steady, despite the emotion gleaming in her eyes.

"Dogs or bodyguards serve a purpose. I would never say they don't. But they are no replacement for someone who loves you, who would sacrifice anything to keep you safe."

Mercy was appalled. "You want me to have consorts so they'll be willing to die for me?"

There was nothing gentle in Vashti's eyes now. "You are a queen, Mercy. You have no idea yet how necessary you are for our survival, but you will eventually understand. Consorts are essential. You aren't just important to our future. You are vital to us having one at all."

alking to teenagers was torture. If she had to listen to one more rambling explanation that didn't actually answer her questions, Mercy was going to scream. Somewhere, she was sure, the old Wolf was laughing his ass off. He had to be. More than once, he'd spoken the fateful words "Someday you'll be having this conversation from my side". He'd been right, and sooner than Mercy ever expected.

Were all teenagers this difficult to communicate with? Had she been? Given all of her secrets at the time, she'd probably been worse. As she listened to Kator ramble on without actually saying anything, Mercy decided enough was enough. She sat forward and slapped her hands onto the desk.

They were sitting in Cannon's office, which he'd graciously donated so she could speak with her new – she didn't even know what to call them. Followers? No, that didn't feel right. She was sitting at Cannon's desk, an antique if she wasn't mistaken. Probably lifted from some high-ranking officer in the Commonwealth Navy. Max and

Kator sat across from her, and for the past hour had managed to avoid giving her a single straight answer. It was unreal.

Kator fell silent at her movement, and he and Max exchanged uncertain looks.

"Forget about that," Mercy said, forcing herself to smile as she waved a dismissive hand. "Let me ask you this: why me?"

"Why you?" Max looked like he didn't understand the question, which had Mercy biting back a sigh.

All she wanted to do was take some time to herself and process the information she'd been given in the past few days. So she could be prepared when Reaper returned, for whatever that conversation entailed. Instead, she was trying to fulfill her obligation to these two, and it wasn't going as smoothly as she'd hoped.

"Yes," she said. "You have a lot of people you could have chosen to swear yourselves to. People a lot more experienced than I am. But you two chose me. Why?"

Neither boy moved to answer, and Mercy thought maybe she'd actually stumped them. Then Kator shifted in his seat.

"Well," he ventured hesitantly, "you're the Queen."

Max nodded emphatically. "Exactly."

Mercy just stared at them. "That's it?"

"Er...what else would it be?" Max looked at Kator again, but the other boy shrugged.

Mercy closed her eyes for a few precious seconds. When she opened them again, both boys were looking at her with identical awkward, earnest expressions that left a sinking feeling in her gut.

"If you guys just picked me because I'm a queen, I'm not sure what I can do for you."

"What do you mean?" Panic flashed in Kator's dark eyes. "You can help us, right? I don't want to learn mechanics. I want to be a pilot!"

Finally, a real answer. "So, go be a pilot."

"You don't understand." Max's shoulders slumped. "That's not how it works."

She looked back and forth between them, wishing Cannon had explained a little more to her than "You're responsible for them now. Mentor them. Sponsor them. Figure out what they want and how hard they're willing to work for it." She wished, not for the first time, that Reaper was here.

When both boys sat looking as morose as if she'd kicked them, she leaned forward. "Well, someone better explain it to me."

"It's like this." Kator looked like he was struggling with how to put it into words. "Max's family is powerful. His Uncle's a Core member, another is a dog, he's related to the king. So he gets to train as a pilot."

"Whether I want to or not," Max muttered.

Kator pointed to himself. "Until me, my family didn't have anyone born with a powerful Talent in years. My Dad can barely float a wrench with his telekinesis. He can't talk to people telepathically unless we're in the same room. My telekinesis is powerful, but that isn't enough on its own. I have to prove myself."

"What do you mean?"

"I come from a family of mechanics and engineers. We fix stuff. We build stuff. So I automatically get assigned to learn those skills."

There was definitely something she was missing here. "Those are good skills to learn."

"Maybe somewhere else." Kator looked down, dejected. "But a mechanic doesn't get many opportunities to do stuff."

Mercy bit back a laugh. She knew a lot of mechanics and ship techs who would argue against that statement, vehemently. She looked at Max. "Define *stuff.*"

"He means like fighting, taking ships. Bringing valuables back to the fleet. Stuff that gets you noticed." He jerked his thumb at Kator. "He doesn't just want to be a pilot, he wants to be a dog. He has to get special training if he ever hopes to earn that place, and to get special training, you have to get noticed, or…"

"Or?" But Mercy was pretty sure she finally knew where this conversation was headed.

"Or be sponsored by someone powerful enough to get you the training."

She sat back and contemplated both boys. She thought about the first time she met Max, and his conversation with Cannon about a secret project. She thought about Kator setting Max up and their fight in the arena. Their body language since then had been anything but antagonistic. Sometime between the arena and swearing themselves to her, the two boys had put aside years of bullying and antagonism. They were at least allies now, if not friends. How did that happen?

"Kator." He looked up at her. "You've spent your whole life bullying Max, until now. Why?"

He looked away, ashamed. "I was jealous. He had everything I wanted, and he didn't even care. He just kept hanging around my engineering classes, taking notes, being the teacher's pet even though he didn't have to be there."

"Max, you don't want to be a pilot?"

"Sure. It's useful. But I like messing with stuff. Taking it apart to see how it works. Making it better. I needed to know more to do what I wanted, so I crashed his classes. Even though it got me beat up a lot." There was no animosity in what he was saying, just a mumbled statement of fact.

"Sorry," Kator said. He sounded genuine.

Max shrugged, like it was all forgotten. Mercy wasn't sure she'd be as forgiving in the same situation. It impressed her that a kid Max's age could be.

"After the arena," Max said, "we started talking. We realized we both want the same thing, and working against each other wasn't going to get it. But you could." He looked at Mercy with shining eyes. "You could get Kator flight sim time. You could even get him the type of training to help him become a dog."

Mercy raised an eyebrow. "And you? What do you want?"

Max shifted his eyes away from hers. "I need some specialized equipment for a project. Really difficult to find stuff."

"*Dangerous* stuff," Kator muttered. Mercy was surprised, again, that Max had apparently shared so much with the other boy. She upgraded their relationship in her mind from allies to friends.

"What's dangerous about it?"

Max sent Kator an accusing look. "Nothing much," he said. "You just have to be really careful with it, that's all."

"What is it?"

"I can't tell you."

Mercy favored Max with a smile. The kind of smile that had him scrunching down in his seat as though to avoid her gaze. "Try again," she said. "And remember that if you want my help, you're not getting it if I don't know *exactly* what you're doing."

He mumbled something she didn't quite catch.

"What was that? Louder, please." She paused. "Or maybe I'm going about this all wrong."

She'd spent this conversation reveling in her new shields, in how airtight they were and how easy it was to keep her own thoughts locked down. Now she tested Reaper's assertion that she could read thoughts with her shields still firmly in place. Especially if the other person was thinking loudly enough.

Max was thinking very hard about what he didn't want to tell her. She stared at him as the thoughts crystallized in her mind. Just stared. She was pretty sure her face was going pale as faint worry quickly escalated to outright fear. Fear for Max, fear for the entire ship. Playing with jump drives was something even serious mechanics took every precaution doing.

"Does Cannon know about this?" Her throat was dry. Max had gone pale as well, but probably because he realized from her face that she'd picked up what he was thinking. He nodded, then shook his head.

"Which is it?"

"He knows what I'm working on. Theoretically. It's supposed to be a mock up, and theoretical. He doesn't know I'm asking you for the parts."

"Because he told you absolutely not."

Max's pale face told her everything she needed to know. She stood up so fast it sent both boys scrambling to their feet.

"If you swore yourself to me because you thought I'd get you what you needed to create a portable jump drive inside some hold on this ship, you are going to be sadly disappointed." Mercy was pleased her voice came out sounding calm. She'd done enough ship repair, talked to enough mechanics over the years, to know exactly how dangerous those components could be. To have heard horror stories.

Every ship with a jump drive took certain risks using it. Every time they entered otherspace they ran the risk of never coming out again. Any captain worth a piss had their drive inspected in every space port, just to be sure and catch any anomalies, errors, or bad components before something catastrophic happened. As long as regular maintenance and inspection took place, jump drives were relatively safe to use. But it only took one mistake to lose an entire ship and crew. One miscalculation to be lost forever. Building one aboard a ship was idiocy.

"I am issuing an order here and now: under no circumstances are you to proceed with building a working model aboard this ship, or any other."

"But—"

"No."

"If you'd just listen to the possibilities. Fighter-class ships equipped with jump drives could—"

"Max." He stopped, his face dejected. Mercy took a deep breath. "I'm not saying you can't ever build one. Just not on a ship. On a planet some-where. In a workshop designed for building jump drives. With the right tools and the right training." And the right supervision, but she figured that didn't need to be said. "I won't get you the parts. But I will make sure you get the training."

Max looked up, a glimmer of hope in his eyes.

"Wolfgang is trained in jump mechanics. I'll speak to him about giving you lessons."

"Really?"

"Don't expect it to be easy. He's a hard taskmaster, even when the subject isn't something that could get you and thousands of people around you killed. And I want your word you won't try to build one aboard a ship. Ever."

"I swear. Never."

Mercy eyed him for a long time, but it felt like he was telling the truth. She switched her gaze over to Kator.

"I'll get you sim time." She paused. "And I'll look into the rest." To prove it, she reached out to the dog standing outside the door. Jaxon was on duty today. But to her surprise, she didn't feel his presence. She'd gotten used to the feel of his mind in the past few days. She expanded her reach, but still didn't find him.

She'd noticed that when he wasn't with her, he visited the infirmary a lot. At first, she'd thought it was to sweet talk Nayla with Doc being gone, but the dog rarely spoke to the young woman. In fact, he spent a lot of time just sort of hanging around the area cordoned off for Atrea. Mercy had meant to ask him about it, but she'd been too wrapped up in her own thoughts lately.

Surely Jax wouldn't abandon his post just to visit Atrea. Reaper would have his ass when he found out. She frowned at the two boys.

"I need to go check something."

"Sure," said Max. "Can we, um, go?"

"Yeah. I'll be in touch about things." She gave Max a pointed look. "And you remember everything we talked about."

"Yes ma'am."

The two boys escaped quickly, chatting excitedly together. Mercy followed them out the door, but turned the opposite way down the hall. Getting to the infirmary these days was a bit more complicated than taking a lift. As long as they were still repairing the explosive damage, it meant taking a lift at the other end of the very large ship, or using emergency ladders.

She felt odd moving through the ship alone. She hadn't been alone since boarding *Nemesis,* especially since the bomb. A dog shadowed her everywhere. But not today. An uneasy feeling washed heat up her spine. She realized she'd moved down several corridors and not run into a single person. That, too, was unusual. She reached out further with her mind, probing.

Cannon?

Vashti?

And, because if anyone would be sure to hear her, it would be him. *Treon?*

Nothing. A resounding silence answered her. The unease turned into full blown adrenaline. She took a couple of calming breaths. Whatever concern she felt, there was no need to panic yet. Maybe everyone had been called to some kind of emergency meeting…and she'd either missed the summons, or not been invited. And somehow, Jax had failed to tell her before he left for it.

No, that didn't sound plausible at all.

Not sure what else to do, she continued to the infirmary. It was the most likely place she'd find Wolfgang, at least. And, in stasis or not, Atrea was there. Mercy picked up her pace to a jog, feeling the whole time like she was one step away from something disastrous happening. Another explosion. A Killer jumping out from the shadows. Reaper seemed concerned about the man she'd met as a child. He was looking into it because apparently no Killer ever gave up on a contract.

But that still wouldn't explain the emptiness of the halls, or the way everyone had fallen silent. She made it all the way to the emergency ladders and still hadn't run into anyone. She stopped mentally reaching out, because now she was afraid of what she might find. She needed to regroup. Hopefully with Wolfgang. The old Wolf would know what to do.

But when she entered the infirmary, it was empty. Nayla wasn't there. Nor was Wolfgang or Jax. Only Atrea, silent in her stasis cocoon. Mercy stood beside her for a few minutes, thinking.

What the hell was going on?

Mercy. The mental voice was familiar and soft.

Tamari?

The little girl appeared beside her, throwing her arms around Mercy's neck, practically choking her. Her small body trembled. *Papa won't answer me. The scary man and the mean lady won't let him. I'm scared!*

Mercy put her arms around the little girl and held her tight. "What scary man?"

The one who came on the ship with Uncle Nik.

Reaper's back? Confusion and hurt warred within her that he would return without letting her know. She pushed it aside. Something else was going on here.

Papa told me to wait. He told Blaine to wait with me, but then Blaine left! Rasa and I got tired of waiting. We went to find Papa, but he's with the scary man.

Mercy sat down, still holding the child. She stroked a hand over Tamari's curls, thinking. *How many people were with the scary man?*

Tama pulled her head back and looked up at Mercy. Her blue eyes shimmered with tears. *Everyone.*

"Are you sure?"

Everyone on the whole ship. 'Cept me and Rasa. And you. And the lady. She put her hand on Atrea's stasis field.

"Where are they, Tamari?"

The child looked down, playing with the hem of her dress.

"Tama, this is really important."

"I'll get in trouble." The words were barely a whisper.

"I promise, you won't be in trouble. I need to know."

Tamari's lower lip quivered. "I'm not allowed to go there."

"It's okay that you went there." Mercy forced herself to smile. "I won't tell anyone, I promise. Please, just tell me where they are."

"The place where people fight."

The arena. Mercy thought about the space. It could probably hold the entire crew. But why were they there? What scary man and mean lady had Reaper brought to the ship? Other Killers?

"Who is the scary man?" she asked Tama.

The child hid her face against Mercy's shoulder. Her body trembled again, and it took Mercy a moment to realize she was crying. A horrible feeling balled in her gut.

"What did the scary man do?"

But the girl didn't answer. Her sobs grew in intensity until Mercy just sat, rocking her. Something bad had happened. Something Tamari didn't want to talk about.

"Did he hurt someone?" Mercy asked softly.

After a moment, Tamari nodded.

"Who?"

Wolf. The scary man hurt Wolf.

*M*ercy fought down panic. Wolfgang wasn't dead. He couldn't be. Getting more information out of Tamari proved impossible. She just kept repeating that Wolf was hurt. The only detail she added was *real bad*, which did nothing to reassure Mercy's fears.

Her first instinct was to run to the arena and see what was happening for herself, but rushing in would be foolhardy. She needed more information. Wolfgang might have left the military, but that didn't mean he'd left everything he knew behind. He'd drilled strategy into her from the beginning, probably sensing that with the secrets she was keeping, she would need it.

A pang of worry and pain filled her at the thought of him, but she had no time for that now. Carefully, she set Tamari on a chair so she could get up and pace. She felt time draining away like sand running through her fingers. She didn't know how long she had before someone came looking for her, but she didn't imagine it would be long. If they wanted everyone on the ship in one place, there was a reason. Someone would come. Unless she went to them first.

She looked at Tamari. "I have to go, but I want you to stay here."

"No! Don't leave." The little girl's lower lip quivered again, her eyes filling with fresh tears. *If you leave, you won't come back. Just like Mama and Papa. I tried to talk to Mama, but she couldn't hear me.* Even her mental voice was shaky and tearful, and Mercy's heart squeezed painfully. *She was standing next to Uncle Nik, but she couldn't hear me. No one could.*

Mercy knelt in front of Tamari. "Tama, I promise you, I will bring your parents back. All right? But I need you to stay safe." Inspiration struck, and Mercy placed a hand on Atrea's stasis cocoon. "I need you to make sure Atrea stays safe. Can you do that?"

Tamari looked up at her and sniffled once, blinking back her tears. *Watch the lady?*

"Yes, I need you to watch the lady for me. It's really important that you stay here with her." And Mercy would lock them in to make sure they stayed safe. Not that locks would keep Tama in if she wanted out. "Will you do that for me?"

Another sniffle. "Yes." It was the most heart-breaking agreement Mercy had ever heard, the child's voice trembling over the word.

Mercy hugged her, and Tamari's arms crept around her. "Thank you. Now, you and Rasa…" An idea occurred to her, and she trailed off.

Mercy?

She gathered her thoughts and pulled back.

"You and Rasa will stay here," she said firmly. "I'm going to go and get your parents back."

And Uncle Nik?

"You bet. Uncle Nik is at the top of my list." She took a deep breath, shifting her focus. *Rasa?* Silence answered her. *What was his full name? Rasalas? If you can hear me, please answer.*

A faint growl sounded from the right, followed by a flicker of movement that had Mercy's mouth going dry. She remembered his teeth all too vividly.

I need your help, she continued, sending on a tight thread that she hoped Tamari wouldn't pick up. She turned in a circle, in the direction she thought he might be moving. *I can't do this without more information. I don't know why Tama and I haven't been trapped like everyone else, but I need your help if I have any hope of unraveling this.*

The air right in front of her rippled, and the huge spotted cat wavered into focus as his camouflage fell. It was a neat trick, and one Mercy wished she had right about now. Green-gold eyes studied her, and the upper lip of his mouth trembled on another sub-vocal growl, flashing his fangs.

Will you speak with me?

He dipped his head. *I will speak with you, human Queen.*

Thank you. Relief washed through her. *You were with Tama at the arena?*

I was.

What did you see?

He didn't answer right away. He moved, standing up and padding closer to Tama's chair.

He stretched and rubbed his head against her. She put both arms around him in a tight hug.

I saw all of the humans. Tama's mother and father, and the rest. I saw people I have never scented before. The leader was a man with a battle wound.

It took a moment for Mercy to process this. Then she realized Rasa meant scar, and the breath froze within her. *Willem Frain.*

There is a stripling human as well. A girl. She is like you.

Like me?

He blinked at her. *A queen.*

Mercy sat down. Another queen. From where?

She smells like you. Not exactly the same, but like… litter mates.

"That's impossible."

I only tell the truth, human. The kith do not lie.

I wasn't accusing you of lying. I just don't have any siblings. Litter mates.

The cat stared back at her, unmoved. *There are others, but they take orders from the two. The man and the girl-queen.* He nuzzled at Tama, and received a tremulous smile in response. *You will retrieve Tama's Mama and Papa?*

I'm damn sure going to try. Were there other children there?

Yes. Many. All but Tama, I think. They were called like the others.

Called?

By the girl-queen.

Mercy tapped her fingers against her leg. She hadn't known a queen could do that. Could *she* do that? Call everyone back, maybe? It explained why she hadn't been pulled to the arena. As a queen, she must be immune. She frowned, looking back at Tamari.

Why wasn't Tama called?

She was. But her bond with me is strong enough that we resisted it. His eyes flashed in the light. *We belong to no queen. Yet.* The way he eyed Mercy made it clear he wasn't sure they ever would.

Thank you for your help. Stay here and guard Tama.

I will never leave her. This was said fiercely, almost like an accusation. His fur practically bristled as he stiffened and glared at her, eyes half-slitted.

Mercy lifted a hand. *Sorry, I didn't mean...I just want her to stay safe.*

I will keep her safe.

Mercy was sure he would. She had to trust that, because she had so many people to worry about right now if she thought about it too closely, she might be sick. Willem Frain had a queen, and he had control of every person aboard *Nemesis*. It was a nightmare come to life.

"Mercy?"

"Yes, Tama?"

Tamari's small hand splayed against Atrea's cocoon. "You should wake up the lady."

Sadness engulfed Mercy. "I wish I could, Tama. But Atrea is still sick. If I wake her up, she'll die." Did the child even understand death?

Tamari shook her head. Her hair was free of its usual pigtails, the curls bouncing with her movement. "No. Tama fixed her." The little girl bit her lip. "Not supposed to without asking, but I couldn't ask. The lady sleeps."

Mercy just looked at her for a long time. She'd

never wanted to believe something so badly in her life. But how could she take the word of a child and risk her friend's life? Even if Tamari could heal Atrea, there was no way she could do it through the stasis field. *Nothing* could penetrate stasis. Right?

"How did you fix her, Tama?" Reluctant hope made her voice questions that couldn't possibly have real answers.

"The lady was sick. Icky dark sickness in her head. It was hurting her, so I stopped it. I…killed it."

"You killed it." What the hell did that mean?

"Uh-huh." Tama nodded seriously. "I could see it. It took a long time. The icky stuff was really hard to touch, but Rasa showed me how I could do it. Then *zap!* I killed it. Just like Papa." She smiled up at Mercy hopefully. The smile trembled a little around the edges, like she still wasn't sure of the response she would get.

Mercy crouched in front of her. "Tamari, this is really important. Are you absolutely *sure* you got rid of *all* the sickness?"

"All of it." Tama nodded sagely. "Every bit." She patted the stasis cocoon. "The lady is all better now."

Impossible. Right? But how many impossible things had Mercy witnessed since coming here? Since being taken by Willem Frain? The *icky dark sickness* Tamari described fit his brand of poison perfectly. What if Atrea really was healed? Mercy could definitely use her best friend's help now.

But even if what Tamari said was true, there was one more problem. One Mercy had created.

"I can't wake her up, Tamari." The words left a heavy weight in her gut.

"Why?"

"Because Atrea..." How did she explain this to a child? "Because unlike you and me, Atrea got her Talent right before the sickness. She doesn't know how to use it, or control it, and it hurts her to try. Even if she was awake, she wouldn't be able to help us."

Tama tilted her head, seeming to consider this. Then she hopped down from her chair and padded across the room to the section with all of Doc's herbs and plants stored in stasis along the wall. She rose up in the air until she could reach one of the cupboards. It slid open, revealing more storage. Tamari rummaged around for long enough that Mercy almost told her to get down, but curiosity kept her quiet. Finally, the little girl picked something out of the cupboard, and then suddenly she was back across the room to Mercy. Immediately, she looked guilty.

"You count as super-ized, right?" She asked, leaning in as if to share a secret.

What? "Um...sure."

"Good." Visibly relieved, Tamari reached out and placed something in Mercy's hand. Looking down at it, it was a small disc no bigger than her thumb nail. It looked like a medical patch of some kind, but more complex. Almost like a circuit board.

"What is this?"

"For the lady. So she can help you without her Talent." Tamari's tone made it clear this should have been obvious.

Mercy glanced at Rasa. The big cat's tail twitched, and she could swear he was laughing at her. *A dampener. Temporary, and limited. Doc uses them for children struggling with their Talent early on. Tamari wore one for a time. Place it on the woman's skin.*

The glimmer of hope became a wild surge in her chest. She could really wake up Atrea. Wake her up, and get her help. Lightheaded, Mercy had to sit down for a moment. This was really happening.

She just had to pray that Wolfgang was still alive. That they all were.

"All right," she said on the heels of a long breath in. "Let's do this." She only hoped Tamari was right, that Atrea really was healed. If not, Mercy would have to re-engage the stasis field immediately.

Shutting down a snow white was just as simple as activating one. Mercy triggered the mechanism before she could think too much about it, and the blue shimmer of the field faded and vanished. The high pitched sound of Atrea screaming filled the room, making Rasa hiss and Tamari duck down, startled. But Atrea came out of the field exactly as she'd gone into it: screaming in agony. It faded to silence in moments, however, as her friend struggled to sit up, blinking around her with confused, wary eyes.

Mercy slapped the dampener against her neck and pulled Atrea into a hard hug.

"Whoa!" Her friend's voice was muffled. "What the hell, Mercy? Where are we? What happened to the space station? Who is that child and what is that giant…cat?"

"It's a lot to explain," Mercy said. She kept holding her friend. She wasn't sure she could let go. "You were in stasis, we were rescued. We're with my family now. The little girl saved your life, and the cat is her…friend."

"You're kind of choking me." Atrea pushed against her until Mercy let go. As usual, she went straight for the heart of the matter.

"Your *homicidal* family?" Atrea searched her face. "Are you serious?" Her hair was still mussed and her face gaunt from their time in captivity. Dark circles and hollow cheeks marred her features, but her eyes were alert and hard as steel. "Do I need to kill someone?"

"Yes." Mercy reluctantly let go of her. "But not who you think. Willem Frain and his people are here. They have my family, and everyone else on this ship under some kind of…mind control." She lowered her voice, her stomach churning. "They've hurt Wolfgang. I don't know how badly."

"Dad?" Atrea swung her legs over the side of the infirmary bed her stasis field had rested on. "Where?"

"In a big, converted room that used to be a cargo hold."

"I need weapons."

"I don't…have any." Mercy looked around, but they were in the infirmary. Weapons would have been out of place here, even on a pirate ship. Still, maybe it was worth searching.

"I know where they are." Tamari was ducked half behind Mercy, watching Atrea with a shy look on her face. "I could show you. I've been there with Papa before."

"Who is this cutie?" Atrea grinned at Tamari, then looked back at Mercy with a quick frown. "You've grown out your hair? How long was I out?"

"Only a few weeks. Look, I promise I'll explain everything later." She looked down at Tamari. "You can show Atrea where to get weapons?"

Tama gave such a serious nod it melted Mercy's heart. "All right then. You two go do that." She snuck a glance over at Rasa. "You three, I mean. Then Tama can show you where the arena is. I bet she knows a secret way into that room." The kid probably knew every hidey hole and passage on this ship.

"There's the place where you fix things," Tamari offered.

Mercy cast about in her own considerable knowledge of ships, but could only come up with the flight deck, which was fairly close to the cargo hold, but not connected.

"You mean the flight deck?" she asked, pretty sure she was wrong.

Tamari shook her head. "No. The place you climb in between."

Mercy and Atrea looked at each other. "Maintenance shaft," they said at the same time. Mercy grinned. It was good having her best friend back.

"I think there are places you can access the cargo hold from there. If I can cause a big enough distraction, you might be able to find a good sniping position."

"Worth a look. What kind of distraction?"

This was the part that was still murky. "I have no idea, but I'm sure something will come to me." She crouched down to Tamari's level. "As soon as you're done showing Atrea where to go, I want you and Rasa to hide. Don't go into the arena, no matter what."

Tama's face took on a mutinous look. "I'm brave."

"I know you are, sweetheart." Mercy pulled her into a hug. "It isn't about being brave. It's being smart. If something goes wrong, you're the only one who can get help. Other ships will come eventually. You can talk to them telepathically, but not if you're stuck with the rest of us."

Tamari thought about that. She looked at Rasa, and finally nodded. "All right. We'll hide."

"Good."

Mercy stood up, and took a moment to search through the room. She knew just enough first aid to be dangerous, but she did recognize the name written on a stash of capsulets she found in one the drawers. She pocketed one, just in case she got in close enough to use it. She also found a storage box of old equipment that contained some useful items. She handed Atrea a comm to hook behind her ear.

"Here. You can listen in to whatever's happening with me. We can communicate this way."

Atrea frowned at her. "Can't you just…" She waved a hand. "You know."

"No. Telepathy is too risky with these people. Old school will be the safest." Mercy couldn't take much longer. She couldn't think too hard about what she was doing. She hugged Atrea again, quick and hard. "Be careful."

"You too. See you on the jump side." Atrea grinned, using the old slang they'd found so funny when they were young.

Mercy smiled back, but she knew it was grim. "Sooner, I hope. Good luck."

"You too."

CHAPTER TWENTY-EIGHT

The closer Mercy got to the arena, the worse her anxiety became. She had a vague idea of what she would be walking into, but that wasn't enough. She didn't know the level of control this *girl-queen* had over everyone. She'd called them to her. Could she force them to do things? Make them turn on Mercy?

Could she force Reaper to kill her?

Because Mercy was pretty sure the whole "can't kill a queen" magic didn't work when a second queen was in play. It was a hunch, but one she'd bet money on if she were a betting woman.

She didn't remember exactly how to get there, but the ship's systems were all working properly. The map of *Nemesis* traced color over the wall as soon as she touched it, and Mercy was able to pinpoint the route she needed to take. She took as much time as she dared, to give Atrea time to get what she needed and find a good position. But every minute that passed chased prickles of anxiety up her spine. Soon, she was certain, someone would be sent to look for her. She wanted to be the one to walk in on Willem and whatever he was planning. She did *not* want to be dragged there.

She stopped in her quarters and retrieved the disruptor she'd picked up on the space station. Doc had given it back to her, but Mercy hadn't felt the need to carry it in a long time. Now, the weight was comforting in her hand, even though she knew Willem would strip it from her the instant she stepped into the room. Hopefully, he wouldn't look too closely to see if she was carrying anything else. The capsulet she'd pocketed was small and easily missed.

Mercy stopped when the lift spat her out on the correct deck. She was still a few corridors away from the arena.

She kept her voice just above a whisper. "Atrea, can you hear me?"

"Copy." Even that one word sounded weary. Mercy remembered how weak she'd felt after waking for the first time in the infirmary.

She hoped Atrea was up to this. "Should have tested these earlier, I guess."

"I'm jump ready. Got the goods."

"Let me know when you're in position."

"Copy. Watch yourself, Mercy."

"I always do."

With no further reason for delay, Mercy forced herself to continue forward. She didn't walk slowly now, but strode with a confidence she didn't feel. When she threw open the doors to the arena, she did so aggressively, as hard as she could.

It was a bit anti-climatic to walk in and find it so crowded with people that she couldn't even see to the center. And those nearest to her didn't even react to her entrance. A few glanced her way, but without emotion, as though marking the movement without taking anything in. *So much for that. Guess I'll have to do this the hard way.*

"Willem!" She pitched her voice as loud as possible, yelling it across the room like she stood on the loudest deck at the busiest spaceport in existence. "Willem Frain!"

The crowd parted before her like the tides on Lunas 7, pulled apart by twin moons. Mercy walked between them all, marking faces as she went. She spotted Cannon, Griffin, Nayla, Doc, Cage, Sanah, Dem, Vashti, dozens of others she'd seen in the mess, or the bar, or passed in the halls. None of them changed expression as she passed, though she thought Vashti's robes might have twitched when she walked by. She didn't dare reach out with her mind to touch their thoughts. She was afraid of what might happen, of leaving herself vulnerable with Frain and his pet queen.

She saw the two of them waiting for her in the center, and stopped dead for a beat. She couldn't help it. Looking at the girl was like looking at a ghost. Or a mirror into the past. The girl looked like Mercy, but like Mercy from ten years ago. She was maybe fifteen, tall and thin with dark hair, bronze skin, and green eyes. Mercy remembered that awkward stage when her body seemed to have a mind of its own and she'd hated everything about how she looked. No curves, just a skinny stick, with coloring she'd had to change and hide using nanites. Looking at this odd reflection of herself now, she could admit she'd been a pretty teenager. Awkward, but pretty. Why were the young always so hard on themselves?

The girl's eyes might have shared Mercy's color, but they glittered with something eager and dark that was absolutely foreign. Willem, dressed impeccably in a suit, stood beside the girl where she sat perched on a crate. No…a throne. Someone had used the nano-graph to build her a Mother-damned throne.

"Are you fucking kidding me?" Mercy thought she whispered the words quietly enough, but she heard Atrea in her ear a moment later.

"What is it? What's wrong?"

"Just a few delusions of grandeur. Nothing to worry about."

"Then why are we talking about it? Don't scare me like that. A few more feet and I'll be in position. Center left, above you."

Mercy didn't dare look up or acknowledge Atrea's words in any way. She was too close to them now. She continued walking, keeping her eyes fixed on Willem's scarred face. He was dressed in what he probably considered his best. An even more expensive suit than the one he'd worn on the space station, this one clearly cut and tailored to him. It was black, the color so deep it looked like velvet, though it wasn't. Mercy imagined it in pieces. That bastard wasn't going to leave this room alive.

Before she took another step, someone moved in front of her. She looked up, and her heart stopped along with her feet. *Reaper.*

His face was expressionless, but that wasn't unusual. His eyes weren't the icy Killer blue that would make her worry, but he also wasn't answering her. She'd reached out to him mentally on instinct, breaking her vow to keep her mind locked down tight. But he didn't answer back. She could feel him distantly. It was like a barrier existed now that hadn't been there before. A wall she couldn't see a way through. It kept her mind from even brushing his.

He took the disrupter from her.

"Reaper." She reached out to touch him, and he stepped away. It was casual, as he turned his back and strode down to hand the gun to Willem. She let her hand fall to her side, and hoped her face was blank. She didn't want to let Willem know how much that exchange had hurt.

Willem eyed the weapon, and laughed. "This is it? You came armed with a disruptor to...what? Shoot me?" He tossed it aside. "As though I'd let you get close enough to use it. It's good to know our time apart hasn't improved you."

"I see you're still an asshole." Mercy couldn't help it. Taunting him in any way was probably a stupid plan, but it made her feel just a tiny bit better. And she remembered how much he'd disliked crudeness, so she deliberately used it. She moved forward again, slowly. Careful to stay mindful of where Atrea would be positioned.

His smile faded, and he placed a hand on the young queen's shoulder. "Have you met the new you? A much improved version. Rani, meet Mercy. She was the source of the DNA we used to rewrite your clone matrix. A bit of a dud, but then one doesn't run across a queen every day."

Mercy shook her head. "It really burns you that

I lived, doesn't it? That you couldn't kill me for all the times you've tried. Maybe I'm not the queen you hoped for or wanted, but that's a bonus in my book. And I'm still here." She crossed her arms, stopping a few feet away from him. "I've got the best of you, *Will.* So what does that say about you?"

He watched her with eyes full of malice and disdain. "Rani, tell Mercy what you've done."

The girl gave Mercy an insolent look that really grated. It made her sorry for all the times she might have looked at Wolfgang the same way when she was that age. *Wolfgang!* Where was he? She didn't see him anywhere, and she couldn't risk looking around too much.

"I claimed them," Rani said. She waved a hand at everyone gathered in the room. "They're mine now. It was stupid of you to leave them unclaimed for so long. You had *weeks.* What were you doing for all that time?"

Fucking learning who I am, brat. But Mercy kept the thought to herself. She was pleased that, for all his bluster, Willem had yet to enter her mind. She wanted to believe it was because he no longer could.

The comm crackled. "I've got you in my sights. And Willem. Wow, still a dick, huh?" Atrea's voice in her ear spread warmth through Mercy. She wasn't alone. "No sign of Dad. Mini-you is kind of creepy."

"Don't get me started."

"Started about what?" Rani glared at her like Mercy had just said something insulting.

"About what I've been doing with my time."

Mercy made herself smile. "It's been a busy few weeks. Meeting family, learning where I come from, recovering from this asshole's hospitality, surviving explosions. You know. Stuff." She tried to affect a bored tone. "So what do you mean by claiming them?"

Rani cocked her head, like she wasn't quite sure she understood the question. Then she laughed. She grabbed Willem's arm, and annoyance flashed over his face before he stiffly removed himself from her grasp.

"You were right," Rani said between giggles. "She has *no idea* how to be a queen!" She practically bounced in her seat, like a child excited about a present. "Let's show her! Can I show her?"

Willem tugged at his sleeve where Rani had gripped it. "If it amuses you, my dear."

Ugh. Mercy was so glad he'd never used that creepy, possessive tone with her. Rani snapped her fingers.

Seriously. It was an imperious and arrogant gesture. And people responded. The crowd parted, and Zion and Jaxon stepped through. Each of them held the arm of a boy. *Kator and Max.* Mercy made to lunge forward, but even as she stepped, an iron arm caught her around the waist and held her imprisoned. *Reaper.* His grip was so tight it was painful. She couldn't break free, could barely move as he held her.

"Let go of me."

Poor Max and Kator didn't look like everyone else in the crowd. They weren't expressionless drones. They looked terrified, wide-eyed and frantic. But, like her, they couldn't break free from those who held them.

"He can hear you, but he can't respond. I won't let him." Rani gestured to Reaper. "He's not nearly as scary as I thought he'd be. All this talk of Killers, and he fell just as easily as the rest of them." She looked at the boys, and her smile thinned. "But not them. You'd already claimed them. I tried to take them away, but a queen's influence once made is hard to throw off."

"Listen." Mercy tried to appeal to her rebellious side. She was a teen. Surely she had one. "You don't have to do what he wants." She nodded to Willem. "You're a queen! You can do whatever the hell *you* want."

Rani smiled again, and something dark glittered in her eyes. "You're right. I can." She looked at Jaxon and Zion. "Kill one of them, or both. I don't care which."

"No!"

"Fuck." Atrea's voice was a distant sound in Mercy's ear. She strained against Reaper's grasp.

Three things happened at once. Jaxon and Zion moved at the same time, and for one horrible instant Mercy thought both boys were dead. Something huge filled her, numbing her hearing and prickling her hands as it swept through her and out. The people standing between her and the boys were knocked to the ground by a wave of force. It staggered Jaxon and Zion just as they were moving, each of them gripping a boy's fragile neck and twisting.

A shot rang out. Blood sprayed and Jaxon went down. Max scrambled away from him, coughing.

Another shot. Everyone hit the floor. Mercy couldn't see who else had been hit, if anyone had been. Willem had grabbed Rani and pulled her down with him. Bodies crowded around the throne, swallowing them up and shielding them.

Get that bitch! Willem's order went out as a broad command, and several people started moving, shoving past each other to get to where the shots had come from.

"Shit. I have to move, Mercy. I know I hit one of them, but I think I missed the other. Too much movement, people crowding the shot."

"I know." Mercy's voice was breathless. "Get out. Get safe."

"Fuck that. I'm not leaving you."

"They'll find you. *Go.*"

A string of expletives filled Mercy's ear, and relief coursed through her. Atrea would go.

That wave had loosened Reaper's grip on her. She concentrated. This was *Reaper*. He didn't belong to some child, some other queen. He was *hers*, on a level Rani couldn't possibly reach or understand. Mercy twisted so she was facing him. With his arm still holding her, she was pressed against him like a lover. That suited her just fine. Chaos still reigned around them. Mercy leaned close and brushed her lips over his. She kissed him, pouring everything she had into it, every desperate emotion. It was hard to drum up passion when she still didn't know who was alive and who might be dead, but this meant more to her than just freeing Reaper from Rani's control.

This might be the only chance she had to show him what she felt.

"I choose you." She whispered the words against his unresponsive mouth. "*You* are my first consort. My heart. My center. You are mine, but I am just as much yours."

She kissed him again, and reached out with her mind. The wall was still there, but she wasn't going to let that stop her. She pressed with her thoughts as much as her body, hammering at that wall. There was flutter of movement behind it. Reaper was reaching for her, she was sure of it.

Reaper, please. You're a Killer. You're stronger than her. You don't belong to her. You said you'd never belong to another queen like Lilith. Let me help you keep that promise. I love you.

Mercy. It was faint, but she could swear she heard her name. Then he started to return her kiss, and she was sure.

Hard, bruising hands grabbed at her, tore them apart. *No!*

CHAPTER TWENTY-NINE

*S*he'd been so close. Reaper stood motionless as she was ripped away from him, his face still expressionless. But she thought she saw a flicker of ice in his eyes now.

Men she didn't know pulled her to the center of the room, closer to Willem and Rani. Mercy struggled against them, reached for the same power that had knocked dozens of people flat, but nothing happened. All she managed was to slow their progress, and the crowd was doing a better job of that. People were still pressed tightly to the center as a human shield for Willem and his queen. Robes brushed against Mercy as she was tugged along, and she saw a flash of Vashti's face, blank and emotionless. But she also felt the brush of her mind…and there was no wall there. A hand brushed hers, soft and wrinkled. *Vashti.*

A whisper answered her, so light she wasn't sure she heard it. Inspiration struck, and Mercy fumbled in her pocket, gripped the capsulet, and pressed it into her aunt's hand a nano-second before she was yanked away and past the older woman. But she'd felt fingers close over it decisively. She was sure that somehow, Vashti was in control of her own mind.

Finally the crowd before them parted, and Mercy got her first glimpse of the tableau near the throne. Max had disappeared, but Kator lay crumpled and still on the floor. Jaxon sprawled near him, a pool of blood beneath his body. *No, no, no.*

No longer caring if it opened her up to Willem, Mercy reached out to touch Kator's mind. There was nothing but blank emptiness. Not even a spark of his mental signature remained. His head lay at an odd angle; his neck was broken. She moved on to Jaxon, was surprised when she felt the flicker of a presence there. Fading fast. She closed her eyes, allowing herself a brief moment of grief.

A boy's life, so much potential, had been snuffed out on a whim. A good man had been forced to do something reprehensible, and another lay dying. Anger rose quickly on the heels of sadness. No more of her people would die today.

Willem stood, and she took a perverse satisfaction in the fact that his suit was hopelessly wrinkled, and even smudged with dirt in a few places. Rani was next to him, looking dazed and more vulnerable than she had moments ago. She almost seemed confused, looking around like she didn't quite know where she was.

Was Willem controlling her somehow?

"Mercy." The way Willem said her name, it might have been a curse. "As usual, you manage to be more trouble than you're worth."

She smiled at him. It was more a baring of teeth. "Fuck you."

"And charming, even in the end."

"Still trying to kill me?"

Anger tightened his face, made his scar stand out starkly white against his skin. "We finally have the queen we need. You are obsolete, and despite your shortcomings, present a threat we cannot allow to stand."

"Which is it, Will? Either I'm useless, or a threat. You can't have it both ways."

He ignored her, turning to put both hands on Rani's shoulders. Mercy took the opportunity to search the crowd around him. She saw both pirates and his people, including the girl who'd teleported him away at the space station. He was confident, but he also had an escape. Mercy set her jaw. No way was he going to get the chance to take it.

Turning, she caught a glimpse of something behind the throne that made her breath catch and her heart stutter. A shock of white hair. She eased to the side and couldn't breath; it was Wolfgang. He lay as still as Kator, and Mercy stared with tears welling, unable to move or look away. She struggled with herself for a horrible, endless moment. She wanted to reach out mentally to check for his mind, but dreaded what she would find. Breath ragged, she forced herself to feel for him. She had to know.

Faintly, so faint she thought she might be imagining it, she felt the familiar whisper of his presence. Still and silent, but there. He was alive, barely.

A muttered curse brought her attention back to Willem. Luckily, his attention wasn't on her. He might not know the old Wolf still lived, and Mercy would rather shoot herself than bring it to his attention. Willem was focused on Rani. He looked unhappy, and anything that he found upsetting had to be good news for her. Rani, she noted, wasn't looking so good. He helped her to sit back on her throne, but her eyes reflected confusion.

"What's wrong, Will?" Mercy shoved aside the worry and fear. She couldn't deal with it now. "Your pet isn't quite the replacement queen you were hoping for?"

He glared at her. "She has never claimed so many at once. Having one of them shot while she was influencing him appears to have overwhelmed her. But she'll recover." He wagged a finger at Mercy. "And don't think you'll be able to use this moment to wrest control from her. These people still belong to her. She just needs a few minutes to recover from the shock."

Interesting. Mercy had no idea how to claim people, exactly, but she reached out and tested the wall that continued to separate her from everyone else. There was a little more give to it, but not much. Not enough. It was heartening to know it was weakened, though.

"Why would I want to claim them?" She shrugged. "Unlike you, having an army of mindless drones doesn't appeal to me."

"As always, you don't look deeper than the surface. This level of influence is rarely necessary. Talented people need the connection of a queen, but only in extreme circumstances is she required to exert this much control."

Mercy flashed an insolent smile. "Pirates aren't so keen to join you, huh? Maybe something to do with the virus your people used to try and kill them all?"

He scowled at her. "Killing them all wasn't the primary goal. Killing Lilith was."

Mercy could swear she felt a wave of shock at his words wash through the crowd. Maybe she was imagining it, but she didn't think so. So they were aware enough to process what was happening. They just couldn't act against it. Yet.

"I thought you wanted a queen? Why go to so much effort to kill one?"

"Lilith was a problem. Her influence was being felt even in the furthest systems where we have Talented agents. She was powerful, and while we needed a queen, we needed one we could control."

"Wow. I really don't think you understand the whole function of a queen."

"I understand much more clearly than you. And I'm done talking. Like your grandmother, you are a problem that needs removing."

Mercy forced herself to act casually. She crossed her arms, looking around with a shrug and a bored expression. "Looks like your puppet isn't working right now, Will. Pretty sure you can't kill me without her."

"I don't need her to deal with you."

"Sounds like you're trying to convince yourself."

Willem smiled, and it was genuine enough to cause worry to stab through Mercy.

"You can't kill me." She was pleased at how confident she sounded. "You've certainly tried enough times to prove that. Hell, you can't even get into my mind."

She wasn't one hundred percent sure of that, but she threw the challenge down anyway. There had to be a reason why he had yet to speak to her mentally. Willem's smile faded around the edges.

"Your shields have improved, that much is true. But I don't need to get into your mind to kill you. In fact, you're going to do it for me."

Mercy was startled into a laugh. "What? You honestly think I'll what…kill myself for you?"

"I already know everything there is to Mercy Kincaid." His arrogance scraped across her nerves. "You care about all of these people. And I think if I start killing them, one by one, you'll do anything to stop me." He raised a hand and pointed. "Let's start with the one I know will hurt the most."

Reluctantly, Mercy followed the line of his arm. He was pointing up. There were numerous platforms high in the room, probably used for storage once. One had several people standing on it. Including Atrea. Her hands were twisted behind her back, and a gag had been tied around her mouth. Mercy's heart thudded hard in her chest, and she had to exert supreme willpower not to take a step toward her friend.

She stayed absolutely still, bile in her throat as she imagined Atrea broken on the ground. *Like Kator. Like Wolfgang.* No. That could not happen. She swept her gaze over the crowd, just a quick glance disguised as turning her head away from the sight of Atrea's plight. She caught the flash of

Vashti's robes near the throne, and fought not to show the surge of hope she felt when she raised her eyes back to Willem.

He was watching her with a knowing smile. "You are going to take yourself to the nearest air-lock – escorted, of course – and walk yourself into it."

"You want me to space myself?"

"Fitting, don't you think? You once imagined me so clearly in the same position."

"Not happening."

"I think it will. It might take a few deaths, but I'm willing to bet I won't get through five lives before you change your mind." He paused. "I'm going to give you five seconds to agree, or your friend is going to plunge to her death."

Mercy hesitated for four. When he raised his hand like he was going to give an order, she made an abortive move forward, and her shoulders slumped. "Wait!" She had to buy Vashti time. A few seconds, or minutes. She wasn't sure how long. "Fine. I'll go."

Willem laughed. "So quickly! I gave you too much credit." He jerked his head at two of his people. Not pirates. He was taking no chances. "Take Mercy to the nearest airlock. Make sure she goes in, and make sure she ejects herself into space."

Mercy stood as stiffly as possible while Willem's people took hold of her arms. "I said I would walk myself."

"I can still have your friend killed."

Mercy allowed herself to be dragged backwards three steps. She reached for Vashti's mind, too afraid of drawing Willem's attention if she looked in that direction. Right now he was focused on her, and she needed that to remain the case.

Whatever you're going to do, do it now. She received no direct reply, but more of a feeling from her aunt. Anticipation, and a grim determination.

Seven more steps. One of the men holding her tripped, lurching to the side. He went down, almost pulling her with him. Confused, Mercy stared at him. The man holding her other arm gave a high, thin scream that jerked her attention to him right before he crumpled to the ground. Their minds were gone, snuffed out in an instant.

The next one to touch you will die slowly.

Reaper!

Willem cursed and spun toward Rani just as Vashti moved. Vashti lunged forward and stabbed the capsulet into Rani's neck. At the same time, Willem flung his hand toward Atrea. *Kill her.*

"No!" To Mercy's horror, Atrea was thrown bodily from the platform, almost in slow motion. After the most excruciating few seconds of her life, Mercy realized it *was* slow. Someone was using telekinesis to catch her, and lower her gently to the floor.

I've got her, Reaper said.

Telekinesis lifted Vashti off her feet and threw her from Rani in a violent motion. She hit the ground hard and didn't get up again. The young queen put a wavering hand to her neck, and then her eyes rolled back and she slumped onto the seat of her throne. Willem was right there, his hands gripping her shoulders, his face a mask of fury as he shook Rani. Her body moved like a rag doll.

The wall came down. Mercy felt it. People all around her started to blink and move and wake up. Rani's iron control faded, and Mercy could touch their minds again. That connection bloomed inside of her, building in a wave of power unlike anything she'd ever experienced. It was the warmth she felt when she touched Talented minds, but brighter, stronger, like comparing the warmth of a summer day to the molten heat at the center of a star. It spilled over her skin like fire, and her breath hissed between her teeth at the intense flash of heat. She went rigid with the pain.

"Mercy."

She heard Reaper's voice as though from a great distance, not because a wall still separated him from her, but because it was everything she could do to hold the power contained. If she let her attention waver even for an instant, it would explode.

Reaper pulled her close. She was vaguely aware of his arms holding her, even as his mind reached through the heat and connected with hers.

Let it go.

No. I can't.

You must.

I don't know what will happen.

Trust your instincts. Trust what you are.

She bit back a sob as the pain intensified. In her mind, her skin had ignited, curling black as though eaten by fire. The longer she held the surge of power, the greater it built, the sharper the agony.

You must release it before it kills you.

What if I kill everyone in the room?

You won't. He sounded so certain.

How do you know?

It's not who you are. Let your instincts guide you. Control it, but let it go.

Mercy took a ragged breath. She could hear a keening cry, and knew it was her own voice. *I'm afraid.*

I'm here with you. I'll always be with you.

Something within her settled, grounded. She let her shields fall.

The power left her in an explosive blast that rocked through the room, the ship, the system and beyond. She felt the shockwave expanding past the hull of *Nemesis*, past planets and stars, in an instant that transcended distance and time. It went on and on, the fire within her dying to heat, and then warmth, until only a trickle was left. She could barely feel it, but it connected her to every mind in the room. To every Talented mind within range.

She wasn't sure what that range was, but in that moment, it might have included the entire expanse of the universe. She took a shuddering breath, and then another.

I can feel them all. They were hers.

Not only their minds. She could touch their Talent. She felt Reaper's ability to kill as though it was her own. Cannon and Sanah's empathy rolled through her, and she felt the wonder and awe as people tested their new connection. Beneath that, she felt their anger and loathing. Not for her. For Willem. For Rani. For what had been done to them now and in the past. Nayla's biokinesis told her every injury in the room, and with it, Mercy reached out and stopped the last of Jaxon's lifeblood from leaving his body. She closed the wound.

Nayla.

Yes, my Queen. The young woman was already moving through the crowd. She knelt beside Reaper's dog and placed her hands on him.

Mercy moved on to Wolfgang. Only his implants allowed him to live. Their repair nanites worked to keep his body alive, but they were losing the battle. It was a function they'd never been designed for, keeping flesh alive and blood flowing. Mercy took over the task, mending the bones that had been broken, knitting back together the torn tissue and arteries that Willem's people had inflicted. The Talent seemed guided by a hand beyond her own. She was afraid to think about it too closely. Afraid that she did, it would stop working and Wolfgang would die.

The flicker of life she felt from him became a steady beacon, small but definite.

Arigatou gozaimasu. For the first time, Mercy understood Doc's ancient dialect clearly as he thanked her while kneeling beside Wolfgang's prone form. *I will take care of him now.* The doctor's tone was more gentle than she'd ever heard it.

Mercy eased back and hesitated over Kator. Even with the seemingly endless bounty of Talent at her disposal, there was nothing she could do for the dead. She gently closed his eyes as she opened her own.

Reaper still held her. Though it felt like endless time had passed, it was only a few seconds. Willem still held Rani. He only now stepped away from her. Mercy could feel his surge of fear as he looked around the room, taking in the hostility of the pirates. She heard his thoughts as he planned his escape, calling for his teleporter, Octavia.

But Octavia didn't belong to Willem anymore. She was Mercy's now. And so was he.

No. Mercy spoke the word without heat or inflection, but Willem still winced when he heard it. He put a hand to his head, no doubt realizing that her voice was well past his surface thoughts. Inside his shields.

Mercy moved through his thoughts and memories. She saw him steal the research Sanah once built and turn it into a deadly virus to kill Talented minds. To kill Lilith. She saw him plan the operation that kidnapped Mercy, saw him coldly decide to take Atrea as leverage. She saw him create Rani, manipulate her, use punishment and reward to build her into someone he could control.

But nowhere did she see her mother. A pang went through her. Pallas had never been with Willem and Veritas.

You—you can't kill me. Willem sounded far too confident. He had not yet realized that the true threat was Mercy, not the pirates facing him. He tried appealing to her. *I have information you need. Your mother! I can help you find her.*

His lies should have angered her, but Mercy looked at him and felt nothing. An emptiness rose within her, Reaper's Talent. A numb cold that was soothing and pleasant. She looked at Willem, and saw a thousand different ways to kill him. Ways to stretch it out and make it last. Ways to cause torment and pain.

You have nothing I need. She chose the most efficient method. She was already inside his shields. It took only a moment's concentration to crush his mind. He never even screamed.

As his body crumpled, the room wavered around Mercy. She realized she felt weak. Somewhere behind this place where she floated among Talented minds and abilities, pain hammered at her head, the kind of nausea-inducing headache that was unbearable. *Burn out.* It seemed even a queen had limits.

She allowed her awareness to drift back to herself, to pull back from all the people who were hers. The moment she did, she doubled over and vomited at Reaper's feet. It didn't improve her headache. Blackness edged her vision.

"I think I'm going to pass out," she said out loud. Because thinking the words hurt too much.

"I've got you."

She felt Reaper lift her into his arms just before the blackness rushed in.

CHAPTER THIRTY

ercy watched the azure blue shell of stasis crystallize around Rani's sleeping form. The sedative loaded into the capsulet Vashti injected her with had sent the young queen into a deep slumber. Mercy tried to remember the ancient fable the snow white name came from. Did the woman ever wake up? It seemed there was something about blood on snow, so maybe not. Maybe Rani never would either, and that might be for the best. Mercy wasn't entirely sure the girl was sane after everything Willem and his cronies had done to her, both physically and mentally. Doc said there were reasons not to clone the Talented, much less whatever Frain had done to create his own cloned queen.

But Mercy couldn't quite bring herself to kill the girl, either. She was a child, used and abused by the people around her, and Mercy would not see her murdered for that. Maybe, between them, Doc and Nayla could help her somehow. Or, as Tamari grew older and into her power, maybe she could. The child seemed miraculous enough at the tender age of four.

A scanner was abruptly thrust into her face, interrupting her reverie. It had Mercy stumbling back a step and sputtering as Doc invaded her personal space.

She glared at him. "I thought we'd reached an understanding."

"Oh yes?" He didn't even look up from his scan. "What understanding is this?"

"The understanding where you respect my boundaries and I won't try and avoid you anymore."

Now he glanced up, dark eyes glittering with something that looked suspiciously like amusement. "And when did we have this discussion? I don't recall."

"We shared a moment when I healed Wolfgang. Don't try and deny it."

His head cocked quizzically. "Healed? You *healed* Wolfgang? *Ie.* No. What you did was triage. First aid. It is not the same as healing."

Mercy's mouth dropped open. "I repaired broken bone! Knit tissue together! What the hell is that if not healing?"

He picked up a bone knitter and waved it at her. "This instrument could do as much. Your efforts kept him from slipping away, I will grant you that. But I would hardly call it *healing*. That is what Nayla does. It is what I, as a doctor, do."

"What's the damn difference?"

He set the bone knitter down and stared back at her seriously, all amusement gone. "The difference is we are trained to heal. You are not. Do you understand? You were lucky. One slip—" He snipped the air with his fingers. "—and Wolfgang bleeds out instead of recovers."

Mercy's outrage drained to worry. "He's going to be all right, though, isn't he?" She craned her neck to look around him, even though she couldn't actually see Wolfgang behind the privacy screen.

There were too many sections of the infirmary cordoned off for patients, from Wolfgang, to Jaxon, to Vashti – who had two broken bones – to a disgruntled and bad-tempered Atrea. She'd suffered a few bruises in her scuffle with Willem's men, but Doc was most concerned about the malnutrition of her previous captivity…and whatever Tamari had done to heal her.

Doc moved Rani's stasis pod to the only free corner of the infirmary. A second stasis pod lay there already, but this one was covered with a shroud. Mercy followed Doc over and touched the shroud with hesitant fingers.

"Has Kator's family been by yet?"

"Yes. They are working with Cannon to make arrangements for the ceremony." He hooked Rani's stasis pod into emergency power, so if anything happened to take main power down on *Nemesis,* her stasis would remain active. "Max has not been by." Doc said this almost casually, as though making a passing comment.

Mercy knew it wasn't. "I'll check in with him."

Doc nodded, like he expected nothing less. "Well, your scans still show a massive improvement." He gave her a look that held accusation. He hadn't quite forgiven her for waking up after the events in the arena with near perfect health. If Doc couldn't explain it, he didn't approve.

"Are you telling me I'm free to go?"

He grunted. "I suppose I have little choice. I'd love to keep you here and take samples and scans to study how you managed this feat, but I suppose Cannon or Reaper would simply come and drag you away before I had sufficient data."

"So I can go?"

He gave a long suffering sigh. *"Hai."*

"Take me with you!" Atrea's cry came from around two privacy screens, but her voice was unmistakable.

Doc said something under his breath that didn't sound complimentary. Mercy burst out laughing as she crossed the room to Atrea's bed.

"You know I can't do that."

Her friend's eyes narrowed. "I know no such thing. You're the Queen, right? You can do whatever the hell you want."

"That's not actually how it works."

"It *could* work that way. If you wanted it to."

"I told you, I'm not taking command away from Cannon. Not now, maybe not ever."

"But you did that claiming thing. Everyone here *belongs* to you now."

"No. Everyone here is *connected* to me now. That's quite enough for me. I'm not looking to control people, like Rani, or rule them, like my grandmother."

Atrea rolled her eyes and crossed her arms. She lowered her voice and leaned close. "Seriously, you can't leave me here. I don't know if you've noticed, but this doctor has a worse bedside manner than the Navy doctors. And let me tell you, that is really saying something."

Mercy tucked the blanket around Atrea a little tighter as she stood up. "I'm sorry, I really am."

"Traitor."

"I'll be back to check on you."

Just as she moved to step away, Atrea's hand whipped out and snagged her wrist. "Mercy, please." Desperation shone in Atrea's blue eyes. "I can't be here when *he* wakes up." She jerked her head toward Jaxon's privacy screen, her face pale.

"You had to shoot him, Atrea. You made the right call, and he'll agree."

"No, I didn't." Atrea sagged back onto her bed. Mercy had never seen such a stark look on her friend's face. It was enough to make her sit down.

"What's going on?"

Atrea looked away. "I should have popped that girl. The queen controlling everyone. I don't know why I didn't. One shot and her control would have fallen. None of the good guys get hurt, and both kids live. Instead, I chose between the two men being controlled, and nearly killed one of them. Fucking shot went low. I missed the other guy completely. So now we have a dead kid, and a bunch of people in the infirmary."

Mercy didn't say anything right away. She took a moment to think about how to approach it. "Wow," she said, keeping her voice mild. "That is a lot of guilt you're taking on for someone who helped me save this entire ship."

Atrea just shook her head. "I'm serious, Mercy."

"So am I. Besides, you only think you could've

shot that girl. But if you'd tried, you would have missed, and both boys would be dead."

Atrea frowned. "The shot was open."

"You still would have missed. Queens can't be killed by just anyone. There's like a…an aversion to it. When Willem tried to kill me, he couldn't physically pull the trigger. The same thing would have happened to you. Or you'd have missed." She squeezed Atrea's hand. "So stop beating yourself up. And don't worry. Jaxon seems like a good guy. I'm sure he'll be understanding."

Atrea laughed, but the sound had no humor. "Right. Most guys are really understanding when you shoot them."

"You'll see." Mercy stood up. "Now, I really have to go. If I don't meet Reaper soon, he's going to come looking for me. And no one wants Doc and Reaper butting heads."

"Yeah." Atrea eyed her with a hint of her old spirit. "You're going to have to tell me more about this guy. I've never seen you like this before."

Mercy rolled her eyes as she walked away.

"No, seriously!" Atrea called at her back. "Does he cook? Give back rubs? The sex has to be great."

Mercy made a rude gesture as she slipped out of the infirmary, and heard her friend's voice dissolve into a laugh. It was good. A sound she was grateful to hear again.

Soon Wolfgang would be back on his feet. Vashti was already nearly healed. She and Mercy were due for a long talk – Mercy wanted to know exactly how Vashti threw off Rani's control when no one else could.

She figured Reaper would be with Cannon and

the rest of the Core. They'd all been meeting fairly often since the arena. Some were pleased with the way things had turned out. Others were definitely not. Mercy was staying away as much as she possibly could. She didn't need to ruffle anymore feathers, and she definitely didn't want people thinking she was setting herself up as some sort of supreme ruler. She'd met with them once, at Cannon's insistence, and told them in no uncertain terms that she wasn't interested in changing anything. Cannon was still the King, and that was that. Of course some people believed her, and others didn't. Bottom line: she couldn't make everyone happy, and she wasn't going to try.

Mercy, where are you? Reaper's voice made her smile.

Hey. Aren't you with Cannon and the other pirate captains? Since most of the Core had their own ships to command, Mercy had started giving them nicknames. Captain Reaper, Captain Griffin, and so on. If the person didn't have a suitably pirate-themed name, she gave them one. "Captain Bloodstar" was her current favorite. Nobody seemed amused by it but her.

I just returned to our quarters, and found you gone. Did you take one of the dogs with you?

I thought we agreed that I was safe now that I've claimed everyone on the ship. Even if Willem's tool is still alive, he definitely can't hurt me now. Not even as intentional collateral damage with another bomb.

There is still the matter of the Killer.

Mercy sighed as she turned down the corridor to their quarters. Reaper just would not let that go. *Have any Killers boarded the ship recently?*

That's not the point.

She opened the door and walked in, crossing her arms over her chest. "Well, if any do, you let me know. I'll happily go back to dragging a dog with me every-damn-where."

Reaper was waiting for her. He stepped close and pulled her against him. "Yes," he said. "You will."

"Enough. I walked across the whole ship by myself and nothing catastrophic happened. Can we just take a moment and be happy about that?"

"You're in a good mood. Wolfgang and Atrea must be doing better."

"They are." A little mollified, she softened against him. "Atrea asked me if you cook and give back rubs."

He grinned, his eyes gleaming with amusement. "And what did you tell her?"

"That we just have really great sex."

"Well, that's true."

He took her mouth in a possessive kiss. It was a constant amazement to Mercy that someone with the ability to turn off all emotion could be such a passionate and attentive lover. His hands threaded in her hair as his tongue swept across hers, and she could already feel the fabric of her shirt parting along her back, the cold air of the room prickling her skin.

You keep tearing my shirts.

Not my fault you don't take them off fast enough.

She grinned against his mouth. *It's a good thing you do cook.*

Reaper chuckled softly. "I really don't. I order up from the galley."

"Well, damn."

He lifted her into his arms and carried her to the alcove. He'd been doing that a lot, since the arena. Carrying her. She wasn't sure what that was about, but figured she'd ask him eventually.

As he laid her down, he said, "The Core wants to know what we're going to do with the rest of Frain's people."

Mercy narrowed her eyes. "You've been waiting to say that since I walked in the door."

"You're the one who refuses to come to meetings."

She closed her eyes and felt the bed dip as he lay down beside her. "What do they want to do? The Core." And damn him for making her ask. He and Cannon had some scheme cooked up between them to try and make her join in all of the politics.

"It's a split vote. Some want to maroon them on the nearest moon, habitable or not. Others want to take them in. Especially the women." Reaper paused. He was playing with her hair. It had grown longer again, long enough now to hang past her shoulders. "Cannon says it's up to you, since you claimed them along with the rest of us."

"Hmm."

He nudged her with an elbow, but she didn't say anything. "Mercy."

"What?"

"What do you want to do?"

She sighed. "Take them in, of course." *And let them be pirates.*

The resort world Ghalos was known for its five star cuisine, offering a selection of dishes that were delicacies on a hundred other worlds. One meal cost more credits than most people saw in a Galactic Standard year, yet Thirteen's breakfast sat congealing on the resort's fancy china. She had no stomach for it.

Since being woken this morning by the shockwave of Talent, she'd been restless. Unable to go back to sleep. Unable to eat. Dread filled the pit of her stomach. She stood by the observation window that filled an entire wall, and stared out at the red giant star framed perfectly by the station's careful rotation.

It was why she came here whenever she could scrape together the time. Whenever she could escape. Ghanos had long been abandoned as a viable planet for life, but the resort station orbiting it still drew huge crowds of wealthy citizens wanting to observe the last days of this system's sun. Even if those last days took another thousand years. No one knew for sure. It could expand and engulf the station tomorrow, ending all of those lives in a moment.

Sometimes, Thirteen hoped it would. But her fascination with the red giant wasn't just the vain half-hope that it might end her life. She felt a kinship whenever she stared at the deep, flaring swirl of red and orange. The closer it came to death, the more brilliant the star became. Eventually, it would explode. Become something new. It was a fate she shared with the star. And, like it, her days were numbered. It might happen tomorrow. Or ten years from now.

But it would happen.

When the contact finally came, it was a relief to get it over with, even as the powerful mind connecting with hers overwhelmed her thoughts and took control. It brought her to her knees.

You felt the claiming. It wasn't a question. The voice sounded like her own, but it wasn't. The power that reverberated through it made Thirteen's bones ache.

Yes, Mother. The Alpha must always be addressed as Mother.

This queen is more powerful than the others. She could have taken those who belong to us if we had not been vigilant. She is an inconvenience.

An inconvenience, never a threat. The Alpha didn't admit to being threatened.

What do you want to do? Thirteen felt her body begin to tremble. The weight of the Alpha's presence was too great. It might take her days to recover after this conversation.

She will be ours.

Shock coursed through Thirteen. Never before

had the Alpha taken a queen not of her own line. Never had she found one she wanted in that way. A traitorous seed of hope sprang up within her at the same time.

Yes, Mother. What can I do?

You will be my eyes. I want to see this queen for myself. Then I will decide.

Thirteen hesitated. Questioning the Alpha was never wise. She kept her thoughts careful, respectful. *Won't that expose us, Mother?*

It is necessary. I trust you are skilled enough to avoid detection. My Chosen could do no less.

The threat was clear, unsaid, but implied. Only the Chosen lived as long as Thirteen. The rest were discarded, empty husks. Thirteen bowed her head.

Of course, Mother. I will not fail.

ACKNOWLEDGMENTS

Mercy and Reaper. Where do I begin with these two?

For those of who read the prequel novella, *Pirate Bound*, you should know that Sanah and Dem came after. I wrote the first draft of Pirate Nemesis – then just Nemesis – over eight years ago. It has seen many versions since then. This was the first book I wrote where I truly understood authors who would do multiple complete rewrites to get the book *right*. I had the character, I had the bare bones of world building from the roleplay universe my co-author had created for them. But that firs draft still wasn't right. I wasn't the writer then that I am today. The world wasn't fleshed out enough. We needed more detail, and Mercy and Reaper needed a lot of work to translate from roleplay to a book.

I started and stopped many drafts of the rewrite. Diana Fox, an agent who read the original version of this book, gave me lots of great feedback to make it better, but I struggled with implementing it. I think I needed those intervening years to grow as both a person and a writer before it finally clicked and made sense. And *Pirate Nemesis* wouldn't be the book it is today without her invaluable advice.

Mercy and Reaper are who they are because of input from many, many people. In the old fandom days, I was on Livejournal writing fanfic. My friends there (you Harem girls know who you are!) were my first beta readers. They saw the beginning of this journey, and many of them are still around to see the culmination now. To my beta readers, then and now, this book would not exist without you. Thank you Heather, Janice, Tamatha, Chaz, Rebecca, Paula, Lea, Veronica, Jade, Eliza, Brooke and Amy. If I have missed anyone, give me a little leeway for the years that have passed.

I must also thank my critique group, Scott Hungerford and Elisabeth Knottingham. You turn a writer's and editor's eye to my work, and you make it better with every bit of feedback you give.

Thank you to my friend Jason, who provided the Japanese words for everything Doc says. He wouldn't be the same character without you.

And, of course thank you to my co-author. She is always there when I need to talk through some bit of world building or future plot line, or just when I need to get away from the writing and talk things through. These books would not exist without the worlds and characters she creates in our roleplay games. Mercy is mine, but Reaper was hers before I ever wrote him onto the page. I always hope when I am putting words onto the keyboard that I do her complex characters justice.

My husband deserves a huge amount of thanks

for his patience, especially during these last weeks when every day went something like "Honey, I don't have time to go to a movie or cook dinner – I have to make my word count!" He is everything supportive, and I promise to make it up to him now that the book is finished.

And last but certainly not least, my eternal thanks to my mother, who always believed I could do this and never lost faith that I would.

If you've finished *Pirate Nemesis*, you know that Mercy and Reaper's story is far from over. There are three books planned that directly feature them. This one, and two more. From there, the series will move on to another character as the central focus, but that doesn't mean we won't ever see them again. Mercy is essential to the overarching plot, and I expect to write more about her in the future of the series. This is a long game. I hope everyone will enjoy the ride.

Finally, I want to thank you, the readers. Thank you for taking a chance on a new author. Thank you for taking the time to read about characters I love and the universe Malea and I have created. In the end, if we wanted to keep it to ourselves, we could just roleplay in it forever. But we wanted to share it with you, and I can only hope you will fall in love with it as much as I have.

ABOUT THE AUTHOR

Carysa Locke has been writing stories since she started with horrible Star Wars fanfic in the 6th grade. (Trust me, it was bad!) Her Telepathic Space Pirates series is based on a series of role-play games her best friend ran which introduced her to this universe and concept, although many aspects changed as the books have taken shape, but some of the central characters and the core of the space pirates themselves were created by her friend, MaLea Holt, for those games.